THE SACRIFICE

THE WATCHER SERIES BOOK THREE

ROBIN WOODS

Second Edition

Epic Books Publishing

Lead Editor Second Edition: Beth Braithwaite

Cover Design by Vera Walker.

Summary: After months in captivity, Aleria Hayes escapes and returns to find that nothing is the same. The Watchers who believed her to be dead no longer know if they can trust her. When Ali turns over a secret communication from someone within the French Coven's ranks, the Watchers and their allies soon realize that Queen Agrona's plans were larger than previously thought.

[Fiction-Fantasy, Fiction-Young Adult, Fiction-Paranormal, Fiction-Vampires]

Paperback ISBN-10: 0985454245
Paperback ISBN-13: 978-0-9854542-4-1

"Hell is empty and all the devils are here."
—William Shakespeare
The Tempest I.ii.

PROLOGUE—NOT YOURS

They had been walking the grounds for nearly an hour in silence. "Dagan?" Bowen said.

"Yes, Sire."

"May I ask you something personal?"

He replied with a little reluctance. "Of course, Sire."

"What is your interest in her? I see the way you watch her."

He exhaled and picked his words carefully. "She robbed me of any peace I had with one question."

"And what was that?"

Dagan walked without responding for a long while. "She asked, 'How could you give up heaven for this?' She knew what I was and was daring enough to ask it."

"Of course," Bowen replied with both admiration and sadness.

"She is like the Helen of myth," Dagan noted.

"But Helen deliberately used her power. I don't think Aleria knows she even possesses it."

"And when she learns of it?"

The question, double-edged, sliced into Bowen, and he didn't know how to respond.

"Your mother fears her."

"My mother fears no one," Bowen retorted, but a slight shake in his voice betrayed his doubt.

Dagan shrugged, feeling no need to defend any of his statements. They walked for another length and peered out over the moonlit cove. The water looked black under the faint light as lazy waves lapped at the shore and stone dock below.

Bowen peered over at Dagan and spoke, his voice low and rough. "She's not happy, is she?"

"No, Sire," Dagan answered directly.

"I thought not," he breathed.

"Her care for you is genuine."

"But?"

"She is not yours to have."

Bowen bent and leaned forward on the wall, needing support. "Will she ever be?"

"Love can grow from obligation, but you will always have doubts, as will she. If she stays, you will never know why."

"My mother will never allow her to leave."

"No, she will kill her, even if she is not needed as a sacrifice."

"Then why say I have to let her go?" Bowen asked, frustrated. He looked out at the distant ocean.

"Your mother cannot control everything," Dagan stated flatly as he turned and walked away. Bowen stood, feeling stricken by the conversation, his world crashing. He watched as Dagan disappeared around the corner and wondered what Dagan knew that he didn't.

AURORA

I didn't think vampires could get cold, which was yet another surprise. Standing in knee-deep snow, I wondered if it was late in the year for this type of weather. Moisture was saturating the legs of my filthy jeans, and my shoes were hopelessly waterlogged. My skin, a crisp 65 degrees, melted the flakes that alighted on me.

Pacing, I hoped this would be my last night of waiting. Tomorrow was the anniversary of Laylah's death. All of my hopes were pinned on Gabriel visiting his sister's grave. I knew of no other way to locate a Watcher or Slayer who wouldn't stake first and incinerate the corpse later.

The sun was about to rise, so I trudged to the mausoleum and slid the heavy stone aside, replacing it once inside. Rats had been my only food for a week, and I hated the unpleasant musk that tainted their blood and the way the fur stuck to my lips. I curled up on the dank, granite floor, wrapped my arms around my torso, and prayed that Gabriel would come tomorrow and stay after sunset.

When I closed my eyes, all I could see was Bowen's face

behind my lids. I choked back the guilt from not really saying goodbye, though he must have known I wanted to. In the months I'd stayed with him, not once had we engaged in more than a squeeze of consolation on the hand or shoulder. My grief for Joshua had crushed my heart.

I'd had two shocks my final day in the castle. The first was when Dagan appeared in the room and handed me the means to my escape. He was the head of Queen Agrona's Royal Guard and the general over the army she was creating. Dagan was the most massive being I'd ever seen—a literal fallen angel walking on earth.

He'd peered down at me with his almost black eyes and had simply said, "Thirty minutes before sunrise," nothing more.

There was an escape route mapped out in the package, followed by instructions. I'd opened the door precisely thirty minutes before sunset to find the guards missing, and I followed his plans without wavering. They led me to London. I was able to get myself to the money and IDs that were stashed in Gloucester, and from there I'd headed to Enniskerry, Ireland.

My second shock was the way I felt with the knowledge that I might never see Bowen again. He'd entered the room not long before I was to leave. I was standing on the bottom step leading to the bed.

He gave me a crooked grin. If my heart still beat, it would have gone into a sprint. When I didn't say anything and continued staring, he did a double take and approached me slowly, a faint smile still on his lips.

"Are you well?" he asked, concern creeping onto his face.

I didn't answer, but held out my hands. He stood before me and placed his hands in mine, looking down at them. His hands were perfect, like everything else about him. He was tall and blond and had the lean musculature of an Olympic swimmer. I ran my thumbs over his knuckles and pulled him a half-step closer. He stepped forward, and I dropped his hands and cupped his face. *People had once worshipped him like a god...he looked like one.*

I traced along his high cheekbones and arched brows and down his perfectly chiseled nose. We stood nose-to-nose with the aid of the step, his blue eyes piercing and full of questions. *He must have sensed something.*

Running my right thumb gently over his lips, I willingly drew his lips to mine for the first time. My impulse to kiss him was a surprise to even me. We'd kissed once before many months ago at the warehouse in California, but it was irreparably twisted by the actions of his twin brother. I'd kissed him because I had to, not because I desired it.

Bowen took in a startled breath at the last moment, clearly not expecting me to actually kiss him. His lips were soft and firm and tasted sweet. My lips moved slowly as I leaned into him. His hands found my hips as my arms encircled his neck. I pulled him against me, feeling the hard planes of his chest press against the softness of mine.

My kisses became more feverish, and I brushed the tip of my tongue across his top lip. They parted as he let out a gasp. I ran my fingers through his blond locks and grabbed on hard, desperation driving me. His hands ran upwards, one accidentally catching the hem at the bottom of my shirt. I sucked in a shaky breath, feeling his hand on the bare skin of my lower back.

Kissing him was nothing like kissing Joshua, where I'd always felt like my body was a network of sparks leaving me breathless. With Bowen, I felt like I had an ocean raging inside me, undulating and pulling at my very core—waves of emotion colliding and collapsing on one another. Our breathing was ragged and fast. He pulled me closer, his arms enveloping me, my feet barely on the ground.

The barriers I'd so carefully built were chaotically crashing in on me. I wished I could tell him everything I was thinking. *I truly do care about you, but I have to leave. I can't be here. You're amazing, and if my heart wasn't broken, a part of it would be yours. Goodbye.*

Tears welled up in my eyes as I pulled myself away. He looked at me in an awe-struck daze, and I caressed his face again. *So beautiful.*

A warm tear tumbled down my cool skin, and I wiped it away with the back of my hand. I caught a glimpse of its color—a tinge of red stained it. "There's blood in my tears."

Bowen pushed some loose strands of hair behind my ear. "Is something wrong?"

My voice stuttered from an onslaught of emotion I had broiling under the surface. "No matter what, know I care about you, and I never wish to see you hurt."

He straightened up slightly and held my face between his hands, wiping the next tear tenderly away with his thumb. "I love you, Aleria. I always have, and I always will."

A sob escaped my lips. "D-don't say that. Please," I whimpered and looked down.

It was obvious he loved me, but hearing him say it aloud for the first time—now—I'd been so careful to keep him at a distance. Pushing past him, I locked myself in the bathroom.

He stood vigil at the door for a long while. He whispered my name and the words "I love you" again and again, as if I needed convincing of their truth. I anxiously watched the shadow of his feet reflected on the shiny marble surface beneath the door. When I finally exited, he was gone, and it was time for me to depart.

Sighing heavily, my thoughts returned to the present. I gripped the locket from Joshua in my palm and rubbed the North Star charm he'd given me, as was my habit to soothe myself.

With some effort, I was able to fall asleep surrounded by the decay of ancient corpses in coffins. Only to have a dream that I'd dreamt before of graveyards, running, and a knife, but it was more fragmented this time. A few hours later, I woke with my chest constricted. Though my bloodlust was under control, my emotions definitely weren't.

This time of year, days and nights were roughly split fifty/fifty. I'd been spoiled in the castle with its protective windows coated by something—something I could never pronounce. It'd made me feel like I was still human, being able to watch the sunrise and sunset. I certainly didn't need twelve hours of sleep; no vampire did. Dark and light, literally and figuratively, had become my eternal struggle.

I wondered how Joshua had been able to cope with the claustrophobic feeling of being trapped by day. *Joshua.* Gripping my chest, it seemed impossible that an unbeating heart could feel like this. Pressing my face against the cold stone, I concentrated on breathing because the last thing I needed to do right now was cry.

If Gabriel did show, I didn't need watery blood streaked down my face. Checking the watch Dagan had provided, I confirmed that the sun had just set, since I didn't entirely trust my instinct yet.

After sliding the stone to the side, the golden light of sunset was but a whisper in the air, the blues and purples of night washing away the sun's warmth. Circling around the side of the mausoleum, I was overwhelmed with joy when I glimpsed Gabriel's large and lean figure sitting slightly hunched on a bench near his sister's grave not a hundred yards away.

His chocolate brown hair and olive skin looked darker in the evening light; the long fishhook scar on his left cheek was pronounced in the shadows, increasing the lethal image he always projected. But what I knew to be grief was evident in his posture. Normally the silent warrior, I was one of the few people he actually talked to, and he'd become family.

Without thinking, I smiled and ran to him, approaching from the side. At the moment I was about to say his name, something stopped me in my tracks. Then I looked down at my chest to find a Durateus blade stuck there like my own personal gravestone.

My eyes were wide when they met Gabriel's—his expression of rage melted into horror when it registered. And I fell backwards like a slab of granite, unable to move; his blade was straight and true and had found my heart. My paralysis was complete.

"Aleria," he cried, sliding up next to me on his knees. My upper body convulsed as he withdrew the blade.

"I'll heal," I said.

But he shook his head, the look of horror still fixed on his face. And then, without warning, I screamed out from a searing pain more horrific than anything I'd ever experienced. My chest burned like a thousand fires. Sweat was beading to the surface of my entire body, a sensation I hadn't experienced since I'd been turned.

I was vaguely aware that I was being carried and loaded into the cab of a vehicle, maybe a truck. Tires screeched as Gabriel accelerated out of the cemetery. Curling my body inward on the bench seat next to him, I wished I could snuff out the blaze in my chest.

He was yelling into the phone. I only caught bits and pieces between my whimpers and moans, something about "training room...ice...antidote...and NOW."

Letting out small pants, I tried to control the pain. Gabriel swerved off of the road and roared to a halt. I heard him throw the door open and launch himself from the cab, leaving me there. He returned after I had taken thirty small breaths, and gently placed a bag of ice on my eyes, then barreled back onto the road.

"Ali, listen to me. I know it hurts. Keep the ice on your eyes. It is the only thing protecting your eyesight. You fight. I thought…" Gabriel paused. "Do *not* give up on me."

I pressed the bag to my eyes and concentrated on that, but it was melting rapidly. *How hot was I?*

Not too much time later, we stopped, and I was being carried again. This time it was down long runs of hallway, one after another. The bag over my eyes was completely melted and warm, so I dropped it as we entered a room with long industrial lights at regular intervals. My vision was dim, even though the lights were bright and piercing my eyes. I squeezed them shut and turned my face towards Gabriel's chest.

A moment later, I shrieked when I was unceremoniously plopped into a tub of ice water— instinctively, I fought to get out.

"Ali! Do not fight me. We have to keep you cool."

I tried not to struggle, but my mind was chaos. The heat was spreading through my body, and the cold felt like knives delving into my flesh. *I'm a freaking vampire. Why do I feel like this?*

Someone put another bag of ice over my eyes. I felt more hands on me, maybe four sets, trying to keep me submerged.

"She is melting it too quickly," Sebastian's distinctively gravelly voice boomed. "Ian, get more ice from upstairs," he ordered.

Ian's alive, I thought in relief.

"On it," he answered, and a set of hands disappeared.

A new wave of pain ravaged me, and I screamed out, arching my body. The bag of ice fell from my face, and I saw Peter as he placed it back on my brow. Then more ice was dumped over me and a set of hands returned.

Gabriel's said, "The antidote is still 15 minutes out. Did

anyone get him?"

"No."

"Peter, go." Another set of hands disappeared.

Sebastian's voice asked, "Is she a threat?"

"I don't think so. I thought she was..." Gabriel's words dropped off.

"Dead. They must have turned her to save her," Sebastian conjectured.

Then it sunk in; all of them thought I was dead—as in dead-dead—not undead. Despite my efforts not to struggle, I threw someone backwards when the next wave of pain hit me.

"MAKE IT STOP. PLEASE." I couldn't take anymore; this was far worse than being turned. "KILL ME," I gasped. "Please. I can't. I can't."

And then I felt someone plunge into the tub with me. I was being held from behind. Arms and legs locked around me like iron, holding my body under the water, so strong I couldn't move. A fresh bag of ice was pressed to my eyes.

"Please, end it. End me. I can't," I wailed repeatedly.

Ice was dumped on me over and over again as my body melted it off. I could hear the drain gurgling with the runoff of water. Finally succumbing to exhaustion, I couldn't fight anymore, even if I'd wanted to. My arms and legs were limp, yet my chest was jerking from quick pants as I tried to breathe through the spasms of pain.

Someone entered, and I could hear another flurry of motion. Gabriel said, "Through the chest, at the entry."

My arms were pulled away from my chest, and the person under me arched me upwards. I felt the jab of a long needle.

An Aussie accent...Uriel instructed, "She doesn't have a heartbeat to push it through her system. We need to do that manually."

Chest compressions started, and if I didn't know any better, I would have sworn that my heart beat a few times. Then my arms and legs were being massaged in a circular motion pushing towards my extremities. I finally started to cool, the pain ebbing, so I relaxed and leaned onto my captor. Whoever it was eased their grip slightly.

Gabriel's voice sounded relieved. "Ali, can you hear me?"

"Yes," I pushed out.

He lifted the ice pack from my eyes. "Can you see me?"

He came into soft focus. "Not well." I blinked several times, and he came into sharper focus, but he was still blurry. "The light." I cringed and squeezed my eyes shut. Then I remembered the name of the toxin he'd mentioned months earlier. "Aurora."

"Yes."

"It works," I said dryly.

He let out a single laugh, and the person behind me pressed their cheek against mine. "Yes," he replied. "It works well."

"Count me out of the next field test, 'kay?"

"Done." He reached in and pulled me from the water, holding me tight. I heard the other person slosh out, water sheeting on the ground.

My voice was slurred. "So tired." I was handed over to someone else.

I heard keys being tossed and Sebastian's voice say, "Peter, open up the other basement room. We'll take shifts."

"No, she stays with me," said the person holding me, his voice unrecognizable.

"No," Sebastian replied firmly.

"She's my wife," he rasped. I sucked in a breath and opened my eyes, still too weak to lift my head. In my blurred vision, I took in dark, wavy hair. "Joshua," I mouthed.

"It's true," Gabriel confirmed.

Sebastian was silent.

I reached up and touched his face, afraid I was hallucinating or had heard incorrectly. My hand dropped to his throat and the deep scar that ran around as far as I could see. He was real, not a dream.

No more protests were uttered, so he exited the room with me and walked swiftly down another hall. He opened a door with his hip, and a moment later, placed me on a bed, not caring that we were both soaking wet. We lay on our sides facing one another, and I couldn't stop touching his face, though it was difficult to move because my arms felt hollow.

His green eyes blazed over at me, full of emotion.

"You're dead," I whispered, still confused.

"So were you," he replied, his voice a rasp of air. He pulled me to his chest and wrapped his arms around me. He seemed to be in shock.

"I watched you die," I said, still in disbelief. My voice muffled in his shirt.

"Gabriel watched *you* die."

"I'm so, so tired."

"Rest, love," he murmured.

"You won't go anywhere?"

"Never again." He pressed his lips to mine and for a moment all distractions fell away. His lips felt warm and inviting, and despite my utter exhaustion, I felt electricity in his kiss. His body touched mine at every point, easing me, calming me, healing me. Then I realized what he tasted like: home.

My energy waned, and I tucked my head under Joshua's chin. Despite my happiness, worry crept into my thoughts. I remembered the coded message I carried, my vision of the coming menace, and my feelings of guilt.

Soon I plummeted into a vision of Moloch rising, his black wings spread wide as he soared over the devastation. The fallen one, who once had led angelic armies, now gloated while the world burned.

2

SAFELY THUS

Something woke me. My eyes flew open and I sat up, unsure of where I was. A deep, dull burn was pressing its way through me, so I clutched my chest trying to dull the pain. I sucked in a breath, though I had no need to breathe at all, and surveyed the room.

Joshua was sound asleep on the bed next to me. His dark, wavy hair twisted on the pillow and stuck up in places like he'd been tossing and turning. Emotion knotted in my throat—I'd really made it back. Shaking my head, I tried to clear my mind and figure out what was real.

"Are you okay?" Joshua rubbed the sleep from his eyes.

"I just...I thought it was a dream," I replied.

He rolled on his side, propping his head on his hand, and smiled. "Not a dream." He looked a little thinner than before I'd been captured, but he still had the same lean, soccer player physique.

I laid back down, rolling to my side to face him. He reached over with his free arm and pulled me closer. "The dreams I was having, they were so..." I trailed off, sorry I'd said anything.

"Prophetic ones? Or just dreams?" He ran his fingers lazily up and down my arm, searching my face. His eyes looked dark, like emeralds, and I couldn't see the gold flecks in them.

"Just normal dreams. Nothing a hot shower and clean clothes won't wash away." I fingered the collar of my shirt and scowled comically at my clothing.

My clothes had been on me for days; they were filthy, still damp, and itchy after being in the ice bath. I tried to fix my face with a pleasant look, but the dreams I'd been having for weeks— there was a darkness in them that terrified me beyond imagination, and that was without mentioning the two visions I'd had the week before I escaped.

He narrowed his eyes at me, knowing me too well. "I…"

A knock at the door startled me, and I wondered if that was what had woken me in the first place. Joshua got up and answered it.

"Sebastian was hoping you could see him now." It was Peter's voice.

"Sure," he turned and looked at me as he exited. "Be back in a bit." But I could see he didn't want to leave me.

"I'll try not to get kidnapped while you're gone," I smirked.

His face darkened.

"Too soon?" I looked at him doe-eyed.

He rolled his eyes. "Uh, yeah, too soon."

I followed Joshua to the door to see Peter. He stood awkwardly outside and stepped back when I came into view. Slipping into the hall, I smiled, leaving the door open behind me.

His light, brown hair was longer than I'd ever seen it. Thick locks hung below his brows, occasionally catching in his lashes as he peered at me with cautious, brown eyes. Gentle curls relaxed on the collar of his shirt. I leaned forward as if to take another step towards him, and he stiffened. I rocked back on my heels, trying not to be offended, but hurt hit me hard.

"Sebastian would also like to see you in a half hour or so, if you are feeling well enough."

Nodding mutely, I looked at the floor: generic, off-white laminate squares glared up at me.

"Ummm. Gabriel will be there too. Just to let you know."

I found my voice. "How have you been?" I asked, my fingers still aching to reach out and give him a hug.

Peter had become my best friend. He was the only person besides Joshua that'd known me for any length of time. I still felt incredibly guilty over drawing him into this life, even though he'd repeatedly told me he had no regrets.

His breath seemed to hitch in his throat, and he took a half-step back and leaned against the wall. He shook his head slowly, the sides of his mouth pulling downwards. When he spoke, he revealed a bitterness I'd never seen in him. "I woke in an alley next to a dead friend, after I watched that monster kill my girlfriend, and kidnap my best friend. How do you think I've been?"

Instinctively, I started to move towards him, but he raised his hands. So, I backed towards the opposite wall and leaned against it.

Peter let out a frustrated huff of air. "Logically, I know you're still you, but I need some time to process. I..." He paused. "I know what you sacrificed for me—again. I feel like a complete jerk."

I slid down the wall until I was seated and stared at my pale hands and the spider web of veins running beneath the surface of skin. My voice was low and rough. "I understand if you don't trust me—or are scared of me—or just hate what I am now. I don't blame you." I dropped my head into my hands.

Peter let out a cross between a sigh and an exasperated growl. "It's just..."

"What?" I looked up at him.

He slid down the wall to join me, our knees just a foot apart. "I'm sorry. I just had this rush of anger the second you came to the door—it's not at you. Gah." He squeezed his eyes shut and hit the back of his head against the wall a couple times, then sat deathly still for a couple minutes.

I waited. I'd been in my own personal hell. Peter and the others had their own version.

"We buried you, Ali."

"H—How?"

"We thought you were dead." He opened his eyes, tears at the brim. He cleared his throat and blinked them away. "Gentry...she was your double. She didn't have any family. Sebastian used an asset in the Coroner's office...changed the report: hair color from red to brown, eye color from green to lavender. Someone helped out and dyed her hair. The cause of death as a car accident...and that we were with you—Tyran had crushed the left side of her face when he threw her into the wall...and there was the broken neck. After the paperwork was done and the story was set, we took 'you' home."

"Home," I repeated with longing.

"Sebastian sent Joshua and me with the body. Gabriel escorted us. Joshua was...he..." He swallowed again. "I convinced your parents to have an evening memorial. I reminded them how much you liked candlelight services. That way Joshua could be there. We thought it might help give him closure."

"Help?"

"Ali, he stopped speaking—*literally*. I mean, he had the neck wound, but the first time I heard him say anything in months was yesterday." The look in his eyes was far away, "The way he held onto your mom at the funeral..."

"My mom..." my voice trembled, and I felt tears streak down my cheeks. Peter's eyes widened. "Don't freak. I know, blood in my tears."

"Your family will be okay. In a way, this could be good. You were never going to be able to go back anyway."

"I know. I just thought, maybe…" My voice strangled.

"I just want to warn you: It's not the same here, without you or Leslie or Gentry here. It's been…"

"A house full of angry men."

"And Uriel."

"Sounds like fun."

"We tried to carry on in the same way. Gabriel finally got Joshua to leave his room. They went out on a couple of missions, even though he still wasn't speaking. Then we were doing some training, and he broke Ian's arm."

I gasped and put my hand over my mouth.

"It's fine. It wasn't a bad break, but Joshua…he sort of disappeared at that point. Like a phantom. I've been delivering books and blood to him. I don't think he would have left his room if there was a bathroom in there. He just kept looking worse. I don't know if he ever slept."

"It's all my fault. I shouldn't have gone out with everyone. I should've." A new set of tears stained my cheeks.

He sighed and slid over to my side, placing his arm around my shoulders and pressing his cheek to my forehead.

"Careful, might be hungry," I grumbled.

"I'm sorry, Ali. I'm an idiot. Of course you're you. You are way too stubborn to let even a DNA reorganization change you."

"It's fine," I laughed tearfully. "I probably need to get used to it."

"Hopefully Josh broke everyone in."

"Doesn't mean I'll get accepted. I've been with the 'enemy' for months." I fluttered my fingers dramatically on the word enemy.

"And I'm sure you gave them hell."

"Hmphf. I wish. I wish I did. Peter, for the first time ever I saw my breaking point. A few more days in that dungeon...I was done. Tyran would have succeeded."

He squeezed my shoulder. "You're back. That's all that matters."

We sat in silence for a few more minutes. I could tell he wanted to ask me something, I could hear his lips part; he took a small breath, and then stopped.

"What is it?" I finally asked.

"Did you really get married?"

"Yeah."

"When?"

"The night before I was taken. Remember, I left town with Josh and Gabriel for a couple of days?"

"Gabriel agreed to that?"

"Reluctantly, I think. It was all a surprise to me. He asked me one night, and the next, we were married. I had nothing to do with the planning. I know Joshua and Gabriel had a few arguments about it."

Peter gave me a sheepish grin. "Soooo. You guys... ummmm."

"Really?"

He laughed.

I rubbed my leg and felt the packet I had taped to my leg. "I'm supposed to get something to Gabriel right away. Do you think I can interrupt them?"

"Come on." He stood and offered me his hand. "I'll show you the way." As he pulled me up, he said, "That will take some getting used to," referring to my cold skin.

"Yeah, it did with Joshua." I paused, "Do you think there are any clothes around here for me?"

There was a small shake in his voice as we walked down the hall. "I think we have a few of Gentry's things that got swept up in the last move. I'll get 'em for you."

"Thanks."

We walked silently down the hall and made a left, then he knocked at the second door on the right. Sebastian's voice answered. "Yes?"

Peter stuck his head in the door. "Ali has something for Gabriel. Can she interrupt you?"

"Yes. Have her come in."

Peter turned to me. "I'll go find you the clothes. Be back here in a sec."

"Thanks." I circled around him and entered the room. There was an odd mix of emotion in there, like the relief someone would have after surviving a tornado, only to find out that a category five hurricane was on the way.

The room was a serious downgrade from anything I'd seen in the past. It was long, narrow, and squished looking. Dozens of dilapidated filing cabinets were shoved into one corner. There was a single desk, some folding chairs, and some oversized, fabric-covered couches that looked like they belonged in the 1970's. The room smelled like dust and stale cigarettes, like someone had spent years in here smoking while they guarded the files. I wondered how much of it I would smell if I were still human.

Sebastian was seated in the middle of one of the couches. He'd aged in the last few months; the grey streak that'd been a stripe through the middle of his beard had infiltrated the sides. His wire-rimmed glasses lay askew on his nose. He still looked tidy, but he had a slightly messy edge, far from his normal immaculate appearance.

Gabriel and Joshua sat on opposite ends of the couch from one another. "You have something for me?" Gabriel asked, sounding surprised.

"Yeah." I held up my finger for them to wait. Gabriel leaned forward; it somehow felt aggressive. *Maybe the aggression was just in my head.* Feeling deflated, I dropped my shoulders somewhat, and grabbed a folding chair. Perching on the edge of it, I hiked up my pant leg, revealing something securely taped to my leg.

The thick, blue, waterproof tape was wound all the way around my leg several times, and had been there since I'd left the castle. My orders were strict—do not to remove it until I'd passed it to Gabriel. I crumpled the tape into a ball and handed the plastic wrapped packet to Gabriel.

"Did you get out on your own?" Sebastian asked.

"No. I—"

Gabriel made an odd sound, and everyone looked at him. He sat looking at the paper in a state of shock. "It's in the language of the angels." He finally tore his dark eyes away from the page and looked at me. "Bowen didn't help you escape? I thought from what Joshua said—"

"No. He didn't know I was leaving. I thought he'd be safer if he didn't."

"So that's from?" Joshua asked.

"Dagan," Gabriel answered, stunned.

"Well, that is the second time he has surprised us," Sebastian commented while rubbing his beard.

"Second?" I asked.

"He's the reason that I'm still alive," Joshua replied.

"He—" I stopped short and thought of those horrible moments. I'd watched Tyran cut Joshua's throat and Joshua fall from the castle wall into the ocean so far below.

"He what?" Josh asked.

"He did what I asked," I said dumbfounded. "Well, not what I asked. What I tried to ask. I was dying. My lung was filling with blood after Tyran accidentally stabbed me. All I got out was the word 'please.' He stood there, towering over me, glaring. He looked like he wanted to finish me right there."

"Accidentally?" Gabriel asked.

"Yes. Tyran and Bowen were fighting. Tyran ran Bowen through with his sword. He was so focused on his brother, he didn't realize I was standing directly behind him. I remember being so happy that I was dying, that I couldn't be used anymore, and—" I paused, and glanced at Joshua for a split-second. "I thought you were dead."

"The queen was screaming at Tyran as I looked at Joshua's blood bubbling up in the water below. My only means to mentally escape was to concentrate on a small light in the trees across the cove that seemed to wink at me. Then Dagan stepped up next to me, bringing me back. I heard the queen say, 'Make sure he is finished.' Dagan spread his wings and looked down at me. I tried to say, 'Please save him,' but after I got the word 'please' out, I started coughing up more blood. He dove off the side, and I thought that was it.

"But it wasn't. Moments later, I felt like a fountain of sparks was just unleashed in my chest. I heard Bowen and Tyran arguing over me. Bowen said, 'Tyran's bite. My blood. Blood trumps bite.' And the queen replied, 'So it is written.' And then Bowen took me. The sword had gone through Bowen and into me, his blood mixing with mine."

"How long did it take to turn?" Joshua asked. I knew he was wondering if I suffered for days like he had.

"Not long…" I looked away from Joshua. "Bowen asked if he could help me. He asked for permission to accelerate the transformation. I told him he could if he promised to keep me from killing anyone. He agreed. It didn't take long after that. Well, I don't think it did. I blacked out at some point."

"Did he keep his promise?" Sebastian asked.

"Yes." I looked him square in the eyes. "I haven't killed anyone." But then I broke my gaze and looked down, a frown pulling at the edges of my mouth, and I spoke more softly. "I would have. I would've killed a lot of people." I felt ashamed; if I could blush, I think my face would have been burning. I just wanted to leave.

There was a knock at the door.

"Come in," Sebastian answered.

"Hi. I just wanted to let Ali know I found some clothes for her."

"Umm. Do you mind if I clean up somewhere?"

Sebastian peered at me for a second. "I have a few more questions."

Gabriel intervened. "Sebastian, why not let her go? It will give me a few minutes to see if I can figure out what the message says."

"I'll come straight back," I offered.

"See you in a few minutes. Peter, would you show her the way, please?"

"Yes, sir."

"Thank you," I said as I ducked out of the room without really looking at anyone and followed Peter back down the hall. Once clear of the room, I breathed a sigh of relief and spoke. "Thanks for digging up the clothes for me."

"No problem." He led me to the bathroom and opened it up. He stepped in, opened the cabinet, and glanced inside. "Anything you need should be in here."

"Thanks."

He squeezed my arm and exited the room.

Every inch of the bathroom was covered in tiny tiles in various shades of teal blue. The shower didn't have a pan; the water simply flowed from the shower area to a drain in the center of the room. The feeling of water running over my body was transcendent. I scrubbed off a week's worth of grime and watched the sudsy water disappear under the curtain on its trek towards the drain.

My chest burned where Gabriel's dagger had impaled me. I

scoured the area to remove the remaining crusted blood that hadn't been washed away in the ice bath. It flaked away, but the skin around the area was still agitated. The edges had knit together, but there was a bumpy line dimpled with reds and pinks. It's common for mortal wounds to scar vampires, but something about this didn't look right.

It still felt like heat was pressing into my chest. My healing abilities must've slowed since I hadn't fed in a day—that and rodents weren't exactly fulfilling. I toweled off and examined myself in the mirror. Feeding was definitely moving up on my priority list. My veining was purplish-blue, the color deep like paint on alabaster. I looked at my chest wound again and cringed. It was way worse than I'd thought.

I pulled on my clothes and headed out to find the others. Peter was waiting in the hall.

"Hey, were you waiting here the whole time?" I asked.

"Nope. Just got back a couple of minutes ago. You—" He stopped and looked at me warily.

"I…?"

"No offense, but you don't look so good. Do you need to eat? Or drink? Or feed?"

I sucked my lips inward. "Yes."

"Come on," he motioned and started down the hall.

I trailed behind him, but after we'd proceeded a few yards down the hall, it felt as if icy fingers ran from the base of my skull, over my head, and onto my face. My vision blurred, and my knees buckled. Peter whipped around and started to reach for me.

"Get away from me," I cried as I hit the floor, deathly afraid I'd hurt him.

"What do you want me to do?"

"Vision. Get back." I slurred as it dragged me under.

. . .

Heavy irons were cutting into my wrists, while my toes only scratched at the floor. The windowless room reeked of mold and soot. The door wasn't visible from where I was confined, only the start of a hallway. I yanked at the chains, but my feet couldn't find purchase, and I had no leverage.

Near my left, a vampire with a stake through his heart was shackled to the floor. The blood around his wound was dry, and the veins in his hands looked almost black in the light. His clothing was torn, like he'd been in a fight and dragged a long distance. Holes were worn through the knees of his jeans that were blackened with dirt. He'd been here for a week, maybe more—he was starving.

I heard the clank of a metal door down the hall. Tyran emerged around the corner. My flight instinct cut in, and I flailed. Trying to break my bonds, I hit my head hard against the wall behind me, stunning myself. He grinned wickedly. I stopped my struggle.

"Back safely thus, I see. Did your precious Watchers not want you?"

He continued his approach and stopped inches in front of me, the smell of salt air on his skin. He raised his hand, skimming the clothes along my side. I sucked in a breath, trying to control my revulsion. He leaned in, his mouth so close that his warm breath spilled across my cheek. "Do you know what a starving vampire will do to another? It is a sight to behold." He ran his fingers down my face on the opposite side in which he was speaking. "It will be a shame to scar this pretty face of yours."

From his pocket, he pulled a small blade with a circular hilt that he slid his thumb into, and he proceeded to cut my cheek. I felt blood gush from the wound. He stepped back and admired his work with a sadistic smile on his face.

He placed the knife back in his pocket and pulled what

looked like a large vial of blood from the other. He walked to the vampire who was motionless on the floor and sank to his haunches next to him. Tyran's hand hovered over the stake for a moment before he tore it out and tossed it into the corner with a hollow sounding clank.

Then he pulled the hood up, revealing just a mouth. He opened the jaw and dumped the contents into the vampire's mouth. I could smell the fresh human blood, which was still warm. A small moan escaped the mouth of the captive. I recognized the voice, and my heart sank. "Time to wake, brother," Tyran said, and with that, he disappeared from the room soundlessly.

A beep drew my attention to a camera in the corner of the room. A small green LED light came on just as Bowen started to pull against the chains. He moaned again, yanking harder this time. Small bits of rock crumbled from the metal plate holding the fetters to the wall. He yanked once more. This time, it made a popping sound, and both chains were loosed from the wall.

He slowly rolled onto his belly, and raised himself until he was up on all fours. Then he grasped at the back of his head, pulling off the hood.

Bowen's brilliant blue eyes fastened on me—glowing as his fangs fully extended. A guttural sounding growl welled up from deep within him. There was no look of recognition on his face. It was that of an animal, fierce and ready to kill. Panic struck and I struggled against the chains.

Wake...I need to wake. In a frenzy, I strained at the chains until I felt blood dripping down my arms. *Wake up. Wake UP.* His body coiled, and he sprang at me, hands and teeth tearing into my flesh.

I screeched. Someone had me. I shoved at whomever was holding me and realized I was back. Joshua was on his knees in front of me, holding my legs, saying my name over and over again. Gabriel was behind me, pinning my arms to my body. I relaxed and leaned against him. "Sorry…sorry…sorry…" I panted, trying to shake the fear pulsing through me.

"So, I see the visions have continued," Gabriel quipped.

"Is Peter okay?"

"Yes. He's with Sebastian," Josh answered.

"I'm okay. You can both let go now."

They relaxed their grip on me.

"What was that about?" Joshua asked.

"The usual." I smiled ruefully and evaded the question. "Gabriel, I need to get away from you." I didn't think Slayer would smell so good.

"How long has it been since you fed?"

"Counting rats or not counting the rats?"

Joshua made a disgusted sound in the back of his throat.

"I know—gross. I didn't have a lot of options in that graveyard. Didn't have a cell to call the Red Cross emergency vampire delivery service. It's been a week since I have had anything…substantial."

I leaned forward so Gabriel could get out from behind me. He stood and gave me some space. "Go. Feed. Get some rest. We will talk when you are up to it."

"Thanks." I stood on shaky legs. Joshua put his arm around me and led me to his room. Once inside, he pulled out a packet of blood from the fridge and handed it to me. I sat with it in my hands, staring down at it.

"It has to be better than rat blood."

"I think anything is better than that."

I pulled the cap off the end of the surgical tube and squeezed some into my mouth. I felt better almost instantly, but it tasted horrible. "It's like eating Tofu straight out of the package, when you were expecting a steak," I groaned.

"Yeah, never said it was good. It's not live blood."

I drank down three units and curled up on the bed. Joshua crawled onto the bed behind me and settled in, spooning me. He rested his hand on my waist.

"Mmmmm. Thank you."

"Get some rest."

"I love you," I said in return.

"And I you." I felt him kiss my hair, and I slipped into restless dreams.

> Dreams of running…
> and crying babies…
> and blood…
> and more blood.

3

BLOOD OF THE SLAYER

I awoke after what felt like a short time. Joshua was still behind me, my head on his arm. I carefully rolled over, trying not to jar him from his sleep. His eyes opened to slits.

"Sorry. I didn't mean to wake you."

"You didn't. Just enjoying being here with you."

"Mmmm." I blinked my heavy lids. After a long pause, I said, "I still can't believe you're alive." I reached over and traced the angles of his face with my fingertips. "Dagan is certainly an enigma. How did he save you and not draw suspicion?"

"There's an underwater cave beneath the stone dock. He dragged me into it and revived me. He said he would send someone I trusted to retrieve me. When he went to leave, I asked about you. He simply said, 'Concentrate on healing,' and dove back into the water at the mouth of the cave. I don't know how much time passed by, but Dagan found Gabriel, and Gabriel got me home."

I ran my finger over the scar on his neck and spoke through downturned lips, my thoughts coming out in fragments. "If

Tyran...two more inches and...I thought...he almost took your head."

"But he didn't," he answered, as if my thoughts were coherent.

A smile flickered on my face. "Your voice, you sound more like you today."

"Do I?"

Speaking about his voice reminded me of how I was told he'd shut down when he'd thought I'd died. "Josh, if something ever happens to me again, I need to know you will be okay. I need to know you will move on."

"We have forever now. Nothing will happen to you." But there was an edge to his voice. He didn't seem himself; like he was shell-shocked that I was back, and there was emotion ready to well up in him at any moment.

"I know. It's just that..." I closed my eyes.

"I *am* angry with you, though," he said, eerily calm.

"About what?" My mind raced, knowing he could be upset about a hundred things.

"You tried to take yourself out—before I could get to you. I felt it." His stare made me squirm.

Closing my eyes for a moment, I felt ashamed. "I did. I'm sorry. I lost hope, and I was afraid that if you came. Well, what happened *would* happen. I tried to use a guard to kill myself, but Dagan intervened and literally tore the guard in half when he went for me."

"That's three for Dagan."

I blanched involuntarily.

"Four?"

I sighed. "Long story short: me unescorted, sunlight, tested with my arm." Joshua winced. "When I went to finish the job, he pulled me back inside. He posted guards after that, and he..." I didn't finish.

"And he what?"

"He said, 'Not all is as it seems. Hope is not lost.' I didn't try anything after that. I felt like he wasn't speaking about anything within the castle. Part of me wonders if he was hinting about you."

"Did you speak with him much?"

"Uh, no. I think that was two of ten sentences he ever spoke to me."

He was quiet for a moment. "What was it like, being exposed to the sun?"

I took in a slow breath, trying to put it into words. "Not what I expected. In the movies, it's always fast. I didn't know if my arm would turn to ash and fall off or explode into flame. I held my left arm in the light and watched. It was the same reaction a human would have, except accelerated by a thousand.

"It turned pink, then blistered. Then it became purple, watered and swelled, and black blotches appeared as the fat started burning up. It was excruciating, but it was better than feeling the way I did. I started to lean forward, and that's when Dagan tore me from the light. It took a long time to heal. Bowen told me that if you don't will yourself to heal, it takes longer." I ran my fingers over the rent in his throat.

He put his hand over mine.

"Mortal wounds will always leave a mark. Your body spends too much time repairing the internal damage, and the scars set in."

"That explains a lot."

"I don't know how you did so well without a Sire to train you." The admiration must have clearly shone on my face. "I don't mean to sound cheesy, but you're amazing."

Before he could say anything, I pressed my lips to his. He gathered me up against his chest. But when he did, the dull ache I had in my chest blossomed into a sharp pain. I smiled and pulled away a little before the kiss escalated into more.

His brows knit together. "You okay?"

"Yeah. I don't think I've fully recovered. I still feel exhausted."

"Do you want to talk about that vision yet?"

"No, but there are a lot of things I need to tell you. Things that happened. Things I did. I just…I thought you were dead." I felt a sense of hysteria rising in me, mingled with guilt and the horror of the last few months.

He stared at me for a moment, and then kissed my forehead. "Rest, love." His voice was warm and kind.

I rolled into him and buried my face under his chin. He encircled me with his arms and rubbed my back. "I love you," I choked.

"Love you."

Worry raced through my body as I drifted off to sleep, and I awoke clutching my chest, squinting at the green letters of the alarm clock. It'd only been an hour since I'd fallen asleep for the second time. Joshua's eyes were darting back and forth rapidly while his lips twitched as if he was speaking in his dream. I ran my fingers over the curve of his neck, and the intense look on his face smoothed.

I carefully sat up, trying not to disturb him. He murmured something I couldn't understand and rolled the other way. I pushed my pillow against his back, and he settled back into his dream state.

Rubbing at my chest, I slipped out the door, and padded down the hall at human speed to the bathroom. When I caught sight of my reflection in the mirror, I noticed that the bags under my eyes were better, and the veining had all but disappeared. But a sick feeling sank to the pit of my stomach.

I stood there for minutes, afraid to look, my fingers trembling while they hovered over the buttons of my blouse. Drawing in a long breath, I unfastened the top two buttons, pulling back the left side to look at the wound that was puckered-looking earlier.

It still looked red and irritated, but now there was a fine net of crimson spider veins creeping out from it in every direction. They were over half my breast and all over my sternum. I buttoned back up and leaned forward on the sink, pressing the heels of my palms against the porcelain to feel something other than panic. All that time wanting to die, and now all I wanted was to stay alive.

Swallowing hard, I stepped into the hall wanting to talk to someone. Showing the infection to Sebastian seemed too much like having to show it to my own father. I didn't want to worry Joshua, not yet. I settled on Gabriel, but I didn't know where anyone was staying in this place. All I'd seen were long runs of hallway and a few rooms. I remembered a reference being made to basement rooms.

So were the others staying upstairs? Were they meeting in that room earlier to keep Joshua and me out of the sunlight?

Walking up and down each of the halls, I listened intently for the sound of breathing—nothing. I found the only staircase that led upwards and started up the steps. When I came to a door and opened it, and a beam of sunlight came through the opening. I jumped back so fast that I put my elbow through the wall. *A little bit of an overreaction,* I scolded myself.

I picked my way down a couple of steps and sat, listening for someone to walk near enough that I could call out to them. *Oh, to have a cell phone again,* I lamented.

It didn't take long. Gabriel jerked open the door about ten seconds later to investigate the noise. He looked at the wall, and then at me.

I shrugged and bit my lip. "Sorry, wrecked your wall."

"Anger management problem?"

"Cute." The smile I had melted from my face, and emotion

knotted in my throat. "Gabriel, can we talk somewhere?"

He looked at me with an unreadable expression.

"Promise, I'm not hungry now." I tried to smile as best I could.

He let out a short gust of air. "I am not worried about that. Come on." He walked past me down the stairs and led me to the room where I'd met everyone earlier. He turned on the lights and eased himself onto the longer of the two couches. He still looked cautious. I couldn't tell if it was distrust or something else.

I sat opposite him on the other couch, curled my legs beneath me, and leaned one elbow on the armrest. Something horrible pricked at my consciousness, and the first thing that came to mind was to not show him the wound, but to ask a question.

Instead of making eye contact, I stared down at the black buttons on my shirt and spoke. "Has a Slayer ever been turned?"

He sat silently for long enough that I finally looked up. His face had darkened with some emotion, and he didn't look like he was going to answer me.

"Please, I need to know."

"Why would you need to know that?"

"Please, just humor me."

"No. Slayers are either immune, or it kills them. Not a single one has been turned in history."

I took in a stuttering breath. "The vaccine you gave me. It was designed for vampires?"

"Yes."

"Does Aurora work on humans?"

"No."

"What about Slayers?"

"No."

"So there is no vaccine for Slayers?"

"I do not believe so. Our DNA is different. It targets the

strain of vampire DNA and superheats it."

"What if a Slayer did need it?" I asked.

"They would be out of luck. By the time we could come up with one, it would be too late."

My heart palpitated. "Thanks, that's all I needed to know."

He looked at me, puzzled, and held my gaze.

My lip quivered. "I..." I didn't know what to say. "My ancestry." My thoughts got jumbled. "Umm. Did Winslow tell you where he traced the Lux back to?"

"Yes, it originated with the Sentinels and the line of Michael. Michael married a Seer, and their daughter was the first Seer to be able to resist vampire mind control."

"So the same bloodline as Slayers, but not a Slayer."

"Correct." Then the color in his face slowly drained away. "Ali, what are you not saying?"

I pursed my lips. "It's nothing. Just working something out. Thanks for answering my questions." I stood and started to turn towards the door. Suddenly, Gabriel's hand was encircling my left bicep. I sighed.

"What are you not telling me?" he pressed.

"I was just curious," I replied, but my voice gave out on the last word.

"Even as a vampire, you are a bad liar."

I slumped my shoulders in defeat. I placed my right hand over my heart, wishing I could cover the evidence of my distress. Gabriel released my arm when I turned back towards him.

My fingers rested on my top button. I looked down at myself for a long moment, and then I met his eyes that were locked onto me. Without taking my gaze off his face, I slowly unbuttoned the top two buttons of my blouse, opening it just far enough so he could see the wound and the veins branching out from it.

His eyes blazed. "No. No," he said firmly, like he could stop what I was about to say and it wouldn't be true.

An odd sort of peace washed over me. "It's okay," I reassured, my voice no longer shaking.

"It is *not* okay." He held up his finger to silence me as he stood abruptly, putting his phone to his ear. "Sebastian, we need to get a blood sample to Research and Development—the group fine-tuning Aurora. Yes...Yes...I will leave in 15." He hung up the phone. "Stay here. I am going to get a syringe to draw some of your blood. You will not be dying on me."

I sank back onto the couch, dropped my head into my hands, and waited. A piece of me—a very large piece—was hoping Gabriel would say I was crazy, that my premise wasn't sound. I'd felt like I was going to fall apart before I'd come in here, but the moment he agreed with my hypothesis, I felt calm.

He swept back into the room two minutes later and sat down next to me. He pulled a large syringe out of some plastic. I unbuttoned the cuff of my shirt and held out my arm. He took my arm in his left hand; his calloused hand felt feverish.

"You need to tell him," he said with a grim firmness.

"Not until we know something for sure."

"Ali, it is not right. You need—" But he stopped himself from saying something else, clamped his mouth shut and flexed his jaw.

"Let's not assume the worst. Can you just keep him busy or have Sebastian keep him busy?"

"Perhaps." He released my arm without drawing blood. "You are coming with me to the lab. It is probably more efficient anyway."

"Okay—when? It's kinda bright out."

He strode to the desk, swiped a pad of paper and a pen, and thrust it at me. "Write Joshua a note. I will get you some gear." Then he disappeared out the door, leaving it open behind him.

I stared at the blank piece of paper and finally scrawled a message:

GABRIEL TOOK ME TO R&D TO SEE THE PEOPLE WHO CREATED AURORA. DON'T KNOW HOW LONG I WILL BE, SINCE I DON'T KNOW WHERE WE ARE GOING.

I LOVE YOU. SEE YOU SOON. –A

I headed to Joshua's—er—I guess—our room. I passed silently through the hall and into the room. I quickly changed my clothes, placed the note on my pillow next to Joshua's sleeping form, and returned to the couch within seconds.

Gabriel came back with an armful of the Daylight gear that the French coven had used. I looked at him surprised.

"We recovered these the day you were taken from the alley. There was one female with them. They should fit. We repaired the hole in the chest."

"Thanks."

I took the leathers and the helmet from him and started shoving my legs through the pants. I pulled on the protective hood to cover my neck before sliding into the jacket. The previous owner had been taller than me, but it was good enough. I held the helmet under my arm and trailed behind Gabriel to the stairs. Once there, I yanked the helmet on and followed him into the afternoon sun.

We took a blue, generic-looking four-door sedan in order to leave the van for Joshua. Gabriel promised to have Sebastian keep him busy. I reclined in the back seat, since I figured it would look rather odd to have someone in full motorcycle gear sitting in the passenger seat. We must have driven for an hour or so—maybe more. I spent the entire time trying to steel myself; I needed to be prepared to hear: "We can do nothing to help you."

I squeezed my eyes shut and prayed fervently. A knot formed in my stomach, and I wondered if God still heard my prayers...if I still had a soul in my body.

MUTATIONS

A t some point during my prayers—or maybe pleadings would be more accurate—I fell asleep. Gabriel wasn't exactly chatty, not that he'd ever been, but I found this new level of silence frightening.

Part of me wished I could delve into his head and know what he was thinking. I woke when the car decelerated and turned onto what sounded like a dirt road. Within a few minutes, we stopped. I'd dreamt of Morpheus and the expression he'd had on his face when I saw him above the maze. I was finally able to put a word to name his expression: *unnerved.* I unnerved him. I wondered if I'd been the only person to discover his presence in a dream.

I got out of the car and followed Gabriel into what looked like a dilapidated barn. Dust rose from his footsteps as he stalked in before me. He stepped in front of a faded metal silo, about six feet in width, and pressed a button on the front of the control panel. Then he looked upwards. I followed his gaze and noticed a small camera hidden in a knot of wood. After a moment, there was a metal clicking sound, and the front of the silo popped open.

"Ready?" He turned and looked at me, his face blank of any expression. I nodded and walked into the opening.

Once I stepped into the circular space, Gabriel moved in behind me and closed the door. Blue LED lights awakened the second the door shut, and the platform started moving downwards.

Gabriel turned around. "It is safe to take the helmet off."

I took it off and tucked it under my arm, looking at him apprehensively. I opened my mouth to say something, but I couldn't put into words what I was feeling.

His non-expression softened, and he placed his hand on my shoulder. "We will find a solution."

I nodded. The elevator stopped, and the door opened. He dropped his hand to his side and turned to face the opening. We must've been a hundred or so feet down, as the coolness of the earth seemed to emanate from the walls.

Everything in the structure seemed to be made of cement, stainless steel or glass, capped with a rough rock ceiling. It appeared that we were in some type of natural cave that'd been converted into a research lab. A small lobby greeted us with sterile-looking white chairs and a wall of thick glass with two sets of doors.

The main lab was just inside the second entrance. Two smaller rooms were partitioned off in the far left and right corners. In the room on the left, I could see people in white, lab-type clean room suits with goggles and long green chemical gloves. The one in the far-right corner was dark. The center section had rows of tall tables with stainless steel tops like you would see in a science lab.

A tall, blonde woman with safety glasses looked up excitedly from her work and beckoned us to enter. She took off the glasses, tossing them on the worktable as she walked over to the inner doors of the entrance and buzzed us in. We stepped through the first set of doors, and once those closed, she buzzed us into the second set.

There was a piece of parchment paper taped to the door with the words, "Abandon hope all ye who enter here" in calligraphy. I recognized the reference; it was the inscription over the gateway to hell in Dante's *Inferno*. I would normally find it funny, but not today.

Once inside, anxiety welled up inside me and I moved stiffly. Gabriel put his heavy hand back on my shoulder. "Beth, this is Aleria…Aleria…Beth."

She looked at his hand on my shoulder, then at my face, and smiled, but there was confusion in her expression. I held out my hand in greeting. "Nice to meet you."

Beth hesitated, then shook my hand after it was left hanging in the air for a moment. "Nice to meet you, too." She looked down at our clasped hands, then let go. When she did, she rubbed her fingers against her palm.

I tried not to be offended.

Beth was physically imposing; she had to have been close to six feet tall. Her face was a pleasant oval with a strong yet delicate nose and deep blue eyes rimmed with dark blonde lashes. She wore no makeup, save a tinted balm on her lips. When she turned to lead us to the other side of the lab, I noticed that her hair was swirled into a bun with dyed electric blue ends sticking out of the bottom.

She unlocked the door to the darkened room in the corner and flipped on the lights. It was an office with a sofa, bunk beds, a kitchenette, and a folding table with remnants of a recent meal all over it. She swiped a waste basket and shoved the pile of wrappers into the can.

"Sorry about this. Go ahead and have a seat."

Gabriel sat with his back to the corner so he could still see everything in the room, as was his habit; my back was to the door.

There was a long pause before Beth spoke. "Sebastian called and said you were headed this way. Something about Aurora?"

"Yes." He looked at me, and then at Beth. "We need you to run a blood sample. We have an anomaly. The antidote was not fully effective."

"There is nothing wrong with the antidote," she said a little defensively.

I spoke up. "It wasn't the antidote. It was the recipient."

"I don't understand."

I looked at Gabriel. I didn't know how much information she needed. His lips tightened. "Ali has some Slayer DNA, but she carries a variation of the gene."

"How is that possible? She's a—"

"Yes, and we do not know," he replied.

Beth looked at me. "I've heard your name before. I didn't realize you were a vampire."

"I wasn't."

"So, you're the one we are talking about, yes?"

"Yes."

"And how do you know the antidote isn't working?"

I looked at Gabriel, and he nodded. I stood and shucked off the leather jacket. I had a zippered hoodie over a black sports bra that I would've felt comfortable wearing by itself. I unzipped the hoodie. Gabriel's eyes widened for a split-second. My eyes shot to my torso. Three wide, blue lines spiraled from the entry wound now, in addition to the network of thin, red spider veins.

I gasped, "It's worse."

"When was your exposure?"

I shrugged. I didn't actually know.

"Thirty-six hours," Gabriel answered.

She pursed her lips. "Okay, let's draw some blood. Why don't you come over to my work station?" She had an air of brilliance, but her demeanor was down to earth and friendly. My nerves eased a little.

Gabriel and I filed out behind her, and she had me sit on a stool while she opened a kit marked "Phlebotomy." She pulled on some blue gloves, then hesitated in front of me.

I smiled faintly and said, "It's okay. I won't bite, promise."

"I'm not used to working with live patients," Beth replied.

"Or undead ones," I kidded and wagged my eyebrows.

She chuckled. "You are my first undead one."

"Have you ever met one of us before?"

"I've only had samples."

"I didn't think so."

"Why do you say that?"

"Your reaction to touching me the first time."

"Oh." She looked slightly embarrassed, but then she got right back to business. "Do you experience pain the same way?"

"Yes, but when you know it'll heal right away, it's easy to ignore it. As long as there isn't too much blood loss, most wounds can heal in a short time. Our skin is thicker even though it looks thin. It's harder to break the skin." Beth picked up the type of needle you use with an evacuation tube. "You will need to use a syringe. I don't have a pulse."

She rolled her eyes at herself. "Of course." She picked up a large syringe and proceeded to stick me with the needle, but had to work to get it through. "Definitely thicker," she said under her breath. Then she drew some blood into a syringe and placed cotton over the needle as she removed it from my vein. When she lifted the cotton, it had already stopped bleeding. "That *was* fast."

Gabriel put his hand on my shoulder. "You okay? I need to

make some calls. Cell phones do not work down here; I need to use the land line in the office."

I looked at Beth, and then back at him. "I'm fine. Thanks."

Beth stopped him. "Gabriel? Would you mind giving me a sample of your blood? Since we are dealing with the Slayer gene, it would be helpful. We don't have any on site."

"Anything you need," he answered and picked up the rubber tourniquet out of the kit to start wrapping it around his arm. He became agitated when it didn't go smoothly.

I lifted my hands to help, but paused to wait for permission. He nodded, and I continued. I tied it off, swabbed the area with an alcohol wipe, picked up the needle, and inserted it. Beth handed me a glass evacuation tube, and I drew the blood.

"I think you can finish this." I handed him gauze and quickly turned away.

My eyes were glowing, and my fangs had extended. I was still under control, but I didn't want anyone to look at me. After a few deep breaths through my mouth, I regained control. When I turned back around, Gabriel was handing Beth a third vial and had removed the needle.

Beth spoke to me while she put the samples in tubes, spread things on slides, and dropped vials in a spinny thing. "Were you a phlebotomist in a past life?"

"Uh, no. *Someone* was just really anal about medical training the first four months of Watcher education."

Gabriel grinned for the first time today. "Necessary, *not* anal."

"Toe-may-toe—toe-mott-toe. You just say that because you benefitted from my mad skills."

"I see you are in better spirits now. I will go make my calls." Gabriel paused and looked at Beth. "Unless you need something else?"

"That was it," Beth confirmed. Once he was out of the room

and his voice could be heard on the phone, Beth asked, *"He benefitted?"*

I looked over at the office. Gabriel was closing the blinds on the door. "Yeah, we had a run-in several months ago in a train station. The vampire was able to mask her presence. She was very well-armed and managed to ambush us. It wasn't pretty."

"You seem to get along well. I've never seen him relate to someone like that."

I exhaled. "He's family."

"How long ago…" She got an awkward look on her face.

"Was I turned?"

She nodded.

"A couple of months ago."

"I had heard about your kidnapping. Well, everyone did. I'm sorry."

"Do you think I'm contagious?" I asked as I gestured towards my chest.

Beth thought for a minute. "It depends. If the toxin did *not* mutate, then a vampire exposed to your blood would simply need to take the antidote. If it *did* mutate, it could be deadly. But at this point, we don't know if it's fatal to you."

"Would it just be in my blood? Or would it be in my saliva too?"

"Again, it depends on mutation. But saliva is easy to check. Let me take a swab." I watched everything anxiously, wanting an answer. She walked to another table, opened a jar with long swabs on wooden sticks, and took two samples from my mouth. She then clipped off the tip of one of the sticks and plopped it into a vial, rubbing the other one onto a slide. She placed the vial into one of the machines and returned for the slide, which she slid under a microscope and peered into it.

As she studied the slide, Beth pulled a blue ink pen from her breast pocket and scribbled in a spiral notebook. When she finished writing, she looked up at me; I was staring anxiously at her. She smiled and said, "This may take a few minutes."

"Sorry," I cringed and raised my hands to back off. I strolled around the lab, looking at equipment I knew nothing about, and found myself asking, "Can you talk and work?"

"Yes."

"Have you worked down here long?"

"My parents were Watchers—my dad a scientist. Been running around the labs my whole life." She paused. "This is all pretty new to you, isn't it?"

"Yeah. I had a pretty picture-perfect California girl life not too long ago. I liked working with the Watchers, but now," I paused to swallow. "Even if I live, they won't be too accepting of what I am." The truth of my statement made me feel sick, so I changed the subject. "How does this toxin work? In dumbed-down terms, please." I gave her a strained smiled.

"It uses some of the same principles as snake venom. It works much like a Cytotoxin. There is an enzyme that binds our introduced molecule to the strain of vampire DNA. But instead of ripping a hole in the cell membrane and causing necrosis, it seals it up and superheats it. The power of the sun from within."

"That's pretty much what it felt like."

I wandered around while she worked. I noticed that there was a huge padded chair with its back to the lobby. It reminded me of an old-fashioned barber's chair, but on steroids. It was made out of a thick metal and appeared to swivel and recline, but it had huge restraints on it. Heavy bolts kept the base in place. I stepped on the footrest and hoisted myself onto the chair. I sat on the burnt orange cushions and settled in. "Funny, this is the most comfortable chair in here."

Beth looked up. "Huh. I guess that is ironic." She must have opened up a container with blood in it. When the smell hit me, my fangs reacted. I took a deep breath and willed them to retract.

The door to the lab in the corner opened, and four men filed out. They stripped out of clean room suits and hung them in lockers I hadn't noticed before. They were so involved in conversation that they didn't notice me until they turned around.

Beth was around a corner out of their line of vision. I saw fear on their faces and realized my eyes must be glowing. I crossed my legs and leaned back in the seat and smiled without showing my teeth, trying not to look threatening. One of them called out, "Uh, Beth?"

"Hey, guys," she answered calmly. "You finish?"

"Yeah," he answered, not taking his eyes off of me.

I chuckled under my breath. "Beth—they think I'm here to eat them."

"Oh. Oh!" She dropped her pen and walked towards them. "Sorry guys, this is Aleria. She's here with Gabriel." She hitched her thumb towards the office. Their relief was palpable.

I waved.

One of them with black hair in little curls timidly walked towards me and held out his hand. "Pleased to make your acquaintance. I'm Thomas."

"Nice to meet you." I shook his hand.

None of the others approached me, but they waved a greeting. In an odd way, it made me feel powerful. The truth was, I could've killed all four of them in under a minute if I'd wanted to—but, obviously, I didn't.

I swiveled one of the restraints over my left arm. It was so large that it covered half my forearm.

They moved almost as a unit past me. A different one spoke to Beth. He had brown hair and a medium build with thick, black-rimmed glasses. "We're going on a food run. Want anything?"

"Yeah, I'm starved. You know what I like. And bring something for Gabriel, too." She turned and went back to her worktable. She shuffled some papers and moved, with her back turned, to the side closer to me.

"Will do," he said.

Thomas looked at me. "Ummm. Do *you* need something?"

I smiled again. "Thanks, no."

"Bye," Beth said without looking up from the scope she was looking into.

She set up another set of test tubes and started cutting off the tips of cotton swabs into them. She got a frustrated look on her face. "Urgh. These aren't cutting," she mumbled to herself and shook the scissors as if scolding them. "Aleria, are there scissors on the table in front of you? These are dull."

"Yes, and please call me Ali. You want them?"

"Yes, please."

I heard the first door buzz, and then the second. There was a long pause before I heard the door shut.

I flipped open the restraint I'd been playing with and snatched the scissors. I took about two steps towards Beth, then felt a crack followed by a searing pain in the back of my head. I stumbled forward throwing my hands out in front of me, but before I hit the ground, someone seized my arm and wrenched me over so I landed on my back.

My head smashed onto the ground. I sucked in air to scream; but before I could, I focused on the Durateus dagger coming down on me. It drove straight into my heart. The only movement I made was the air escaping my lungs in a hiss.

I looked at the man hovering over me, who I'd never heard coming, even with vampire hearing. He had striking black hair that was shaved on the sides with the rest pulled into a ponytail.

His skin was olive-toned; he looked like he could be of Persian descent. Then I spied the Slayer tattoo on his right shoulder. *Figures.*

He pulled out another blade and stuck it in the side of my neck as if I was going to jump up and needed to be held here. I then realized he must have fractured my scull. I could feel the tickle of the back of my head getting wet. I could also feel blood pooling under me; the blade had gone clear through. The blood reached the backs of my arms on both sides. *Not good.*

Two other figures flanked him: a man and a woman. The Slayer with the knife poking into my throat spoke. "Beth, are you okay?"

I heard glass smash on the ground and Beth's voice. "What are you DOING?"

Then the sound of the office door jerk open and thunderous footsteps. "Stop…NOW," Gabriel's voice boomed.

All three of them backed away. Then Gabriel was at my side. The dagger was wedged between my ribs, and he had to jerk hard to remove it. He held my face between his hands. "Ali, speak to me."

I blinked my eyes. "Ouch," with a weak grin was all I could manage.

A little relief spread on his face, but not much. He unzipped my hoodie and looked at the wound. "Get me something to slow down the bleeding." Beth handed him a pile of gauze. He pressed it to the wound with his left hand, and I felt his right hand slip under my head. "Damn it." That was the first time I'd heard a foul word pass his lips. "Kez, Amara, Samael—what are you doing here? I thought you were still in France."

The one who'd stabbed me answered. "A whole lot of France is coming here. We were tracking three different hit teams. We came here to pick up some supplies while it's light."

Gabriel looked down at me and lifted the gauze from my

chest. "This is not slowing down at all. You should be half-healed by now." His expression was alarmed as he looked over at Beth. "Do you have a blood supply here?"

"Nothing pure. Everything has been used in some sort of experiment. Our new supply is coming in tomorrow."

"What does it matter?" The other one, with the light brown hair and flared jaw, muttered. "One less parasite to kill later."

Gabriel's jaw flexed. "Samael, she is one of us."

"That *thing* is not one of us," Samael replied flatly.

"Yet you fought alongside Joshua without complaint."

His voice didn't sound as confident. "That was different."

"This is Aleria. I know you have heard of her. She is under my care and is Joshua's mate. You *will* help her." I closed my eyes. "Ali, open your eyes and focus."

"Why is she not healing?" the woman, Amara, asked. She sounded North African.

He lifted the gauze again, and I felt a new wave of blood ooze down the side of my chest.

"All three of you are donating blood right now. Beth, draw their blood." I heard grumbles from one of the men, but they followed her to the other side of the room.

Gabriel rubbed his cheek, leaving a huge smear of my blood on his face. My lids were getting heavy. I gazed up at him again. He shifted and pulled my upper body onto his lap and leaned against the side of one of the tables. He looked like Atlas, the weight of the world was on his shoulders, but then his grim expression softened.

He placed his wrist over my mouth. "Take it. I'm immune."

I turned my head away. "No way," I moaned.

"The hard way then, as always."

He reached into his boot and I heard the familiar sound of a knife being drawn. He cut his wrist and held it over my mouth. I still resisted, but when the warmth of his blood touched my lips, my body took over. Shame washed over me and tried to will my fangs to stay put, but they wouldn't. I bit Gabriel.

His eyes tightened for a second, then I released the hormone and he relaxed. There was a closeness in the feeding, but not intimacy. I concentrated on his heartbeat. It was more robust than anything I'd ever heard. His blood was different too, stronger somehow.

My senses started sharpening as I drank. His eyes narrowed to slits. I felt the slowing of his heart, and more than anything, I wanted to keep going. I tried to move my arm and was able to— barely. I licked the punctures and the cut to close them up. Then I reached up and pushed his wrist from my mouth.

I turned my head away from him and again had the sensation of a few phantom beats of my heart. I wished it could be true, but it only added sadness to my humiliation.

Gabriel seemed to come back to his senses. He lifted the gauze once again and said, "It is slowing." His voice was sleepy.

"Thank you." I wasn't able to look at him.

"Consider it penance. As I said, you are not going to die on me." Beth came over a minute later and handed him a bag of blood. He ripped the tube out and lowered it to me. "Cheers."

I rolled my eyes, wishing I had enough strength to do this on my own. After being force-fed two more pints, I rolled off his lap onto my side. "Please just give me a few minutes. This is horrible, Gabriel."

I felt his fingers on my back, and then in my hair. "These have closed up."

I glanced at him as he stood to his feet. Scarlet stains were splattered all over his clothes, and he was standing in my blood. He stepped to the edge of the pool, kicked off his shoes, and walked over to the others in the back of the lab.

Beth was asking if I needed more, and Gabriel was saying to give me a few more minutes. She asked him another series of questions, but I tuned out. The others were silent. I put my arm over my head to block out the light and curled into a fetal position, wishing I could transport myself somewhere else. I'd never wanted to feed where anyone else could see me, much less feed off of someone I knew.

Still drained, I struggled to a sitting position and pushed myself backwards against the table leg. Then I heard Gabriel's tone turn sharp. "Why would you attack her unprovoked?" The tension in the room was palpable from here.

I chimed in, knowing exactly what went wrong. "It's not their fault," I said from across the room. "They thought they were protecting Beth from me." I twisted around and used the table to pull myself up on my feet, but had to lean forward on my elbows to keep from going over.

The Slayer with the dark complexion spoke. "She got out of that chair and headed towards Beth with those shears." Amara stood not far from him, looking defensive.

"Like I said, they thought they were protecting Beth. It happened. No blame on anyone."

Gabriel's forehead smoothed. My knees got shaky, so I shifted to the side and eased myself onto a stool.

One of Beth's machines beeped. She walked over to it and removed a vial. A moment later, her printer spit out a report, she pulled it out and started perusing the paper. She had a pen in her hand and incessantly clicked the tip in and out while she read. Nerves hit my insides the longer she read without saying anything. Finally, she looked at me. "Good news. Your saliva is clear."

My shoulders sagged in relief. "How long until we know about the rest?"

"It will take me days. Sorry. It's complicated and not my specialty."

I was confused. "You didn't create Aurora?"

"No. The creator of it is deceased. She had some seriously inventive thinking on this one."

I asked, "Who is *she?*"

"Neka Rousseau—this was a personal project of hers."

"She's not dead," I said.

"What?" Samael questioned, exchanging a look with Kez.

"She's alive or, she was two months ago. She's a prisoner in Agrona's castle. I was in the cell next to hers for weeks."

"It's been years," Beth said quietly.

"They removed her from the cell each day to work on something. She was treated better than most of the prisoners. She looked fragile though. I never saw them feed on her." I thought for a moment. "She's the only one I never saw them feed on."

"They fed on you?" Amara asked, her tone gentle.

"I...I can't." I lost my breath. I shook my head, despising my reaction. The room went quiet.

Samael turned towards me. "How fortified is the castle?"

"There are hundreds of them. And their numbers are growing."

Gabriel leaned in. "Growing?"

I told them about the maze surrounded by dungeons. The games they played—the feedings. And how they painted the contestants to indicate how many games they'd survived: purple, then blue, and finally red if they made it to the final challenge. I explained how it reminded me of the Coliseum in Rome—how they watched the killing for pleasure and toyed with their prey. Then I told them, "If the contestant survived the third meet, their reward was to be turned. They want warriors—survivors, to add to their army."

They continued to ask questions for an hour, giving me a few breaks to regain my strength. By the end of it, I'd sketched out as much of the floor plan as I knew. I indicated where guard stations were and routes I knew about. But I hadn't seen entire wings of the castle.

The hostility I'd felt earlier towards me lessened.

"Where do they keep Neka?" Samael asked intensely.

"The farthest corner of the dungeon." I stood up and added, "Don't even think about it. All of you. These questions. I don't care how awesome all of you are—it's suicide."

"You got out; there has to be a hole in their security," Samael pushed.

"No, there isn't. I had help. I would never have gotten out."

"Maybe they will help again," Kez said, with hope painting his expression.

"I don't think so. And I have no way to contact the inside."

"Or maybe you don't want to bring them down?" Samael challenged.

I slammed my hand onto the counter so hard the stainless steel top dented. "No one wants to burn that place down to the ground more than me. And to make sure Tyran—"

Amara gasped loud enough to stop me short.

My body was shaking, and I was so angry I was on the verge of losing control of my emotions. I quickly turned my back to them just as my fangs sprang. Putting my hands over my face, I disappeared into the bathroom.

My eyes were glowing lavender, and my hair was matted with blood. Needing focus, I grabbed onto the sink and stared into the mirror. Blood was simply everywhere. I stripped off the hoodie, wet down a wad of paper towels, and started sponging myself off.

The door opened, and I spun to face the corner to hide my fangs. I expected to hear Gabriel's voice, but it wasn't; it was Amara. She was about my height and very exotic-looking. Her dark skin was smooth, her eyes the color of cinnamon, and her head thick with tiny braids.

Something about her voice was very comforting. "Beth gave me some scrubs. She said there's a shower in the back corner."

"Thanks." I kept my back to her; I was trying to hold back tears.

"For what it's worth, I don't think you're protecting the French coven."

"Why don't you think that?"

"I'm an Empath. I can sense what you're feeling."

"And what does that tell you about me?"

"I know you are fiercely loyal to Gabriel, and that is enough for me."

Worry hit my stomach when I remembered an overheard conversation in the castle. "Are you from the Abacha family?"

She tilted her head. "Yes."

"Then you're in danger."

"How so?"

I leaned my head against the wall, still hiding my face. "The French coven is trying to raise Moloch. They need an Empath from your family, unless they already have one."

"As far as I know, no one is missing from my family."

"Then you need to be careful. Don't let them draw you out." My teeth finally retracted. I turned holding the hoodie in front of my chest.

"What else did they do to you?" she asked.

"Who?"

She leveled her gaze at me. "Your emotional response, when you said you wanted to burn down that coven. I haven't felt something so strong in a long while."

"I'm going to go ahead and get that shower."

Her face fell a little. "You aren't alone. Others will accept you. Don't let the hot-headed Slayer, Samael, get to you."

I touched her elbow as I passed by her. "Thanks."

When I got into the shower, my mind flooded with

information: cytotoxins, mutations, a lot of the French coven headed this way, and meeting my first Empath. I tried to process everything as I washed all the blood away. I didn't know if it was my imagination, but it seemed like the veining over my torso was getting better.

I toweled off and pulled on the green scrubs that Amara had dropped off. I fingered through my wet hair, trying to work through the tangles, and pulled open the bathroom door.

As the edges of my sight started going dark, I looked wide-eyed at Gabriel as a vision pulled me down.

I was back in that room with Tyran and Bowen. Tyran asked, as he pulled the stake out of his brother's heart, "Do you know what a starving vampire will do to another?"

But this time, I said something else. "Tyran, please don't do this. It's a death sentence for him."

Tyran looked at me and smiled malevolently as he unlocked the shackles on Bowen and left the room.

I came out of the vision sprawled on the floor, gasping, with Gabriel and Amara at my sides. Covering my face, I rolled on my side.

My voice was strangled, and my vision blurred with tears. "It mutated, Gabriel. Aurora mutated."

5

INSTINCT

G abriel pulled me into the office and shut the door, leaving the others in the lab. "The tests are not in yet. You do not know it mutated," he said firmly as he practically pushed me onto the couch.

I shook my head. "But my vision—"

"What did you see?" He asked as he ran his fingers through his hair and paced back and forth.

I recounted the whole thing: the chains, Tyran gloating, and Bowen starving. Then, I told him what I said to Tyran, that letting Bowen bite me was a death sentence.

"Ali, you could have been lying."

"I don't think so," I stammered. *Maybe that is why I had the vision? So I could lie?* "I felt genuinely panicked and protective of Bowen."

"I might feel a little 'panicked' if a starving vampire was about to be unleashed on me."

"Yeah right, *you* panicked," I muttered.

"Do not lose hope. You only have a piece of the story."

I nodded. "Okay." But I was scared to let myself hope.

"When you walked out of the bathroom, you smiled before the vision hit you."

"I did? Oh." I stood and hiked the shirt up to reveal the map of veins. "Does this look better to you?"

"Yes. The veining is lighter." He put his hand on my shoulder and started ushering me towards the door. "You need to show Beth, but... " He paused. "Be careful around the others. I do not want them to know you are of the Lux. It is not that they cannot be trusted."

"Amara seems to know I'm different."

"Suspecting and knowing are two different things. Let us go."

I walked out just ahead of Gabriel to Beth. Samael, Kez, and Amara were gathered around a table on the other side of the lab, speaking in hushed voices. The other scientists must've gotten back while Gabriel and I were speaking. There was a bag of food next to Beth, and they were pulling on their clean room suits again.

We headed over to Beth.

"How are you feeling?" she asked in her upbeat manner.

"Getting back to normal, but something changed, for the good I think." I turned so my back was to everyone else in the room. I revealed my torso.

She cocked her head and stuck the back of her pen in her mouth. "That definitely seems to have improved." She leaned back on a stool and thought for a few beats. "Slayer blood," she said matter-of-factly.

"You think that makes a difference?" Gabriel asked.

"It makes sense."

Beth abruptly stood and started smearing things on slides, peering into the microscope. She worked while explaining her theory, but her techno-babble got to the point that I couldn't really follow. Once it got past the basics, I was lost.

Gabriel seemed to be following well, so I tuned out and

waited for the translation. She had Gabriel look at something, and the discussion continued. I shifted over and sat on a stool, putting my head on my arm while I waited. I felt tired, which was a rare sensation since I'd been turned.

"Ali, you mind coming over?" Beth asked. She was radiating excitement.

I stood up and rubbed my eyes as I walked over. "I'm here to serve."

"I would like to make some markings on you." I nodded, and she made dots where the deep blue veining became light. She swiveled around and held out a small beaker of blood. "Please drink this."

I hesitated, not wanting to drink it in front of anyone. I reached out and took it, but then just stared at it. I finally stepped a couple of feet away and turned my back. When I returned, Beth was jotting something down in her spiral notebook again.

"Okay, I'm going to wait a half hour and draw some blood, then we'll see what we see."

"That was Slayer blood with something else mixed into it, wasn't it?"

"Very good," Beth grinned.

Gabriel looked at me thoughtfully. "You can tell the difference?"

I pursed my lips. "Slayer blood tastes stronger, and I get more of an energy surge, like there's more nutrition. Maybe that's the wrong word, but I *do* know that wasn't your blood." My eyes flickered over at Kez and Samael. Samael met my gaze for a split-second. His eyes weren't as filled with contempt as they were before, but they weren't friendly either.

Gabriel must have seen the exchange. "How about you go get some sleep in the office. Someone will get you in a half hour."

"K." I slowly walked away. As I turned to shut the door,

Amara gave me a comforting smile. Once inside the office, I plopped onto the couch and curled into a ball. I must've been exhausted because I was out almost instantly.

I woke in what was obviously a dreamscape. The colors were too intense—the stars above shined like it was midnight, yet the landscape itself seemed to be bathed in the most beautiful golden light, like those perfect moments before the sun dips below the horizon. The ocean was in the distance and sculptured gardens teaming with life filled the entire way to the shore. A majestic oak stood not far off, shading a significant area.

The figure of a man was sitting beneath the tree, so I started picking my way towards him. When I was a few yards away, the man jumped up, startled. His infuriated voice asked, "How are you here?"

I stumbled back a step because the wave of emotion coming off of him was overpowering. It took me a moment for my mind to catch up. "Morpheus?" I said, more questioning him than identifying him.

"How are you here?" he screamed.

I didn't know what he meant. "Where?" I finally managed.

"*My* dream."

My mouth dropped open, and just as I was about to ask another question, someone gently shook me.

I opened my eyes. Amara's kind face was hovering over me.

"Beth would like to see you again."

"I'm awake," I replied, my voice thick as I sat up completely disoriented. *Did what I think just happened, happen?*

I walked back behind Amara, shuffling my feet and trying to get my wits about me. My chest was marked again and I was made to drink another round of Beth's Slayer blood cocktail, followed by another. After two hours of this, she came to a conclusion: Slayer blood would slow the progression of the illness and regress it if I drank enough, but it would not cure me.

She saw this as extremely positive. It would hopefully give her enough time to find an antidote that would work. I, on the other hand, was not happy. *Slayer blood, great. I'm sure they'll all line up to donate. Maybe they should just stake me now.*

I groaned internally, but Gabriel saw it race across my features.

"It gives us time," he said gently.

I rolled my lips inward and tried to smash down the negativity I was feeling.

"You will need to suck it up and accept help."

My neutral look became a glare, but I didn't say anything. Beth turned her head, but I caught the beginnings of a smile. She was apparently amused by the exchange.

"It's sunset," Kez said from across the room.

I knew it was without him saying so. I felt it, but I wondered why he was pointing it out.

Gabriel responded, "I know. I was hoping to be on the road already. Sebastian will be glad to see all of you."

I was a little confused. *They are going back with us?*

"Let's get some supplies together for you," Beth said as she stood and grabbed a bag, packaging packets of blood-drawing supplies.

Gabriel turned to me. "Would you gather up your belongings?"

"Sure."

The daylight gear was in the office. While in there, I pulled on the leather pants over the scrubs, put on the jacket, and shoved the neckpiece and gloves into the helmet. Then I went into the back room, grabbing the blood-stained jeans I'd been wearing earlier. My hoodie was trash, as it had two sizable holes in it.

When I exited, everyone was standing by the door waiting for me. I strode over and followed them out into the elevator. I made sure I was on the side opposite of Samael, and as I did, I noticed Kez's hand on the small of Amara's back for a brief second. It seemed—tender.

We walked through the barn, and the sound of nightlife was all encompassing. A surveillance van was parked next to the sedan Gabriel and I had arrived in. When we pulled out, the van took the lead. We were farther out in the country than I'd thought.

We drove for forty-five minutes and didn't see much more than hedgerows. Gabriel was very silent. I cleared my throat. "Did you translate the message from Dagan?"

"Not completely."

"Soooo...?" I prompted, trying to prod him into saying more, but he didn't. I crossed my arms across my chest and leaned my head back. The collar of the leather jacket had a button to secure the hood, but since I wasn't wearing it, my hair kept getting caught. I parted my hair in the middle and braided it into pigtails.

I was quiet for a while, but a question kept nagging me. "Gabriel?"

"Yes."

"Why do you trust me even though I'm one of them now?"

He exhaled and thought for a moment. "A few reasons. The look on your face in the graveyard the split-second before the knife hit you. The fact that vampires are flawlessly deceptive, and I can still read you clearly. And, I trust my gut. You have that same something that Joshua has."

"Have you ever been bitten before?"

"No."

"Then how did you know you were immune?" I asked, a little upset that he would put himself at risk.

"Everyone in my line is—one of the Angels of the Four Corners. Perfect immunity. No sickness. Prolonged life."

"I forgot, Super Slayer. I can add 'super' before your name before I say it each time if you like," I smiled.

The corner of his mouth twitched up, but he kept his eyes on the road. "There are advantages to my ancestry."

A short while later, the van in front of us rolled to a stop and Gabriel's phone rang. He hit the speakerphone. "Is there a problem?"

It was Kez. "There appears to be a two-car collision in front of us. I see bodies, but no movement." He paused. "I don't like it. Something is off."

"I will come up to help you check it out." Gabriel cut the engine, opened his door, and picked up the sword he had on the floor in front of the seat. "I want you to wait in the back of the van with Amara."

"Gabriel, I'm not helpless anymore. I can help."

"No arguments. Just do it."

I got out and followed him to the side door of the van. He knocked twice, and it popped open.

"Amara, I want her in here with you while we investigate."

"Come on in, Ali," she beckoned.

I looked back at Gabriel; he gripped the sword in his right hand while his fingers went over the throwing knives on his belt. I turned to protest one more time, but he pulled on my pigtail and said, "In you go."

The passenger door opened as Samael stepped out. So I ducked into the back of the van quickly, before we could make eye contact. As soon as I was inside, I walked to the bank of monitors and started turning them on. I gave Amara a worried grin. "Just because we're stuck in here doesn't mean we can't watch."

She slid into the seat next to me and we scrutinized the scene.

Two cars were blocking the road, and one was on its side. I couldn't see a driver in that car, but there was a circular spider web of cracks in the windshield and blood on it. The other car must've still been idling, as billows of hot exhaust were rising into the crisp night air. Once the three Slayers went past the cars, I couldn't see much.

"Where are they going?" Amara wondered.

"Maybe someone is hurt on the other side?" I surmised.

"Maybe. Kez is right though, this doesn't feel right."

I stood from my chair and opened the weapons closet. It was almost empty. "How many weapons did they take with them?"

"Ali, you were told to stay here," she warned.

"I just want to know what's here."

I looked through the closet. There was a sword, a couple daggers, and a crossbow. I returned to my seat, and we watched the monitors.

"Is this the only view? Or does this van have thermal imaging?"

"I think..." She looked at the control panel on her side. "Here we go." She pressed some buttons, and one by one, all the monitors blazed with a rainbow of colors.

We could see that the people in the cars were dead, their bodies cooling. The heat of the exhaust acted as a curtain, muddying the signals beyond. When they emerged from the plume of the exhaust, all three of them were moving back and forth. There also appeared to be some bodies on the ground. Then we started seeing movement to the left of the van in the tree line. All three of them stood, but we couldn't tell if they sensed the oncoming danger.

I looked at Amara. "Are those–?"

She already had the phone on her ear. "Kez, you have company coming from the east."

Within three seconds, we heard the clash of blades.

"How many are there?" I asked, my voice rising.

"Ten…maybe."

"Three to one or more."

"They'll be fine."

I stopped breathing and stared at the monitors. One vampire fell. Then another and another. The fight moved closer, and the exhaust from the car cut off the view. We switched back to video feed. It was still two to one. Then, I sensed something.

Standing, I moved behind my chair without taking my eyes off the screens. I pointed at the rearview camera, behind our car. "There. More of them," I whispered.

They came around the front of the car and hung at the back of the van. We counted three of them. They each chambered a round in their automatic weapons. "They're just going to mow them down." I went to the weapons locker again and grabbed the sword, two daggers, and a holster for the second dagger.

"No. You were told to stay here," Amara hissed, grabbing my arm.

"Just keep the door locked."

I opened the roof hatch and lifted myself through it. I stood on the roof watching them split up and rejoin at the front of the van, then move swiftly to cut the distance in half between the van and the scene of the accident.

They stood maybe a yard apart. The tall, slender figure on the left looked vaguely familiar. Taking a deep breath, I placed the dagger in my right hand and the sword in my left. I paused for a split-second and thought, "You don't see me." Instinct I didn't know I had took over, like it was hardwired.

My wish came true—they didn't sense me. Everything was crystal clear, like a choreographed dance. I launched myself into the air, landing silently behind the one farthest on the left, thrusting the dagger through his heart from the back. Before he had the chance to tumble to the ground, I switched the sword to my right hand and spun in a circle, fully extending my arm, and took the head of the second. A spray of blood hit me, as his head was loosed from his body. Then I was onto the third one.

He caught my approach and turned, jerking the trigger on the gun. I dove, somersaulting forward and avoiding the spray of bullets that he had no time to aim. When I came out of the roll, I was too close, and he knocked the sword from my hand with the gun. He went for my discarded weapon, but I twisted around and freed the other dagger from its sheath. I then drove it up under his ribs and into his heart. He fell backwards. I seized the sword from the ground and raised it high, ready to take his head.

Movement started coming at me from over one of the cars. I took a defensive stance and realized it was Samael, and it appeared as if I was going to attack. I dropped my weapon, hearing it crack against the asphalt when it hit the ground. Raising my hands in surrender, I stumbled backwards, beginning to shake with the realization of what I'd just done. I'd never taken a life before.

Then Samael stopped short. He stood there looking at me, his chest heaving gulps of air. He surveyed the area around me: one dead and two immobilized vampires, then lowered his weapon.

I glanced over into the trees and saw a ghostly face linger for a moment before it disappeared. We made eye contact, and acknowledged one another. The second he was gone, sickness hit my stomach. It was Morpheus. That's why he'd felt so close in the dream—he was—and he now knew my location.

Kez jogged between the vehicles to Samael's side, and a moment later, Gabriel strode up from around the car on the right.

"What are you doing out of the van?"

Before I could open my mouth, Samael said, "Saving our asses, apparently." Gabriel blanched, and Samael quickly corrected himself, "Sorry, protecting our flank."

I looked away from Gabriel to the vampire on the left that I'd taken down first. Now that I could see his face, I recognized him and pointed. "If you want to know more about the castle, that one. His name is Kyle; he was human last time I saw him, and he worked in the castle."

Some looks were exchanged between Samael and Gabriel, but I felt numb. I stared at the blood on my hands and backed up until I hit the grill of the van and leaned back. Logistics about who was going where were discussed, but I couldn't focus on the conversation.

I just kept gazing at the spots of blood like inkblots on my pale skin, totally disassociated from what was going on around me. When I finally looked up, Samael finished the job on the second vamp I'd immobilized. Kyle was picked up and shoved in the back of the van where Samael stayed. The other bodies were piled into the wrecked cars and set on fire.

At some point Amara had come out of the van, I noticed a very discreet hand squeeze as she passed by Kez and went back inside. Gabriel gently took my arm and ushered me to the sedan; we followed the van for a short while, and then peeled off in another direction.

"Are they not going back with us?"

"Later. After the interrogation."

"And after they kill him," I added.

"Yes."

I frowned. "Morpheus, he was in the woods. He saw me."

Gabriel nodded, his eyes tight.

We drove the rest of the way in silence.

I got out of the car woodenly and followed Gabriel into the house, or maybe home base would have been a more appropriate term. Gabriel stopped me before I got to the stairs and said, "Take a few minutes and change. I would like you to be with me when I brief Sebastian."

I nodded mutely and made my way to the room. Joshua was reading on the bed and appeared calm, but I could sense tension in the set of his shoulders. He exhaled slowly, the way he does when he is trying to keep his cool.

"Hey." My voice sounded forced. "I just need to change and get back." I smiled faintly because it felt like I should. I turned and opened the top drawer of the dresser, searching for something to wear beside scrubs and leathers with blood splatters.

"What happened to your clothes?"

"You really don't want to know."

Joshua's hands snaked around me from behind; there was tenderness in his touch, though I knew he was upset. "I really do want to know," he said against my neck.

I sagged slightly.

He ran his hands down my arms and stopped my search. I stopped breathing. He turned me around and kept his hands on my biceps. He found some droplets of blood on my face.

"Blood?" He paused. "It's not human."

"No."

"What happened?" He repeated.

Pulling away, I shrugged out of my jacket and shucked off my leather pants. "There was an ambush on the road on the way back. Kez, Samael, and Amara will be here shortly. Gabriel wants me there for the debrief."

Holding a clean shirt loosely in my fingers, I turned to change as nonchalantly as possible. Whipping off the scrubs shirt and jamming myself into the clean one, I noticed that the veins on my chest had darkened once again. I buttoned it as quickly as I could, but my hands shook and I fumbled with the buttons. My locket got tangled on the collar, making me jerk like I was caught doing something wrong. I smoothed both my necklaces and turned around.

"Ummm, you do realize we are married; you don't need to hide." His tone was light, but he leaned his head to the side, like he was thinking.

"Habit," I muttered, almost inaudibly. Hiding my illness was killing me, but Beth said it would be another day before we would know anything. Josh said something else, but my mind was still on the reemergence of the veins. He walked over to me and touched the back of my arm, and I jumped.

"What is wrong? Why are you pushing me away?"

"I-I'm not. I—"

"But you are. You know you are."

"I...please..." I looked at him pleadingly. I didn't want to have this conversation until I had more information. *Just one more day.*

He exhaled, dropping his hands to his sides and staggering back a couple steps. "You said, 'there's a lot of things I need to tell you. Things that happened. Things I did. I thought you were dead.'" He backed up and sat down hard on the bed. "Did you–" he swallowed and his voice broke, "Did you sleep with him?"

"No. I did not," I answered immediately, meeting eyes, but then I broke eye contact. I sat down on the floor and leaned against the dresser, unable to look at him.

My shame was burning me up. "But, I kissed him. Once. The day I left. I was trying to say goodbye without telling him goodbye, and I...I'm so, so sorry." I felt like a horrible person. The pressure was unbearable, I had to get out...to leave, so I stood and bolted to the door. But he was already there, blocking me, so I turned my back to him. "Please just let me go."

He stood there and didn't say a word. He took a few deep breaths, and it seemed as if he was going to say something, but then he refrained. I walked over and sat on the bed, still not making eye contact.

"Do you want to be with him?" he asked, his voice low.

"No. I would be lying if I said I didn't care about him. I was grieving over you, too much so to even seek comfort with someone else. When I thought you were gone, it was over for me. When my heart stopped beating, I simply went into survival mode. Everything I did was to learn as much as I could so I could get out. I felt like I was using him, but I didn't mean to. He was good to me."

"If it's not about him, why are you pushing me away?"

"It has nothing to do with Bowen," I cringed. "I love you. I am committed to *you*." I finally met his eyes.

He came over and knelt in front of me. "I know you love me," he paused. A pained look gripped his face, "You thought I was dead. It hurts, but I do understand."

I took in a stuttering breath, trying not to cry.

He raised himself onto his knees and moved forward. He wrapped one arm around me and placed his hand on my lower back. With the other, he ran his fingers over my face. I closed my eyes as he touched my eyelids...cheeks... lips...chin...neck...collarbone...his hand stopped on my sternum and I flinched, almost imperceptibly, but he paused. I leaned in and kissed him. A slow, languid kiss, but my heart wasn't in it.

He put his lips to my ear. "Our connection was severed. If we drink from one another, will it be reestablished?" His hand drifted to the top button on my blouse. I placed my hand over his, but it wasn't a smooth movement.

"Maybe," I replied unconvincingly, though I knew the answer was yes. "I really need to get back."

"I've hardly seen you. I think they can spare you for a little while longer." He leaned in and kissed me just under the jaw line, then moved down my neck. He paused. I realized what he was considering.

I not-so-gracefully wrenched myself free of him, jumping a few feet away. I was breathless, and there was hysteria creeping into my voice. "You can't. I need to get back." *Lame reason.*

Practically panting, I gripped at my shirt, covering my heart, not able to control the torrent of conflicting emotions pulsing through me.

"Then what is it?" His voice was escalating into anger.

"Please, I just need some time."

"Time for what? Why won't you let me touch you?" he said, topping my voice.

"I'm sick." It popped out of me like a cork—unfiltered, loud, and terrible. My voice dropped. "I'm sick."

I watched the understanding wash across his face. He stared at the hands over my heart, and then he met my gaze. Slowly, he stood and moved towards me. Placing his hands over mine, he pried them away from my chest and carefully unbuttoned my shirt. His face darkened when he took in the maze of veins that were now twisting their way almost to my bellybutton.

"Why? Why didn't you tell me about this?" His tone was sharp.

My voice trembled. "I didn't want you to worry. I wanted to see if there was any hope. I—"

He actually yelled. "You don't keep things like this a secret. It's not right. What were you thinking? You leave while I am sleeping, and you think it's okay? You leave a freaking note? You don't violate trust like that." He turned his back to me and uncharacteristically cursed under his breath, clenching his fists.

My throat constricted. "I didn't mean..."

He drew in a breath and exhaled slowly while turning to face me again. "What is it?"

My lips twitched downward. "A reaction to Aurora."

"*We* did this to you?" he said incredulously.

"It was an accident; no one is to blame. It's my freaky DNA. They're working on it."

"That's where you disappeared to with Gabriel?" His voice

rose and became heated again. He looked at the door as if he wanted to charge out of the room to speak with Gabriel.

"Yes, but don't get angry with him. I made him not tell you. He really didn't want to keep it from you. The first thing he told me to do was tell you. I was hoping they would have a solution for me."

"Did they?" he asked, a little more composed.

"I should've told you." I didn't answer his question.

"Yes, you should have. You are my wife, and we have to be a team. You don't ever need to bear a burden like this on your own." His voice was still frustrated.

"I'm sorry."

His anger seemed to ease. "I know," he replied and pulled me to his chest. He tucked my head underneath his chin. "It's going to be okay."

"Josh, we need to be prepared. If there is no—"

"No. I won't accept that."

I held onto him like I would never be in his arms again and prayed.

6

WON'T BE WITHOUT

Our bodies sat frozen on the bed, arms entwined around one another for who knows how long. We'd talked for a while, but the gravity of my illness was overwhelming, so we sat in comfortable silence. Well, as comfortable as could be under the circumstances.

Joshua's phone buzzed, breaking the stillness. He raised it to his ear. "Yes....Yes." He hung up. "The others are here."

"I should go."

"We should go. I don't care if they invited me or not."

I let out a relieved breath.

As we walked slowly down the hall, I remained tucked under Joshua's left arm. It felt as if he was emanating this barrier that would protect me from all harm. We arrived at the meeting room and hung outside the door for a moment.

We could hear conversation through the door. Positioning myself in front of him, I captured his face between my hands. I pulled his lips to mine and kissed him with such intensity he gasped and looked at me with both desire and confusion.

Placing my index finger on his lips, I said, "I wasn't keeping anything from you; I just didn't get a chance to tell you about the last 12 hours. Just sayin'. Just in case."

"I don't think I like the sound of that," he said warily.

Shrugging, I slipped back under his left arm as he opened the door, and we entered. Kez was perched on the back of the couch with his feet on the cushions. When he saw Joshua, he immediately stepped off the couch and came over, extending his hand.

"Good to see you again." His greeting seemed warm and genuine.

"Good to see you too, Kezef." Joshua shook his hand.

"I am sorry for the misunderstanding with your girl, here." Kez motioned to me.

Joshua looked at me, but before I could open my mouth, Sebastian cleared his throat and said, "Now that we are all here, let's begin." Everyone quickly took a seat. I sat next to Joshua, who never let go of me. I don't know if he ever would again.

Sebastian's opening question surprised me. "Kezef, do you make it a habit of trying to assassinate members of other teams?" I thought he was joking at first, but his face was very serious. I glanced around and realized Gabriel wasn't here.

"I am sorry, Sir. I was just about to apologize again when we started. I—"

"Sebastian, Sir," I interrupted. "I would have staked me, if I'd seen things from their perspective." The set of Sebastian's mouth eased, but not completely. *Something was wrong. And why wasn't Gabriel here?*

Kez continued to explain how I was sitting in the chair and removed the restraint, picked up scissors, and headed towards Beth. He said he had hit me in the back of the head with the hilt of his dagger and then pinned me to the floor with it. I hadn't realized that Gabriel was on the phone with Sebastian when Kez took me down. He'd heard some of what had happened over the open line.

Joshua appeared calm on the outside, but his body stiffened ever-so-slightly, and he squeezed my hand. I looked over at Amara; she was observing Joshua, and then she closed her eyes, head bent down. She appeared overwhelmed.

The door opened, and Gabriel took a seat. He had a notebook in his hands that he was gripping so hard, his knuckles were white. I made eye contact with him, but his expression didn't change. It felt like a stone dropped into my stomach, and the stress rippled through my body. Then I caught myself and tried to calm down.

I peered over at Amara, and sure enough, she was watching me now. She returned the half-smile that I managed to give her. It was an odd having someone read my emotions with perfect clarity. Joshua had the ability to sense intentions, but since mine were usually pure, I'd never really thought about it.

Samael started going over the ambush, so I tuned back into the conversation again. He explained, "Gabriel met us at the van and had Aleria wait with Amara." He paused. "I didn't approve of Amara being left with the...with Aleria, but it wasn't my call." He nodded at Gabriel.

"We proceeded past the wreckage and found three humans on the ground. Two were dead, and the third was in the last stages of bleeding out. We sensed something was off. Kezef's phone rang; Amara called moments before twelve vampires converged on the three of us. Ten of them engaged us at once. They were from the two, six-man teams we had been tracking. We now know that they took out the Watchers we had observing them. They were due to check in about the same time as the ambush.

"Two of them hung back; we assume that they were the

leaders. One was a tall male with shoulder-length, black hair and a square jaw. I hadn't seen him before."

"Broad shoulders, grey eyes, and an angular nose?" I asked.

Samael thought for a moment. "Not sure about the eyes, but yes on the others."

"Morpheus. He's one of the Oneiroi. I saw him in the woods before he disappeared."

"The Oneiroi? From Greek mythology? I thought they were a fairytale."

Sebastian exhaled. "Unfortunately, no. They were awakened and are quite real."

"Are they able to infiltrate dreams?" Amara asked.

I peeked at Sebastian for permission and he nodded in assent. So, I explained, "Yes, but they need to have your blood. They need the blood bond to get into your head. It appears that they don't need to actually feed on their victim to establish the bond like most vampires."

"How long ago did they start infiltrating your dreams?" Amara asked, automatically knowing it had happened to me.

"A week and a half before I was captured. I was poisoned, and some of my blood was stolen while I was in the hospital."

Sebastian steered the questions back to the ambush. "You said there was another vampire hanging back?"

"Yes, a woman," Kez answered.

"Did you know her?"

"No. She disappeared with the one you call Morpheus."

I rubbed my chest. "Was she about my height with wavy auburn hair, really full lips, a mole on her left cheek, and large dark eyes?"

"Yes," Samael answered.

"Zahra. She and Morpheus liked to hunt together in the maze."

Then Samael continued, "Both Morpheus and Zahra stopped

and stared behind us, like they were expecting something, and disappeared. I put down the vamp I was fighting. At that moment, I heard gunshots and thought Amara may be in trouble. So I proceeded in the direction the two leaders had been focused on. When I got there, I found a vampire with glowing eyes and blood all over her in a defensive position.

"I raised my sword and was about to engage when she dropped her sword and stumbled backwards a few steps. I realized it was Aleria and that she was standing over three enemy bodies. I hadn't sensed any of them, including her. They were equipped with automatic weapons. I believe the leaders, Morpheus and Zahra, bugged out to avoid the weapons fire."

Samael took a deep breath. "If Aleria hadn't intervened, I don't know if we would've survived." He squinted at his hands for a moment, fidgeted, and finally locked eyes with me. "I didn't thank you before. Thank you, I owe you one."

I nodded. It seemed difficult for him to say that to me.

"Ali, did the vampires you engaged sense you coming?" Gabriel asked.

"I don't believe so. I came at them from behind and immobilized the first and took the head off the second before the third realized I was there. And I think the only reason he noticed me was because when I took the head of the second, it rolled into his view."

"So you had to fight the third?" Sebastian asked.

I shrugged. "Briefly. When he saw me coming, he fired at me, but I was able to roll and avoid getting hit. Then I was at his feet, and he knocked the sword out of my hand. When he went for that, he lunged forward. I buried my dagger in his chest hitting his heart. He fell instantly."

"You took on three by yourself," Joshua said.

"Well, yeah. There was no one else," I answered.

Joshua turned his head away from me.

Samael continued. "I took the head of the one she'd fought. She identified the first one as someone that had worked in the castle, so we questioned him."

"Did you learn anything from the captive?" Gabriel asked.

"Yes. We have a more complete floor plan. It matches with everything that Aleria gave us, so we believe he was telling the truth. But he was a neophyte and not trusted with much information."

"Kyle. He was less than a month old," I added.

"I'm surprised they would send out someone so young," Amara commented.

"Depends on the target," Sebastian said.

"What do you mean?" Kez asked.

"If they are tracking a vampire who doesn't like to hurt anyone." Sebastian paused and regarded me. "Ali, did you realize who it was before you engaged?"

"No."

"Would you have hesitated?" Sebastian questioned.

"Maybe…" I thought for a moment, "No. I did the right thing. I would have protected everyone, just as I did. Kyle made his choice."

"What was he to you?" Kez inquired curiously.

Not wanting to answer, I dropped my gaze and stared at the hem of my shirt, squeezing the bottom button until I heard it crack in half. I glanced over at Sebastian, and he was actually waiting for an answer too. I sighed. "He was a familiar."

"Did you feed on him often?" Sebastian inquired.

"Every other day for a month or so." The room went cold, so I felt the need to explain. "There is no bagged blood in the castle. You use familiars or starve and I had help. I never killed anyone." I swallowed hard and felt rising stress radiate through me again. "That is, until the vampire I killed a few hours ago." It became hard to breathe and I suddenly felt exhausted—like my head weighed a thousand pounds.

"Ali, I think you need to take a break and feed," Gabriel interrupted.

"I'm fine."

Joshua leaned forward and inspected me. "No, you're not."

Amara stood and walked in front of me and offered me her hand. "Come. I will go with you. Let the boys talk." I took her hand and let her lead me out.

We went to my room, and I immediately caught sight of the emergency. A blue vein was snaking up my neck and wrapping under my jaw. I opened the fridge and noticed new blood pouches marked with my name in Gabriel's handwriting. I picked one, sat on the bed, and stared at it. I felt too embarrassed to drink in front of Amara.

"I'll sit over here and turn my back," she volunteered.

"Thank you," I said quietly, surprised she was willing to turn her back on a vamp she doesn't really know. I sat with it in my lap, still not wanting to drink, but after a couple of minutes, I finally acquiesced and fed. Afterwards, I took a few deep breaths and walked to the mirror almost afraid to check. The vein had almost disappeared.

"You feel better?"

"I guess so. I just feel tired. Other than that, I don't feel that bad, but I'm sure that will change at some point."

"Hopefully there will be a solution soon."

"Yeah," I replied, but my tone was dismal.

"You aren't expecting one, are you?"

"Things are never that easy."

"You ready to go back?"

Nodding, I moved towards the door. We strolled down the hall in silence. Questions bubbled inside me about what she was sensing, but I couldn't seem to muster a coherent thought.

When we reentered the room, Kez and Samael were gone, and it felt like there was no air in the room. Gabriel was hunched forward with his head in his hands. Joshua and Sebastian had unreadable expressions. Amara closed her eyes and bent her head forward for a brief moment.

Sebastian looked at Amara. "Blackthorne called. He is dispatching the three of you for a quick opp. We will see you again in a few hours. They are waiting upstairs."

"Thank you. I'll see you soon." She turned and peered at me like she was trying to communicate something. Then, she squeezed my arm and departed down the hall.

I sat down next to Joshua; he reached over and took my hand. He felt cool even to me. The room remained hushed. "Did something happen?" I asked hesitantly. I realized everyone was actually looking at Gabriel. "Did you finish translating the letter?"

He sat up with a haunted expression. "Almost." Then he got to his feet and left the room.

"Did I say something wrong?" I asked.

"No," Sebastian answered.

"Did he say anything before I came back?"

Sebastian pursed his lips. "He said that something else was done to you in the hospital, besides removing your appendix."

"And...?"

"That is all he said," he paused, "We will meet again later. Let him process whatever it is."

"Have you ever seen him like this?"

"Not like this, no."

"Uncool," I said under my breath. I felt worry expand inside me until it felt like there was no room for anything else.

How could he say that they did something to me and not explain? When Jess had run the ultrasound wand over my belly after the surgery, she and Gabriel had exchanged a look. He already knew they did something else to me. This was just his confirmation.

I cringed and pressed the bridge of my nose with my fingertips. I thought I saw Sebastian nod in agreement when I said uncool, but I wasn't sure. All of us sat in silence, maybe waiting to see if Gabriel was going to return.

Then Josh stood without letting go of my hand and pulled me out the door. We headed towards our room. As we walked down the hall, I could feel an odd energy rolling off of him. It was frenetic and wild and made me concerned. When we walked through the bedroom door, Joshua spun around and picked me up, pulling my legs around his waist and pressing me against the door. I gasped and looped my arms around his neck.

His lips came crashing into mine. He tasted of desperation, a low moan escaping from deep in his throat, and his breath was instantly ragged. There was no gentleness in his kisses; each was grasping, like all the emotion he'd controlled for months was surging out of him. I felt a knot of emotion in my throat as I returned the frantic kisses.

Running his hands up my spine, he sent sparks through every nerve in my body. Then carried me to the bed, lowering me without letting his lips leave mine even once. His weight settled on me as he kissed me under my chin and down my throat, lingering on my collarbone, his breath still rough. He pulled back for a split-second and gazed down at me. The only way I can describe his expression was reckless and intense, like he was afraid I would melt away like tissue paper in the rain.

Josh reached behind his head, grabbed the collar of his t-shirt, and pulled it off in one, smooth motion. Then he lowered himself back onto me. The sensation of his skin made me feel crazed. I gulped air, trying to catch my breath.

His mouth was at my ear as he said, "I need you." His warm breath spilled down my neck.

More than anything, I wanted to repeat the same phrase, to lose myself. Then reality hit me. With strength from somewhere, I rolled us over so I was straddling him from the top. I pinned his shoulders down as I gasped for air, trying to get control of myself.

"We can't. We don't know yet if you could get sick."

He rolled me off so we were on our sides and pulled me close again. I couldn't think straight.

"I don't care."

The words spilled out of me feverishly between kisses, "No, you have to care. I won't get you sick."

"I won't be without you again." Then, he had my shirt open, and I could feel the skin of our bellies pressed together. His body felt warm compared to mine, and I could feel it through the lace of my bra.

"No. What if they fix me, and it changes, and they can't fix you?"

"Just be with me," he said breathlessly. "Just be my wife. My lover. My partner. Just be." He twisted his hand in my hair at the base of my skull and pulled my lips to his to keep me from a rebuttal. My hands were moving over his back urgently, my body on fire.

"I…" The words strangled off in his mouth. Another desire welled up in me, overpowering my senses: the desire for a blood bond with him and the need of his blood to seal that bond. I felt my canines unsheathe. I panted, digging my nails into his back; he groaned. This was something I could do, I realized. *The virus wasn't in my saliva.*

Running the fingers of my right hand upwards, I caressed his shoulder blades and his neck. I grabbed onto his hair and kissed his neck while I rolled so I was more on top of him again. Pulling my head back enough to meet his eyes, I knew mine were glowing, and that my desire was clear.

He offered his neck to me and rasped, "Do it."

I drew in a deep breath and bit down on his neck. His blood hit my tongue, salty and metallic and perfect.

He let out a stuttering breath.

I released the hormone, and I felt him relax beneath me, the calm coursing through him. The hand that was still knotted in my hair relaxed, went to my back, and gently pulled me closer as I drank. He let out a quiet moan that I could feel vibrate in his chest. I finished, sealed the punctures, and rested my head on his bare chest.

The frenzy was over; our breathing became slow and synchronized. I was linked to him now, though he couldn't drink from me and reestablish the bond that had saved my life more than once.

After a long while, I asked, "Are you okay?"

He sighed. "I'm not sure."

"Did you not want me to?"

"Not that. Just everything else. I'm frustrated."

"I thought I was the impetuous one." I lifted my head to look at him.

Words poured out of him in a whispered gush. "I just kept thinking: you're my wife, and I love you. I love you more than anything. And we only had one night together before you were ripped away from me. I want to make every moment we have together count."

"Just one more day, and we'll have more information."

He raised his head and kissed my forehead.

"If we get bad news, I—"

He cut me off. "It won't be bad news."

I cringed and put my head back on his bare chest. "I'm sure it won't be." I lied. "I'm sure it won't be," I repeated one last time before drifting off to sleep.

7

DO WHAT YOU MUST

I was back and completely startled by the familiar landscape. The sky was pale on the horizon, pushing up the velvety darkness. Only one star twinkled above the rolling hills in the distance; the sun poised to creep above the horizon soon. Following the slope with my eyes, I found the oak tree reaching into the sky like it had been sketched with black ink. I sank down next to a large rock and kept still. I wasn't sure what to do or how I'd managed to get back here.

The edge of the sun crested, and I felt its warmth on my face. It made me feel hollow, and I wished this could be real. Suddenly, I felt a heavy hand grapple my shoulder and tear me out of my reverie.

"You! You *were* here. How are you here?" Morpheus boomed as he wrenched my arm and pulled me to my feet.

I stammered. "I-I don't know. I just went to sleep."

His face was a mask of terrifying anger. "Get out. Get out of here."

My terror melted away, and it was replaced with defiance.

"So it's okay for you to invade *my* dreams, to twist them into nightmares?"

"Orders," he clipped.

"You enjoyed it," I accused, narrowing my eyes at him.

"It's what I do," he shrugged, without apology. He seized me by the throat. Spittle flew out of his mouth as he spoke. "Never come back here again." Then he began to squeeze. I fought and flailed, trying to make some sort of impact on his massive figure, but I felt as if the energy was being sucked from me.

He slammed me to the ground, keeping my throat in his ever-tightening grasp. In desperation, I reached for his face, trying to fight dirty. He started to ask me a question, but a horrible whirring was in my ears, and everything was twisted into shades of grey, like I was spinning.

Fighting the sensation, I pictured the sun smoldering his flesh. Seconds later, Morpheus screeched and released me. I scrambled to my feet to find him down on one knee clutching his face.

"I don't have to be your enemy," I said with a tremble in my voice, fighting to keep myself in the dream.

He spread his fingers and looked at me between the gaps, still keeping his face hidden. He opened his mouth, then snapped it shut. I couldn't see enough of his face to read the expression.

Then his mouth twisted into a snarl, and he launched himself at me. I could see the last bits of his scorched face were healing as he knocked me to the ground, his weight crashing on top of me. Morpheus pinned my chest down with his left forearm and pressed the fingers of his right hand into my throat. He was so heavy that I couldn't wriggle out of his grasp.

Suddenly, an epiphany spread across his features, like something he should've seen before had hit him square in the face. He eased his grip slightly.

"Your transformation into one of us." Morpheus smiled and

cocked his head. "It didn't alter your powers; it only made you stronger. The queen will be most pleased." He stroked my cheek with a single finger and said in a forced whisper, "What a beautiful sacrifice you will make."

Shrinking from him, the whirring returned, and I welcomed the blackness.

I awoke gasping with Joshua howling my name. He was holding a cloth to my face that smelled like him. I could feel my eyes rolling back into my head involuntarily and could sense the fingers of Morpheus around my throat again.

"Ali. No...no....concentrate. You need to wake." I felt Joshua grab my face with his other hand.

My eyes fluttered open, and the dream faded once again. I was laying on the bed, and Joshua was hunched over me on his knees, shirtless.

"I was..." I placed my hand over Joshua's and took over, applying pressure to my nose. It was then that I realized he was using the t-shirt he'd taken off and tossed on the floor before we went to sleep. "I was in Morpheus's dream," I said half-dazed. "I invaded *his* dream."

Joshua sat up, still on his knees, and placed his hands on his thighs. "Have you ever done anything like that before?"

"It happened yesterday, but I wasn't sure if that was what really had happened. But it was. I know that now."

"Do you want to tell Sebastian? Or Gabriel?"

"I probably should, but I don't know what good it would do— the ability I mean."

"It must be good for something." He motioned to my nose. "Have you been getting these often since you were turned?"

"No, this is the first one. It must be an Aurora thing."

I pulled the shirt away, and I felt another gush go down my face. I sighed and closed my eyes. When I opened them, Joshua's glowing eyes were fastened on me, fixed with concern. I sat up and swung my feet off the bed. I started to stand, but felt light-headed.

"What do you need? I'll get it for you."

"Got it." I padded to the fridge, dragging out a unit of blood marked with my name. I used my teeth to pull out the stopper and squeezed some into my mouth, flinching at the cool temperature. But I figured this would be the only thing to help me heal. After finishing, I checked my nose again and the bleed had stopped.

"The bleeding. You aren't healing, are you?" He moved to the edge of the bed and put his feet back on the floor.

"Not like normal."

"Is that why there's blood marked with your name?"

Internally cringing, I leaned against the wall and focused on my feet, knowing that I was taking way too long to answer his question. I exhaled harshly. "It's Slayer blood."

He raised his eyebrows.

I moved to the bed and sat down next to him to explain everything. I kept my head down as I went over every detail of my trip that he hadn't heard in the debrief, including the parts I wanted to leave out, like feeding on Gabriel. He remained quiet while I spoke, his breathing remained calm and even the whole time.

He finally asked a question after a prolonged silence. "Does human blood do you any good right now?"

"Yes, but it's like eating cereal when you need protein. You feel better, and it tides you over, but later that day, you still need to eat the protein."

"So, if you become injured..."

"I don't seem to heal well without it. And when I get stressed, my energy wanes and I feel myself getting worse."

"Did you fight to stay in that dream?"

"Yes. I didn't know. I thought maybe, now that I'm not

human, it wouldn't have the same impact on me."

"Please, if it happens again, just wake."

I nodded in agreement.

"Are you actually going to listen to me?" I could hear the mock astonishment.

The corner of my mouth quirked up. "Yes."

"See, miracles do happen." There was a smile in Josh's voice, and when I glanced up at him, he wore a crooked grin.

"I always listen. I just don't always follow well."

Sunset was approaching. Joshua had gotten dressed and headed upstairs before me after getting a text from Sebastian. I lingered a moment to feed again. There was a knock at the door. I checked the mirror to make sure there was no remaining blood on my lips and opened the door.

Peter stood looking very pleased with himself.

"You look happy. Wait, where have you been?" I said slowly, wondering what the catch was.

He held out a phone and shrugged. "I'm still taking classes, and I'm smiling because Sebastian sent this down. He's lifting the embargo on recruits having phones unless on an opp." He held up another phone in his other hand and wagged his eyebrows.

"He still considers me a recruit, eh?"

"You're still one of us—recruit or not. I programmed my number in, so you can text me now."

I smiled. "Like a little bit of home." I shoved down the surge of homesickness I suddenly felt.

"Seriously. We have all these cool gadgets, and we aren't allowed to use anything. I'm still going through tech addiction withdrawals. Growing up in Silicon Valley, it's painful to have your tech limited."

"Maybe that won't be the only embargo lifted—" I paused, "So what classes have you been taking?"

"Mostly reading since you...while you were gone. That and the normal physical and weapons training. I think I may be able to school you with a crossbow now."

I looked at him through hooded lids. "Not likely," I patronized.

"Sorry, but you're going down Al."

"Oh, it's on then," I said with a flourish and curtsy.

"Come on. You're going to love this," Peter smirked and trotted from my room.

I trailed behind him down the seemingly endless hallway adjacent to mine. We came to a set of double doors at the very end. It was a small room with the same industrial laminate tiles, but in brown instead of white.

Peter strode through to another set of double doors, and when he swung them open, I was hit with the scent of hay. I came to a stop next to him as he held his arm out like a showman, revealing a shooting range that looked like it had once been a cafeteria. The hay I smelled was piled at one end of the room, backed with thick sheets of plywood, and pegged with well-used targets. He indicated for me to wait next to a long counter piled with weapons.

"Milady, your challenge awaits," he said with a theatrical bow in response to my earlier dramatics.

Peter jogged out, put new targets up, and returned to set up the bows. I sat on the counter, watching and splitting stray pieces of hay in half. They were still moist enough that they only made a dull squeaking sound as they were shredded.

"You're staring," Peter accused.

"Intimidation technique. Is it working? Are you scared?" I curled my lips into a wicked smile.

"I don't know. Does my manliness and superiority scare you?" Peter retorted.

"Quaking with fear," I replied, trying to suppress a giggle.

He handed me a loaded crossbow. Taking my place behind the line chalked on the floor, I took aim, purposely hitting the outer ring of my target. The crossbow was already my weapon of choice, and now with my increased abilities, it was cake.

"Ooooh, too bad, champ," he said in mock consolation.

I moved aside, and he fixed his eyes on his target. He let go and pierced the second-most inner ring.

"Wow. Lucky shot," I teased.

"And whose arrow is closer to the center?"

"Hmmmmm." I stepped back and let my arrow fly, hitting the same spot on the opposite side.

Peter took his turn and hit just to the right of his last arrow on the edge of the third ring. Each of his shots were closer to the center than mine. We alternated back and forth for another four shots.

"You wanna do the last one at the same time? Or are you afraid it'll be too distracting?"

I made a pouty face. "I think I might be able to handle it."

We lined up next to one another and let loose our last arrows. Mine hit dead center, his almost did. He had a tighter grouping at first look. But, I waited for him to notice what I'd done.

I heard a sharp intake of breath. "You suck."

I grinned. "I don't understand what you mean?"

"You know you ripped that off from a movie," he replied with faux judgment.

"It doesn't make the smiley face any less funny," I said as I stuck my tongue out at him.

"That's it—my illusion of vampires is shattered. I thought you were supposed to be all serious and broody now. Not all flaunty and superior."

"I've always been superior to you," I said batting my lashes.

"The other way around, darling, and now it's time for handguns."

We spent the next hour in playful competition that didn't tax me too much physically. He legitimately beat me using the handguns. I actually forgot about the outside world for that hour. That is, until the vein on my neck decided to make an appearance. I slumped onto a bale of hay and told Peter about my illness. He got quiet and pale and just listened.

When I finished, he didn't offer any false hope; he simply hugged me. He held tight for a long while, and the warmth of his embrace made me realize that I didn't need to keep things locked up inside. I had people to rely on who accepted me despite my being turned. As we strolled back towards the inhabited rooms, I looped my arm in his.

"Thanks, Peter."

He smiled, but there was a sadness in it. "You bet. We'll rematch next week." He winked and loped off down the hall in the direction of the stairs.

My hands that were smudged with dirt and had a lingering metallic smell from loading ammo into clips. I headed towards the bathroom, and when I rounded the corner, I found Gabriel sitting in the hallway. I stopped short, as this was completely out of character for him.

"Hey, you okay?" I asked, my voice a little shaky.

He met my gaze, obviously troubled, still clutching his notebook. He didn't look like the thirty-something warrior that embodied all things badass. Tired lines crowded around his eyes, and the slope of the shoulders lacked their normal confidence.

"We need to talk."

I felt like ice filled my chest. "Okay. Here? Now?"

He stood to his feet stiffly and noticed my hands. "No, go

ahead and clean up." He started to turn away, then halted. "And feed."

I sighed.

"Do it—and bring Joshua. I am not talking to you without him. No secrets." He pointed to Sebastian's office as he trekked down the hall away from me.

I had the horrible feeling that I didn't want to know whatever he was going to tell me. With purpose, I washed away the grime before darting to my room. Joshua wasn't there, so I pulled out my newly acquired phone and cycled through the numbers Peter had programmed into it—all five of them, and found Joshua's number.

I typed in a text: "G wants to meet."

Joshua immediately texted back: "When?"

"Now ok?"

"Where?"

"S's office."

"Down in a sec."

While shoving the phone into my jeans pocket, I noticed how soiled the bottom edge of my shirt was. So I tossed it onto the growing pile of dirty clothes overflowing the basket in the corner of the room. My hand landed on a fitted black shirt with grey graphics that reminded me of Leslie. I struggled with the sudden feeling of loss and locked it away, quickly yanking on the shirt.

I went for the fridge and fed as ordered. It was the last pint of Slayer blood. As I reached for the doorknob to go, it turned, and Joshua appeared.

"Ready?"

"Yup."

"You know what this is about?" he asked, putting his arm around me. I tucked myself in circling his waist with my arms as we walked down the long hall.

"No, but Gabriel had that notebook in his hands and he didn't seem himself."

Josh didn't reply, but he stopped breathing and pulled me a little tighter to his side.

When we arrived at Sebastian's office, Gabriel was sitting on the couch, leaning forward, elbows on knees, with the notebook in both his hands. We slipped noiselessly into the room and sank onto the seat across from him. He didn't look up at us.

"You finished translating the letter?" Joshua asked.

"Yes."

"May I see it?" I asked.

Gabriel looked at me reluctantly, but he didn't move. I leaned forward and put my hand on the notebook. He allowed me to pull it from his hands. The original letter was on the left, and he'd neatly scrawled the translation on the right. I was surprised at how much Dagan had written. I looked over at Joshua and felt my face turn pale. His lips thinned into a line, and he nodded at me. We began reading together silently.

GABRIEL,

DO NOT MISTAKE MY ACTIONS FOR ALLIANCE. I SENSE MICHAEL IN HER AND HAVE CHOSEN TO HONOR AN ANCIENT DEBT THROUGH HIS HEIR. THE SPIRIT I SEE IN HER HAS BROUGHT UP REGRETS I HAVE LONG SINCE FORGOTTEN, WHERE MISGUIDED LOYALTY EXILED ME FROM THINGS I LOVE. MY SINS ARE TOO GREAT TO BE FORGIVEN, BUT THEY DO NOT BLIND ME TO WHAT IS COMING. THE WORLD DOES NOT NEED TO BE LOST IN DARKNESS AS IT ONCE WAS. PROTECT HER. PROTECT HER CHILDREN.

LAZARE, WHO I ASSUME IS DECEASED, WAS TASKED TO HARVEST NOT ONLY HER BLOOD FOR THE ONEIROI, BUT ALSO A MEANS BY WHICH AGRONA COULD PRODUCE A MEMBER OF THE LUX FOR HER OWN PURPOSES. USING WHAT WAS STOLEN, THE QUEEN HAS SEEN

TO IT THAT A DOZEN SURROGATES HAVE BEEN IMPLANTED. ONLY ONE PREGNANCY HAS MADE IT INTO THE SECOND TRIMESTER.

IF THE CHILD IS A FEMALE, THEY WILL WAIT TO CONFIRM THAT SHE HAS THE POWER OF THE SEERS. ALERIA MAY BE SPARED FOR A TIME, BUT IT WILL NOT LAST FOREVER. THE DIVISION SHE HAS CAUSED IN THE QUEEN'S FAMILY WILL NOT BE IGNORED. *IF THE CHILD IS MALE, HE WILL BE RAISED IN THE CASTLE. ONCE A LUX IS PROCURED FOR THE SACRIFICE, HE TOO WILL BE SACRIFICED FOR HIS SLAYING ABILITIES.*

DUE TO CIRCUMSTANCES IN THE PAST, THERE WERE TWO TYPES OF PEOPLE MOLOCH WAS NEVER ABLE TO DRAIN FOR THEIR ABILITIES. HIS DESIRE FOR THEIR POWER BECAME THAT OF OBSESSION, AND THE QUEEN WISHES TO GIVE IT TO HIM ON HIS RETURN. MOLOCH WANTS THE POWER OF A SEER OF THE LUX AND THAT OF A SLAYER FROM THE ANGELS OF THE FOUR CORNERS.

THE PAST HAS A WAY OF IMPACTING THE FUTURE. YOUR ANCESTOR WAS RESPONSIBLE FOR DESTROYING THE NEPHILIM, AND MOLOCH'S CHILDREN WERE AMONGST THEM. I FELL WITH MOLOCH, BUT I DID NOT HAVE ANY CHILDREN WITH THE DAUGHTERS OF MAN, AND THEREFORE DO NOT BEAR THE SAME GRUDGE AGAINST YOUR FAMILY. AGRONA MEANS TO HONOR THE REVENGE SWORN BY HER HUSBAND. HER FEAR OF HIM IS AS GREAT AS HER LOVE FOR HIM. SHE HAS RESOLVED TO BOTH BRING HIM BACK AND ENACT THIS REVENGE AT ANY PRICE.

THE ATTACK ON THE GENETICS LAB THAT TOOK MICHAEL'S LIFE WAS NOT RANDOM. THE CHILD THAT GROWS IN THE BELLY OF THE SURROGATE IS ALSO YOURS. DO WHAT YOU MUST.

STRENGTH BE WITH YOU.

The closing was some sort of symbol that I assume couldn't be translated.

It was too much. I sat in stunned silence, breathing shallowly. Joshua handed the notebook back to Gabriel, who upon taking it, leaned back, balancing it on his left leg, and looked at us exhaustedly.

Joshua took my right hand in both of his.

I finally found my voice and asked Gabriel, "You knew, didn't you, that they stole my ovary?"

"Yes."

"Jess noticed, didn't she? When she removed the tracker, that's what she showed you."

"Yes." Gabriel's voice sounded choked for the first time ever.

"Why didn't you tell me?" My voice came out more hurt than angry.

His mouth pulled down at the corners, and he shook his head slowly from side to side. "You had just had emergency surgery, and we were on the run. Maybe I should have," he exhaled harshly. "Part of me had hoped you were born with only one, no matter how remote the possibility."

My voice was low as I asked, "A child, what do we do?" I looked at him pleadingly like he might have the answer.

He met my eyes. "I do not know."

I shot out of my seat and paced back and forth, unable to attach myself to one single thought. Emotion was lashing at my insides almost painfully, a raging tempest, so much more powerful than when I was human.

"A baby. Mine and yours. It's so..."

"Awkward," Joshua answered, speaking for the first time.

Gabriel let out a single, solemn chuckle and ran his fingers through his hair.

I continued pacing, unable to calm myself. I felt as if I would shatter into pieces with such an explosive force that I would decimate anything around me. I *had* to move. I had to go. I had to do something, even if it was only going outside.

My chest was heaving like I was going to hyperventilate, and I couldn't stop myself even though breathing wasn't necessary. I glanced at Joshua, who was perched on the edge of the couch watching me fearfully, his fingers lifted slightly like he was itching to reach out to me.

I waved him off, despite feeling the wildness of my expression. "I'm sorry. I have to get out of here."

Without any other warning, I bolted through the door, down the hall, and up the stairs. Both of them were calling my name and the sound of pursuit echoed behind me. But I just wanted to be alone, as selfish as it was. Another staircase going upwards came into view, and within seconds, I was on the roof.

I slammed the door behind me and found that the weather matched my mood. The moonless sky was cracked by lightning, followed by a blast of thunder, and then the heavens let loose a deluge of rain to drown out the city. It smelled of wet stone and cold.

My clothes were already plastered to my body. I pushed my soaked hair from my eyes and spun in a circle to survey the roof. I needed to run. So, I backed up a few steps and jumped to the next roof that was nearly twenty feet away, and I landed lightly and kept running. Running, jumping, running, jumping to the next roof and the next.

I'd never been outside like this to use any of my physical abilities. It felt freeing, like the world was dropping away. Pushing harder, I kept going until I came to the ledge of a building and a flash of light caught my attention. Looking down at the busy street below a neon sign flickered, casting a glow on the people with umbrellas who were scurrying in the darkness, into buildings, or into waiting cars. Rubbing at my eyes, I backed up a few steps, and lighted to the next rooftop. I thought I heard my name, and stopped and looked around, but saw nothing.

I continued on until I was in the heart of downtown, and then I missed—my emotion distracting me. Flailing, I desperately grasped at the slick roof, but everything was smooth.

Then I was weightless, falling through the air, clawing at nothing, and hit the ground hard on my side, knocking the breath from me. Glancing upwards, I counted four stories. The smell of wet trash invaded my nose. I'd fallen into an alley next to an overflowing dumpster with a couple squeaking rats trying to keep dry.

My shoulder felt dislocated, but it didn't seem like anything was broken, and I couldn't smell blood. I lay there motionless, trying to work up the energy to stand. "I'm an idiot," I murmured to myself.

To my horror, an unfamiliar voice answered. "Yes, it's not wise to be out on your own on a night like this."

I struggled to my feet and found the source of the voice. A vampire was sitting on the landing of a fire escape just across from me; he hadn't been there a moment ago. He was kicking his legs like a child would in an oversized chair. I could sense what he was, but even with my eyesight, I couldn't see him clearly. Holding my left arm, I tried not to show the degree of pain I was in.

"Nasty fall. Where is your Sire?"

"Close," I replied, holding up my chin confidently.

He smiled and leaned forward so that his face was in the muted light from the street. He had black hair, a sharp jaw, narrow lips, and a hooked nose all running with water.

He pulled his lips to the side. "Or are you a refugee? Or a nomad, perhaps?" I felt like a bug under glass, awaiting a pin.

"It's none of your business." I let go of my arm and started towards the street, but he was instantly in front of me, joined by three others. Cringing backwards, I assessed the situation—I was out here alone and without weapons. I'd just fed, so I still had energy, but I needed to relocate my shoulder. I raised my right arm peacefully. "I don't want any trouble."

"But we do," Hook Nose replied with a sinister grin.

"What do you want?" I asked, my voice surprisingly calm.

"Just a little fun. Humans don't last long. And when they go missing, the powers that be get so out of sorts."

A tall, thin one behind him spoke up; he looked like a red-headed Q-tip. He was incredibly thin with a giant, round mop of hair crowning his head. "Aye, but a wayward vamp, no un 'ill miss 'er."

The one with green hair next to him laughed eagerly.

I nodded. "You miss the hunt."

Hook Nose smiled to show his shockingly white teeth. "Precisely."

"Will you give me a second?" I swallowed. "In the interest of sportsmanship?"

"Of course." He bowed slightly.

I moved towards the back of the alley looking for a bar or something I could use. Some pipes were protruding from the side of the building, and unfortunately there was no time for finesse. Using my right arm to loop my left around the bar, I grabbed onto my left wrist and took a deep breath and jerked back. It clunked back into the socket making me want to vomit, but I stayed on my feet.

Testing it, I moved it around like a prizefighter before a match. This fight had to be won by sheer skill—there was no element of surprise like at the ambush. Stretching a few extra times, I glanced around to formulate my plan of attack.

This was as ready as I was going to get, I walked back and stood before them weaponless, and addressed Hook Nose. "I will save you for last," I said with some bravado.

He laughed.

I bent to my left, slipping my fingers under the edge of the dumpster and sent it soaring towards Q-tip and Green Hair, plopping it on top of them like you would drop a cup over a mouse. I jumped over the leader and came down with my knees in the chest of the fourth vamp, Gigantor, throwing him on his back. He padded the landing. When his head hit the pavement with a deafening crack, he dropped the stake in his hand. I seized it and planted it in his chest.

The moment I thought I was doing well, someone grabbed my hair and pulled me deeper into the alley. I spun around, my hair still in his hand, to see that Hook Nose had me. He kicked me in the stomach as he let go of my hair, sending me hurtling into the back wall.

Blinking away the stars, I jumped to my feet. My energy was quickly depleting; I was still healing, but not for long. Pain was starting to radiate from my previous chest wound.

Hook Nose was standing with Q-tip and Green Hair by the dumpster, but they left Gigantor paralyzed in the mouth of the alley.

I glanced around for another weapon—nothing. Taking a deep breath, I turned to face them head on. At minimum, they were going down with me. When I got halfway there, a shadowy figure dropped in between us and engaged them. Within three seconds, two of the henchmen were extinguished, and the third was on his knees with a dagger to his throat. It was Joshua, and he'd been so fast, I hadn't had time to even help.

"You want him alive?"

Hook Nose looked at me horrorstruck. I shook my head, indicating no. Glaring at him, I mouthed, "Saved you for last."

And with one swipe and a spray of blood, the leader fell lifeless onto the sodden ground. I helped Josh drag the bodies under an overhang in the back corner of the dead-end.

A car rumbled to a stop a couple of minutes later, and Gabriel got out. His posture screamed of fury. Josh hadn't uttered a word to me since asking if the leader should be kept alive. Gabriel flicked the lid off a bottle, and it made a hollow sound as it hit the ground.

He dumped the contents on the bodies and set them ablaze. They quickly succumbed to ash and were washed away by the continued rain. Lightning flashed directly overhead, drawing my eyes to the roofline. I thought I saw a flicker of movement; I watched for a moment and determined it was the storm playing tricks on me.

I walked between Gabriel and Joshua to a car, like a prisoner being escorted to a transport. We returned to base in a quiet so complete I wanted to jump from the moving vehicle.

All I could think over and over again was...

I'm an idiot...
I'm an idiot...

8

NEWS

O bviously still agitated, Gabriel swung the back door open. I despised feeling like I'd disappointed him. He'd said a few things under his breath as we walked up the back steps, but peels of thunder smothered some of the words. Something about me being "faster than I should be," "a magnet for trouble," and "GPS on my phone." I suppose the latter is what saved my life.

Fat droplets of water shed from our clothes and splattered on the linoleum tiles as we made our way down the hall. We hadn't made it ten steps when the door opened again behind us, and Ian slipped inside, his eyes expectant.

I hadn't seen him since the night of my return. He was one of my classmates who was about to graduate from the academy and had saved my life in Germany. His strawberry blond hair was stuck to his head and darkened by water, trails of liquid running down his face.

He didn't have a jacket to protect him from the rain and his shirt was soaked, revealing the sleeve of tattoos on both his arms. When he turned to shut the door, I could see the ink of another massive tattoo through his shirt that almost covered his entire back.

His eyes met with Gabriel. "We found her. She came back to town like you thought she would. Got off a flight from Belgium. Sorry, I tried to reach you, but it went straight to voice mail."

I was a little confused. *Found whom?*

"Does she have anyone with her?"

"She appears to be alone. Sebastian wanted to be there. I came back to escort him."

"Is Uriel there?"

"Yes. Do you want to be there also?"

Gabriel thought for a moment. "Yes, I do not want her hurt." He turned and pointed at me. "You stay here. Joshua, chain her up if you need to."

I deflated. "I won't go anywhere."

Joshua asked, "Do you want me to go with you?"

"Let's not agitate her any further. You are—" Gabriel paused.

"Hated. I got it." Joshua shrugged.

Sebastian appeared at the end of the hall. He didn't have on his normal scholarly garb of a tweed suit. He was wearing an all-black tactical uniform under an open black, trench coat. The military boots he was sporting made a soft-squeaking sound as he marched determinedly down the hall towards us and stopped next to me.

My confusion must've shown on my face. Sebastian put his hand on my arm. "Aleria, we are bringing in Rousseau. You may have reasons to be angry with her, but I'm going to ask that you refrain from any action against her. I ask that you trust me."

Nodding, suddenly everything made sense. Crina Rousseau was the mole, and she was responsible for more than one of the ills that had befallen me in the last few months. She was the one who must've poisoned me and divulged my location so I could be captured.

I stopped breathing. Then I realized that Sebastian was waiting for more than a nod. "I trust you. Do what you need to do. I won't interfere." He squeezed my arm again and brushed past me before disappearing through the door with Ian and Gabriel.

Joshua and I continued on to our room and turned on a single, low-watt bulb in the corner, making the room a soft yellow. We stripped out of our wet clothes. I stood shivering in my underwear as I hunted for something warm to wear. My chest was aching enough near the entry wound to make me want to double-over in pain. I kept my body turned away from Josh as much as I could; my veins were screaming beacons of sapphire.

"Are your teeth chattering?" he asked surprised.

"Mmm hmm."

"You shouldn't be cold unless it's below zero." He yanked a heavy blanket from the bed and hurried over to me, draping it around my shoulders.

I adjusted it so it was wrapped around both of us, locking my arms around his waist. He slid his arms inside the blanket and encircled me. His bare skin felt feverish to me as he rubbed my back. I melted against him, feeling a little better, and the shivering soon subsided.

My voice muffled as I talked into his chest. "I'm sorry. I shouldn't have freaked and run off like that. I feel like a complete screw-up."

He leaned away slightly, moving his hands to my face. "Am I still a little angry? Yes. Completely at you? No. This situation..." he sighed. "I wanted to freak out too. You just seem to have really, really bad luck sometimes. It's like you need your own personal force field that repels villains."

"I would laugh, but I think you're right."

"You warming up at all?"

I leaned my head back a little more and smirked at him. "It

was all a ploy to keep you in nothing but your boxers."

"Yes, I could tell by the blue lips and violent trembling."

"Mere play-acting," I replied theatrically.

"Mmmmm. Yes." He kissed my forehead.

A vision of whirling black fabric flickered through my memory. "Did you see anyone else on the rooftop before you dropped into the alley?"

"No."

"Mmmmm."

"Why?" he asked.

"I...nothing," and Joshua let it drop for once.

"Should you feed? Is that why you're so cold?"

Needing to lay down, I pulled away, and curled up on the bed, pulling the blanket tightly around me. I couldn't cover my feet, and it sent spiked chills up my legs. "I will in a little while. I just need to rest for a minute."

I could feel him looking at me for a moment before he finished getting dressed. Afterwards, he crawled onto the bed and spooned me from behind. His clean scent made me feel more at ease, despite that the desire to feed was growing more urgent. But I knew I was out of Slayer blood; I'd consumed the last of it before the meeting when Gabriel let me read Dagan's letter.

My mind drifted. "So it *was* Rousseau?" I asked.

I felt him shrug. "She magically disappeared after the assault at the pub. It doesn't bode well for her. I doubt she anticipated the magnitude of what happened."

"I thought it was Phineas."

"You weren't the only one."

"Where is he?"

"I would suspect that he is on his way here."

"Awesome. Two of my favorite people." My tone was venomous.

Joshua reached around and felt my forehead. "You're still freezing." He got out of bed and pulled clothing out of a couple of his drawers. He knelt in front of me with the garments tucked under his arm. "Sit up."

I groaned.

He lifted my arm, forcing me to sit up and gathered the sweatshirt to pull it over my head. When I dropped the blanket, his eyes lingered on my chest, then ran down my torso; it wasn't a "checking me out" type of look.

His shoulders squared, and he pressed his lips into a narrow line as he helped me into his sweatshirt. I pushed the hair out of my face as he tugged the legs of the sweatpants over each of my feet.

"Stand up."

I stood and yanked up the pants around my waist and cinched the drawstrings tight. He rolled the pant legs up as I eased back onto the bed, and he grabbed my foot, gently working a thick sock over it. He repeated the process with the other foot.

I smiled, knowing it was a tired one. "You take good care of me." He ran the back of his hand over my cheek and walked over to the fridge. The refrigerator light created a silhouette as he hunched his body and looked at the contents.

"You said you would feed later because you knew you were out of Slayer blood," he said without turning.

I didn't answer.

Then he was sitting next to me with a unit of normal human blood. "Better than nothing, I guess."

I placed my hand over his with the blood in between. "I'm sure it will help." Then, I twisted my body away and drank, not wanting to ingest it even in front of him. Part of me wondered if I would ever get over my reluctance to feed in front of people. Maybe not, since I never wanted this life—never wanted to be turned. Within a minute, I'd drained the bag and tossed it into the wastepaper basket across the room with perfect accuracy. I let my body fall backwards onto the bed and felt the weight of a million worries working their way through my skin.

Josh leaned back on one elbow next to me, his gaze as heavy as my thoughts.

"You are going to give me a complex watching me like that," I grinned crookedly, but didn't turn my head to look at him. When he didn't answer after a few moments, I returned his gaze.

"Weren't you supposed to get a call by now letting you know if the toxin had mutated?"

My lips turned downward. "Yes. I was trying not to think about it." I paused. "I feel like Beth would've called with good news right away. So I—"

He finished my sentence. "Have been thinking no news is bad news."

The sound of heavy, booted feet reverberated through the floor above; we both fixed our eyes on the ceiling and listened.

"They must be back," I commented. "Do you think they got her?"

We listened for a while longer.

"Yes, I think so," he said slowly. "Their movements wouldn't be so quick if they'd failed." His body seemed to tense slightly.

"Go ahead and check it out. I'll be fine down here. I still want to rest a bit."

He assessed me with intensity and measured what I said. He picked up my legs and swiveled me onto the bed. He then wrapped the blanket around me, tucked it tightly and kissed my temple.

Joshua vanished from the room, not making a sound. I closed my eyes and curled farther into the blanket. My thoughts dimmed as I felt sleep approaching.

. . .

Adrenaline surged through my body as I launched myself through the air, hitting my target with such force that I felt a cool, metal table bend beneath us. I closed my eyes as I sank my teeth into his neck. The gush of warm blood pouring into my mouth was intoxicating.

My body ached for more. Greed overcame me as I twisted my hands in his clothing and wrenched him closer. His heart rate slowed, but I didn't stop.

I needed more, despite his life slipping, and his heart struggling, but I didn't stop. Reality pierced my bloodlust. My eyes flew open to the face of the man, though I knew who it was. I knew his taste.

I shrieked in horror and self-hatred at what I'd done. A wail of anguish rose up, and I screamed and screamed and screamed.

My name was being yelled, and I was being shaken. I cracked my eyes open, trying to wake the rest of the way. Light from the hall was flooding inside the room. The door was open all the way, and Gabriel was leaning on one knee hovering over me.

Screaming, I twisted myself from his grip, scrambling to the corner of the room, where I cowered.

"What is wrong? I am not going to hurt you."

Tears pricked my eyes. "Gabriel, I'm going to hurt you."

He sat on the bed the rest of the way. "I do not believe you would."

"My dream. I was…I was killing you."

His expression darkened, and his eyebrows knit together. "You will not." He stood and offered to help me up. I pressed myself into the corner and turned my face away, unable to look at him.

"Come. That is an order."

"Am I even a Watcher? Can you even order me around anymore?" My voice sounded sulkier than I meant.

"I can order around family." He offered his hand a second time, and I took it. It was the first time he'd called me that.

I'd described him as family, but he'd never used the term to describe me. Emotion knotted in my throat, making the dream that much worse. He looked at my hand, and then felt my forehead. He dropped my arm and went to the fridge. "How much are you going through now?"

"The other is working fine." My face twitched into a smile. "Did you get Rousseau?"

"Yes. Now, how much?" he pressed, not distracted by my change of subject.

"To feel normal—four units a day. To heal—probably more." I sat back on the bed again. "It's hard to estimate what I consumed before Aurora, since I didn't have bagged blood until I got here. Judging from the feeling of fullness, it was probably one, maybe two units if I was really physically active." I twisted some threads that were poking out from the hem of the blanket. "Shouldn't we have already heard from Beth?"

He picked up the chair from the desk and turned it around, straddling it in front of me. "She called while we were out. We were not able to speak. How about you feed, and we will get Joshua to do a videoconference in the office. We can all hear together." Then he rolled up the sleeve of his shirt and offered it to me.

"You're trying to kill me, aren't you?"

"You going to make me go upstairs and bleed into a bag and bring it back down? You drank from familiars every day before. This is no different."

"It feels different." I bit my lip. "Gabriel, there's something in me now. It scares me. I've never had to work at being good before." I was ashamed, but I looked into his eyes anyway. "Part of me wants to kill. There's this darkness."

"There is darkness in everyone, Ali. You are simply

experiencing it on another level. Being good has always been harder; if it were not, the world would be a better place." He offered his wrist again.

I dropped my head into my hands and shook my head. "You hate me. You really hate me. I make a dreadful vampire."

Gabriel chuckled and thrust his arm in front of me again. I let out something between a whimper and a groan, even though I wanted to feed—more than just wanted. The taste of his blood still lingered in my mind from the dream, and it terrified me. But I relented and started to drink.

He leaned forward and rested his head on his other arm, which was resting on the chair back. I closed my eyes and felt the same sensation I'd had twice before. It felt as if my heart beat a few times. Gabriel seemed to twitch, and his heart rate started to slow. I sealed the punctures.

He sat very, very still. It made me worry after a few minutes.

"Did I take too much?" I asked hesitantly.

He rolled his head to the side; he looked more peaceful than I'd seen him in a while. "Fine, just thinking."

"Good. I was worried you wimped out and fainted on me or something."

He raised an eyebrow.

"So, what is the plan with Rousseau? And where is Joshua?"

"We have her locked alone in a dark room right now. Mild sensory deprivation. Joshua and Ian are constructing a proper interrogation room."

"I guess Josh's summers working at his dad's construction company are still coming in handy."

There was a faraway look on Gabriel's face. He stood abruptly. "They may be helping more than you know." He headed out the door, but a moment later, he popped his head back in. "You coming? We have a call to make."

I grabbed my shoes and followed him down the hall. He

swung the phone to his ear. "Sebastian's office. One minute."

When we reached the other hall, Joshua was already leaning against the wall outside the office. I caught the scent of freshly cut wood and something metallic and noticed there was a light dusting of sawdust across the front of his shirt.

"What's up?"

"We're calling Beth back," I informed him.

Joshua didn't say anything, but I watched him swallow hard as he reached for my hand. When Gabriel turned to go into the room, Josh bent and tried to lightly kiss me, just a brush of his lips, but they were too firm. It made me realize that he was more nervous than he was admitting. He gently pulled me behind him through the room to one of the couches.

Gabriel set up the videoconference so we all could see and clicked to connect. The sound of each ring jarred me. I realized I was actually flinching with each buzz when Josh squeezed my hand. My eyes darted to his face. He smiled, but his eyes were tight. I wondered what I looked like. A mess, I was sure.

Beth appeared on the screen, and Gabriel spoke some obligatory greetings. Maybe they weren't obligatory. I just wanted to get to the point. He looked over to see if I wanted to speak, but my throat felt clenched. I nodded at him to continue; I'm sure she could see my nervousness.

Gabriel looked at the console. "Beth, what were the results?"

There was a long pause, and she licked her lips like she was suddenly parched. "I'm sorry, Ali. You were right. It mutated. I'm working on it, though. I made some calls to some specialists, but without being able to actually reveal exactly what I'm working on, it's difficult. Vampire DNA is different than human DNA, and it would be obvious to anyone in the field almost immediately. We have to maintain secrecy.

"It's just that Neka made some mental leaps I just don't understand. It's not my specialty." She began talking more quickly, her face a mask of concern. "Don't lose hope. We have time with the Slayer blood. I'll keep working. I already sent an appeal to the Concilium requesting a soon-to-graduate geneticist with a specialty in bio-chemical engineering for recruitment." She kept speaking, but I couldn't listen any longer.

Then I realized the phone conversation was over, and Gabriel was looking at me. His face was twisted with worry and guilt and a dozen other emotions. "It is not over."

I nodded, but my face was expressionless.

"I will give you two some privacy. I..." He nodded and exited the room, his unfinished sentence swirling about with the emotion-laden air.

Turning, I buried my face in Joshua's chest, and in the shelter of his arms, let myself go. I sobbed until my breath no longer hitched in my chest, and my limbs felt like empty rubber tubes. And for the first time, I felt his emotion layered with mine.

After the Herculean winds of feeling stormed by, I realized that even though I had drunk from Joshua, I still hadn't been in tune with him—until now. In fact, the only other time I'd felt the blood bond with anyone had been when Kyle, my familiar, had been executed after his interrogation.

Leaning back, I looked at Joshua's soaked shirt, and to my surprise, had found no blood in my tears. I wrinkled my forehead. With his thumb, he wiped away the errant tear that tumbled down my cheek when I sat up.

"What?" he asked concerned.

I wiped at my face and looked at my fingers. "No blood in my tears."

"They don't stay that way. It's like you have to clear out the pipes. It goes away."

"Really? I thought I was going to be a circus freak forever, besides the fact that most vampires don't cry."

"Maybe they do. Isn't that what you said bathroom stalls and bedrooms are for?"

"Humphf. I guess I did. I guess I can't picture most vampires hiding in a bathroom stall to cry."

"Funny picture though."

I shrugged. "What are you thinking?"

"That I love you."

My bottom lip trembled. "What are you really thinking?"

He made a soft, exasperated sound and tucked a lock of hair behind my ear. "That is what I'm thinking. I was also wondering what else Rousseau might know."

"Should we go help finish that interrogation room?"

"You and your vast construction experience," he joked.

I held my chin up proudly. "I'll have you know my dad taught me a few things while you were away at school. I helped him build two new sheds out back from scratch. I am power tool proficient."

He pulled me a little closer. "That's kinda sexy."

I wagged my eyebrows at him as I stood up; I offered him my hand this time. "Come on. I need to keep busy."

"Sounds good. Just don't push yourself too hard."

I saluted. "Yes, sir."

Ian and Gabriel were working away when we arrived. I assisted the boys in constructing a legitimate interrogation room complete with two-way glass, video surveillance, and spotlights. I had the feeling Gabriel was up to something. There were definitely some sidelong glances at me, and I could see the wheels turning in his head. He had Josh wire up some non-standard items in the room, such as emergency lights that could be shut on and off from the control room. The fact that two control rooms existed caused me concern too.

They moved her into the room the next day. I wasn't allowed

anywhere near her. Another two days ticked by. Nothing. She had not so much as uttered a word. On the third day, Sebastian called a meeting in the office.

I sat between Josh and Peter on the smaller couch and watched as Kez, Samael, Amara, Ian, and Uriel filed into the room over the course of a few minutes. When everyone was assembled, Sebastian looked at Amara. "What is her emotional state today?" he asked.

"She is tired, but she is nowhere near to breaking. When she is questioned, she vacillates from anger to defiance to protectiveness. It is troubling." Amara's face became thoughtful.

I felt self-conscious asking a question, but I felt like I was missing something. "What's troubling?"

Her dark eyes of cinnamon met mine. "I have not sensed fear in her. Not once."

A sound escaped my lips that had a "well duh" type of sound to it. I covered my mouth and cringed, apologizing and shaking my head.

"What are you thinking?" Sebastian asked.

"She knows you won't kill her," I said bluntly.

Gabriel spoke to Amara. "What is she reacting to?"

"She has a strong emotional response when her niece, Neka, is mentioned. And also, when she hears Aleria's name."

Gabriel smiled. I didn't like the smile, especially when he turned it towards me.

I sank back into my seat a little farther. "I'm not going to like this, am I?"

"Nope," Gabriel replied, "but you are going to do it."

He spent the next hour laying out a plan, and I saw the reason for the two control rooms. And he was right.

I hated the plan.

Gabriel had too much faith in me.

I feared I would snap.

9

ILLUSIONS

This was real. Not a dream. I entered the control room from the hall, and both Ian and Peter whirled around to look at me. I grabbed a chair and sent it sailing through the glass and into the interrogation center, where it clattered to the floor.

Ian charged at me from the corner, and I sent him hurtling through the air and into the computer panels and equipment, tearing wiring from the ceiling; they shattered in a cacophony of sound. The lights went out, and flashes and sparks flew from the damaged ceiling. They burned light into my eyes, but I only saw stars for a moment. My eyes recovered faster than a human's would.

Peter bent over Ian to check on him. Then he seized a dagger from the counter and tried to stop me, but hesitated. I took it from him like a parent would take something dangerous from a child. When I slid the blade into his side, I watched his expression, first surprise, and then nothing. I held him there until his face went slack, then I dropped his body on the windowsill between the two rooms.

His blood poured in thick streams down his arm that dangled

out the window and into the interrogation room, puddling onto the floor. I jumped onto the control desk, sank to my haunches over his slain body, and peered at the prisoner. The scent of salt and sweat was heavy in the room.

Ian's hand came down hard on my shoulder. Without taking my eyes off of Rousseau, I swatted him to the opposite wall and heard a dull thud as he hit the floor.

Rousseau's small figure was struggling, strapped to a large metal chair on the far side of the room, a few feet behind a large-stainless steel table. Her red hair shone like a halo in the intermittently flickering light, and her dark brown eyes grew wide when she peered at Peter's lifeless figure. She knew he was my best friend, and she'd watched me dispose of him like refuse in mere seconds.

It was a symphony of chaos. Ian moaned from the floor behind me, and a crackle of sparks showered from the ceiling. And now I could smell it: what I had been wanting—fear. My lips curled into a horrific smile.

I watched her delicate nostrils flare and force herself to control her terror. She sat calmly in front of me, no longer tugging at her bonds. There was doubt in her eyes.

She didn't know if she could believe what she was seeing. I leaned forward aggressively, as I silently alighted on the floor inside the room with her. Gabriel, who'd been questioning her, moved defensively in front of her, obscuring my view and effectively blocking my path.

"Ali, do not do this." There was a warning in his voice.

"She did this to me," I lashed.

"You can stop this. It is not too late."

"The moment I touched *them*, it was too late," I spit back jerking my finger behind me. "It feels good, Gabriel. This is what she made me. What I'm embracing, and she's going to pay for it."

With that, I launched myself at him. I hit him so hard, he

stumbled back a few steps, but he managed to pivot his body and throw me into the wall back towards the door. He drew a blade, and angled it towards me, ready for an attack.

My fangs elongated, and I ran at him again. I tried to disarm him, but I was tossed back into the door, giving way this time, and I tumbled into the control room. The lights faltered again, and I flew at him in the darkness, knocking him on top of the stainless steel table mere feet from Rousseau. I felt the table legs groan and bend, but they didn't give out. The dream I'd had the day before, about killing Gabriel, came rushing at me, almost blotting out what I was doing.

A single flood light came on from the emergency lamps behind Rousseau, blinding me and bringing me back to the present as I crouched over the top of him. I dropped onto one knee and straddled him. Then, after glancing at Rousseau one last time, I plunged my teeth into Gabriel's neck. With the hand closest to Rousseau, he tightly grabbed my bicep and pushed away. But it was too late; I released the hormone and felt his grip soften. He exhaled and closed his eyes.

I drank for a moment and pulled back, eyeing Rousseau, who sucked in a breath and squared her shoulders when she saw that the wound was real. No Slayer would ever allow themselves to be bitten.

Blood dripped down my chin as I returned to his neck. His heart slowed, and I lifted my head once again, still straddling his body. I got nervous for a moment until Gabriel squeezed the hand she couldn't see. I returned the squeeze, ready to finish our drama.

Bending to his neck once more, he let the hand that was gripping my arm drop dramatically. After another two beats of time, I sealed the wound, then jumped from the table. I shoved him to the floor with a disgusted look to keep her from seeing that I'd stopped the bleeding.

I stood there, chest heaving with jagged breaths, while I glared at her with glowing eyes. Her eyes darted to Gabriel's unmoving body on the ground, and then to me. I felt the tickle of his blood as it trailed down my jaw and over my collarbone. All the doubt she'd previously had appeared to melt.

Prowling forward, I leaned into her, placing my hands on the armrests of her chair until we were nose-to-nose. My smile was cold when my cheek brushed hers like a feather, and my mouth hovered over her ear. "Tell me the truth, and you won't suffer." It was taking every ounce of my self-control not to snap her puny neck.

She let out an uneven breath, and a bead of sweat streaked down the side of her face. I eased back a little to look her in the eyes. "You poisoned me."

There was a hesitation, and her bottom lip quivered. I wiped two fingers across my face and looked at the blood, then smeared it across her face. She let out a whimper and sucked in a breath, holding it longer than I thought she could. She finally nodded as she exhaled.

"How? The chocolates?"

"No, it was in the tea."

"But I watched you pour it."

"I put it in the cup itself, so you could watch me pour a cup for Sebastian from the same kettle," she confessed.

"Where did you get the poison?"

"I had Phineas pick it up from a courier."

"Did Phineas know what he was getting?" I leaned in closer.

"No. He never knew anything."

"You were setting him up."

"No. I wasn't trying to set him up."

At that moment, there was a loud crash in the control room and I whirled around to find Kez and Samael in the doorway. I stepped to the side of Rousseau just as Samael threw a dagger at me. The blade pierced my heart, and I crumpled to the ground, my head cracking on the table as I fell.

Grinding glass crunched underneath their feet as they moved around the room towards Gabriel's location.

"Does he have a pulse?" Samael asked.

"It's faint."

"Should we finish her?" Samael asked Kez, referring to me.

There was a long pause. "Rousseau, as we came in you said, 'I wasn't trying to set him up.' Who were you talking about?"

She took a few short breaths. I wished I could see her face. "Phineas. She was asking about Phineas."

"Why was Aleria after you? Why would she do this?"

Silence.

In a soft voice, but loud enough for Rousseau to hear, Samael said, "Kez, Gabriel must've had Rousseau in here for a reason. My money is on her being the mole. I need to know if she knew that Neka was alive this whole time."

I heard the shifting of feet and Kez's voice aimed at Rousseau. "Start talking, or we pull the blade out of her and let her finish what she started. We can just as easily kill her in the hall after she's done with you."

Silence.

Someone moved towards me. Samael came into view and paused next to me. He reached for the Durateus blade.

"I'll tell you what you want to know. Please, don't," Rousseau said hurriedly. Her voice cracked under the strain.

"Samael, drag Gabriel out of here and see if you can find some help for him. And get rid of the other bodies. I have questions for my friend here."

I heard him drag Gabriel out through the control room and into the hall. Shortly after, I was scooped up and carried out. The light in the hall seemed horribly bright, but I wasn't able to even close my eyes. I was placed in Joshua's waiting arms, and Gabriel immediately pulled the dagger from my chest.

The second I was able to close my eyes I did, and pressed my face into Joshua's chest. Our theatrical took so much out of me, all I wanted to do was sleep for a year—maybe two.

Moments later, I heard the shuffle of Peter and Ian being dragged into the hall, not sure in which order. Then, the door to the control room was firmly shut—followed by an audible sigh of relief from all involved.

Peeking through slits, it was still too bright, so I closed them once again. I was carried down the hall into the second control room where the whir of computers greeted us.

Sebastian was saying, "Ask her how she was contacted."

Kez repeated the same question in the other room. I squinted at Amara who was seated next to Sebastian, counseling him on Rousseau's reactions.

Josh stood me on my feet, but he held me to his side, as there was no way I could stand yet. He cupped my face with his free hand, tilting my head up to meet his eyes. We had a silent exchange, and I smiled to let him know I was unharmed. I'd just fed, so I would heal, at least for a little while.

"Ali, how are you doing?" Gabriel asked.

I looked over at him and said, "I still hate you. Making me bite you and getting stabbed in the course of ten minutes is unforgivable."

He smirked.

"Did I hurt any of you?" I looked specifically at Ian, since I'd heaved him across the room twice.

He pulled his shirt over his head and loosened the Velcro straps on the custom hard-shell armor he was wearing under his clothing. "Nope." He knocked on his chest. "This worked really well."

Then I looked at Peter, who was unstrapping the depleted

theatrical blood-bag from his side. He realized I was looking at him. "I'm waiting for my Oscar," he bowed dramatically.

I rolled my eyes.

Josh noted, "I guess we're lucky she didn't notice that your fangs didn't unsheathe when you stabbed Peter."

"Yeah, I tried," I said, a little disappointed.

Sebastian's chair creaked as he swiveled to address our band of thespians. "All of you did well. You cracked her. I think we will get whatever we need now. You may all go ahead and get cleaned up. It will be a long night."

We filed out and lingered in the hall for a moment. Then Peter and Ian headed to the showers on the upper floor. I tested to make sure I had my motor skills back; I was shaky, but able to move under my own power. Joshua and I turned to head to the showers on that level, but Gabriel told us to wait. He disappeared back into Control 2 and emerged with a bag.

"From Kez and Samael—their idea."

I raised a questioning brow as I reached for the bag. I opened it and saw two units of blood. "They volunteered this?"

Gabriel nodded. "If you can win Samael over, many more are to follow."

"Thanks."

He turned and moved towards the stairs. I folded down the top of the bag and dropped it to my side. Joshua leaned over and kissed the top of my head as we started walking towards the showers. "You did good, babe."

After cleaning up, we settled into bed. Even after feeding again, I was still exhausted. All I wanted was to be held. I curled my body into his arms, growing heavy with sleep. The last thing I remembered before drifting off was the horrible sensation of knowing Bowen was in trouble and in an unspeakable amount of pain. It was the first time I'd felt the blood bond between us, and I was sure it wouldn't be the last.

10

SPEAK INTO DARKNESS

I woke to a puzzle of conflicting emotions; all of the things no one was talking about seemed to be raining down on me. Rousseau's capture seemed to supersede everything else. I'd woken more than once during the sleeping hours of the day, with thoughts of the surrogate carrying my child. Bowen had haunted my dreams, as well. Everything was surreal and unsettling. I knew he was still in a dreadful amount of pain.

I wiggled closer behind Josh and buried my face in his back, breathing in his scent, as I tried to push thoughts of Bowen and babies elsewhere—there was nothing I could do about either at present.

Joshua stirred a few minutes later and rolled over. Dark circles were stamped under his eyes, and his expression was melancholy. I ran the tip of my finger under his eyes.

"You didn't sleep, did you?"

He shrugged. "A little."

"I snore, don't I?" I grinned.

"Yes, I'm surprised no one called the cops for disturbing the peace." A smile played at the edges of his lips, but it didn't touch the sadness in his eyes.

"I thought that might be the reason, 'cause staying up worrying would be just downright silly."

"Yeah, silly," he said with a slightly guilty look.

"Do you think it might be possible to get out tonight? To not think about Rousseau or sickness or anything but us?"

"I can't. I'm accompanying Kez. We're bringing in some of the people Rousseau used. Need to see what they know."

"More interrogations."

"'Fraid so."

"As long as we don't have to put on anymore theatrical productions. I think I've been stabbed enough," I said lightly.

He got quiet. "I don't think I could watch that again."

"You watched?"

"I was in Control 2. I couldn't *not* watch. Even though I knew it was an act, it was almost impossible."

"I can see that. When I left you in the hall, I thought you would stay there, for some reason."

He fell silent, but I could see a question on his face. I finally nudged him and raised my eyebrows proddingly. His eyes tightened. "You were talking in your sleep."

"I was?"

He pursed his lips. "You kept saying, 'Bowen,' over and over."

"Oh. It's not—" I stopped to gather my thoughts. "He's in trouble. I felt the connection between us for the first time last night. I finally know what it was like for you when I was in pain." I paused. "Did you ever feel *good* emotions? Or was it always the negative ones?"

"All heightened emotions when I was able to tune into them. But it's easier to sense the more negative ones like fear and pain." He smiled genuinely. "I did feel your joy when I proposed and when we were married."

"Best days of my life." I kissed him, my lips soft and beckoning. He took my cue and left the rest of the conversation alone.

At sunset, we stood in the hall for a long while, foreheads pressed together and hands bound to one another's in tight knots. With a sigh, we parted reluctantly. Joshua went to join up with Kez, and I went to Control 2 to see if there was any new information.

Slowly, I opened the door and poked my head inside to make sure it was okay to enter. Sebastian waved me in. He and Amara were seated at the long table butted up against the interrogation room that appeared to be vacant. They were turned towards one another, going over some notes. Gabriel was leaning over one of the two circular coffee tables, resting his head on his arms, sleeping like the dead.

I bobbed my head towards Gabriel. "He finally succumbed to sleep, eh?"

"Involuntarily—he went down fighting," Amara replied.

"Where's Rousseau?"

Sebastian's voice sounded haggard, on top of the normal gravel. "We brought a cot into the interrogation room. She is asleep. She was too tired to give us anything useful."

"Is she resisting anymore?"

"She doesn't seem to be. Amara doesn't sense any deceit in her."

"So, if she was doing all this to get Neka out, why didn't Queen Agrona release her?"

"They wanted you, the genetics lab, and something else she hasn't revealed." Sebastian twisted some strands of his beard between two fingers. "When abducting you in Germany didn't work, they accused her of warning your team. While they waited for another window to capture you to present itself, they had her poison you to prove her good will. She believed it was simply to implant the tracker. She wasn't aware of their secondary plans."

"What do you think the third thing they want is?"

"I cannot even begin to venture a guess," he said.

I nodded and wished that Amara wasn't busy. Part of me wanted a girl to talk to, even if she was ten years my senior. It was the quiet times that made me feel the hole Gentry and Leslie's deaths tore in me. "Is Peter around?"

"I had him doing some research on the computer in my office. I doubt he is done yet."

"Thanks. I think I'll go find him."

When I said goodbye, Amara gave me a knowing look. She had to have sensed my emotional distress, though I probably appeared relaxed. I felt lonely and worried and overwhelmed. But maybe worst of all, was the sense of foreboding.

Peter was still in Sebastian's office. He was leaning his head on his left hand, while his right was clicking the mouse like he wanted to punish it.

"Graduated to research assistant I see."

He leaned his head back, arched over the chair, and looked at me upside-down. "Please, kill me now."

"Really? I thought you would be at home here."

"I think you have me mistaken with you. *You* are the research queen. I love dramatic literature and poetry, and that is not exactly helping me with these tedious tasks." He swirled his hand in the air, still looking at me upside-down. "I should be done here in a little bit. You wanna go to the shooting range and get in some practice?"

I thought for a moment, biting my lip. "I don't think I'm up to it. We have any movies or something mellow to do?"

He sat up and swiveled around to look at me properly. "You look like crap, Hayes."

"Thanks, I love you too."

"No, seriously. Not trying to be mean. Even sick, I thought you would be fully recovered by now. You know, with your mad vampire abilities."

I shrugged and gave him a withering look.

"You want to hang out in here until I'm done? Probably another twenty minutes."

"Sure." I ambled over to the couch and curled up on it to watch Peter work. My eyes drifted closed while listening to him peck at the keys and click the mouse. I was jostled awake when Peter bounced onto the couch next to me.

"It is time to wake, oh-you-of-the-drooly-mouth," he announced while shaking my shoulder. "It's been an hour."

I rubbed my eyes and surreptitiously checked my chin for drool. *Lies.* "An hour?"

"Yeah, when you fell asleep, I went ahead and finished another small project for the boss man."

I pushed myself up into a seated position. After a long moment, he gently grabbed my hand, rolled my arm over, and looked at the dark veining on it. He didn't say anything, but gave me a look. I pulled my arm away and wished I'd worn long sleeves. "It's been an hour and a half."

"What?"

"Since I fed. It's what you were wondering."

"Mind reading now. Guess I'll have to watch myself." He winked and stood, fluttering his fingers in an offer to help me up. "Let's go watch a horribly bad Sci-Fi movie and make fun of it."

"Sounds like heaven."

When we entered the hall, he put his arm around my shoulders, like he had done so many times in the past, and led me to the small sitting area upstairs. Ian was munching on cereal in front of the TV. When we appeared, he glanced up and caught with the spoon a drop of milk that was dripping down his chin.

He grinned and moved to one side of the couch to make room for us. I sat between the boys, and lucky for us, we found a movie so bad that the zippers in the monster costumes were visible. Ian joined in as we added our own dialogue.

Peter tilted his head to rest it on mine when I leaned my head on his shoulder. He put his hand over mine and held it, only making one teasing comment about my being so cold now. It was platonic and comforting and just what I needed. A knot developed in my throat, and it grew larger as the movie progressed. When the movie ended, I wished I could hold onto times like these forever.

After that, I must have dozed off, I woke when Ian said Gabriel's name. I blinked a few times and realized a different movie was on, and another hour had passed by. Gabriel was standing at the end of the couch looking blankly at the TV with his hands laced behind his head. He hadn't shaved in a couple of days and his hair was sticking up on one side, both out of character for him.

Peter squeezed my hand. "I should probably get some sleep. It's really late."

I sat up straight, allowing him to get up. "Thanks, Peter."

He gave me a lopsided grin. "See you tomorrow."

"I'm out too," Ian groaned as he stood and stretched.

"Night."

He mussed my hair as he passed.

Gabriel was still standing there like a statue, barely acknowledging Peter and Ian as they brushed by him.

After a few moments of inspecting him, I said, "Maybe you should go and get some more sleep, Gabriel."

He dropped his hands to his sides and looked at me as if he hadn't noticed me there, then sat down.

I scooted back to give him a little more room and turned sideways to face him. My voice came out a little shakier than I'd hoped. "It's been a couple of days. Have you heard any news from Beth?"

He closed his eyes and ran his fingers through his hair. "We approached the geneticist that she thought might be able to help, but it did not go well."

"Has Beth made any progress?"

He looked at me with that same sad look Joshua had when we'd woken up. "No."

I nodded.

"You are worse." A statement, not a question.

"Yes."

He leaned forward, resting his elbows on his knees and resting his head in his hands. "Ali, I did this to you. I will go and get Neka out of that damn castle myself if I need to."

My eyes bulged. "Ummm…*hell* no."

He sat up and looked at me surprised.

"Gabriel, this was an accident. I didn't realize you were still feeling this guilty. Don't, seriously. I don't blame you at all. So knock it off, and be the scary, intimidating, bad-ass I know you to be."

He let out a humorless chuckle.

"Go get some more sleep, so you can be back to your overly-serious self tomorrow," I ordered. "I'm sure someone will wake you if you are needed."

"Yes, ma'am." He paused and looked at me a long moment, then nodded as if answering his own question. He stood slowly, like he was stiff, and drifted from the room.

I sat by myself in front of the television, wishing I wasn't alone. Eventually, knowing I should feed again, I wandered back to my room. The horribly cold blood was sooo not appealing, I held it in my lap, procrastinating. There was a knock at the door.

"Enter at your own risk."

Amara opened the door and leaned against the doorframe. "You seemed like you wanted to talk to me earlier."

"I thought you could only sense emotions?"

She smiled.

"I'm doing a lot better. I hung out with Peter and Ian. I think I just needed some friend time."

Amara looked at me with those cinnamon-colored eyes seeing more than she should. Then, she walked in and made herself comfortable on the desk chair. I'd been wishing just a few minutes ago that I wasn't alone—now I wanted nothing more than to be alone.

"Sebastian said you were pretty close to the Watchers who were murdered—Gentry and Leslie, was it?"

"Yes. I was."

"How are you dealing with that?" Her question would have seemed a little too therapist-y without her enchanting North African accent. She tucked a few of her braids behind her ear.

I smiled and dramatically deflected. "Was I supposed to deal with it? Or just shove it in a 'deal with later' compartment?"

"Sebastian also said you would use humor to brush off serious questions."

I narrowed my eyes. "He's such a traitor."

Her expression was kind while she waited for me to speak.

"Days like this, I really miss them, but I have mourned them. Believe me. I spent most of my evenings in captivity dealing with what had happened just prior to it."

"Have you spoken with anyone about what happened while you were imprisoned?"

I shrugged. "I went through most of it in the debrief."

"That helps, but you left things out, didn't you? Things you didn't think would impact the report?"

"Honestly, I think I'm okay."

"There is something that is upsetting...or unsettling. Something new."

"I can suddenly sense Bowen."

She looked concerned. "Is he near?"

"I don't know. I don't think so. It's just, I think he's in trouble. He's in pain."

"And you care for him?"

I exhaled and pinned my eyebrows together. "It's complicated."

"I can sense that. This is something you didn't talk about in your debrief."

"It's not like everyone doesn't know, and I've talked about it to a certain extent with Joshua."

"But?"

I sat on the bed and stared at the unit of blood still in my hands. "Do you know our background?"

"Just bits and pieces."

"I met Bowen almost a year ago in a coffee shop. Some friends of my ex-boyfriend were harassing me, and he stepped in and saved me. We spent weeks meeting at the coffee shop, getting to know one another. I really liked him. I couldn't even admit at the time how much I did because I was still reeling from breaking up with my boyfriend. And then, I was attacked.

"I thought I was losing it. One day, he was kind and amazing, and the next, he was—not. I thought it was Bowen, but I later learned it was his twin, Tyran. Everything bad that had been done to me was all Tyran. Bowen genuinely cared for me, and Tyran interpreted his brother caring for me as betrayal. He's been making Bowen pay for his affections ever since."

"So what is your current concern?"

I shook my head. "I obviously don't like that he is being hurt. After Tyran abducted me, Bowen protected me. And when I was accidentally turned during the first escape attempt, I made

Bowen promise to not let me take a human life. He kept it. He is in love with me, yet he never laid a finger on me unless it was completely necessary. Part of me feels obligated to him, I guess."

"How does Joshua fit into all of this?"

"In a nutshell, I grew up with him. I've known him my whole life. He went away to college, and that's when he was assaulted and turned by Tyran.

"Two years later, Tyran and Bowen came to California trying to find me. Tyran wanted to hurt me to inflict some sort of revenge on Joshua. They found me, and then I was attacked by Tyran. Josh, Gabriel and Sebastian interrupted Tyran. If they'd gotten there five minutes later, I would've been dead, or worse. I've been with Josh ever since."

"Did you date Joshua before he went to university?"

"No. There's a three-year age gap, so it didn't really occur to me before. I was shocked by my feelings for him when he returned. He said it was much the same for him."

"What is it you're worried about?"

"See, I can't even explain all this so it makes sense."

"If Tyran hadn't attacked you, would you have fallen for Bowen?"

I fell backwards on the bed and looked at the ceiling, feeling done in. "Maybe. I don't know. I would say there was a high probability." Then a word came out I wasn't expecting. "Yes." The truth of that single word jarred me. "But everything with Bowen was tainted." I ran my thumbs over my eyelids.

"It doesn't matter though, Joshua is it for me. He is part of me; he's been a presence in my life every single day, even when he was away at school. He's all I want. When I thought he'd died…" A wave of emotion shot from me, and I couldn't finish the sentence. I heard Amara suck in a short breath, probably sensing my inner turmoil.

"Then why do you feel guilty?"

"I'm connected to Bowen through a blood bond. Every time I think something about him or sense something from him, I feel like I'm betraying or hurting Joshua, and I feel like seeing Bowen again is inevitable. I don't know what to do."

"I wish I had a simple answer for you."

"Yeah, I wish I had ruby slippers and could click my heels together."

"Would you really leave all this behind?"

I sat back up and slouched forward. "No, but I would undo the deaths of my friends and this." I held up the blood. "I wouldn't be undead."

"During war, if a soldier is captured and held prisoner for months, do you think that soldier should talk through everything that happened after they are released?"

"Of course they should. They…" I closed my eyes and bit my lip, catching up to her analogy. I cringed at how slow I was being.

"This is war, precious girl. You need to talk to Joshua. He is a good man. No good things can come from keeping your pain from him."

"You sensed him struggling, didn't you?"

She gave me a long look, but didn't answer my question. "I should let you rest and eat."

I looked at the blood still in my hand and shrugged. "Next time I get to ask the questions," I smiled.

"Deal."

"Will you dish on Kez and Samael?" I asked.

"If it doesn't violate my trust with them," she answered.

"Nice. I really want to know about the funny looks they exchanged when I mentioned Neka's name in the lab last week."

She walked to the door and opened it. "That one is easy. Neka and Samael were engaged." She nodded at me.

Then I risked a guess. "And Kez…"

"What about him?"

I looked at her more seriously. "You and Kez…"

She jutted her chin in the air, but didn't deny it. "Sleep well, my friend."

"Thank you." And with that, she shut the door. I finally drank the blood that was now up to room temperature.

I woke to fingers gently running through my hair–Joshua was back.

"Mmmm. That's nice," I murmured. I was lying on my side, and he was seated on the bed, cozy in the C shape of my body. He smelled of chimney smoke and metal and leather.

"Sleeping day and night now," he said with a ghostly smile on his face.

"A cat nap really." *While dreaming that you were horribly injured.*

"You were talking in your sleep again."

"Great." I opened my eyes wider and looked up at him a little worried, but his expression was still soft.

"It's okay, you were saying my name this time."

"Phew." I yawned. "What time is it?"

"3:00 AM."

"Did things go well?" My eyes drifted from his face.

"They…went." He put his hand on the zipper of his leather jacket and then paused, like he thought the better of it, and dropped his hand.

"What happened?"

He pursed his lips. "We met a friend of yours. Kez said it was the female that escaped the ambush."

"Zahra?"

"Yes."

"She's in Dublin?" The thought of her being so close made me shudder. I still had nightmares of her chasing me through the maze, her dark auburn hair flying behind her as she jumped from the tops of the walls, examining her prey scurrying below. I'd watched her do it time and again as she hunted. *And now she was here.*

"Yes, in Dublin. We had Rousseau's contact, and she used a crossbow to kill him from the rooftop, just as we were loading him in the car."

"And you went after her."

"Yes. I jumped to the roof, and Kez soon followed."

He moved, and the scent of blood puffed out from beneath his jacket, so I grabbed the pull and unzipped it. I could see he wanted to stop me. "Blood. Yours and…Did you kill her?"

"No, we fought, but she wasn't alone. One of them sacrificed himself to secure her escape."

"One of them? How many were there?"

"Four, that we saw."

"So the operation was all for naught."

He thought for a moment. "The fact that it was important to keep that specific person from us may actually help. Sebastian has a theory, but he said he isn't ready to share it yet."

I sat up and thought about the slight waver in his voice when he said "we fought." I put my hand on the lapel of his jacket. He placed his hand over mine, then drew it to his lips and kissed it. I asked, "I wasn't dreaming you were in pain. You *were* in pain, weren't you?"

"I'm okay. No need to."

"Fret." I grumbled as I pulled my hand from his and peeled his jacket away to examine his shirt. Two slices across his abdomen were edged with crimson and a hole over his heart was saturated with blood. I placed my fingers in the hole and moved the fabric to look at his chest. There was an aggravated scarlet line caked with crusted blood. "She—"

"Is really good, but she missed, barely." He kissed my forehead. "I need to go shower."

I nodded.

He shrugged his jacket the rest of the way off and tossed it over the chair. Then, he walked to the dresser and rifled through a couple of drawers, pulling out clean clothes. There was a hole in the back of his shirt where the blade had gone clear through him.

My voice came out a little shaky. "You want company?"

"In the shower?" He blinked at me a little surprised, and then his face slowly spread into a grin. "That might be nice."

"Might be?" I raised an eyebrow.

He walked over and knelt in front of me, tossing the clothes on the bed. "Sorry, would be."

"Better."

"You okay?" he asked.

"Yeah, I'll meet you there in a second."

He stood and headed to the bathroom. I grabbed a pint of blood from the fridge and drained it. The sensation of strength trickled through me as I watched the spider web of veins beneath my skin pale. Part of me wondered how long it would last though. Feeling better for the moment, I padded down the hall to meet him, with my robe draped over my arm. I wanted to feel normal for a little while, and needed the closeness of doing something like an ordinary married couple.

The steam from the shower churned around with the new air from the hall, billowing in graceful swirls. I locked the door. Joshua's silhouette was visible through the curtain, and I suddenly felt nervous. I watched the water run out from under the curtain to the drain in the center of the bathroom. I hadn't noticed the odd light that reflected off the thousands of tiny blue tiles.

The bluish cast seemed to emphasize the pallor of my skin.

The tiny mole on my forearm stood out like a beacon. I undressed and noticed that the scar on my knee looked like a silver streak, even though it was almost invisible in normal light. *Perfect, lights that emphasize flaws.* I folded my clothes, placed them next to the sink, and stood there in all my nakedness. I drew in a deep breath and stepped around the curtain.

Part of me expected my heart to quicken; he was worthy of a classical sculpture. He had his back to me. His hands were on the wall on either side of the showerhead as he let the water run over his head and down his back. The bluish light made the blood running off of him look like trails of amber.

Joshua turned his head to the side and looked at me from the corner of his eye. "I was wondering if you'd changed your mind."

"No," I returned, sounding hoarse.

Stepping forward, I felt compelled to touch the scars on his back. The light made them appear a faded purple. I rubbed the most recent scar and scrubbed the remaining dried blood away. He had two scars inside his left shoulder blade, one wrapping all the way around his right side, and the one on his neck. I looked down and saw another scar on his thigh.

"Why do I still feel like I'm doing something illicit?"

His back was still to me. "We really haven't been able to enjoy being married, have we?" He caught himself. "Not that I haven't enjoyed it, just that we haven't had much time together." He stopped talking and turned around.

I smiled, meeting his gaze. "I know what you mean."

He touched my nose, leaving soapsuds behind.

I touched the scar on his side. "What is this from? Why haven't I noticed it before?"

He shook his head. "While you were...gone. A couple of months ago."

I ran my fingers over the evidence of battle on his chest, his neck, and his shoulder. "How many scars till I lose you?"

His face darkened, and he ran his fingers down my neck. I knew he was looking at all of my scars. *Stupid lighting.* "You said he fed on you, but you didn't say that it was so often."

"I didn't think it mattered." I moved under the water and let it run over my head for a moment.

"You've been hiding them. There must be thirty sets of punctures here." He furrowed his brow. "So many."

"Thirty-three," I breathed. "If you include last summer."

He tore his eyes from my neck and peered at me, his emotion broiling beneath the surface.

I frowned. "I'm sorry. I thought my coming in here would be —intimate. I didn't think it would stir up old wounds. I shouldn't have." I started to turn.

He grabbed onto me and pulled me to him. "We need to see each other's wounds if we want to overcome them, to help each other heal. We've been so wrapped up with surviving and everything else that's been going on, that we haven't taken the time to notice actual physical scars on one another."

"When you've been naked, I've been a little preoccupied."

"Agreed."

"Bad lighting doesn't help either." I grinned.

"No, it doesn't, but that's not what—"

"You're right. I know I glossed over some of the details, but it's hard. I just felt so violated. When Tyran fed on me, I felt like I was cheating on you. And I know that hearing some of those details are hurtful to you."

"I can handle it. You need to deal with it, and I want to be there for you. To help you."

"I'm not ignoring them." I could hear Amara's voice prompting me in my head while I considered. "Is *not* knowing worse?"

"To me, yes. I have a very vivid imagination."

I nodded. "Because of you, I'm feeling whole again. If you

want, I will tell you every single detail I withheld and more. But..."

"But?"

"Can we have that conversation in our room and in the dark? It would be easier if I can't see you."

"Yes." He held my face between his hands and brushed my lips with his, like I was a sculpture made of sand that would crumble to powder.

"Thank you."

He closed his eyes, and that same ghostly smile passed over his face. He opened his eyes again, and in the odd light, they looked more blue than green. He ran his hands down my neck to my shoulders and looked at me—this time it was like all the scars weren't there. His right hand drifted down my side, and I let out a little gasp. "You're beautiful, you know that?"

If my cheeks could have flushed, they would have. "You say that to all the naked girls you shower with."

He rolled his eyes. "Just take the compliment."

I took an unsteady breath before I told him, "I came in here for two reasons. The first: to have my back scrubbed." I turned around in his arms and offered my back. He chuckled and lathered me up. The fragrance of the soap wafted through the steamy air, and I felt the trails of sudsy water tickle down the backs of my legs.

While scrubbing me, he leaned close, and his lips brushed my ear as he asked, "And the second?"

I looked over my shoulder with a coy smile and breathlessly replied, "I think you will figure that out in just a moment. There are things we *can't* do, but there are certainly a lot of things we can."

·   ·   ·

Sometime later, we strolled to our room after our excessively long shower. I glanced at the clock. It'd been ninety minutes since I fed, and my energy level was already starting to wane, disappointment weighed on me.

After trading the robe for a tank top and a pair of Josh's well-worn, pajama bottoms, I decided to walk up and down the hall, needing to move and work out some of my restless energy. Josh needed to feed anyway. So I paced slowly, hearing the pant legs drag with each step as I plodded in a very un-vampire-like fashion.

I felt nervous for the second time tonight. I was going to give Josh all the details he wanted. I'd already told him about the kiss, the one act of my own volition. I did some deep breathing and tried to get my head straight. The compound was eerily quiet. It was always this way in the pre-dawn hours, even with the crazy sleeping schedules of the Slayers, but this seemed strange. I hoped Gabriel was getting some serious rest.

I'd delayed long enough. I returned, and Joshua was already in bed. When the door shut, it was pitch black, so much so that even with my preternatural vision, I couldn't see. He clicked on a flashlight and shined it on the ceiling.

"Dark enough for you?"

"Yeah."

He held open the covers, and I crawled in next to him, although not in my normal sleeping position—where I lay with my head on his chest, arm around his waist, and my leg thrown over his. Instead, I lay on my back and reached for his hand.

He looked over at me. "Are you still in the mood to talk?" he asked.

"Yes."

He turned off the flashlight. I swallowed hard before I spoke. "Part of me feels like you won't want me anymore."

"You know that's not true. You didn't do anything wrong."

Taking a deep breath, I started. I talked into the darkness for what seemed like hours. It must've been hours. He said very little, which is what I needed; he simply asked an occasional question and squeezed my hand for encouragement, once in a while.

In addition to the past, I spoke of future fears, like the fate of the baby. I mentioned every hurt and worry, save one thing: the fact that I was getting sicker by the day.

When I was finished, Joshua rolled on his side, gathered me to his chest, and held me tight. After a long silence, he said, "I will always want you."

And, for the first time since I'd escaped, I felt like there was nothing between us, nothing keeping us apart.

I soon drifted towards sleep, at peace, but my tranquility was interrupted when my thoughts drifted to Zahra and Josh fighting and its inevitable consequence: Tyran would now know that Joshua was alive.

11

HELP UNTIL

Urgent knocking startled me from sleep. Joshua swung the door open. Peter was standing there, but before he could open his mouth, I said, "We're evacuating."

Peter looked at me blankly. "Yes. Here." He thrust two bags at Josh. "Daylight gear. We'd like to be out in forty minutes." Peter turned and disappeared down the hall.

Josh shut the door and looked at me questioningly.

"If Zahra saw you with a Slayer, it wouldn't be hard to figure out who you are. Up until now, you were assumed dead. And if they know you are alive and in Dublin, it wouldn't be hard to figure out that I'm here too."

"You were just spotted by one of the Oneiroi last week."

"But when Morpheus saw me, we were way out in the countryside; our destination could've been anywhere."

He knit his brow, pulled a couple of duffle bags out from under the bed, and tossed me one. I pulled my drawer out of the dresser and dumped it into the bag. Packing done.

I felt Josh next to me. "I should probably give this back to you." He handed my journal to me.

"You kept it," I caressed the leather cover.

He kissed my forehead and returned to packing. Upon opening the fridge, Joshua suggested, "Maybe you should drink this."

I looked at the unit of blood he held in his hand. "It's my last one again. Shouldn't I save it?"

"Perhaps." He tossed it into the cooler with the rest. "You ready?"

"I don't know. It was hard packing my single drawer of stuff. I may have missed something."

"A 'yes,' would have been sufficient, O facetious one." Josh responded with a wry smile.

The second we were in the daylight gear, Josh's phone buzzed with a text.

"Gabriel wants us to go to the stairwell."

We headed off with the bags, and his phone buzzed again. He looked at me, a scowl threatening to overtake his features. "We're in the van. Rousseau is riding with us. She'll have a hood on, but Sebastian wants us to avoid speaking at this point."

"She still doesn't know it was all a ruse, eh?"

"Guess not. She just found out Gabriel 'survived' the attack."

We shoved the helmets onto our heads, picked up our bags, and headed up and out to the alley into the awaiting van. New roofing company decals adorned its sides and back, complete with ladders strapped to the flat roof.

Gabriel was leaning against the back door as we approached. He still didn't look very well-rested, but he was clean-shaven, and the circles under his eyes were half the size they'd been yesterday.

He nodded in greeting and said, "If you need to say something, just do it via text."

I gave him the thumbs up.

This was the vampire-friendly van with a small compartment

in the back so humans could come and go without frying us. Gabriel opened the back door, and Joshua and I pushed through the inner door immediately, since we still had our gear on. We did it with enough speed that Rousseau would have thought only Gabriel boarded the van.

Once the doors were closed, we stowed our helmets under the command table. Gabriel followed us in, cut through to the front of the van, and knocked on the dividing door. The engine started up and pulled out of the alley.

Rousseau was on the bench seat all the way in the far corner next to the cab. She had a black hood over her head, and her handcuffs, with several inches of links between them, were fastened to a metal ring low on the wall next to her. She was restrained, but she was able to sit comfortably. I was amazed at how diminutive she appeared. She moved her head once in a while, like she was trying to hear us.

Gabriel sat down hard on the bench seat, just two feet away from her. Josh sat in one of the captain's chairs in front of the monitors, and I stood there near the back door, holding a handle on the upper cabinet as the van swayed. After a moment, I sat on the other side of Gabriel, figuring he would want the other chair by the monitors at some point.

I pulled out my phone, noting that it was 11:00 AM. After making sure it was on silent, I typed a message to Gabriel: "Peter?"

Gabriel glanced at me, and then typed: "With Uriel and Ian in the sedan."

I typed another message: "Evac precaution or necessary?"

"Both," he typed, then looked at me with a controlled expression.

"Amara?"

"With Kez and Samael. Meet us tomorrow."

I nodded and leaned my head against the side of the vehicle.

My body felt heavy. I closed my eyes, feeling the rhythmic swaying of the van as it sped down what seemed to be a major freeway.

My eyes flew open in alarm to look at Josh. The air rushed from of my lungs. I tried not to make a sound to alert Rousseau of my presence, but I don't know if I was successful. The edges of my sight became blurred as the vision hit me hard. I struggled to reject it, but it was no use.

I was on damp grass, lying on my side, in thick mist. My hands and feet were bound with shackles and heavy chains, and I was in that same, sheer white dress I'd been wearing in other visions. My mind felt thick, like I'd been drugged, so I tried to blink away the feeling. Muffled voices were not far off, but maybe it was just in my mind. I concentrated to make them out.

Someone walked towards me, but I could only see booted feet on stone, then grass. My head was jerked to the side by my hair, and I was hoisted to my feet by my tresses. Once I gained my balance, the hand that had my hair moved to the back of my neck and marched me forward. My captor pushed me faster than I could walk with my chained feet, and I stumbled repeatedly. I felt lost in all of the mist rising from the damp terrain.

Finally, my foot struck a stone step, and I looked upwards. Rising from the ground were a series of steps that looked like they'd been recently unearthed. Dirt was haphazardly removed from each of the steps. I attempted to turn away, but the hand disappeared from my neck, and an arm locked around my waist, dragging me upwards through the fog. It was so thick that it kept our destination hidden.

We reached what appeared to be a precipice, where there was a fire blazing in a stone basin directly next to a stone table. When I tried to scream, a hand covered my mouth and I was carried the rest of the way to the sacrificial table that had haunted my dreams. I was chained down, and the bonds cut into my wrists and ankles as I fought, pulling so hard that I felt the iron bite into me and blood trickle down my wrist. I'd only succeeded in causing myself pain.

I recognized all of this and knew that a robed man would come out and pull a glowing red instrument from the fire and begin carving symbols into my flesh. The only thing that was different from before was the temperature. Last time, the weather had been miserably hot. Something had changed the timeline, but the result was the same—I was destined to be sacrificed according to the vision.

Yanking at my bonds once again, the hooded figure, his face completely shrouded in shadow, emerged from what appeared to be the mouth of a cave, rather than the top of a temple, like last time. This was a different location, not the one I'd seen before. He slowly walked to the fire, removed a slim rod, and approached me.

In terror, I tried to wake. Everything in my being tried to shake the vision. He ripped my dress open. He first took the red-hot iron and brushed it along my belly in a broad circular motion. Then he made swirling slash marks through the center. I screeched in pain and watched him place the rod back into the fire and grab a new one. Again, I tried to wake before the iron reached my skin. This time, he marked my chest. It felt like he was making long waving lines across my collarbone, spanning onto my breasts.

Another robed figure appeared with an iron and began branding my feet. I must have bit my tongue, because all I could taste was blood. Screaming and arching my body, I writhed in pain, wanting to beg them to stop, but I knew it wouldn't do any good.

The vision rippled, and I became aware that both Joshua and

Gabriel were near me. I made an effort to expel myself from the vision again and succeeded. I opened my eyes, finding I was on the floor of the van with my legs twisted awkwardly. They each had one of my arms, and Josh was on his knees with his other hand behind my head. I wondered what I'd been doing in reality. I waved my hands and nodded at them that I was back in reality. They slowly eased their grip and released me.

Gabriel eased back onto the bench seat, but Joshua hovered next to me waiting. I twisted my back leg around and pulled my knees to my chest while squeezing my eyes shut. I felt tears plummet down my cheeks as I tried to take a few breaths as silently as possible. Josh put his hand on my elbow, and I met his eyes.

I mouthed, "I'm okay."

He moved back to his seat, but sat perched on the edge of it, facing me. Warm liquid trickled from my nose, so I wiped it with the back of my hand. Blood. Josh leaned forward, but I pointed at him in warning.

He rocked back in his seat.

Gabriel nudged my shoulder and handed me a rag just as my nose seemed to let loose. I pressed the cloth to my nose and leaned my head back on the bench seat, wishing I could mutter and complain. For some reason, the nosebleed made me feel angry.

I stared over at Rousseau; she didn't seem to be paying attention. Maybe I did keep myself quiet.

But then she spoke, "I recognize her breathing." She paused. "Gabriel, you outdid yourself. I would never have believed you would let her bite you. Risky, but very cunning indeed."

I cringed, I must have made more noise than I thought.

"Silence, Rousseau," Gabriel barked.

I looked at him wide-eyed for a moment, and then held my hands up towards him, wrists together, and mouthed,

"Prisoner?" Then I felt my nose begin to bleed again, so I quickly raised the rag to my face.

He ran his fingers through his hair and flexed his jaw while he weighed the options.

She spoke again. "How long has she been amongst you? It's hard to keep things from the Council, and yet you have not made so much as a whisper."

"I said silence," Gabriel warned, his voice louder and more clipped than before.

I switched to holding the cloth with my left hand, pulled out my phone, and typed a message to Gabriel. "Do what u need to do."

He responded: "Still thinking."

I motioned to my nose, then typed: "Blood could be convincing."

He looked at me and twisted his mouth to the side.

"Bind me. J has gear 2 stay btwn the inner & out doors."

He shook his head and typed: "We do not have bonds that would hold a vampire."

I grimaced, not believing that I was suggesting this: "Then stake me."

He shook his head no: "Your body cannot handle the trauma now."

"Can if I need 2."

He shook his head again and handed Joshua the phone. Josh read through the conversation thread and handed the phone back to Gabriel with a blank look on his face. He was keeping his emotions enough under control so that I couldn't tell what he was feeling. I checked to see if my nose had stopped bleeding. It hadn't, but it was no longer gushing.

"Is it important R thinks I'm a threat?"

Gabriel tilted his head to the side. "She has not told us the third demand."

"Then, yes?" I typed. I picked myself up off of the floor and slid back to my spot on the bench seat.

Gabriel glared at the roof of the van; it seemed like he was having an argument with himself. Then he seemed to turn a little green, and his face twisted with torment. I looked over at Joshua, and he sank farther back into his seat, closing his eyes. It wasn't hard to see the conclusion to which Gabriel had arrived.

Gabriel picked up a helmet and handed it to Josh, who held it frozen for a moment. Then he abruptly stood and pressed his lips to my forehead, clearly not happy. He disappeared noiselessly through the back door, tucking himself into the small nook.

I took a stuttering breath and tried to ready myself. Gabriel made a few hand motions, giving me a basic plan. He sent a text, I assume to Sebastian, and shortly after dialed a number, pressing the phone to his ear. "How far out are we? The sedatives we used are wearing off."

There was a pause. Then I heard Sebastian respond, playing along. "Another forty-five minutes."

"Do you want to stop for more tranquilizers?"

"No. Restrain her."

"Understood." Gabriel shut off the phone. He walked to the supply cabinet and pulled out a few sets of cuffs. I sat there and held out my hands while he put all three sets of cuffs on me. I huffed and groaned a little as if I was fighting in a drug-induced state. We waited a few more minutes to give me more time for the supposed "drugs" to "wear off."

I sucked in some air loudly and strained my arms, breaking the outermost pair of cuffs.

"Ali, stop. Do not make me hurt you. I will put you down if I have to," he warned. His voice sounded a little rough.

I struggled some more. I actually felt some hysteria welling up, as if something was giving me more strength to get through this. "Go ahead," I challenged in what came out between a moan and a wail.

I ran at him from in front of the back door, and he pushed me into the opposite wall. The action was exaggerated and made more sound than it actually hurt. We continued the pattern a few more times. Rousseau started thrashing her head back and forth as she got more agitated. I knocked into her hard enough to scare her. She screamed.

And then came the finale. Gabriel placed the dagger over my heart and stood there. I looked at him and nodded my consent; the strain on his face was evident. Again, I nodded at him as I reached out and grabbed his wrists from beneath and pushed the blade harder into my chest without breaking the skin.

He winced, but didn't shove it all the way in.

I smirked nervously and mouthed, "Be the bad ass."

But he didn't move; he just shook his head, so I sucked in a deep breath and lunged forward, pressing the blade into my heart. It felt like it hit my ribs in the back, stopping it from going all the way through. I let out a guttural sound as my body went limp. He eased me to the floor. At some point my nose had started bleeding again. My eyes were open, and my head was pointed in Rousseau's direction. I could see from her body language that she didn't believe what was happening. She made a scoffing sound.

Gabriel lashed out. "Do not test my patience, Crina. I told you to be silent."

"I fell for it once Gabriel. I won't again."

"You think this is a game?" he asked, his voice booming in the small space.

"No, I think it is playacting."

As if to add to the turmoil, we turned onto an unpaved road that began rocking the vehicle. Gabriel stormed over and ripped the hood from her head, grabbing her face and forcing her to look at me. He had my blood all over his hands, so her face slipped from his grip leaving behind scarlet smears. "You call that acting?"

"I…" Her eyes lingered on me. She looked like she desperately wanted to look away, but she couldn't. "I…"

Gabriel pointed at me, and his face turned red as he yelled, "You deserve that stake in the chest, not that little girl. She was innocent and should have been protected, and yet you delivered her up to demons like she was a pawn in one of your games. Even now, she is better than you could ever hope to be."

"Neka was innocent, too." She screamed back at him, the last vestiges of control finally shattered.

"She was, but that gave you no right. No right. To take someone else's life from them. She deserved better than this. You taint everything Neka stood for with your actions."

"I had to do something."

"No. You bring it to the Council, and *we* do something. Not you—we."

She bit her lip. "But, I."

"No, 'I.'"

She swallowed and leaned back, her eyes drifting to me once again.

"What else do they want, Crina? What else?" Gabriel pressed, anger still lingering in his voice.

The blood drained from her face, and she grew silent once again.

Gabriel picked up the hood, harshly put it back over her head, and tightened the cord around her neck, covering her blood-streaked face. He immediately went over to some of the computer monitors and flipped them on, I assume to create some additional cover noise besides the sound of the vehicle.

A second later, he pulled the blade from my chest. He picked up the rag I'd been using on my nose and pressed it to the wound. I saw him glance at the back door and then back at me. He held up a finger and stepped over to let Josh back inside, then he ripped the lid off of the cooler and dumped all of the red bags on the floor.

He searched through the pile for one marked with my name and found my last unit of blood. He sat on the floor next to me, pulled me up so my head rested on his leg, then tore the plug out of the blood pouch and stuck it in my mouth.

While Gabriel worked on me, Josh stood there stone still just inside the door. He finally removed his helmet, placing it under the command table. He looked pale, even for a vampire. He proceeded to pick up the other units of blood strewn all over the floor and return them to the cooler.

I finished feeding and closed my eyes—my tiredness almost incapacitating. Gabriel moved, and my eyes flew open. I may have lost consciousness for a second. Joshua had started moving towards us.

Gabriel pointed at him, motioned to the chair, then waved the bloody rag at him. Josh nodded. He couldn't be near me until the risk of blood exposure was gone. He slowly sat back, his face bleak.

The blade hadn't even been in that long, and I still couldn't move much. Gabriel was keeping pressure on the wound, so it was a safe bet that was I was still bleeding.

A short while later, the van stopped. It sounded like the driver's side door opened, and I heard a gate or door of some type creak open. It was familiar somehow. The driver's door shut again, and we drove for a very short distance before the engine shut off completely.

It sounded like another vehicle pulled in behind us, followed by the clank of the gate or door again. A key rattled in the lock of the side-door, and it slid open. I involuntarily flinched, expecting light for some reason, though I know Sebastian would never endanger us that way. We were parked inside something made of old stone. Sebastian's eyes widened in surprise for an instant, then he yelled outside the vehicle, "Ian, I need you to escort Rousseau to her room. Please place her in the last room on the left. Secure her to the bedpost."

Ian stepped inside. Gabriel handed him the handcuff key. He unhitched her from the side of the van and led her out of the vehicle. Then, Peter and Uriel appeared outside the open door of the van. They had the same stunned reaction. *This must be something worthy of a horror film.*

Sebastian spoke again. "Peter, if you could help unload. We will be here for a couple of days, until we can secure passage back to England, so we won't require everything. Leave the bags I marked with the yellow tags."

Gabriel lifted the cloth once again and replaced it with a new one and even more pressure. I sighed. He looked out the open door. "Uriel, you willing to…"

"Where's the kit?" she inquired.

"In my pack in the cab, passenger side."

"Back in a few ticks." Uriel disappeared.

Sebastian asked Joshua to go downstairs to keep away from my blood. I looked over at him. "Where's here?"

"You have been here before. The Church of Angels."

I smiled as I remembered the beautiful stained glass in the main sanctuary. I'd longed to see it again. This is where we'd met Winslow months ago while I was recovering from my poison-induced appendicitis.

"Will there be a full moon tonight?" I asked.

He cocked his head to the side, and his hand went to his beard. "I'm not sure. I'll find out." He pointed at Gabriel. "Meet you downstairs in a few minutes."

"Yes."

Then I was alone with Gabriel. I started to sit, and he held me down. "You are still bleeding and need to feed."

I made a disgusted sound in the back of my throat. "You were waiting till everyone cleared out."

"Yes." He offered his wrist. I fed and felt bitter during every moment of it.

Afterwards, I still couldn't stand without help, so he carried me downstairs and straight to the shower. Uriel followed us with a stool into the bathroom and stuck it in the shower. Gabriel sat me down on it and left the room, closing the door behind him. I would've been mortified that she had to help me so much if I hadn't been so exhausted. Soon my clothes had been removed and warm water was running over me. I guess it wasn't the first time she'd helped me with a shower, although the last time she'd dumped me in it and threatened me.

When I was sparkling clean, she helped me get dressed and into the other room. I wanted to stay up with everyone and hear what the plans were, but I was so fatigued that it was almost painful to stay awake. I ached for sleep like never before. Josh escorted me to the room we were to use. There I fed yet again on the blood Uriel had just drawn.

Joshua tucked me into bed and asked, "Do you want me to stay with you?"

"No, I'm fine. I just need to sleep, but could you leave the door open?"

"I can stay," he offered once more.

"I'm good."

He kissed my temple and made his way out of the room. I think I was asleep before he had time to make it to the door.

. . .

I dreamt of Dagan for the first time since my escape. He was trying to tell me something, to warn me, but there was a great wind that stole his words away. He looked sad and conflicted.

He ripped his jacket off, revealing a silver breastplate. A fierce-looking fish with jagged teeth adorned the front, along with a swirl of other symbols. He spread his massive black wings, the feathers fluttering in the wind. He yelled one last thing before the current caught him, and he seemed to rise a few feet off the ground.

I yelled back, asking him to stay, saying that I didn't understand him, but he disappeared with the winds into the distance.

Waking, I heard the muted voices of Gabriel and Joshua speaking in the next room. Josh's voice was low and resolute. "This is the last time. You can't ask this of her again. She will help until it kills her."

"I know," Gabriel said, sounding hollow. "I know she would."

12

PROMISE ME

I woke and felt for my phone, wanting to know what time it was. It wasn't in my pocket. *Uriel must have put it somewhere when she helped me undress for my shower.* I rolled over and felt for Josh, but he wasn't in the bed. I knew he'd been there at some point. I remembered sleepily kissing him when he got into bed and feeling this overwhelming sense of love for him that had made my chest ache.

I took a deep breath; it felt like I'd been in here a long time, but my sense of reality was off. Muffled voices drifted through the thick door. It was closed now. Even now, with my improved senses, I had to concentrate to make out what they were saying.

I felt my way to the door and flipped on the lights. Someone had laid out clothes for me and placed my phone on top of them. I pulled on my jeans and the soft black sweater, then opened the door.

I hadn't even glanced at the main room yesterday when I was carried through it. It looked exactly the same as it had months ago: an enormous room tiled with large pieces of slate. The walls had been plastered and painted with warm tones. It was a four bedroom layout with a bathroom in the far corner and a large, dark fireplace. The oversized table was beautifully carved and had comfortable custom stools that fit beneath it. They were square and heavy with padded tapestry tops.

Everyone had arrived while I was sleeping and were now settled around the table. A fire roared in the fireplace, and everyone's spirits seemed to be much higher than when I went to sleep. Joshua looked over at me and smiled.

I took a small breath and grinned back at him. He scooted one of the stools around in front of him, making a place for me amongst the group. Sitting, I leaned back onto his chest, and he wrapped his arms around me. He rested his chin on my shoulder, and I turned my head until I felt his cheek. It felt warm and wonderful pressed up against mine.

Sebastian looked at me. "Your sacrifice yesterday helped. Rousseau gave us the last demand this morning."

"I'm glad." My voice sounded froggy. Josh gave me a little squeeze. "What was it?"

Gabriel answered, "Inferno."

"What is that?"

Samael fielded this one. "It was the predecessor to Aurora. Neka named it Inferno, as a nod to Dante, because it was supposed to dispatch the leeches to hell. But it failed miserably; it had the opposite reaction. It didn't superheat the cells; it protected them."

I thought about this for a moment. "You mean?"

"Yes, it allowed vampires to tolerate the sun."

Suddenly, I wanted it.

"But there was a problem," Kez remarked, leaning forward.

"It caused madness within a week on the test subjects," said Gabriel.

Suddenly, I did not want it.

"So if the queen had it, she could have daylight-loving-super-warriors until they lost their minds," I surmised.

"Yes," said Gabriel.

Joshua spoke. "Or, they want Neka to fix the formula. That would be a game changer."

I thought for a moment. "They removed her from her cell several hours a day. She would never say what she was doing. It could've been lab work." I paused. "All the new vampires...Do you think that's why they've been increasing their ranks? So they have an expendable army once Moloch is raised?"

"That is one of our theories," Sebastian answered after a long moment of silence.

I slyly pulled out my phone and typed a text under the table to Gabriel: "Do K, S, & A know about the baby?"

"No," he texted back.

"K."

Thoughts churned in my head, but there were too many to focus on just one. I looked at my phone again. I'd been in bed for almost eighteen hours; it was now late afternoon the following day. I couldn't believe I'd slept that long, especially since I felt like I either needed to feed or go back to bed again.

I realized I'd lost track of the conversation when Raphael's name was mentioned. He was a Slayer who'd evacuated with us from London to Dublin, lived with us for a while, then been called away. He'd often partnered with Michael, another Slayer, one whose ancestry I had found that I'd shared. Michael had been killed before I could speak to him about the discovery.

And there was something about another Slayer named Ariel coming in from Canada. I thought about there being a Uriel and Ariel here at the same time and found it humorous. It was like having Darcy and Marcy in my English class the year before.

I tried to refocus, but it proved to be impossible. I patted Joshua's leg, and he opened up his arms. I leaned forward and gave his leg a squeeze as I got up and shuffled towards the bathroom. When I passed by Kez and Amara, I noticed Kez withdraw his hand from her knee under the table.

After inspecting myself in the mirror, I realized it was admirable that no one had reacted to my appearance. My skin was so pale that it looked almost translucent, the circles under my eyes looked like bruises, and even my hair looked haggard. I used the facilities and decided that the lumpy bed was calling my name.

As I passed everyone to go back to my room, I could only manage a wisp of a smile. Joshua and Gabriel both watched me closely; I nodded my head in acknowledgement and exited to my room. I crawled to the center of the bed, collapsed onto my side, and closed my eyes.

There was a knock on the doorframe and then, "Hey, biscuit. I think it's time for you to feed." *Uriel's Aussie accent seemed thicker today.*

"Mmmm hmmm." I opened my eyes and turned my head to look at her. "I know it's bad when even you look concerned."

"Awwr, you're just a little bushed." She sat down next to me and put three units of blood on the bed. "I want you to drain all three of these. We have more."

"Thanks."

"Keep your chin up, chicky. There's always a way." She strolled to the door and pointed to the blood. "Cheers." Her mouth smiled, but not her eyes.

I did what I was told, but I still felt like I needed more sleep. I closed my eyes, and the heaviness of sleep overcame me. When I woke later, Joshua was pressed up behind me. I pulled his hand to my mouth and kissed it.

"There's a full moon tonight," he murmured.

"Mmmm. Can we go upstairs?"

"Whenever you're ready."

"Let's go."

He held my hand as we walked up the stone steps to the sanctuary. The moonlight filtered in through the panes of glass and covered the inside with squares of shadowy, jewel-toned color. All of the depictions were of angels, and I quickly found my favorite: "The Faithful Three," which was a scene of an angel protectively covering Shadrach, Meshach, and Abednego from the flames of the fiery furnace.

"Is this one still your favorite?"

I answered without looking away from the pane. "Yes." I sat down in a pew in front of it and turned sideways in the seat to continue looking at it.

"Mine too." He sat down in the row in front of me and swiveled to the side so that we were next to one another.

There was a long silence.

"I'm dying."

Joshua bowed his head. "I know." He choked.

"I want my death to be worth something."

"I don't want you hurt. I want you for as long as I can."

"Unless something drastic happens, by the time—"

"Don't. I know."

I climbed over the back of the pew and put my arms around him. He let out a long, uneven breath and sagged against me. Talking about it didn't make me feel any better. It just made me feel Joshua's pain as well as my own.

When dawn threatened to crest, we retreated to our room. I didn't want to sleep; I was tired of sleeping, but it overtook me anyway. I awoke a few hours later with Joshua's arms around me; he was sound asleep. As I was trying to calm the chaos in my head, I heard Amara and Samael leave. Shortly after that, Ian and Peter were tasked with something upstairs. I disengaged myself from Joshua's arms and wandered into the main room.

Sebastian and Gabriel were at one end of the table discussing assets in different locations. Uriel and Kez were at the other end going over how to draw out one of Rousseau's contacts. I hovered near Sebastian, not wanting to interrupt.

After a couple of minutes, he looked over at me and asked, "What's on your mind, child?"

"May I sit down for a moment? Do you have time?"

He glanced at Gabriel and pulled out the stool at the end of the table in between them. As I sat down, I looked back and forth at each of them, then thought for a moment. I refocused on Sebastian. "Does the French Coven know that we have Rousseau?"

"We do not believe so. She would go off grid for weeks at a time. They will not think anything of her disappearance."

I nodded. "Do you think they would give up Neka, if they had their demands?"

"It would be much—" Sebastian started.

"I know we can't let them get their hands on Inferno. But, do you think they would honor their agreement if we had something else they wanted?"

"I don't know." Sebastian clicked his pen shut.

I asked another question on a slightly different track. "Do you think Neka could synthesize the antidote to Aurora in the castle? Or would it require her old lab?"

"Neka could, but she would most likely need her notes and samples. Beth has them," Gabriel answered.

"What are you thinking?" Sebastian asked.

"A trade, but I don't know if it'll be enough," I replied.

"What did you have in mind?" Sebastian asked cautiously.

"Me for the baby and Neka. They have a guarantee if they have me. The baby is still an unknown."

"We cannot do that," Gabriel said firmly.

"Why not? They don't know I'm sick. I can gorge myself, so I look well, and buy some extra time. Without Slayer blood, I won't last long. They will end up with nothing. Meanwhile, you can have Neka work on a cure. There's always a chance I'll get out."

"They can still sacrifice you," Gabriel said.

"I am not a virgin, and therefore, no longer a pure sacrifice. There is no way for Moloch to absorb my abilities. The risk to the world is not nearly as great as it would be for him to have our child." I paused, feeling awkward about saying 'our child.' I drew in a breath. "And besides, do they even have everyone they need?"

"We do not think so, but that is not for certain."

"Are my odds higher with Neka on the inside or on the outside?"

Sebastian exhaled harshly.

For the first time, I noticed that assault plans were being drawn up. I placed my hand on the stack of papers and pulled them towards me. I shuffled through them and found incomplete blueprints for the castle.

"You're planning to attack the castle? You'd be slaughtered. You can't seriously be considering this. What are your objectives?"

Gabriel looked at me. "Neka, surrogate/baby, and frozen embryos, if possible. Burn the rest."

"You're crazy. There are hundreds of them—*hundreds.*" I flung my arms wide.

"We have done this before—when there is an imminent threat to humanity. This is no different."

"On this scale?" I gaped.

"Yes," Gabriel replied.

"How long will this take to plan? And get the resources together?"

"Three more weeks."

I closed my eyes and pressed my fingertips into my forehead.

"There is a lower risk to Neka and the baby with my plan. We need to do this quickly for me to have a chance."

Sebastian gave me a hard look. "This is not a yes. When would you like to do this?"

"Tomorrow, or as soon as possible."

Sebastian leaned towards me. "Have you discussed this with Joshua?"

"No, she hasn't," Joshua replied. Apparently, he was standing in the doorway.

I cringed.

Josh's voice was quiet and firm. "So this was your plan when you said you wanted your death to be worth something." He sounded remarkably calm, but I could feel a swell of emotion. "May I talk with my wife alone, please?"

"Of course." Sebastian let out a little whistle. Uriel and Kez prairie dogged in our direction. "We are going upstairs." They looked a little confused, but they followed Sebastian and Gabriel. Joshua trailed them and closed the door at the bottom of the stairwell.

He turned, raised his hands a little, and then let them fall to his sides. "You can't do this." He paused, his face pained. "How could you mention this to them and not talk to me first?"

"I wasn't intending on discussing it with them now. I had a few questions, and then I kept going." I walked over to him. "How much did you hear?"

"I heard your whole plan."

"Then you know it makes sense."

"How can I let you do this?" His tone turned urgent and pleading.

I placed my hand on his cheek and looked into his eyes. "You're fighting me. But you know what I'm saying is true." My voice came out calmer than I thought possible. "I'm the only one that can do this. The French Coven needs me, and offering Inferno to them is much, much worse."

He stepped away from me and paced back and forth. His chest started heaving, like he was going to burst. He spun back towards me and bellowed, "No. NO. There must be some other way."

I'd only seen his eyes brimmed with tears twice before: at his parents' funeral, and when I'd returned. Suddenly, he was in front of me, his fingertips under my chin as he searched my face. His voice had failed him.

"Don't you understand? We need Neka to save *me*. If there is a full-scale attack, it could mean hundreds of lives lost. Maybe even Neka's. I can't have that on my conscience. Nor can you."

His voice broke. "We'll find another way."

"We are out of options, love. And I'm running out of time. You know that."

He grabbed my upper arms. "Please don't do this. Please. I can't lose you again."

"If I stay you *will* lose me. If I go, I-I have a chance." I placed my hand over his, pulling it to my mouth, and kissed his palm. My voice broke this time. "This is me fighting to stay with you. I'm not giving up. I'm just betting on the long shot."

He nodded, but he wouldn't look at me.

I pulled out my phone and sent a text to Sebastian: "If u agree with my plan, set up the trade."

A moment later, we heard voices in the stairwell. I cupped my husband's face and kissed him. "I'll be in our room. Speak with Sebastian, then come spend some time with me."

He swallowed and nodded again, still not meeting my gaze.

I went to the room to rest, leaving the door cracked open so I could hear. My exhaustion was complete; feeling his emotions, on top of my own, had drained me. I tuned in and out of the conversation while I fell in and out of sleep. Later, when I opened my eyes, it felt like a long time had passed. Something was not going well in the other room. I slid off the bed and entered the main living space.

Gabriel was settled on the table, hunched over while looking at his phone with downturned lips, while Josh sat expressionless on a stool a few feet away. I didn't feel anything from him, but there was a weird energy in the room.

Peter and Ian had returned and were sitting quietly at the far end of the table, appearing uneasy about the activity. Sebastian was pacing to and fro, listening to a conversation on his phone; he hadn't noticed me.

Sebastian spoke to Gabriel and said, "The familiar Rousseau used as a contact has cleared out. The apartment is empty."

"Was that her only contact?" Kez asked. He was standing two doorways down from me.

"Yes."

"Can an emissary be sent to the castle itself?"

"No," Gabriel replied. "When I was surveilling it months ago, anyone not invited was eliminated. Not even vampires were spared."

"Guess that's out," Kez said under his breath.

"Maybe the whole idea should be out," Josh muttered.

I spoke confidently as if I hadn't heard Josh's comment. "What if I infiltrate Morpheus's dreams? I could speak with him."

Everyone turned to look at me, making me feel a little uncomfortable. Gabriel asked, "You figured out how to do it?"

"I think so." I took a deep breath and moved forward a little farther into the room.

Sounding both skeptical and surprised, Kez asked, "Infiltrate dreams?"

I bit my lip, realizing he didn't know anything about my being part of the Lux. I eyed Sebastian apologetically and mouthed, "Sorry." I obviously wasn't at the top of my game. It was getting hard to keep track of who knew what about me.

He gave me an understanding smile, and then addressed Kez. "Aleria is a Seer with some unique abilities."

Kez scrutinized me, but spoke to Sebastian. "A Seer with the ability to infiltrate the dreams of the Oneiroi? Are you sure we should do this? Trading away that kind of power..."

I clenched my fists. "Kez, it won't matter. I'm not going to be around much longer. This—"

Josh stood, his stool loudly scratching on the floor. He looked ill; he moved by me into our room before shutting the door softly. It didn't come across as a tantrum, just the inability to listen to the topic.

My bottom lip trembled and I closed my eyes for a moment. I glanced at Sebastian. He jerked his chin toward the door to my room. I nodded, turning on my heel. I paused at the door, leaning my forehead against it to collect myself, and then opened it, stepped through, and closed it behind me.

The room was black as pitch. I used the light from my phone to see. He was sitting at the edge of the bed with his head in his hands.

"I apologize. I just can't hear you say it. I just need a minute." His voice wavered like he was trying to control himself.

"I'm sorry."

He exhaled wearily. "Go ahead and meet with them. I'll be out in a bit."

"Are you sure?" I was cautiously trying to assess if that was what he truly desired.

"Yes, I'm sure."

I returned to the other room. Then, asked Sebastian, "Did you make a decision?"

His lips were pressed into a thin line, making it look like his beard had swallowed up his mouth. "We will try your plan. Contact Morpheus."

He gave me a list of talking points and things to avoid. I read it several times to commit it to memory. Josh hadn't returned yet, so I proceeded into the room Gabriel had been staying in and stretched out on the bed. They left me alone to concentrate.

Once settled, I relaxed my mind and thought of the eternal sunset in Morpheus' created world. A wall of resistance met me, but I pushed through the veil. Then, experienced the sensation of being in liquid, behind a shimmering wall of color.

Again, I focused my thoughts on the sunset and the tree on the hillside where Morpheus would sit. My entire body quaked, as if I was being squeezed. The moment the feeling became painful, it ceased and I was there—and so was he. I walked towards him, silently passing over the grassy hills, until I was standing less than two yards from him.

His shoulder-length, black hair was fluttering in the breeze. He peered up at me, but this time he didn't look shocked or angry. His grey eyes still retained the look of an oncoming storm.

"Couldn't stay away?" he said in a low voice.

"I needed to speak with you. I have a proposition."

"So you figured it out? You came here of your own volition?"

"Yes, and I'll keep coming until you hear my proposal."

"I never said I wouldn't." He twisted a blade of grass between his fingers, releasing the smell into the air, and leaned his head back on the burly trunk of the tree. He appeared contemplative.

"I want to make a trade," I said, my voice strong.

"And what do you have to bargain with, Seer?"

"Me."

He raised his eyebrows in surprise. "And what do you want for 'you?'"

"The surrogate carrying my child and Neka the scientist."

He took a moment to comment; I could see the wheels turning in his head, but he kept a poker face. "You seem to be well informed."

I grinned, not showing my hand.

"And what makes you think *you* are worth *both* of them?"

"The queen likes guarantees. I am of the Lux. She doesn't know if the baby will even carry the gene. How many embryos did they lose trying to conceive just that one child? She knows she has a sacrifice in me."

Morpheus tilted his head. "Very well-informed indeed."

"Yours isn't the only mind I have been in."

He clenched and unclenched his jaw. "The baby... maybe, but Neka? I can't see Tyran giving up his pet."

"One pet for another," I replied, pushing the sale.

"You did seem to be his favorite," he said, as a wicked little grin played at the corner of his mouth.

"Will you present my offer to the queen?"

"I have nothing to lose by doing so."

I gave him the number to contact Sebastian and coolly walked away after he had repeated it back to me. He almost seemed amused.

Once over the hillside and out of his view, I sat down and tried to wake. Blood started to flow from my nose as I strained to return. It worked on my fourth try. I opened my eyes to Gabriel, who was on a chair next to the bed, holding a towel to my nose. His breathing was unusually labored, but his expression was smooth. There appeared to be a torrent raging inside him.

"I'm back." I took over placing pressure on the bleed.

"Did it work?" he asked.

"Yes. He said he would contact the queen. Actually, he said he didn't have anything to lose by presenting the proposal. I suspect he will contact Tyran instead."

"Tyran will bring it to his mother."

"Yes, I suppose he will," I replied, thinking about how Tyran was on the outs with his mother after he'd turned me.

"Go and clean up as soon as that stops. Then get some rest. We will take care of the rest." He stood and started towards the door.

"Gabriel?"

"Yes?"

"Are you okay with this?"

He turned to face me. "You made a compelling argument," he answered without much expression.

"You didn't answer my question."

"No. I am not okay with it."

"Am I making the wrong decision?"

Gabriel scrutinized me with an anguished expression, but didn't answer.

It felt hard to speak the next words. "Sebastian doesn't think I will make it, does he? It's the only reason he is allowing it."

Gabriel met my eyes with reluctance. "No, he does not think you will live, but he has other reasons to take the risk. Sebastian is the strategist," he stated, sounding as if he had been overruled in the debate.

He proceeded towards the door, then stopped, resting his hand on the doorframe. Without looking back, he stated, "Tyran will hurt you after the exchange. It is in his nature." And with that, he left the room. I stared at the empty space he'd left behind and felt unsure of everything.

After the bleeding had finally stopped, I cleaned up in the bathroom and returned to the main room. Joshua still wasn't there. The others were discussing ways to guarantee that the surrogate was the real deal, not just some random pregnant lady they'd kidnapped and used mind control on. I walked over to the table.

"Sooo, you heard from them then?"

"Initial terms are set. Contact in four hours to discuss the place of exchange," Sebastian said, in a very business-like tone, but he was twisting one of the buttons on his shirt.

"When?" I asked.

"Tomorrow after sunset," Sebastian answered.

My insides went liquid. I swallowed and nodded.

Sebastian started to give more details, but I held up my hand to stop him. Knowing more felt overwhelming. I just needed to know the where and when. They could take care of the details. I wanted nothing to do with them.

When I turned to go to my room, Peter was standing in my path a few feet from the table. He'd been so quiet, I'd forgotten he and Ian had been sitting in. Peter's brow was furrowed and his lips pressed shut. He looked almost betrayed. He stood uncertainly, the slope of his shoulders heavy, like he was burdened and didn't know what to say or do.

I walked forward and put my arms around him. He held onto me tight, shifting his weight from one foot to the other, rocking us ever-so-gently. He didn't say anything; he didn't need to. I finally pulled away and kissed him on the cheek. "I love you, Peter."

"I love you too," he replied, then let me go.

I entered the bedroom, and I could hear the sounds of deep sleep coming from Joshua. *That's why he hadn't returned.* I put on a tank and PJ bottoms, fed yet again, spooned him, and drifted off to sleep myself.

. . .

Fragments of different dreams pelted my consciousness as I drifted from dream to dream. I awoke. It must have been the middle of the night. No sounds could be heard from the other room.

Josh was still asleep. I rolled onto my back and felt for my phone that I'd stashed under the pillow, turning on an App that made the screen flicker like flames, I put it on the bedside table. Joshua had fallen asleep in his clothes. I watched him in the synthetic candlelight and memorized all the angles of his face, though I had no need to. The heaviness of a thousand planets hit me—this could be our last night together.

He stirred, and I pressed my lips to his, unable to restrain myself any longer. He sleepily returned the kiss, and as he awoke, the intensity of the kiss increased.

My breath turned uneven as I pushed his shirt up, and he pulled it off and tossed it to the floor. I fumbled with the button on his jeans with shaking hands. He kissed me, and I could feel the smile on his lips as he helped me disrobe him. Soon, there was nothing between us but my lace briefs.

Our hands explored one another with a mixture of desperation and tenderness. My mouth lingered on his neck, and he pulled me on top of him. I wanted our connection to be stronger. Even if all I could feel was his pain after the exchange, I would still be feeling him.

He offered himself to me without hesitation. My fangs elongated, and I bit down, tasting the perfection of his blood. I didn't know if it would increase the blood bond or not, I just wanted more of him. He let out a soft moan and crushed me to him as I drank.

After I finished, he looked at me for a long moment, and I would have felt self-conscious if his expression hadn't been so absolutely full of love. He seemed to be thinking about something. He let out a ragged breath and rolled on top of me, his reverie over.

He kissed me feverishly, and he tugged my underwear down over my left hip.

"No," I whispered and looked at him.

His eyes were glowing, and he didn't stop.

"Please," I begged, "I need you well."

"I won't be *well* without you." He ran the tip of his tongue down my neck, and I lost my breath; his fingers were still resting against my hip, his thumb latched to the side of my underwear.

"We talked about this," I gasped.

"Tell me you are going to fight to live," he said as he trailed kisses across my collarbone, igniting sparks all over my body.

"I'll fight," I moaned, feeling his weight settle on top of me.

"Tell me you want to live." He kissed up my neck and under my chin; I arched in response.

"I want to live. I want to be with you," I panted.

"You promise?" He stopped kissing me and looked into my eyes, his expression fierce.

"I promise—whatever it takes."

"You come back to me."

"I will." And I believed it.

"You promise you will come back to me," he pressed one more time.

"I promise," I said breathlessly.

He kept his eyes locked on mine for another moment, assessing my commitment. All I wanted was him. And I wanted him everywhere—all around me—inside me.

Husband and wife.

One flesh.

He eased the lace down over my right hip. "No," I breathed, but it didn't sound convincing.

"Let me…" His voice was honey against my neck.

My voice came out almost as a whimper. "I'm not strong enough to keep saying no."

"Then. don't. say. no," he said between kisses.

"I always want to give you everything," I said, barely audible, breathless.

He sat up on his knees and eased my underwear off slowly, never taking his eyes off of mine, his expression serious. I looked at him worriedly, torn by my desire. But when his mouth crashed back onto mine…

the rest of the world fell away…
there was only us…

13

OH, HELL

Samael was placing throwing knives in his tactical vest while we waited for the others in the main room.

"Do people ever call you Sam?"

He looked surprised, then smirked crookedly, letting out half a laugh and shaking his head. "You are about to give yourself over to the enemy, and you want to know if I have a nickname?"

I shrugged and twisted my mouth to the side. "Yeah?"

"No, no one has ever called me Sam," he replied, with softness in his voice for the first time.

I pinned my brows together. "Isn't that weird?"

"You never call Gabriel, 'Gabe,' do you?"

"But he doesn't shorten anything. He doesn't even use contractions or abbreviate in text messages. It would be sacrilegious to shorten his name."

He focused on the paper he'd slowly been folding into a small square. The pleasant look he had on his face melted away, and I could feel him getting more serious. He cleared his throat. "I'm sorry I kept calling you a leech. You are far nobler than I expected."

I grinned. "I assure you, this is purely selfish. I need Neka to work on that antidote."

We made eye contact again, his dark brown eyes seemed almost black. "You know what the odds are. It's not selfish."

My voice cracked a little. "Sure it is." My smile became a little more wistful.

"You seem awfully calm," he commented, his eyes steady on me.

"She's not." Amara came in from the stairwell. "This girl is a bundle of worries."

I gawked at her with mock disapproval. "Now that's not fair. I was working hard on this frosty veneer," I said, waving my hand in a circle around my face.

She sat down next to me and took my hand. "Are you sure you want to do this thing? We can still back out of the exchange." Out of the corner of my eye, Samael watched me expectantly.

I felt like there was an iron press on my chest. "Yes, I'm sure," I replied. "I know I told Sebastian I didn't want the details, but can I have some of the details now?"

Amara nodded and her voice took on a professional tone. "In order to establish that the surrogate's child is yours, a medical test was agreed to. They met at a neutral facility a couple of hours ago to do an amniocentesis. It takes a long time to get full results, but they can check three important markers within two hours. No vampires or Slayers were allowed; only two familiars and two Watchers, plus the medical tech. I think you have met the med tech. Gabriel said she helped you once. I believe her name is Jess?"

"Yes, I know her. She helped remove a tracker and stitch me up after the whole poisoning-appendectomy-thing." I paused. "Which Watchers went?"

"Ian and Phineas."

I was startled; I thought I'd hear names I didn't recognize.

"Phineas?" Distrust immediately welled up within me, but I was calmed by the thought of Ian being there. I trusted him, and I knew that boy could fight. I had a brief flash of memory of his fending off all those henchmen in Germany; if he hadn't, Crooked Teeth would've captured me for sure.

Amara waited, seeing I was off on some tangent in my head. She then started speaking again, her manner reassuring. "I think Phineas is trying to make amends for the damage he caused helping Rousseau."

"Mmmm. That would be a stressful two hours of waiting," I commented.

"Yes, I'm glad I didn't pull that duty. They will wait there until you are traded for Neka. A phone call will be made during the trade, and the surrogate will be released."

"So what duty did you pull?"

"I'm to be at the exchange with you, Samael, and Kez."

"What?" I cried incredulously, "You can't. It's too dangerous."

Samael interrupted, "Too dangerous?"

"He doesn't know, does he?" My voice was openly accusatory.

She took a breath and stuck her chin in the air, locking eyes with Samael. "'Twill be fine. I won't let you go in there blind."

Samael leaned forward, questions on his face.

I met his gaze. "The French coven needs an Empath from the Abacha family for the sacrifice. It's no secret they're trying to raise Moloch."

"Amara," he sputtered.

"Joshua can sense intentions. He should take your place."

"He has been forbidden to attend," Samael informed me.

"By whom?"

Amara answered, "The other side. They may know about his skill or they may be afraid he would try to intervene. But I don't think Sebastian wanted him there either. He will stay here with

Peter." She must've been feeling my disapproval still. She added, "They do not know who I am. I will not be captured."

"I don't like it. If they don't want Joshua there, it sounds like they're planning something," Samael thought aloud. He shifted his body towards Amara and pinned her with a look.

"That is why you need me. The decision has already been made," she said.

My mind was racing. *Had I not told Sebastian and Gabriel about the need for an Empath for the sacrifice in the debriefs?* I couldn't remember. *Or did they know and think it was an acceptable risk?*

"Does Kez know?" Samael asked Amara.

"You will not go in blind," she repeated, sounding almost threatening. "He doesn't need to know."

I looked to Samael, but he shook his head, helplessly in obvious disagreement.

After a couple of minutes, I asked, "What about the others? Where are they going to be?"

"The exchange is on a private airstrip, as the vamps will be arriving via plane. Probably so they can do a flyby and make sure we are alone. There are hills a quarter of a mile away. Gabriel is already in position with a sniper rifle. He's using a sniper's ghillie suit to evade detection. It obviously won't kill the vamps, but it can slow them down to aid an escape.

"We have already set up video surveillance, which Sebastian will command from offsite. Kez, Samael, and I are to accompany you. Kez handled all the negotiations. They don't even know Sebastian or Gabriel were involved after the initial call. We kept it to only Conclave members or unknowns."

"Any other backup?"

"Raphael got in this morning. He will have a team standing by near the exchange with the surrogate. Uriel will be a little over half a mile away from our exchange; it's as close as she can be without violating the terms of the exchange. If something happens, she can be there in less than two minutes."

Samael got a text. "Time to go up," he said.

I scanned the room, wondering where Joshua was. I took an uneven breath and followed them upstairs, through the mudroom, and into the attached garage. It was dark, save for a few yellow lights that cast everything in amber. It reminded me of sunset, when there was only a warm glow that was being swallowed up by shadow.

Josh and Peter leaned against the back door of the van. Peter hugged me hard, then retreated down the stairs, his face flushed. Amara and Samael stepped into the van and closed the door, leaving Joshua and me alone.

I immediately circled his neck with my arms. He held me so tightly, I could barely breathe. He eased his grip, and I looked into his face. Tears tumbled down his cheeks, and I wiped them away. Bottom lip quivering, I stretched onto my tiptoes and kissed him. I pressed my cheek to his, and his breathing became ragged.

He kissed my neck and nuzzled me for a moment, then gently knotted his hand in my hair and sank his teeth into my neck. I tried to jerk away, but he held me there and drank. I felt the euphoria of his bite wash over me and my anxiety dissipate. He didn't drink much, just enough to reestablish a blood bond, and then he sealed the punctures. It wasn't enough to weaken me.

I squeezed my eyes shut. "Joshua, what did you just do?"

He pressed his mouth to my ear. "I'm sorry. I have to know if you're okay. My choice," he said resolutely. "My choice."

I pulled back and regarded him, feeling too many emotions to speak: everything from anger to adoration. I reached around the back of my neck and removed my locket, pooling the chain in my hand. I pressed it into his palm. "Just in case."

He opened his mouth to protest, but I quickly placed my fingers over his lips.

"I can't bear the thought of losing your mother's locket. I plan on getting it back." I swallowed. "Peter helped me put a temporary picture in it. It's just on paper, but..." I didn't finish the sentence. I liked the thought of our faces pressed together inside the locket.

He nodded wordlessly.

Someone knocked from the inside of the van door. He cupped my face and kissed me hard before I tore myself away from him, feeling like I was leaving half of myself behind. I opened the van, climbed in, and shut the door behind me. I sat down on the bench seat in the back, a complete and total mess. I felt my phone buzz in my pocket. It was from Joshua: "Remember your promise."

I typed: "I will," in response.

I peeped across the aisle of the van at Samael and Amara; they were both watching me, unapologetically. I rubbed my neck, making sure my collar was covering the evidence of my encounter with Joshua. It should've healed, but I couldn't be sure without checking in a mirror.

Samael's eyes were filled with anxiety, which seemed very out of character. I couldn't imagine being in his shoes, thinking all those years that your fiancée was dead, only to find out it'd been faked and she'd been imprisoned the entire time. I wondered if he worried about what he was going to get back, if she was going to be the same person at all.

Amara handed me four units of blood. "Bottoms up."

I sighed. She hit Samael on the leg. He looked at her, startled, and realized she wanted him to turn towards the monitors to give me privacy. He did.

It was easier with their backs to me. I drank down the contents quickly. The vehicle came to a stop, and my nerves felt frayed again, like a worn-out cable that has been supporting more weight than it could bear. I threw the empty bags away and sat back down.

Amara swiveled around to look at me. I tried to give her a little bit of a smile, but I felt like my face didn't work, and all I'd managed was a weird lip twitch that probably looked like a mild seizure. I felt stupid. She moved alongside me and put her arm around me. I leaned hard against her, blinking back tears.

A short while later, I felt the sun set, followed by hearing Kez's voice over the radio: "Aircraft approaching from the South. ETA four minutes."

The jitters hit me when we heard the plane touch down; its wheels briefly skidded on the landing strip as it returned to the earth. Its engines whined as it taxied towards our vehicle. Once it geared down, we opened the side door so we could observe what was going on: they were about a football field away and had turned the plane around, positioning it for takeoff. The door in the side of the small jet unfolded.

Kez opened the interior cab door, and he and Samael appeared, dressed in identical, black, combat gear. The engine was left running. Samael made a last check of his Durateus throwing blades that were lined in his tactical vest.

Amara pulled a Beretta from her holster, chambered a round, and returned it. Kez appeared to be laden with weapons already. We stepped out of the van, and I glanced towards the hills where Gabriel was positioned, then the other way so as to not inadvertently give away his location. The boys stood in front of Amara and me.

Traces of pink were still in the sky, but the sun had been down long enough that I could tolerate it. A chilly wind whipped around us, flapping the collar of my fitted, black shirt. The scent of fresh-cut grass wafted through the air, reminding me of the blade of grass Morpheus had pressed between his fingers when I'd infiltrated his dream.

I peered over at the plane and saw a single figure emerge. I recognized Morpheus' brother, Icelos. They looked similar, but he sported a shorter version of Morpheus' wavy, black hair. He was tall and imposing, though not as broad shouldered as either of his brothers.

When he reached the ground, he looked around for a moment, then motioned behind him. Zahra appeared with Neka in tow. She looked about the same as the last time I'd seen her, except she was clean this time. Her dark red hair was neatly braided and hanging over her right shoulder, contrasting sharply with her pale skin, which shone bright, even in twilight. She was all angles and bones that seemed as frail as flower petals.

They descended the steps leisurely. Samael leaned forward a little, almost imperceptibly. Then the final vampire materialized in the doorway of the plane—Tyran immediately fixed his eyes on me and smiled broadly. My skin crawled, and I slowly exhaled, trying to stay calm, and wishing I didn't have such a visceral reaction just at the sight of him. *I can do this.*

He descended the stairs and stood just behind Icelos. Tyran said something to the others, but the wind swept away his words. He peered over at me again. I didn't realize I was taking tiny, panting breaths, like I was about to hyperventilate, until Amara touched my hand. I immediately calmed down.

Kez squinted over his shoulder, concerned, and asked, "Are we still doing this?"

"Yes," I said firmly, getting myself under control.

Kez nodded and said over comm to Sebastian: "We are a go."

Both groups walked towards one another; we closed half the distance quickly and slowed down. Icelos took Neka's arm and pulled to the front, as Zahra and Tyran dropped behind them. We did the same, and I moved to the front with Samael.

When we were about ten feet apart, everything seemed to move in slow motion. Amara yelled, "Trap!" and pulled at the back of my shirt.

At the same moment, there was a shift in the wind, and I caught the scent of another vampire—Morpheus. There was a flicker of movement coming down from the wheel well of the plane as he moved behind the tire.

Immediately, I heard two cracks from a rifle slice through the air, and Kez fell backwards on the ground about five feet behind me, dust puffing up beneath him as he hit the ground. Amara froze with horror.

Samael sped forward and rammed Icelos hard as he grabbed Neka around the waist. He spun around her and pulled her towards us. Icelos then sprang forward, drove a knife into Samael's side and left it there, but Samael didn't slow down. He was moving quickly towards the van, half dragging Neka.

I heard repeated popping sounds in the distance. I watched Zahra crumble to the ground, and Icelos a moment later. I realized it was Gabriel with the sniper rifle.

There was another pop, but Tyran moved and reached behind his head, completely calm, as if chaos hadn't broken out around him. When he drew his arm back, he was holding an odd-looking pistol.

His sights were on Amara. *He knew exactly who she was.* My veins went to ice, and I dashed in front of her just as he fired. I looked down at my chest and uttered, "Oh, hell," as I paused for a couple of beats. There was a tranquilizer dart firmly planted in my chest. I brushed it off, but I already felt its effects.

I stumbled towards Amara to protect her, as I felt another dart hit my shoulder and yet another in my thigh.

She was standing there like stone, focused on Kez. I observed her wide-eyed, and then surveyed the scene falling apart around us.

Samael had collapsed twenty yards from the van, and Neka was trying to drag him the rest of the way. Her tiny body strained as she dragged his bulk, looking so delicate, as if her bones would burst through her skin. There was a tumult of crimson gushing from his side.

I twisted towards Kez. His feet were scratching at the ground, the rocks grinding beneath him, but he was unable to stand. I could see a wound in his shoulder and another in his stomach. He rolled toward us, his eyes on Amara. I kept hearing Gabriel plug away with the sniper rifle.

Tyran was moving in our direction. There was a pop, and he was knocked flat on his back, but he sprang back up immediately. He was hit again, but he did the same thing. He was too old—too powerful, and he wasn't just a vampire, he was half fallen angel.

Suddenly, I felt like I was standing in thick fluid, my body wanting to surrender to the drugs. I turned towards Amara again. She was backing up as a tranquiller hit her in the arm. Fear flashed across her face as she gaped at it, and then an icy calm passed over her features.

She made eye contact with Kez and pulled the Beretta from its holster. She mouthed something to him, and I heard him shriek "no" so loudly I thought it would shatter my heart. Within an instant, she placed the pistol to her temple and pulled the trigger. Blood sprayed across my face and into my mouth as I screamed and screamed.

Tyran got back on his feet, with his tranquilizer gun still pointed towards the empty space where Amara had just been. He cursed and moved his murderous eyes to me. I tried to move backwards, but tripped over Amara's body and came crashing down. I frantically looked in the direction of the plane.

Morpheus emerged from behind the wheel, slinging the rifle over his shoulder, and running with purpose to Zahra and Icelos.

They were both moving, but they were unable to walk on their own because of their head wounds. He dragged their bullet-riddled bodies towards the plane while glaring in Gabriel's location in the distance.

I tried to stand, but all I did was flail around like a fish in shallow water. Tyran seized my arm, hoisted me over his shoulder, and moved in the direction of the plane, slower than expected. He must've been more hurt than it appeared. As we trudged up the steps, I could see that Neka had Samael almost to the van.

Kez had crawled to Amara, still screaming as he lay next to her, cradling her lifeless body to him. And there was a black van, probably Uriel's team, barreling down the frontage road, not twenty seconds away from us. The door to the aircraft closed and the engines of the plane ramped up just as the drugs swallowed me whole.

14

NOT...RIGHT

I didn't need to open my eyes—I knew exactly where I was. I could feel the cold iron scoring my wrists as my body hung heavily from the cuffs. My arms were stretched high above my head, and my feet barely scraped the floor. My back was pressed against a stone wall, and the heavy chains jingled with each breath.

The room smelled of dank stone that hinted of mildew, just like it had in my dreams. I knew I wouldn't be in the castle when I opened my eyes; this was some other hideaway Tyran had procured in order to fulfill his plans—whatever they were. Perhaps it was some way to regain his mother's affections.

I also knew that when I opened my eyes, Bowen would be suffering on the floor near me, with a stake in his heart to keep him immobile. I was no longer capable of tuning out our blood bond; he was too near.

A door opened, and I tried to steel myself. I'd already seen all of this: the short hallway with the entrance around the corner and the windowless room with a security camera so he could observe his victims. I could sense him standing in front of me. I didn't struggle like I had in the vision. I knew my fetters would hold. I opened my eyes and met his gaze, with all the hate in the world evident in my eyes.

Tyran had cleaned up. He had on a crisp, white shirt with an absence of bullet holes. I'd seen Gabriel pump six sniper rounds into him, but he'd gotten up each time like they'd been rubber bullets that'd simply stung him. He smelled like citrus soap, and his blond hair was still damp.

I spoke first, my voice sounding dead. "Why are you doing this to him?"

Tyran cocked his head to the side. He seemed to notice I hadn't looked around the room, yet I knew Bowen was there. "You do seem to be in the know." He smiled, but his eyes tightened ever-so-slightly. "Morpheus said you seemed to know things you ought not."

He stepped forward, so close that I could feel the energy from his body, and ran the back of his fingers down the side of my face. "Whose heads can you get into?" he asked in a stage whisper, his lips brushing my hair.

"He's your brother," I said, not leaving the subject I'd started.

He stepped closer still, so almost his entire body was touching mine. "So there is something you don't know. You can't quite grasp my relationship with my brother."

Tyran prowled towards his brother. Bowen was on his back chained to the floor with his arms stretched out painfully tight. An old floral pillowcase was draped loosely over his head. Tyran removed it and swiveled Bowen's head, so his face was pointed towards me. It was painful to see him like this; he was emaciated, and his skin looked like heavily veined marble.

Then Tyran manually opened Bowen's eyes. "Did you know, even in this state, a vampire is fully aware?" He ran the back of his hand over Bowen's cheek, like he was showing off his pet.

"He can see you. Feel how near you are. Feel your pain. And yet, he can do nothing."

I lifted my chin insolently. "This is low, even for you."

Tyran drifted back in my direction and firmly grabbed my face. To my astonishment, he kissed me—a slow, lingering kiss that I did not return. "She does taste good, doesn't she, brother?" He eyed Bowen with cruelty. "I think I forgot to tell you. Your competition survived, somehow."

He turned back to me, his gaze hard. "How did your beloved *Joshua* manage that?" He said Joshua like it was a disease. "What else is in that pretty little head of yours?"

I held my breath and looked to the side.

"Joshua survives, and you escape? Someone helped you." He ran his hand down my side, making sure his thumb brushed the side of my breast. I flinched, and it didn't go unnoticed. A smile crept across his face, as I'd finally given him a reaction he wanted.

"No one helped," I said, my voice steady and even.

Tyran narrowed his eyes. "Someone helped you," he said firmly, his voice controlled. He leaned forward and ran his nose under my jaw as he spoke against my neck. "Brother, did you help her?" I felt his breath against my skin. He rested his hand on my hip for a moment, then ran it upwards, catching the bottom hem of my shirt. When he felt the skin at my waist, he stopped and ran the tips of his fingers back and forth leisurely.

I didn't react this time. "No one helped me," I said as patronizingly as possible. I hoped he would bite me and expose himself to Aurora, but I knew that prodding him to do so would probably backfire.

Tyran leaned back and searched my face. I was hoping my recent forays into acting were helping my ability to lie, but I wasn't sure. At least I didn't have a pulse to betray me this time. He seemed to be assessing me.

He pulled me away from the wall and slid behind me, while lifting me a little at the waist to relieve the pressure. He reached up to the hook that held the chain on my left arm and adjusted it so that my arm hung at my side. Then he added a couple of links worth of slack to the other hand. He stayed behind me, a hand on each wrist, and bent down to kiss my neck again. I still didn't react.

"Do I still have a pure sacrifice?" he whispered in my ear almost sensuously. "You smell of *him* again. Are you still chaste?" He ran his hands down my arms, over my sides, and held them flat over my belly. "What do you think, brother? Has your love given herself to *him*?"

He ran his left hand up to my sternum and pulled me hard against him, as his left hand drifted down to my hip. I let out a whimper and pressed my eyes shut. I felt a tear trickle from the corner of my eye.

Bowen made a faint, guttural-sounding exhale.

Tyra's voice was filled with amusement. "I don't think he likes me touching you."

"Just let him go. He didn't help me," my voice a soft cry.

"So it wasn't him?"

"No one helped me, especially not him. Do you really think he wanted me to leave?"

"He certainly put on a show after you left. Part of me wanted to believe him."

I peeked at Bowen, my eyes welling up with more tears, feeling horribly guilty. I hadn't thought that he would've been punished for my escape. "He didn't do anything wrong," I said almost inaudibly.

"Oh, he has done plenty of wrong, and none of us escape what we deserve. You are going to tell me who helped you, and you are going to tell me evvvveeeeryyything." And then he was gone. He moved so quickly from the room, it was as if he'd evaporated. *Poof.*

I pulled at the chain on my right arm, but I was already weakening.

A knot lodged in my throat. "I am so, so sorry. I thought not telling you I was going to escape would keep you safe. I didn't want you hurt." I cringed and examined the wall mount holding the shackle on my right arm. I was about to make another attempt at my bonds when I noticed that Tyran was already back. He had a vial of blood in his hand—just like in my vision.

I decided to come clean about my illness. I didn't want Bowen exposed. Words rushed from my mouth. "Tyran, please don't do this. I'm sick. If he attacks me and drinks from me, it could kill him. Do you really think they would trade me, if they thought I could be used against them?"

"Nice try. We-Don't-Get-Sick," he said venomously, looking a little ruffled.

Agitation crept into my tone. "I didn't *get* sick. I was exposed to a drug. Do you hate him enough to risk his life?"

He took a breath and smiled. "You almost had me. You know what's coming, don't you? You've grown more powerful, haven't you?"

"I'm not lying," I said, defeated.

"If you saw it, you know what a starving vampire will do to anything with blood. The second he smells it, instinct will take over. He won't even remember it's you until he regains his senses. Which I promise you, will take a while." His voice was hoarse, yet somehow full of glee.

"Please don't do this," I pleaded.

"You will tell me everything I want, just to make it stop, and he will hate himself for hurting you. It's perfect, really. Two birds." He walked over and knelt next to his brother, prying his mouth open.

Tyran poured the contents of the vial into his mouth and unlocked the shackles that were pinning him to the floor. There was almost an immediate reaction. Tyran stood and walked over to me.

"When you see that I'm not healing, you'll know I'm telling the truth."

He scoffed and pulled a small blade from his pocket. "It's a shame to scar such an attractive face, but I do like to leave mementos." He cut deep into my face, running the blade below my cheekbone, then made another slice at the base of my neck. The warm, metallic aroma of my blood filled the air as it gushed out of me.

He stepped back and looked at me like an artist would a canvas. He leaned forward and made one more swipe at the wrist dangling above my head. The blood tickled as it ran down my arm and dripped to the floor, making soft splats on the ground; my body wasn't even attempting to stop the bleeding.

He grinned at me. "Rumor has it Joshua wouldn't bed you. Does he not really want you? Is that why you were allowed to be traded away? He's done with you?" He pivoted on one foot, walked to Bowen, pulled the stake out of his chest, and disappeared once again.

An almost animalistic growl emanated from Bowen's direction; I didn't want to look, but I did. He rolled onto his hands and knees. His eyes were glowing, and there was no recognition in them. The normally intense blue looked almost white, like he had thick cataracts and pinpricks for irises.

I held my breath as he launched himself at me and tried not to scream. He hit me with such force that the shackles were torn free from the wall above me, and I felt my head smash hard into the stone. His hands grasped my arms like claws, and I felt his fingers hit bone as he latched onto my neck. I shrieked, praying to pass out, and moments later, I did. I welcomed the black void as it swallowed me up.

. . .

An odd tugging sensation on my face dragged me from oblivion. I tried to lift my hand to swat it away, but my hands were being held down. The hands were cool—a vampire.

Everything felt wrong. My eyes were glued shut, like I needed a damp cloth to work them open, reminding me of when I had pink eye as a kid. I tried to swallow, but gagged on some sort of tube down my throat. A small moan escaped me. I imagined that I'd been put into a blender, and the operator had hit puree.

Finally, I managed to pry my eyes open to reveal that I was pinned to a table. A severe-looking woman with white hair and thick glasses was hunched over me, and the infernal tugging was her stitching my cheek closed. Bowen was holding my arms, but he was twisted around so that he wasn't looking at me.

The woman's eyes met mine for an instant; they were pale grey and gleamed like my mother's silver. She spoke, but didn't stop stitching. "I was beginning to think you would remain unconscious through the whole thing."

Bowen's back straightened.

Her voice was craggy, like she'd been a smoker for a million years. She parted her lips a little while she concentrated on the knot, revealing worn, yellow teeth. "This is a first, sewing up a vampire."

I blinked at her, not saying anything, and spied four nearly-empty, units of blood were dangling from a rod above me. The dangling tubes were taped to my cheek and shoved down my throat, scratching my esophagus. They were relatively small tubes; not like the breathing tubes I'd seen being used on my grandfather. I could probably talk if I had wanted to. I made another gagging sound as I tried to force the tubes out with my tongue, but they were too far down my throat.

"Almost done," she cooed, as she checked her work. She

gently ran her fingers over my throat, arms, and the back of my head. Then she pulled the feeding tube out. I coughed convulsively for a moment.

After I'd settled down, she addressed Bowen and asked, "Is there anything else you require, Sire?"

"No, thank you." Bowen's voice was rough.

"At your service," She bowed and exited.

He released my hands, keeping his back to me.

I closed my eyes again, feeling exhausted and not knowing what to say. Minutes ticked away. I could hear him breathing shallowly; it was so quiet, that every sound seemed to be exaggerated. I shifted, and the old wood table I was laying on creaked in protest.

I tried to think of what to say to him, wishing he would speak first. My growing anxiety was going to drive me mad. I took in a halted breath and spoke two simple words. "I'm sorry."

He exhaled. "Any wrong you feel you have done me was just washed away by my actions."

"Tyran's actions, not yours. I blame him," I said, with no judgment. I swallowed, trying to right my throat after having had the tubes crammed down it.

He shook his head while clutching the table and leaning forward. The veins in his arms popped out from his lean muscle. He looked remarkably better, but not quite right: his skin was alarmingly pale, and I noticed his eyes were glossy and tired. He finally turned his head to make eye contact; his blue t-shirt was the exact color of his eyes.

"I..." he pressed his lips together. "I just attacked you and three other people." His voice haunted. "I haven't drained a human to the point of death in four hundred years."

"To the point of death, as in you killed them?" I asked, shocked.

"Tyran sent in his familiars when he knew something had

gone wrong. It was the only thing that would have pried me off of you. You were bleeding out; none of your wounds were closing. And even though I had ripped the shackles from the wall, you didn't have the strength to fight me."

"I told him I wasn't lying," I stated.

There was an uneasy silence.

"I don't blame you, if you hate me," he said.

"You have just as much of a reason to hate me."

He let his breath out. "And why would I hate you?"

"I left without a word." Guilt swelled in my chest.

Bowen looked away. "I knew it was inevitable. Someone I trust told me that you are not mine to have. That you felt obligated to me, and I would never know if you felt anything for me if you stayed."

I carefully rolled on my side to face him. "You know I care about you. How could you ever doubt that?"

He shifted like he was uncomfortable, his voice hesitant. "Did you see this in your vision? Did you know I would attack you?"

"Not everything in my visions comes to pass," I said evasively.

"Please answer the question," he requested quietly.

I sighed. "Yes, I saw it."

"And you knew if I did, that I might get sick."

I felt so immensely dim-witted—the obviousness of it. Somehow, in all the frenzy, I'd forgotten. After the initial vision, I had never, for one moment, considered that I would be putting him at risk. My thoughts had turned and been so occupied with what was happening to *me* that I'd never considered the consequence again. *How had I not?*

I remembered telling Tyran it was a death sentence for Bowen. I cringed and rolled away from him. "Bowen," I whispered, feeling the pain of my monumental stupidity surge through my body. "You should hate me. I didn't think. I was trying to...I didn't..." I couldn't complete my thoughts.

I heard him move to the other side of the room and slide down the wall. He sat hard on the floor. "He's alive?" His voice was brittle.

"Yes." I rolled onto my back again.

"And he knew that you were being exchanged?"

"Yes."

Bowen considered this, obviously confused, but I wasn't going to explain anything further when I knew Tyran could be listening. "I would never have allowed—" He didn't finish, but I knew what he was saying; he wouldn't have let me do the trade.

"I don't want there to be any confusion. I belong to Joshua, but I do care about you. Please don't question that. I'm an idiot. If I had thought, I wouldn't have risked you. I would have just died. I owe you too much."

"Just like he said, you feel obligated to me."

I exhaled, hearing Amara's questions echo in my head. I winced and looked at the ceiling. Beige water stains in the shape of ragged rings, discolored the ancient paint in the corner. "If things were different." I stopped. I didn't know if I should admit this.

After a minute, he prompted me, "If they were different?"

I squeezed my eyes shut and clenched my jaw. "I was falling for you. If your brother hadn't...the apartment that night." I sucked in a breath. "That was the first violence of any kind I'd experienced. I realize he's done far worse to me since, but that night—it changed everything; I still have a hard time with it. If that hadn't happened, I would have..." My voice trailed off.

"You would have loved me," he finished.

I rolled away, unable to look at him. "But my heart is taken, and you know me well enough to understand what that means."

Bowen was quiet for a moment. "He wouldn't..."

"Wouldn't what?" I couldn't track with his train of thought.

He sounded uneasy. "Joshua—my brother said—he *wouldn't* sleep with you? Is that true?"

"Both of us believe you should be married first. So no, he wouldn't." An honest answer, though not a complete one. I kept the marriage to myself.

He was silent.

"How are you feeling?" I asked, cautiously.

"Not...right."

It made me wonder how Josh was feeling, if he was sick. I took a deep breath, trying to feel something through our blood bond, but I was too disconcerted to feel our connection. I heard the locks on the door being flicked open. Tyran entered with both Morpheus and Icelos, who hung back near the entrance.

Apparently, he felt the need for bodyguards. I imagined launching myself at him and going for the jugular. It was a pleasing thought. I sat up and dangled my feet off of the side of the table, since I felt too vulnerable lying down.

Tyran locked a deadly gaze on me. "Is there a cure or some sort of antidote?"

"So you do care?" I asked, dripping with sarcasm.

"Answer the question."

I wanted to mess with him and make him squirm, but I couldn't with Bowen sitting there.

"Is Neka safe? Is she with the Watchers?"

"Yes, she is with them."

I felt relief wash over me. It may be too late for me, but maybe not for Bowen. I examined the nearly empty bags of blood they'd been funneling into me, knowing that they did only a fraction of the good they should've done. "If she is with them, hopefully there will be one soon."

"They didn't have an antidote, and yet they exposed you anyway? I have a hard time believing that," he said.

"It was an accident, and it mutated. The antidote didn't work properly."

"And why wouldn't it work on him?" He closed the gap between us by halfway.

"The same reason it wouldn't work on me: Our ancestry."

"Our ancestry? We are nothing alike."

"And that is where you are wrong. My ancestry began with the Sentinels."

I saw shock on his face for a split-second. "The blood of the angels." Then his expression became far-off.

"The existing antidote, it won't work on Bowen."

Suddenly, he had me by the throat, his lips pressed to my ear. "You are not long for this world. I will burn what's left of your soul from your body, and when Moloch rises, he will use your power to make the world lie prostrate before him." He shoved me away, and I latched onto the table to keep myself from tumbling over backwards.

I regained my composure and smiled at him, knowing that Moloch might rise because of me, but he would never have my power.

Tyran raised his hand in the air as if he was going to come back and slap me across the face. Unexpectedly, Bowen appeared between us. He was so close, his body pressed against my knees while he placed his hand on Tyran's chest. Tyran glared at Bowen with a hellish light in his eyes and stepped back. A hiss slid between his teeth, then he vanished.

Morpheus and Icelos lingered for a moment, and then turned to leave. Before he exited, Morpheus stared at me with an incomprehensible expression that made my chest tighten. There was some sort of dark emotion bubbling inside. Bowen stood there, with his back to me until the door shut. Then he moved to the side and sat on the edge of the table.

"You don't need to protect me. I was the one antagonizing him."

"She will really work on a cure?" he asked.

"That was the plan."

"What good would it do with you here?"

"That was the one flaw I couldn't solve, but I think there might be something he would agree to."

"And what would that be?"

I grinned at him. "Despite his actions, he's just proven he loves you."

"That's meaningless."

"No. It means everything."

15

FORGOTTEN

I felt the sun rise, set, and rise again, and with each ticking moment, I felt myself grow weaker as I tossed and turned. I'd spent all my time atop the table that was now shoved into the corner, save the single trip to the tiny bathroom in the hallway near the door.

Bowen still sat in the same corner—an immovable object, a silent pillar holding up the corner of the room. I didn't know it was possible, even for a vampire, to sit without movement for that long.

I wondered if he was beginning to hate me. It would be easier that way, I thought. Whatever he was doing, he was keeping his emotions under control. I couldn't sense anything from him. I shoved my fist into my stomach and rolled over so my back was to him. The table creaked, and I heard him shift. His first movement since yesterday.

I'd been fighting sleep, and my mind raced with questions. *Where are we located? How close is Tyran to accomplishing his hidden agenda? Did Kez and Samael survive? Do they have the surrogate? Is Neka working on the antidote? Is she mentally capable of creating it? Is*

Joshua sick?

My list was unending. Part of me was afraid I wouldn't wake, but I felt it coming for me: the dull throb of exhaustion overtaking the clawing pain of my wounds that itched and ached; I released a slow breath, and dreams came to claim me.

Suddenly, I was sitting in the Church of Angels with my legs drawn to my chest, staring up at the stained glass. I was in a white hospital gown with tiny blue polka dots and worn, grey sweatpants underneath. My hair was pulled into pigtails, which always made me feel younger. Beautiful afternoon sun was streaming though the panes, warming my skin.

I looked at the pew next to me, wishing Joshua was there, that he could see it in the light, and then I realized I wouldn't be able to see it in the light either. For a moment, I'd forgotten what I was, a child of the night, cursed by darkness. I sighed. Dark and light, opposing forces—now both of those forces were actually inside me, and it felt inescapable.

Somehow, the normally comforting smell of lingering incense seemed smothering. I felt someone behind me. I closed my eyes, knowing exactly who it was, and wearily asked, "Are you my enemy?"

There was silence. I opened my heavy lids and returned my gaze to the window in front of me.

"I know you're there." I heard my voice echo off of the walls of the empty church.

He walked to the pew in front of me and sat down, the slope of his broad shoulders making him appear troubled and his long, black hair lacking its normal luster. "You are of the Lux, aren't you? You aren't just a Seer that they procured for the sacrifice."

"Morpheus, why are you here?" I asked.

"Please answer the question."

"I am too tired for mind games, just leave me alone."

"Please," he said with surprising gentleness.

"I thought you were in the inner circle and would know all the details," I commented, still not answering. The tiredness I felt was creeping into my voice.

He exhaled. "When you want to sleep for centuries, you take an elixir that the ancient Egyptians developed for our kind. First, you gorge yourself and get as much blood into your system as possible. Then you take the potion. It slows the body down to the point of hibernation. It thickens the blood and keeps it in your veins to keep you from starving. The sleep aid in it is so powerful that you actually don't feel the pain of your body shutting down." He paused. "When I went to ground with my brothers, the world was a different place. We were still gods. It was a harsh, cruel world."

"What does this have to do with the Lux?"

He swiveled to the side and looked at me. "Have you ever lost someone you loved?"

I didn't see the harm in answering honestly. "Yes."

"Did you worry that you would forget what their voice sounded like? Worry that you would forget what their face looked like?"

"Yes," I acknowledged, feeling the sting of the day I could no longer remember my grandfather's voice.

"When you sleep for centuries, it dulls memories, especially those from when you were human," he said, his voice weighted with something—sadness maybe.

"I can imagine," I replied, not understanding where he was going with this.

"My mother was Roman—she was young and beautiful in a time when the Goths were regularly attacking the Empire. She was captured in a raid and taken to Northern Europe. The invaders recognized something in her. She wasn't violated and sold off, as most of the women captured in battle were.

"She was given to a chieftain, and she actually fell in love with him. They married and had four children: myself first, then a year later, a daughter, and five years after that, fraternal twin boys." He stopped speaking for a moment, and I couldn't help but wonder why he was telling me this.

He continued, "In late fall, when I was about eleven, our tribe came under attack. There were very few of them, but they were so fast that I could only see blurred movement as they went from one warrior to another with their bloody blades in hand. Their eyes glowed, their feet made no noise, and they spoke in a Celtic dialect.

"I could only pick out words here and there. Within a short time, they had decimated our protectors. My father had been slain along with all of the elders. I heard them asking for someone. They used a Latin phrase, and I thought it was odd at the time.

"When they entered our home, I expected to be killed right away. I remember holding my sword up and trembling, trying to protect my family, but the intruder never even acknowledged me. I was knocked to the ground like a dog; he was so strong, it was as if he had been made of metal.

"The leader was masked, but I saw his glowing eyes smile when he set his sights on my mother. We were quickly herded outside. When it was clear that we were to be put in a cage and carted away, I remember her exchanging solemn looks with my sister. Almost immediately my mother fought with one of the guards.

"When she was thrown to the ground, she slyly drank the contents of a small vial she kept on a leather strap around her neck. During the distraction, my sister drank the contents of her own vial. She was roughly a year younger than me, only ten." He lingered on that for a moment, then continued.

"The warriors began burning everything. A man grabbed me and began shoving me into a cage. My mother turned to me and told me 'not to be afraid,' but before she could be loaded in behind me, she collapsed, and white foam frothed from her mouth. A moment later, my sister did the same. I remember screaming. And I remember their leader yelling out in utter anger as she died. With all their strength and power, they couldn't stop the poison." He stopped speaking and rested his head in his hands.

I spoke, my voice sounding loud even though I was speaking quietly. "She killed herself, rather than be captured?"

"Yes. My brothers and I were the sole survivors. Everyone else was massacred. We were taken prisoner, led to an encampment about two days walk from our home, and kept there about a week or so. But on a moonless night, the coldest one of the season so far, our captors came under attack from their own kind, more inhuman men with glowing eyes and preternatural abilities.

"The victors took us to a fortress four days walk from the raiders' encampment. But this time, we weren't treated as slaves. We learned about the world that lived in the shadows, about vampires and other immortals. The three of us were educated and trained to fight. When we were old enough, we became familiars."

"How old?" I asked.

He seemed distracted. He looked at me a moment before he answered, like my question hadn't caught up to him yet. "I was sixteen when I became one, my brothers were a little older. I was always protective of them, being almost six years their senior, and the queen respected my wishes.

"On my twenty-first birthday, they offered me immortality. I refused. I didn't want to be turned until my brothers were of age, and then, only if they chose it. Of course, my siblings had been raised by vampires since they were small children, so naturally that is what they would want. They hardly remembered our parents.

"So, six years later, during the season of their twenty-first birthdays, we were all turned. My brothers and I found that we had powers that no other vampires had and were rewarded for it. As I said, we were gods."

"Morpheus, I don't mean to sound rude, but why are you telling me this?"

"Something about you has bothered me from the moment I saw you. You have been the only person to be able to break through the illusions I have created. You entered my dream, though you have never tasted of my blood. And then I remembered....I thought I had forgotten."

I waited for a long while, and then timidly prompted him, "You had forgotten what?"

"I had forgotten what my mother looked like." His shoulders lolled slightly, then he shimmered like a mirage. It appeared as though Morpheus was no longer sitting in front of me; instead, sat a tall woman with long, sleek, jet-black hair. Her skin was a rich and beautiful olive. She had elegant, chiseled features and high cheekbones. The curve of her collarbone and lilt of her shoulders were sensuous. She was turned towards me on the pew, just as he'd been, but her eyes were closed. Then she, or he, looked straight at me. Two lavender eyes peered at me, and I suddenly understood exactly why he'd chosen to share his story with me.

I spoke slowly, the dawning realization in my voice. "Your mother was of the Lux."

"I had blotted out the memories of that night, and the Latin words they had used: '*Lux Casta.*'"

"'Pure light,'" I translated. "She was of the elite, even amongst the Lux." I paused, "Your ability to infiltrate dreams..."

"It would explain many things: Why I wasn't slain. Why they educated and trained me. Why they made it appear as if I had a choice to be turned. It is always easier to control willing participants. They knew there was a high probability that any child of the Lux would have heightened abilities of some sort, even males."

"But you said that a rival group took you."

"Yes. That is how it appeared, but now, I wonder. It could have easily been staged to gain our confidence."

"So what does this mean," I asked, cutting to the bottom line.

"Maybe nothing. I am what I am."

"Are you my enemy?" I asked again.

His jaw flexed. "I am not your enemy, but neither am I your friend," he replied. "I will not enter your dreams without permission in the future. You know how to contact me." He turned to leave.

"Morpheus?"

"Yes?"

"I'm sorry about your family."

He nodded his head in acknowledgment and disappeared.

I sat there, not knowing how to feel. I reclined on the pew, stretching out and crossing my legs at the ankle. I laced my fingers behind my neck, needing to rest my brain—it felt very, very full. The old lacquer on the pew was slightly sticky, and I felt the skin on my back cling to it through the opening of my hospital gown.

I wondered if I could go from my dream to someone else's. I was obviously lucid. I cleared my mind of everything but Joshua. He was the only person's dream I could enter without permission. I pushed at a barrier. For a flickering moment, I saw him sitting in the gazebo at my parent's house. He turned and saw me and yelled out my name.

Then I felt myself being torn from the dream, and someone else was screaming my name. I looked at Bowen through slits. He was sitting next to me and had my upper body cradled to his side, while propping my head in his hand. He was holding a wad of gauze to my nose that the medic had left behind. I closed my eyes and felt a tear streak down my cheek.

"Is this part of the illness?" he asked tentatively.

"No, just me. When I try to use my abilities, there are consequences."

"You did this to yourself?"

My voice was pinched from the plugged nose. "I wasn't thinking about it. I just—"

"Well, think," he chastised angrily, cutting me off. I had never heard him speak in this tone to me. "I'm sorry. Please don't do anything to weaken yourself further." There was genuine concern in his eyes.

I took over holding the cloth to my nose, and I tried to sit up. My head began to swim, and I pitched backwards. Bowen caught me and eased me back onto the table. I gritted my teeth, feeling frustrated. I stared up at him. He looked worse, and it was all my fault.

"I'm sorry, Bowen. If I said it a million times to you, it wouldn't be enough."

He nodded, but didn't say anything.

"Do you think Tyran would let me make a phone call?"

He raised an eyebrow at me.

"I want to see if they have made any headway with an antidote. They won't talk to any of you, but they will to me. And I don't think either of us dying of this is in Tyran's master plan."

"He won't let you go," he said flatly.

I furrowed my brow. "I'm not worried about me."

"Do you have any idea how frustrating that is?" "What?"

He shook his head. "Never mind."

I looked at him, confused.

The lock on the door slid free, and Tyran appeared at the edge of the room sans the bodyguards this time. He had four units of blood in his hands. He paused for a moment, like he was assessing our hostility level. The thought of going for his jugular was still pleasing, but I could hardly sit up, much less launch myself at him. He walked towards us and handed us each two units, then backed towards the door and left us alone. No taunts or snarky remarks. *Another miracle.*

I wondered if Tyran didn't trust us with familiars or if they were all dead. We both fed, and from the looks of it, Bowen was not used to drinking cold blood from a bag. He grimaced, but never said anything. He would've before. His silence saddened me, and I had the horrible realization that I didn't want him to hate me, but I could never give him what he wanted.

My strength increased, but it was like eating half a sleeve of fries and only being able to smell the hamburger.

He startled me a little when he spoke. "How long do you think you have?"

I frowned at the packet of blood. "A week, maybe. It's a guess. You have probably twice that."

"Why did you kiss me like that before you left?" The blue of his eyes seemed to burn.

I held my breath and looked away. "Honestly, I don't know. It surprised me, even when I was kissing you." I turned my head back to look at him.

Bowen seemed to be percolating on my words as he peered across the room for several long moments. "That was quite a kiss for someone who doesn't love me," he commented, almost under his breath.

I opened my mouth, but I didn't know what to say. It audibly snapped shut. He rose and returned to his place in the corner, holding up the wall once again. He had smudges of my blood on his face and staining the front of his blue shirt, in addition to the hole from the stake and the periphery bloodstain. He seemed to notice; he smoothed his hand over the stains, then he dropped his head in his hands, his blonde hair poking through his fingers like silken threads. Somehow, he still looked good, despite the fact that he hadn't cleaned up since who knows when.

The door opened again, and this time, Tyran entered with a phone. He sat on the edge of the table and placed it in my hand, keeping his hand locked over mine. I wanted to whip my hand away, but I controlled my revulsion.

"Save him."

I wanted to make some comment about eavesdropping, but he'd refrained from threatening me. "May I talk alone? Would you let Bowen out of here while I make the call?"

His mouth started to form the word no, then he thought the better of it, and consented. He walked towards Bowen, turning his back to me. I knew then that he realized how sick I was: I was too weak to attempt an attack or an escape for that matter.

Tyran offered Bowen his hand to help him up, but Bowen waved it off and stood like a creaky old man. He walked ahead of Tyran out the door. Bowen made eye contact with me for one second before slipping out, but I couldn't read his expression.

I stretched out on the table, then bent my knees and pressed my feet flat on the table. I thought through what I was going to say. I had a dangerous amount of emotion battering my insides, and I needed to be clear. I struggled to sit up and was thankful that feeding had cleared my head enough to think straight.

Easing off of the table, I stood, but my legs wouldn't hold. Causing me to sit so hard on the floor, my teeth clanked together. I pushed myself backwards under the table and leaned against the wall. I couldn't sit up straight, but I felt safer under here—not as exposed now that the camera couldn't glare at me.

I stared at the keypad on what looked to be a disposable cell. I punched in the secure cell number Gabriel had made me memorize. He picked up on the first ring. "Yes?"

"It's me."

"Are you…"

This horrible whine welled-up within me, and I let out this high-pitched sob. "Gabriel, my vision. I forgot about my vision. It happened." My breath hitched in my throat as I tried to control myself. I tried to speak, but only let out a garbled wailing sound. *So much for clarity.*

"He was starving and attacked you," he filled in, his voice low. He'd remembered when I hadn't.

"Mm hmm," I labored through stuttering breath.

"What can I do?"

I started getting a handle on myself: "Is she working on the antidote?"

"Yes."

"How close is she?"

"She is doing what she can, but is struggling without you being there. She needs fresh blood samples. It seems that the necrosis of the cells kills the samples within hours of defrosting them. She does not understand how you are still alive."

"Stubbornness." I let out a humorless chuckle through another sob. "There is no way he'll let me go, but they might…"

"Send him," he said resolutely, reading my mind.

My voice still wavered. "Will you protect him? He doesn't deserve this. I owe him my life many times over."

"Yes."

"Promise?"

"Need you ask?" he said reassuringly.

"No," I admitted.

"Is he strong enough to travel?"

"Yes, I believe so, but he seems to be progressing faster than I did."

He paused. "I will text an address to this phone. Tell Bowen to come alone; he will not be harmed. We will leave a set of directions in the phone booth."

"Gabriel, tell Joshua it was me this morning."

"Aleria—you did not try—"

A hand reached beneath the table and yanked the phone away. Tyran was bent next to me, resting on one knee. I hadn't heard him come back in. I kept my face lowered to hide my tear-streaked face.

"You get all that?" I asked, my voice rough.

"Of course, darling," Tyran replied, sounding a little more like himself. I heard the phone chime with what must have been a text. "Looks like he will be off just after sunset." It sounded like he was working hard to keep his voice light.

"They won't harm him. You, on the other hand…" I managed a grin and look over at him.

He made a scoffing sound, stood abruptly, and slowly drifted to the door. "That is always how it has been. One of us loved, the other…" A moment later, Bowen returned with Morpheus and Icelos, who each had a thick bedroll with pillows and tossed them on the floor before retreating.

Bowen rolled them out at 90-degree angles on opposite walls, the heads of each almost touching. He plopped ungracefully on one, almost making me cringe; he'd always been like this sinuous, jungle cat in his movements. He looked over at me when I didn't move.

Bowen spoke, filling the silence. "I convinced him that being uncomfortable burns unnecessary energy. Energy we don't have."

"Smart."

His tone turned concerned. "You can't walk over here can you?"

I shrugged and expelled the air from my lungs. "I can crawl." And so I did.

We lay there, heads inches apart, in silence for a long while, and then I finally heard the sounds of sleep coming from his direction. I rolled on my side to look at him. He was on his side, and his head was tilted back, like he'd been watching me. The title of Robert Frost's poem, "The Road Not Taken," popped in my head.

The lights in the room went out for the first time since we'd been in here—only an eerie red glow from the LED light on the camera. Eventually his deep breathing stopped.

Almost inaudibly, I said, "Bowen, I do love you. I just can't the way you want me to." I don't know if he heard me or not. Soon, I was in a dreamless sleep while the rest of the daylight hours ticked away.

16

DEN OF OUR ENEMIES

My eyes fluttered open. All the lights were on, so I scowled at the too bright room. I could sense the sun was still up, but sunset was not too far off. I'd slept so soundly, that I wondered if Bowen was still here—my eyes quickly darted to his bedroll. He was sitting up, leaning against the wall, his thoughts elsewhere.

A newly visible network of veins had surfaced under his skin, causing a surge of guilt roll over me.

He cast his eyes in my direction for a moment. Then he sighed, "I believe that you didn't mean to infect me. You are not a treacherous person. Even now, as one of us, you seem..."

"Seem?"

He gave me a weak smile. "It doesn't matter." The look on his face made me let it go.

A question hit me with such force that I made an audible sound. When I looked up, Bowen was searching my face for clues.

"How did they know?" I asked slowly, as it formed more clearly in my mind. "How did they know who Amara was? How did they know she was an Abacha? Her identity has been hidden since birth."

"I don't know, but there is another prisoner."

"Where?"

"I noticed what looked like a new padlock on a door down the hall when I was originally brought in, and there was a low moan coming from within the room."

I tried to force my exhausted brain to work. Something else had been nagging me—Tyran's choice of words.

"Tyran said Josh *wouldn't* sleep with me."

"Yes?" Bowen replied, a question in his voice. He was perhaps wondering where this was going.

I was thinking out loud, still lying on my back. I stared at the water stains on the ceiling. "There is only one person I know that has the ability to research the identity of someone so guarded and has been privy to that particular part of my personal information."

I thought of my last conversation with the only person it could be. "He was livid that we were clinging to our morals; he said we were endangering the world. He even suggested that—" I caught myself. I thought for another moment. "But still, I can't imagine him betraying..." I didn't want to think his name. I wanted to think better of him.

"Tyran can be very persuasive, or he could have compelled him to speak. Though he much prefers torture to mind control, he delights in watching the shame blossom as his victim betrays everyone he or she cares about."

An involuntary disgusted sound escaped me, and then I worked to sit up and lean against the wall. When I finally had managed to, I felt really accomplished and smiled over at Bowen. My smile melted away when I saw his expression.

"What?"

"You can hardly sit up."

I pursed my lips and shrugged. "I'm sitting up just fine; getting there is the problem." I paused, and gave up on my feeling of triumph, responding in a subdued tone to his serious look, "Maybe I don't have a week."

The door opened, and Tyran came in with an armful of clothes and tossed them on Bowen's lap. "It will probably look better if you show up without her blood all over you. If loverboy is there, he will know it's hers."

"How very kind of you. How long?"

"You have an hour until we leave."

Bowen peered back at him coolly. "I need a stool from the other room."

Tyran stared at him blankly and didn't move.

"Just do it. You can't still be angry with me."

Tyran rolled his eyes and tossed one of his hands up in the air. "Fine." I was surprised by this interaction for some reason, it was so—brotherly.

"And the clothes you already have for Aleria," he yelled before Tyran disappeared through the door. I started to open my mouth, but Tyran was already back with a small pile of clothing and a short stool. He put the stool down with a clank, leaving the clothes on top. He gave his brother a measured look, then left once again.

Bowen regarded me for a moment, then asked, "Would you like to get cleaned up?"

I did—desperately—but I knew I couldn't do it without help. I gave him a deflated look.

"The stool is for you, so you can sit in the shower." An odd expression glided over his features. "Have you looked in the mirror?"

"No. It looked like Tyran removed the one that had been in the bathroom."

He nodded. "Potential weapon." Then his tone softened

further. "It would be good to get cleaned up. It has been a couple of days, and..." There was something in his voice that worried me, maybe something he saw.

I reached up and felt the side of my hair that felt matted and crusty. There were tiny pieces of something hard, dried into what I assume was blood. I pulled out one of the dull shards and looked at the jagged piece of ivory for a moment, wondering what it was.

Bowen softly said, "Don't think about what it is. Let's just get you cleaned up."

I gazed at him confused. He stood gradually, like it caused him some pain, but once he was upright, I wouldn't have known he was ill. He moved towards me as I inspected the miniscule object in my hand.

He plucked it from my fingers, shook his head in disapproval, and pulled me up. Unfortunately, my legs wouldn't hold. He pinned me to his side and bore most of my weight as we walked. He paused by the stool and leaned to gather it under his other arm.

We walked around the corner into the hallway; it was about three yards long, with the bathroom door halfway down the wall on the right.

Once inside the bathroom, Bowen eased me onto the toilet seat, pulled the shower curtain to the side, and placed the stool in the shower. Yellow mineral stains on the once white shower basin lined the edges. He folded the clothes over the towel bar within arm's reach and helped me into the shower. I leaned against the wall and waited while he got the water going.

Bowen glanced at me. "I checked. There are no cameras or listening devices in here. You are safe to speak." He handed me the showerhead and slid the shampoo down the shelf so it was next to me. Then he backed out and closed the curtain. "Just let me know if you need anything." A moment later, he hung a towel over the curtain rod.

"Thanks."

I didn't bother trying to remove any of my torn and bloodstained clothing. I held the nozzle up to the left side of my head and tilted my head as I worked on the snarl of tangled hair, blood, and... I rolled another ivory colored fragment in my fingers. When the epiphany of its origin overwhelmed me, a whimper escaped my lips as I tried to stifle the sound. My body convulsed with the emotion I hadn't allowed myself to feel yet. I heard Bowen's hand run over the outside of the curtain.

"Are you still dressed?"

I managed, "Mmm hmmm," between two sobs.

He opened the curtain just as I fell to pieces. I held two fragments in my right hand while I hooked the shower head, still gushing with water, over my shoulder with the other hand. My eyes latched onto his—wide and tragic. I pushed out three words through heaving breaths and closed my eyes. "Bone fragments…Amara."

I felt his hand close over mine and ease the shower head out of my fingers. Without a word, he started washing away the rest of the evidence from my hair. I kept my eyes closed. I didn't want to watch the blood go down the drain, now that I remembered that not all of it was mine. I concentrated on the fresh smell of the shampoo and tried to block out the smell of the newly wet blood.

When he was done, he knelt on his knees in front of me, not caring that he was getting soaked. I met his gaze.

"I wish I could bear the pain for you." His hands hovered in the air like he wanted to comfort me, but he didn't touch me.

"I don't understand why you are so kind to me," I choked. I wasn't being self-deprecating. I just didn't understand why. Everything was so complicated.

"Because you are worthy of it, and I am very, very good at waiting."

I exhaled. "Can you just be my friend? I can't—"

"I am your friend."

I folded my hands in my lap and leaned forward, resting my forehead on his shoulder, feeling as if my head was much too heavy. I took an occasional stuttering breath as the remnants of my sobbing worked themselves out.

"Why is your brother so angry with you?" I asked into his shoulder. There was a long silence, filled only by the sound of running water and the gurgle of the drain.

"I may have killed some of his men," he said hesitantly.

"May have?" I raised my head and leaned against the shower wall so that I could look at him. It seemed like he still didn't know what to do with his hands; he finally grabbed onto two of the stool legs.

"There was a redhead that Tyran had been extorting for information. He sent out one of his teams after he'd leaked her location to draw out some Watchers. Apparently, she was a Conclave member; he'd figured only a select group of Watchers would know she was trading information. And that those same Watchers would be involved with you and be privy to your location. Tyran's team were to intercept them, kill any Slayers, and capture a couple of hostages. From there, they'd hoped to capture you."

I thought for a moment; if Tyran had succeeded, Gabriel and Uriel would've both been dead, and Ian and Sebastian would have been dead or captured. I looked at the shower head spraying the corner of the shower uselessly.

"How did you know?"

"There are people loyal to me."

"How many were there?"

"Eight," he answered, as if he'd said one.

"You killed them all, by yourself?" I asked, my voice rising.

"They were young. Aleria, make no mistake, I am a killer—as are you, from what I understand. Morpheus returned from an ambush with an interesting story about you."

It took me a moment to recall what he was talking about—the trip back from the lab, with the wrecked cars blocking the road. "Oh," was all I said, but the fact that he'd spoken to Morpheus was interesting.

"He said you immobilized two vampires and killed a third within seconds."

"Yeah," I frowned.

"You did what you needed to do to protect your people."

I returned to the original topic. "So, you killed his men, and he decided to stick you down here and starve you?"

He handed me the shower head again. "You're shivering." He frowned. I wasn't supposed to be cold. I ran the warm water over my clothing and looked at him expectantly. "When I returned, we fought. He had stabbed me twice, so I finally returned the favor."

There was something in his voice. "What aren't you telling me?" I demanded.

"He has everyone he needs, save the Empath from the Abacha family. Tyran has kept me down here to keep me from stopping him."

"He didn't realize you were working against him until you took out his team, did he?"

"No," he replied with an odd tone.

"Do you think your mother knows?"

"No. She would be furious, but I would be back at the castle, not in a basement in Ireland."

"Where are we?"

"We must be close to Dublin. The meet is in Dollymount, just outside of the city. We have to be close."

"So the plane at the trade was to hide how close he was," I mused.

"We need to finish up in here. Tyran is not going to like not being able to hear us for so long."

I nodded.

He stood slowly and closed the curtain again. The fabric of my clothes was so heavy from all the water, it was difficult to remove them. I wiggled them off an inch at a time, while taking breaks, and finally let them fall to the ground with a loud splat. I was painfully aware that Bowen was just on the other side of the curtain. It made me feel both comforted and vulnerable.

Once I had my clothing off, I managed to wash away the rest of the crusted blood, and then shut off the water. I pulled the towel off of the curtain rod and dried myself. As I did, the sheer volume of stitches sunk in; I must've had a hundred or more. There were long, jagged lines circling each of my biceps, a row under the left side of my ribcage, some at the base of my neck, and some under my right cheekbone, that I could definitely feel right now.

"Are you okay?"

"Yeah, just realizing I'm stitched together like Frankenstein's monster is all."

He was quiet.

I cringed, forgetting he was the one who tore me up. *I'm an idiot.* "Sorry. I'm not blaming you. I just didn't realize I had so many stitches. Please, forget I said anything."

"They will scar," he said with regret.

"It's okay. It looks like she did a good job. Clean stitches. The scars won't be bad. I'll look intimidating," I replied, sounding rather convincing.

"The one on your face."

"You didn't do that." I paused as I reached my arm out of the curtain and grabbed the clothes from the towel rack. "Tyran cut me. I don't know how much you remember while you were incapacitated. He blocked your view while he cut my face, neck, and arm. That's why you were so frenzied when you attacked me. I was already dripping with my own blood."

I felt a wave of anger come from him, the first emotion he hadn't controlled in the last day. "I thought," he paused. "I remember him taunting me and touching you. Telling me Joshua was alive. Then I don't remember anything until I came to my senses with the bodies of Tyran's familiars around me. You were lying in the corner and looked so broken with chains twisted around you."

I tossed my towel on the floor at my feet to soak up some of the water before I attempted to put on the sweatpants. On my third attempt, I got them halfway on. I sat there, trying to catch my breath, as I held the pants up mid-thigh.

Bowen hadn't said anything in a couple of minutes, so I spoke. "Tyran said something. He said one of you has always been loved, and the other...he didn't finish. What did he mean?"

He was quiet and must have been deliberating. "The past. I will tell you about it someday."

I wormed the pants the rest of the way up, then pulled the curtain open. "That sounds suspiciously like you expect me to be around in the future." I made my best attempt at a smile.

He grinned. "I plan on complicating your life for a long, long while." He stood and took a step towards me, snaking his arm around my waist again. He helped me stand and took on most of my weight as he helped me return to what was passing for my bed. Once I was settled, he returned to the bathroom and got himself cleaned up.

I leaned against the wall and wondered how much time had passed since we were told we had an hour. It seemed like forever. I closed my eyes briefly and tried to figure out what I wanted to tell Bowen before he left.

Bowen returned in black jeans and a deep green Henley shirt. I patted the mattress next to me; there was a brief look of surprise, and then he took a seat. I leaned in close to him and whispered into his ear, feeling the camera glare at me, "Are you nervous?"

He leaned his head against the top of mine. "Will you think less of me if I say yes?" he whispered back.

"No. Gabriel will keep his word," I reassured him.

"I know. He has honor." He paused, looked at the camera, then said, "Are you nervous?"

I swallowed and moved my lips back to his ear. "I am nervous for you, and..." My words hung there unfinished.

He pulled his head back questioningly.

I sighed and leaned in again. "It worries me to be here without you. Believe it or not, Tyran is softer when you're around."

I backed my head away a couple of inches and saw his jaw flex. He took my hand in his and squeezed. Then he whispered back, "We will both be in the den of our enemies."

"Bowen, I wish—"

"Stop," he said gently. "You can tell me next week."

"There's that positive thinking again."

We heard the lock on the door. Bowen put his arm around my shoulder, kissed my temple, and said, "Stay strong, and try for once not to antagonize him."

"Okay."

He stood creakily and walked towards the door. When Tyran appeared, Bowen took one last look in my direction and said, "See you soon," his voice a little hoarse.

"Of course. You have a story to tell me." I beamed.

Then he was gone, and I felt very, very alone. I pressed the charm on my necklace between my fingers and prayed.

17

CONSEQUENCE

I could feel Tyran through the walls. I didn't need to be able to sense his emotions—they were blaring. It reminded me of the evacuation through the catacombs when I'd been temporarily incapacitated by a shock wave emanating from him.

The night wore on, and I kept expecting Tyran to come in and be evil: maybe stroking a white cat, or having a metal-toothed henchman, or opening up the floor to reveal his ravenous pet sharks. After listing my worries and counting many sheep, I finally managed to find some fitful sleep.

I woke and immediately knew I wasn't alone. Tyran was settled cross-legged on Bowen's bedroll with his eyes locked on me. He was so close that he had strands of my hair laced through his fingers. It seemed as if he'd been there a while. I kept my expression blank, controlling my emotion.

"You are beautiful when you sleep," he said with a mixture of dreaminess and something I couldn't identify.

I was pretty sure that was the first nice thing he'd ever said to me. But suspicion gripped me, so I remained silent. I think I may have been too stunned to say anything anyway.

"What? No sarcastic remark? Or disapproval of some sort?" Tyran said with faux horror.

"Is that why you're here? Your verbal sparring meter ran down?" I asked, turning my head away, exhausted.

"If he doesn't survive..." he responded, his tone darker.

I moved my head, resting it on my arm so I could make eye contact. "Are you seriously going to threaten me? Really? I believe it will be a moot point. If he doesn't survive, then neither will I, genius." I cringed and rolled my eyes, remembering I told Bowen I wouldn't antagonize his brother.

"You are insolent, aren't you?" His reply didn't really sound angry.

"You need me. You have nothing to threaten me with. I know you need to make me well, just so you can kill me. It isn't exactly inspiring a lot of love on my part. Would you please just leave me alone?"

Before I could close my mouth, he had scooped me onto his lap and had his arms around me. He had his right hand twisted in my hair, holding my face just a few inches from his. I held my breath and relaxed, forcing him to support all of my weight. I didn't want to expend any energy on something I couldn't win. He ran his nose down the side of my face while breathing in my scent, then he gently kissed my neck.

"What is it about you that inspires such devotion? That would make my own flesh and blood turn on his family? That would make Slayers risk themselves for a vampire?"

I didn't say anything. Frankly, this scared me more than the knife-wielding Tyran with the snarky comments. It took everything in me to keep from trembling, save a slight quiver in my lip. But he didn't miss it. He leaned back a little and ran his left thumb over my bottom lip for a moment, then buried his face in my hair. He remained there for what seemed an eternity.

I actually wished I could see into his messed up head and figure out what he was thinking.

He eased me off his lap and back onto the bare mattress. "It has been twelve hours. In another twelve, I will have you call them and check on their progress."

I nodded, not trusting my voice.

He eyed at me with what I could only describe as confusion, then departed from the room. Once the door shut, I started to breathe again. I wished I could shower again. His scent was clinging to me. With nothing better to do, I rolled towards the wall and gathered the pillow to my chest, trying to sleep, just to pass the time.

The dream was peaceful. I was lying on a comfortable bed, and I felt amazingly good. Fine sheets caressed my skin as I moved my legs, while fingers leisurely glided up and down my bare back. I kept my eyes closed, enjoying the pleasant tingling sensation. I felt lips, feather soft, brush my left shoulder blade as a hand came to rest on my hip.

When my fingers drifted to my belly, I realized I had no control in this dream and that I was pregnant—very pregnant. I looked at the hand on my stomach—it was mine. I wasn't observing through someone else's body. There was a ring on my left finger that caught my attention, and I gazed at it confused.

It was spectacular and very obviously a wedding ring, a cushion-cut diamond surrounded by at least a dozen radiant-cut diamonds encircling the center stone and on both bands, but I didn't recognize it. I would someday be able to wear Josh's mother's ring, once it wasn't necessary to keep our marriage a secret. And this was definitely *not* that ring.

Rolling over, my expectation was to press my lips to Joshua's, wanting the dream to be real, but it was Bowen's blue eyes that met mine. His expression was soft and thoroughly happy. It was comfortable, like I was meant to be here, and I felt...enraptured.

Wrenching myself from the dream, I woke drenched with sweat, strands of hair plastered to my face and neck. *I shouldn't be perspiring.* Gasping breaths rocked me as tried to discern what type of dream that was, but I couldn't tell. I was so thrown. *Did I have it because Tyran had just been holding me? Was this the future?*

Squeezing my eyes shut, I attempted to swallow passed the knot in my throat. I'd already made my choice, and if I wasn't with Joshua, I could only draw one conclusion. I felt as though I'd been punched in the gut.

Just a dream. Just a dream. Just a dream.

But I knew one thing: during my phone call today, I had to find out if Joshua was sick.

Almost immediately, the doorknob clicked as someone entered, but it wasn't Tyran. And it hadn't been locked this time.

"Here." It was Morpheus. With some effort, I rolled on my back so I could see him. He had two units of blood in his hand.

Nausea rolled through me. "No, thank you."

"I was told to force feed you if necessary."

"Just leave them here. I'll drink them."

He pulled the stopper out of the first bag and handed it to me. "It will be more agreeable the easy way."

I lifted my hand to take the blood and felt like my arm was twice its weight. "You drew the short straw, I see."

"No, we are preparing to move locations. Everyone else is otherwise occupied."

I put the tube to my lips and drank. He watched me from the corner of his eye, looking studiously unconcerned. For the second time today, I wished I could get into someone else's head. *What was my non-enemy thinking?*

When finished, he handed me the next one. After emptying it, he bent to retrieve it, keeping his back turned to the camera. He made eye contact with an expectant, almost pleading look on his face. I remembered his last words to me in my dream, that he wouldn't enter my dreams without permission. I nodded at him, and he nodded in return, then left the room.

The pain in my body eased. I rolled back on my side, away from the camera once again. The hair around my face was still damp and gave me the chills. Closing my eyes, I held onto the North Star charm on my necklace, and prayed for sleep once again. Curiosity about what Morpheus had to say was overwhelming.

Soon I was in the Church of Angels again. It made me wonder if the sunset land that Morpheus had always been in was by his choice or if he simply ended up there. I sat on a pew on the other side of the building and stared at a different stained-glass window. A mighty angel had his white wings spread wide. Five lions surrounded him—three were behind him and appeared to be backing away in fear, and his hands were closing the mouths of the other two. In the forefront, was a profile of a young man looking upwards, as if saying, "thank you." The inscription at the bottom said, "Daniel in the Lion's Den."

Sensing Morpheus, I swiveled around to see him. He sat in the row behind me, and rubbed his eyes for a long moment. I waited for several seconds and then asked, "I'm to be moved?"

He dropped his hand and looked at me. "Yes." He drew in a long breath. "Tyran and Bowen had words before they reached the drop off. Bowen calmly told Tyran that if he ever imprisoned him again, he would kill him. Bowen does not make idle threats, and I have never seen either of them like this.

"Tyran is not planning on letting the two of you see one another again. He plans on getting the antidote, keeping some samples for duplication, and hiding you until the sacrifice. He wants my brothers, Icelos and Phantasos, to keep Bowen occupied. I can see no good in this. I know how Bowen feels about you, and I'm not sure if he can allow you to be slain, even if it is for his own father. I'm afraid my brothers will be collateral damage."

"You think Bowen would harm them?"

"Bowen has never liked violence, but when he is forced into a corner, he is lethal. He is stronger than Tyran, but his love for his brother has always made him stay his hand. He is not one to impose his will on another being, whereas Tyran…"

I nodded, not really knowing what to say.

"Do you understand?" he asked, obviously not satisfied by my subdued response.

"Yes. I do. I know what needs to be done," I said with tremor in my voice.

"And what is that?" he asked cautiously.

"Warn Bowen without implicating you."

"And how will you do that? Tyran will cut your phone conversation off the moment he suspects anything."

"I'm going to have to do the worst thing imaginable, Morpheus." Then repeated, "The worst thing imaginable." I looked over at him and saw the anxiety on his face. "Don't worry, I won't betray your trust."

He nodded.

"I do have a question, though. How do you alter your appearance in dreams?"

He studied me warily, and then explained for a few minutes. I asked if he needed to be asleep in order to enter someone's dreams, and he said no, that he uses a relaxation technique. I requested that he step me through it, and he obliged. I was surprised by his openness, but he said I would have figured it out on my own in time. The moment I'd entered his dream of my own volition, he knew that I possessed the power to invade dreams.

After he was through with what had become a pretty extensive lesson, he exhaled in what seemed to be a relieved breath. "I need to get back."

"Morpheus?"

"Yes?"

"Thank you," I said earnestly.

"You are welcome," and with that he faded from sight.

I turned back to the pane of *Daniel and the Lion's Den* one last time and shuddered.

I woke and exhaled a little overdramatically while rolling to my back, then became deathly still. No breathing. No movement whatsoever. Within a couple of minutes, Tyran entered. I could feel the intensity of his stare on me as the minutes ticked by. Finally, he approached, dropping to his knees, and shook me. I flopped as though lifeless. He picked me up and hugged me to him in one last effort to see if I was still part of the living dead.

When my face was against his neck, I took in a small breath while my fangs elongated, and bit down. I didn't need much blood, just enough to establish a bond. I drew strength from somewhere and held on, taking two long pulls, pumping as much of the relaxant hormone into him as I could.

Tyran hesitated for a moment, then let out a small gasp as his body went pliant. A surge of energy washed over me as I drank— there was so much power in his blood. He must've just fed. Then the thought hit me: *I could take it all and end it right now*. I didn't stop. He fell backwards, and I went with him. He was growing weak. I was so close to draining him when hands dug into my shoulders and tossed me, like I was weightless, into the wall.

My skull bashed into the stone and I fell to the ground. A gash just behind my temple oozed. Red washed over my vision, but I could still see Icelos come for me with a murderous expression. Phantasos and Morpheus were at the ready behind him.

"Stop," Tyran said in a weak voice.

"But, Sire." Icelos turned towards Tyran, but Tyran didn't say anything about being questioned.

Tyran gave me a hard look and asked, "Did you infect me?"

I groaned, wishing I could say yes. "No, it's only in my blood." I responded with defeat.

Tyran's face was unreadable. I wondered if he'd allowed me to bite him to punish himself for Bowen being infected. "Morpheus, attend to her wounds. Icelos, I need to feed." He tried to stand and faltered. Phantasos helped him to his feet and moved him towards the door. Icelos trailed behind them, hatred burning in his eyes.

Morpheus glanced at the camera, and then at me. "Attacking him was unwise." He turned his back to the camera, and I could tell he didn't mean what he was saying.

"He likes to mess with my head. Now I can mess with his."

Morpheus walked to the table and put on some gloves before picking up the last of the gauze, then knelt on one knee to examine my head. "This isn't bad. It appears to be healing already." He probed a little more with his fingers, and then wiped the blood from my eyes. My vision cleared. He pressed the cloth to the side of my head, just behind my temple. *I guess Tyran's blood was good for something: no stitches needed.*

I gazed at Morpheus, wanting to ask him more questions, but refrained. He ran his fingers over the stitches on my face and throat. "These have healed. If you promise not to attack me, I'll find something to remove them."

"I promise. Thank you."

He nodded and left the room for a moment. When he returned, he offered me his hand. "Let's get you on the table."

I took his hand and was able to stand for the first time in two days, but not for long. I felt like Tyran's blood was burning off, like mist in the morning sun. After one step, I fell hard to my knees. Helplessness well up, but I stuffed it back down.

Morpheus helped me to the table, where I was able to sit up while he snipped and removed the sutures. When I removed my sweatshirt so he could get to my arms, I felt very vulnerable in only a thin t-shirt. After he finished with my arms, I quickly pulled the sweatshirt back on and reclined on the table to give him access to the jagged line below my ribcage. It seemed to take forever, even though I knew he was moving faster than any human doctor could hope to.

"One hundred and forty-two."

"Pardon?" I responded.

"The number of stitches. I'm done now. Would you like help back to your bed?"

I blinked at him for a moment, still processing the number of stitches, and nodded yes.

"Actually—" I paused. "Could you help me to the restroom?"

He nodded and didn't bother taking my hands and helping me walk. Rather, he picked me up and carried me to the bathroom. It seemed slightly less mortifying to ask Morpheus for help than it did Tyran. At least I didn't need any help with my clothing. He waited outside until I called him, and then he carried me to the bedroll. With his back to the camera, he mouthed, "Good luck. He's resting." He moved towards the exit.

"Thank you," I replied.

He glanced back with an odd smile on his face and exited.

I wiggled into a comfortable position on my back and took some deep breaths, focusing my thoughts. A grin spread across my face when I decided how to appear to Tyran: a fury from

Greek mythology. It seemed apropos, as they were born of Nyx like the Oneiroi, but were deities of vengeance—the angry ones —those that personify the anger of the dead.

Sliding into his dream was almost effortless this time. I half-expected him to be torturing someone in a dungeon, slaughtering kittens, or flouting his power, but he wasn't. He was sitting on a bench above the Seine River in the middle of Paris.

He was facing the slow-moving waters and viewing Notre Dame, which was sitting proudly on the bank not far away, the warm glow of sunset gilding everything in gold. Tyran wore an expression I'd never seen—he appeared utterly miserable.

Concentrating, I felt my form change; bat-like wings grew from my back and my hands twisted into ghastly talons. My skin became a mottled dark-greyish color. I took to the air behind him, dove silently into the water, and came up again directly in front of Tyran. Water flew from my wings as I hovered a couple of yards in front of him. His mouth gaped, and his eyes widened as he watched me.

"Someone must speak for the dead, for those whom you have sent into permanent darkness," I hissed, my voice unrecognizable.

He met my eyes and simply replied, "I know."

"Even now you plot the destruction of mankind," I accused.

"No. I desire—"

"Your father, I know. But with him lies the ruin of all."

"No—"

"The consequences of your actions will be great. Greater than what you may be willing to give."

He stood, his hands clenched into knuckle-splitting fists, and then relaxing. He looked around. "She is here, isn't she?" His voice sounded haunted.

My smile must've been a horrific, judging from his step backwards. "She has seen some of your secrets," I hissed and dove towards him, knocking him flat on his back before I disappeared back into the water.

When I came out of my trance, blood was running down my face. I swept it from my mind, though I was concerned it would draw attention to what I was doing. I had one more visit to make —Gabriel. I exhaled and prayed that Gabriel was sleeping, for once.

I found him near his sister's grave.

"Gabriel," I said, announcing my presence.

He peered over at me as I walked towards him, stopped, and leaned on a tombstone a few feet in front of him. He furrowed his brow, "Am I dreaming?"

"I'm really here. I don't know how long I can stay. I don't think I have much strength left."

"You should not be weakening yourself," he admonished.

"I had to. There's four things I need to tell you: 1. Tyran has everyone he needs for the sacrifice except an Empath. 2. I believe he has Winslow prisoner, but I haven't seen him. 3. Tyran is planning on keeping some of the antidote to replicate it. 4. He is also planning on keeping me and Bowen apart. I won't have Bowen's protection when he returns."

"Anything else?"

"Is Josh okay?"

He paused for a split-second. "Yes." The pause made me worry that he was telling me what I wanted to hear in order to protect me.

"I will be calling for an update soon. If you remember all this, please say that Bowen's eyes are more pale. I'll know you understood. You need to remember all four points."

"Done," he replied.

I walked forward and touched his shoulder. "It's good to see you, Gabriel. You need to wake."

Instantly, everything went black, then I woke. A fresh stream of blood gushed across my cheeks. The strength from Tyran's blood had been used up, and I could tell I'd stopped healing—the consequence for using my power. My eyes drifted closed as I let out an uneven breath. The weakness was crippling. I couldn't fight sleep, and within moments, I drowned in darkness once again.

ANYONE CAN BE REDEEMED

I was awakened abruptly, making me feel jarred and more than a little grumpy. I just wanted to sleep off what appeared to be some weird dream-invading-hang-over. Apparently, the bloody noses hadn't been enough. My fingers slid over my face and lingered on streaks of crusted blood.

Tyran sat next to me and handed me the phone.

"Call." His humor was no better than mine. "And make sure you speak to my brother to prove he is still alive."

I dialed the number, and there were a series of delays and clicks. The call must've been getting forwarded to the underground lab. It finally rang a good thirty seconds later. Tyran reached over and hit the speakerphone, his fingers brushing my cheek. I cringed and held the phone a foot in front of me.

"Hello?" Gabriel answered with tension.

"It's me."

"Are you all right?" he asked, both worry and relief in his voice. I wondered if Joshua or Bowen had informed him of my emotional state when I'd attacked Tyran.

I hesitated for a single beat before answering. "Yes. I'm fine." Tyran leaned forward. "I've called to see if there's progress."

"Neka said we should be ready for a test tomorrow."

"How's Bowen?"

"He is holding up, but he is weaker. His energy level is declining, as if he was being drained, and even his eyes appear to be more pale." I closed my eyes, feeling relief. Gabriel had remembered everything I'd told him in the dream.

Tyran nudged me. "May I speak with Bowen?"

"Yes, just a moment." Gabriel's tone was formal.

A few seconds later. "I'm here," Bowen said, sounding vaguely like himself.

Tyran glared at me, so I asked, "Are you being treated well? Are you okay?"

"Very hospitable. How are you?"

"Causing trouble, as usual," I said, as lightly as I could. Tyran gave me a look that said he wasn't amused.

"Save your energy," Bowen said, with an inflection meaning he knew that I was causing a truckload worth of trouble.

"You do the same."

Tyran took the phone. "We will call again in twelve hours to check progress. Be well, my brother."

"Be well," he replied, and the line went dead. I didn't know if Tyran naturally said that, or if he was mockingly using the Watcher's farewell greeting.

We sat side-by-side in silence for a long while. Tyran stared at the phone as if it would come to life. I was trying to find the right word for the emotion I'd been getting from him, and then I finally found it: regret. I tried to shut off my connection to him. I wished I could sit on a dialysis machine for a decade to clean out any of his blood remaining in my system. As I'd told Morpheus, being in Tyran's head was the worst thing imaginable. I exhaled, not meaning to make an audible noise. Tyran stiffened next to me, and I felt a wave of anger.

"If you ever attempt to bite me again, I will end you."

"You still need me," I said weakly.

He paused for a long moment. "You said I have nothing to threaten you with, but you are very, very wrong." His manner made the blood in my veins go to ice.

I didn't have the strength to sit upright any longer. So, I slumped over onto my side, no longer able to support my weight, and hit harder than I'd intended, making an "oaf" sound.

Tyran was still taking up half my bedroll, so I remained in an L shape, not that I had the strength to move my legs either. I squeezed my eyes shut and chastised myself for making that promise to Josh. I didn't want to fight. I wanted to close my eyes and fade away, hoping that I did still have a soul that would go to a better place.

Against my own better judgment, I decided to ask a question. "You could have stopped me from biting you. At least, at first you could've. I sensed you hesitate. Why didn't you pull me off?"

He gazed down at me, and I wasn't sure if he was going to answer. The corner of his mouth pulled up a little. "I sensed your enjoyment. You were doing something harmful to another being, and you were enjoying it. Despite all your goodness, there is a little bit of me in you after all." That wasn't the only reason—I could feel it.

"You would have let me kill you? So I would join the 'dark side?'"

"You wouldn't have killed me, but I did want you to taste the power of it. I knew you would never risk killing anyone else."

"I didn't take pleasure in it. I am nothing like you."

"My brother may be your primary sire, but I bit you first."

"And Joshua bit me second. Doesn't that give me three sires?"

He didn't answer. After a few minutes, he rolled onto his

hands and knees and swung my legs around so that I was lying flat on my back. Then he proceeded to lie on his side next to me. I could feel his warm breath on my face and neck. It was a labor to keep my emotions in check.

"I can feel your contempt, how uncomfortable you are to have me so close." He was the one taking pleasure in it.

I chanted to myself over and over—*Save your strength, and don't take the bait*. My eyes watered, and I felt a tear trickle from the corner of my eye. He reached over and wiped it away with his index finger. Then I could swear I sensed regret in him, but for what?

I finally broke the silence. "I'm going to sleep. Try not to wake me with your evil plotting."

His eyes looked amused. I expected him to leave, but he didn't. He rested his head on his arm, still looking at me. I was too tired to care; if he was trying to annoy me to death, I would sleep through it. I closed my eyes. The ache of my body slowly breaking down was growing sharper with each passing day.

When my thoughts became clear again, I was dreaming of the past, and there was no other place I would've rather been. It was my last night with Joshua before the ill-fated trade. I didn't even know I was capable of having a good dream. I knew it was a dream, but I lost myself in the feeling of flesh against flesh and being encompassed by love.

I woke, even crankier than the last time. Someone had my arm and was painfully pulling me to a seated position. My mouth felt like paste, and my eyes like sandpaper. I kept my eyes closed and let out a small whimper under my breath as I tried to slump back onto the bedroll. Whoever it was then grabbed my other arm.

Without looking, I rasped, "Please just let me sleep." It was difficult to push out even so few words.

"It's time to call." Tyran sounded impatient.

I finally opened my eyes. "It's been twelve hours?" I felt like I had just closed my eyes.

"Yes." He shoved the phone into my hand.

"I attempted the last number you dialed when you didn't wake, but it was disconnected."

"I know the next number." I blinked repeatedly to moisten my eyes. I couldn't stay sitting up, and slowly started to slide to my left. Tyran sat next to me, placing his arm on my shoulders to prop me up. Clenching my teeth, I dialed the number, trying not to think about his arm around me. The phone took even longer to connect this time, but it did eventually go through. Tyran hit the speakerphone again.

"Hello?" It was Joshua's voice this time.

"It's me," I said, with a small quiver.

"Are you okay?" he asked.

"As well as can be expected."

Tyran nudged me. "I am calling to check on the progress."

There was a long pause. "Neka ran the first test today, but there was no change."

"Okay," I responded with disappointment.

"How is he?"

"Weaker, but doing well."

"Put my brother on," Tyran interrupted.

"Here," and there was the sound of the phone being handed off.

"Brother," Bowen answered.

"Your treatment?" Tyran asked.

"There is no need to worry. I am not being treated like a prisoner. I could ask you to treat Aleria the same."

He let out a humorless chuckle. "Why brother, she is in an unlocked room."

Bowen caught his meaning straight away. "Is she that ill?"

"Tell those Watchers to hurry. She doesn't have long. She can't even hold up her own head."

"Ali? Are you there? Is that true?"

I swallowed, not wanting to answer. "Yes, it's true," I finally admitted.

"Next contact in twelve hours," Tyran said and hung up. He sat there, with his arm around me.

"Please just let me sleep, Tyran. *Please.*"

"We are moving locations within the hour. I will send someone to collect you in a short while."

I didn't respond.

Tyran waited a moment, then eased me back down onto the bedroll so gently it was almost like he cared—almost. Shortly after that, the door shut.

My eyes involuntarily closed and I must've fallen asleep. Later, stuck in a soupy grogginess, a damp cloth was on my face scrubbing off the crusted blood, followed by hands sliding under my body. I tensed slightly, then peeked and realized that it was Morpheus. I relaxed, grateful that it wasn't Icelos or Phantasos.

When I was carried into the night, I could hear the faint hum of cars on the midnight streets and smell the lingering hint of exhaust in the air. We were in the city, not the country like I'd thought.

I was lugged into the back of a van and placed on the floor on top of some thick carpet that smelled like burned rubber. I rolled my head away from the odor; wishing I was well enough to sit up.

Something was placed behind me, and I heard a soft, pained moan. It was warm and smelled of human blood. I cringed as my instinct to feed reared itself.

My fangs sprang so quickly that they pricked my lip. I guess my body was instinctively doing anything it could to survive, not that I could have fed. I wasn't strong enough to roll over and see who it was. Then my thoughts cleared as the initial bloodlust waned, and when the smell of him washed over my senses further, I realized I knew exactly who it was—Winslow. I was right in telling Gabriel when I invaded his dream.

Winslow had worked painstakingly to translate all the prophecies for Gabriel, Sebastian, and me in York. He was one of the few people Gabriel had trusted with the information. My earlier suspicions must've been correct: everyone had their breaking point. He had to be the one that'd betrayed Amara. We'd had a horrible fight the last time I saw him. Winslow had discovered that Moloch would gain my power as a seer if I'd remained a virgin and was sacrificed. He had suggested that someone bed me just to block the possibility. It ended in a heated argument that was never resolved. He had no idea that I'd gotten married.

"Winslow," I said, keeping my voice low.

"Who is that?" he replied.

"It's Aleria."

"Oh, dear one," he stammered. "I did this, didn't I?" The self-loathing in his voice was evident.

"No, I did this." But I felt anger well up in me. "Although, Amara is dead. That is probably because of you," I jabbed.

He made the most pathetic sound I think I've ever heard, and then I felt bad. I couldn't see the condition he was in, and I had no idea what they'd done to him. If his voice was any indication, then he wasn't doing well.

"I'm sorry. I shouldn't have said it like that."

"It *is* my fault," he answered, and then fell silent.

We drove for what seemed like an hour, then pulled onto a gravel road and stopped—maybe it was a gravel driveway. The side-door opened, and Winslow was being dragged out none-to-gently.

"Come on, old man, use your feet," Icelos growled, as if Winslow's weight would've had an impact on him. He could've lifted ten men with ease.

Tyran carried me this time. I watched to see if I could figure out our location, but had no idea—some cottage out in the country. A two-story with tightly shuttered windows on the outside. My almost limp body was lugged across the threshold and into a room. He stood, swiveled to the left and right briefly, then brought me into what looked like the living room with two suede couches facing one another, separated by a glass coffee table.

A shelf hung on the wall crowded with creepy baby dolls with glass eyes. I was pretty sure one of those dolls was going to come to life and try to kill me. It was a mercy when he put me on the couch with my back to them. I don't think I could've handled all those little eyes focused on me. Irrational I know, but whatever. *I guess some human fears carry over.* I thought for a moment. *Yup, still hated clowns, too.*

He sat down on the couch next to my side, pressing me into the back a little. He ran his fingers over my forehead, and then took my hand, pressing it to his cheek and keeping it there. "You are cold."

"Yes."

"Does it hurt?"

"Yes."

He furrowed his brow. "I need to know where the lab is."

"Tyran, honestly, I don't know."

"You were there."

"I was in daylight gear hiding in the back seat of a sedan. All I could see was the occasional tree top whizzing by."

"I don't believe you."

"Seriously?" My voice was incredulous.

"You will tell me," he demanded in a tone that made me want to kick him in the shin.

"I can't, but I wouldn't if I did. But it doesn't matter, because I don't know. And double-crossing them would not be a good idea. There's no reason for it. They're helping Bowen. I don't understand."

He glanced over his shoulder and said, "Bring him in."

Icelos appeared with Winslow and tossed him onto the adjacent couch. It took all my concentration not to react to his appearance. His long, gangly body was emaciated. He didn't have a surplus of body fat to tap into to begin with. He had the burns from the attack fifteen years ago, but they had been topped with fresh ones that went clear up over to the left side of his face. There was a bandage over his left eye, and the way it sagged inward made me wonder if he had an eye there at all. I felt sick.

Tyran smirked, but it wasn't the humorous kind. "You said I had nothing to threaten you with, but I do."

"Tyran, please don't do this. I have nothing to tell you."

My pleas made no impact. Tyran started torturing Winslow to get what he wanted. The sounds that Winslow was making were inhuman. I was powerless. If I'd known the location, I didn't know if I would've been able to withstand. Winslow didn't deserve this.

After what seemed like an eternity, Icelos called Tyran from the room. Many rooms away, an intense discussion followed. Something had happened—all four of them were involved in the conversation.

Winslow and I were left alone in the room; I thought that this was my only chance to speak to him without prying ears, maybe.

"Winslow, are you conscious?" I asked almost inaudibly.

"Yes," he breathed.

"I'm sorry."

"You don't know, do you?" he said.

"No."

In the most melancholy of tones, he spoke, "I'm glad. When I wouldn't talk, they burned me, took my eye, and killed Stephen."

I thought for a moment, trying to remember who Stephen was. "The boy who worked for you in the store with the curly hair and thick glasses?"

"Yes. He was just a boy. He knew nothing of Watchers or vampires."

The knot in my throat made it hard to speak. "Winslow, what do I do?" I asked, panic setting in.

He replied calmly, as a man who has accepted his fate, "Dear one, you let me die."

"I don't..." I didn't know what to say.

"I want to apologize for the last time I saw you. I was scared and angry. Forgive me?"

Tears spilled down my face, and I was too weak to wipe them away. "You had a rational argument. I disagreed, but I never hated you."

"There is hope—anyone can be redeemed."

"Who? Who do you mean?" I asked, not understanding. Was there something in the prophecy? Was there someone that he thought could be reached?

Tyran stormed into the room, his face consumed with dark intentions. "Are you going to tell me the location?"

"Tyran, I will do anything you want. Please don't do this. I don't have the information you want," I whimpered. I wished I could jump up and fight, that I could *do* something.

"You are lying," he accused, his voice intensifying. Tyran stood behind Winslow, hoisted him up, and wrapped one arm around his chest and the other arm around his head. Winslow strained in Tyran's arms. Slowly Tyran tilted Winslow's head to the side, exposing his neck. His expression became fierce as his eyes started to glow and his canines unsheathed. The hair on Winslow's neck rose. He stopped fighting against Tyran and made eye contact with me, his expression soft and at peace. Tears lined the rims of my eyes as I held Winslow's gaze. He knew this was the end. "You can stop this at any time," Tyran said coldly.

I didn't look away when Tyran bent his head and started feeding. I kept looking in Winslow's one good eye as I watched him grow pale. He sagged in Tyran's arms, and his breathing became shallow. Then finally, the light in his eyes disappeared.

Tyran held him there for a moment examining my expression. I'd managed to hold a mask of sympathy for Winslow's sake, but now it melted into hatred and horror. He let Winslow's body fall to the floor like a wet dishrag, his head making a terrible thump as it hit the wood flooring.

Tyran watched me as he wiped a tiny bit of blood from the corner of his mouth with his thumb and licked it off. I sensed no remorse in him. I closed my eyes, wishing I could roll onto my other side and bury my face in the couch. There was no sound of movement, but my upper body was suddenly being lifted as Tyran sat beneath me.

"Get away from me."

The corner of his mouth twitched in amusement, then he bit his wrist and shoved it in my mouth. I held my breath and tried not to take in any of the blood. A small, tearful moan escaped before my body took over. As hard as I tried to resist, my fangs were rapidly embedding into Tyran's flesh. But I didn't release any of the hormone. I wanted him to feel the sting of it. By default, he was forcing me to drink my colleague's blood.

He made an exasperated sound. "I am trying to save you. My blood after a recent feed was the only thing that has had a positive impact on you. I'm giving them more time to find an antidote." I relaxed my jaw a little, but still glared up at him.

His expression softened as I drank, and he looked down at me through heavy lids. A moment later, there was a figure standing over us, and fingers under my chin.

"That's enough," Morpheus said.

I complied.

Tyran let his head fall backwards and rested it on the couch. His breathing became slower and deeper. I tried to move off of his lap but was unable. His blood didn't give me the strength it did last time. I was better, but there was no way I could sit up.

"Sire," Morpheus said. "You need to feed and rest. May I help you to a room upstairs?"

Tyran shifted beneath me slightly. "Put her in a room upstairs. Stay with her; I'll be along shortly." He picked up his phone and glanced at it. "Three hours until next contact. Aleria, there are other things with which I can threaten you. Don't you worry."

I couldn't think of anything witty to retort. "Do your worst, you—"

Suddenly, Morpheus was bent on one knee in front of me, placing his hand over my mouth, stopping me from saying something stupid. He scowled as he said, "Are you able to walk?" He removed his hand.

"Doubtful," I said, still feeling a little too much ire.

He lifted me from Tyran's lap and carried me upstairs, walking all the way down a long hall smothered with floral wallpaper. Five white doors lined the hallway. He shouldered open the third door on the left and placed me on a full-sized bed that was dripping with pink ruffles.

It appeared to be a child's room. A very, very girly one, the kind a barrel of Pepto-Bismol exploded in. There were more dolls in here staring at me with their beady, little doll eyes that said they would dine on my brains while I slept. *Stupid dolls.* I glanced at the dresser. At least there weren't any clowns.

"Did you gain any strength?" Morpheus asked.

"Yes. For a moment, I was almost too weak to tell Tyran how much I hated him."

"You shouldn't antagonize him so much."

"That's exactly what Bowen told me."

"Tyran is dangerous."

"What does it matter? He's down there planning my death right now."

"I've seen him take out entire families for saying a fraction of what you say."

I rolled my eyes.

"He still has ways to hurt you—hurt *you*," he emphasized. He used the same words Gabriel had.

"No promises, but I'll try…a little."

"Get some rest," he said and vanished. I thought Tyran had told Morpheus to stay with me; he was probably in the hall.

I looked away from the creepy dolls and closed my eyes. My arms had barely enough strength to pull a blanket over me. I wished it could protect me like blankets could when I was a kid. I wished that the monsters would go away. Then I remembered that I was a monster. I bit my bottom lip and willed myself to sleep, trying not to think about Winslow lying dead on the floor downstairs.

I prayed there would be good news in three hours.

I needed good news.

19

I KNEW WHAT YOU WERE

Upon waking, I felt distressed, my thoughts on Bowen. I wasn't sure if I was sensing something from him or if it was a dream. My physical weakness made everything feel muddled. Dread washed over me when I sensed a body next to mine, an arm gently resting across my torso. Tyran was sound asleep next to me. I guess if I'd tried to get away, he would've noticed, but why not place one of the Oneiroi as a guard? I didn't understand this new need to be close to me, unless I was the only connection he had to his brother.

I both heard and felt Tyran's phone buzz. He lifted his arm off of me and retrieved it from his pocket. When he held it up, I could see that it was an alarm. It'd been three hours. He noticed I was awake. "Time to call," he said sleepily.

My arm didn't respond to take the phone, even though I'd tried. I swallowed hard, frustrated that Tyran's blood hadn't done more. On my second try, I was able to grip the phone. Tyran watched studiously as I dialed the third memorized number, and then he hit the speakerphone.

"Hello?" Gabriel answered, his voice cool, and I instantly

knew something was horribly wrong. I labored to control my emotion and not let Tyran know.

"I have called to check on the progress," I said mechanically.

"We are moving forward. Bowen is currently undergoing a treatment—"

Tyran spoke over the last word. "I want to speak with my brother."

There was a long pause. "We need an hour."

"No!" Tyran sat up and thundered. He pulled me into a seated position with my back against his chest. "My brother now, or I will do things to her from which she will never recover."

He wrenched my hand backwards into a wrist lock and tried to make me squeal. I took in a deep breath, but didn't utter a sound into the phone even after he prodded me. I bit my lip in pain and tasted blood as it trickled into my mouth.

"Please, one hour," Gabriel requested in a controlled tone. The please must have been hard to say.

"Put. Him. On. The. Phone. Now." He released my hand, almost tossing it away. He paused, then slowly slid his hand up under my shirt. I cried out softly into the phone before he reached my breast. He stopped short of touching me, and I winced, knowing he knew exactly what he could do to me.

There was a shuffling sound over the phone. "I'm here, brother," Bowen said, his voice rough and strained like he was in agony. I realized instantly it was his pain that had woken me.

"Have they done something to you?" Tyran asked.

There was a pause. "No. The antidote. It will work soon," he replied, his voice breaking once.

"Are they forcing you to say this?"

Bowen's voice cleared for a brief moment. "Touch her again, brother, and Slayers will be the least of your worries."

Tyran let out a single laugh. "There's my brother. Contact is in two hours."

The phone line went dead. He pushed me off of him, knocking me flat onto my back. He stood and paced back and forth in the room. I could feel his helplessness; it was exactly how I felt.

He pointed at me, jabbing his finger in the air like it was stabbing me. "You behave," he commanded as his voice broke. I could feel his emotions spinning out of control. "You did all of this. You took him from me."

"I told you he would get sick," I protested, more raw than I wanted.

"You took him long before that," he accused, his voice low, angry, and resolute.

"I am not your competition. I'm not even *with* him," I said bewildered. "Besides, hasn't he been married before? Did you hate his wife as much as you do me?"

"She was one of us."

"You mean born a vampire or that she was twisted and evil like you?"

He took a deep breath while a cruel grin twisted itself across his face. Then I was in his arms; he was holding my head a few inches from his face. I felt his warm breath on my skin. He looked at me under heavy lids. "If my brother dies, I will make you pay. I know exactly how to break you, just as I promised so long ago."

And then starting at my chin, he kissed his way down my neck. I could feel his tongue linger on my skin between each brush of his lips. A small keening whine escaped me, even though I desperately tried to stifle it. I hated him, knowing he was getting to me.

He released me suddenly as if some dark force had dragged him away. I wished I had enough strength to pull a blanket over me, still wanting the cloth to be a magical cloak of protection. And with little warning, sleep engulfed me.

. . .

I was standing just inside an entrance to a chamber that appeared to be carved into a mountainside. Turning a slow circle, I scanned the room. A carved stone table was stationed near a vast fire pit with metal rods sticking out of it.

Curtains partitioned off the remainder of the room; it appeared there were no other entrances or exits to the chamber. I finished my circle and faced the entry again. A heavy curtain hung between pillars, and fresh air moved from beneath it. I leaned against a smooth, grey column and peaked around the drape.

The room I was in was perched above a vast platform, or maybe a veranda. I counted seven uneven steps. When I scrutinized it closer, I was instantly filled with horror. It was different than past dreams, but unmistakable.

A massive, circular cover stone was wedged in the center of the platform, and it appeared as though everything was sloping towards it. On the edge of the cover stone closest to me was an altar topped with an intricately carved stone table. A channel was cut into the ground leading from the table to a deep groove in the cover stone. It appeared as though it was lined with precious metal.

Around the rest of the circle were seven raised slabs that were tilted towards the stone. They too had channels glittering with silver that led from each slab to the groove around the cover stone. There was an outline of a human body on each one, with symbols scoring the surface.

Beyond the veranda, a magnificent set of steps spilled down the mountainside—there had to have been a hundred or more. The stairs gradually narrowed to a couple of yards in width as they went down the slope into thick trees growing in perfect lines, like they had been planted long ago.

Somehow I'd been so focused on my location that I hadn't taken in the fact that there was a battle waging below. The action reached deep into the forested area and seemed to be in slow motion. Sparks from the clash of swords lit the night like shooting stars. Moving out onto the stone stairs towards the chaos, smoky air swirled around me. Where I could taste the ash that was settling on the ground like snowflakes.

When I came closer to those fighting, I realized that their clothing was from another time period. They wore ancient-looking battle gear with chainmail, leather, and other materials with which I was not familiar. It occurred to me to check what I was wearing, it was in the same sheer white gown with nothing underneath it, but this time the fabric pooled on the ground.

The hands weren't mine—a light dusting of freckles cast a warm glow on her hands and arms. Her nails were short, as if they'd been chewed off out of nervousness. Thick red hair spilled over her shoulders to mid-thigh. When I looked down, I could see everything inside the loose-fitting dress, which included a scar that ran between her breasts and all the way down her torso. I had no control in this dream; I simply had to watch.

Guards came forward, carrying struggling figures dressed in long, beige tunics. They strapped the prisoners down to six of the seven stone beds. Once secure, they walked to the edge of the platform and turned to watch the battle below. No one seemed to notice me...or her, I should say.

Tyran was in the distance, fighting his way towards the awaiting sacrifices, but the moment she saw him, she wasn't afraid—she was relieved and filled with joy. When the last opponent in his path fell, he rushed past the guards—who stepped aside—and straight to her.

He pulled her back into the chamber behind the curtain, wrapping one arm around her waist, and hugging her to him so tightly her feet barely touched the ground. He pressed his lips to her ear. "She is away. My mother will have to postpone. We'll ride as soon as it is safe. I can't take you through the melee." He indicated the battle below.

And then he kissed her, and it wasn't just a kiss. It was the sort of kiss that said, "I-love-you-I-would-die-for-you-you-are-my-world," sort of kiss. And that was the way she returned it. She wasn't using him for her escape. She loved him. She loved Tyran.

In an instant, his mother's voice shattered everything. Just on the other side of the curtain, she asked, "Is she prepared? We have recaptured the Empath. We do this before they break through our lines."

A growing terror unfolded in his eyes as he listened. He stiffened and slowly turned towards the voice, loosening his grip on his love. He held back the curtain. The queen had her back to him, holding a sword up towards the impending threat; it appeared as though she hadn't seen the kiss.

Over her shoulder, she commanded, "Get the seer to the altar. She is first."

"Mother, our lines won't hold. We won't be able to complete the sacrifice. We should retreat and regroup."

She pivoted on her heel to face him. "I will not wait another day. Do not question me." Then dismissed him by turning her back.

Tyran dropped his hand from the curtain, and it fell shut once again. The hopeless expression he gave the girl at his side was heartrending.

She strained on her tiptoes and whispered into his ear. "Taranis, there is no escape. If she knew it was you, we would both die."

"I can't. I am supposed to be the one..." he choked.

"You will. There is no need for you to perish." She peeped

around him through a small crack in the curtain at the throng of people pressing towards them. "Your mother won't succeed," she said.

His arm slid to her bicep, and he kissed her again. Tears that were warm compared to the night air spilled onto her face, but they didn't belong to her.

The queen's voice boomed outside. "We have no time to waste. Why do you delay?"

I or she wiped the tears from his face before he pulled back the curtain, and they slowly descended the steps past the queen to the magnificent granite altar. She climbed on top of the cold stone slab and sat upright staring at him. I noticed the top of the altar was hollowed and sloped to holes drilled through highly polished stone at each of the pulse points to catch the blood.

Queen Agrona was suddenly standing next to him. "Secure her and begin the ritual." Agrona eyeballed her. "You are first." The queen's lips curled into a grin, and then she turned away. She walked to the cover stone in the ground at the center of everything and sank to her knees. She had her back to Tyran and started chanting something.

He looked around, fraught with desperation, then leaned in once again. He held her upper arms gently in his hands. "I'll stall. We'll run now."

"Look at your mother's guards." A dozen immortals surrounded them, all facing away, but completely blocking every exit, not to mention the battle below where both sides would be trying to stop or kill them. "We won't make it, and you'll die too."

"More time," he said, as the breath went out of him.

"I accepted my fate the moment my identity was discovered. I am prepared to die." She put her hand on his chest. "Remember how this felt. You make your future—you do not have to be trapped by it."

He stood there like a statue for a long moment, and when he

met her gaze again, his eyes were glowing. "It won't hurt. I won't let it," he said as he nuzzled her neck. I felt his teeth sink into her flesh, but he instantly released the hormone and kept releasing it, flooding her. Euphoria surged through her body, all the pain and fear melting away. He eased her head down to the table, pulling a knife from a sheath on his thigh. He held the knife to her wrist, his hand trembling.

Before I could see what happened, I was catapulted from the dream, though I didn't wake. It felt like icy cold talons were pressing into the top of my head and into my brain. I cried out in pain, and when I opened my eyes, I was on the ground, my back pressed against a cold gravestone. Gabriel was sitting on his bench not three feet away. I looked at him confused. Was I in his dream? I hadn't tried to enter one.

He looked down at me, looking equally confused. "Aleria?"

I gripped my head and moaned. "It's me, but I don't know why. I didn't try to enter your dream. I feel like I was thrown here."

"Are you hurt? Are they doing something to you?" Then he was on his knees next to me.

"I don't know what's wrong with me." I gasped and tried to get as much information to him as I could. "Winslow is dead. They killed the boy who worked for him too. We moved locations. I think they may know where another Empath is. I'm sorry. I'm sorry. I don't know how much longer—" A torrent of blood rupture from my nose. He said something to me but I couldn't understand him.

I woke to the smell of a lot of blood. It was pooling on the pillow behind my neck, and there was a new level of pain. It was no longer a dull pain in the background of my consciousness. It was acute and present and couldn't be ignored.

The door opened in a rush. Morpheus entered with a bowl and washcloths. He sat down hard next to me. "You need to save your strength," he said in an irritated tone while pressing the cloth to my face.

I looked at his now bloody fingers, trying to keep the pain from my voice. "Aren't you afraid of getting infected?"

"No. I wasn't planning on licking my fingers."

"Probably a good plan." I closed my eyes, pinning my brows together. "Have you ever entered a dream on accident, just get thrown into one?" It took extra work to speak.

He looked at me confused. "No, never. Whose dream did you enter?"

"It doesn't matter." I couldn't tell him it was Gabriel. He would know I'd fed on Slayer blood and that could have far reaching implications. If they figured out that that is what was prolonging my life, then every Slayer would become a target for the extra healing ability.

He watched me for a moment as he continued to clean me up. "When you infiltrate dreams, there are always repercussions —a backlash. You need to refrain from doing so until you are well."

"You have ill-effects?" I asked, surprised.

"Yes, and so do my brothers."

"Bloody noses?"

"No. I used to lose my vision entirely. Now, it is simply blurred for a time."

"So it gets better?" There was hope in my voice.

"It could." He paused. "You need to feed."

"I just want to sleep," I said, a little pleading in my voice.

Morpheus raised his left brow. "Easy way or hard way? Or would you prefer Tyran feed you?"

"Give me the bag."

"I thought that might expedite things." He almost smiled and attempted to hand it to me.

I wasn't able to lift my arm; I just wiggled it, and it lay there, almost as lifeless as the creepy dolls lining the shelves. He nodded and held the bag to my mouth.

I felt stupid and helpless and wished he would have let me sleep. As I drained the unit of blood, my mind drifted to the Tyran I saw in the dream, and I remembered Sebastian telling me that no member of the Lux had ever been captured. It made me doubt the dream, or maybe it was simply that: a dream.

"Has your coven ever captured a member of the Lux before?"

He thought for a moment while he started me on the second unit of blood. "I have heard rumors that it happened once before. But it was long before my time, and they may have been just rumors." He tilted his head to the side and pulled his lips inward. "Did you dream about it?"

I paused drinking. "I'm not sure, with the way I feel. I'm having a hard time telling the different types of dreams apart."

"There are different types?"

For some reason, I kept thinking he would have prophetic dreams too, but he wasn't of the Lux. I wondered if he would've ever have tapped into them as a human. I doubted it. I answered after a long pause. "Just regular dreams and prophetic ones."

"And the ones you infiltrate." He thought for a moment. "And historical ones."

"What do you mean?" I played dumb.

He gave me a measured look while he rolled the two empty blood bags together and placed them on the dresser. "My mother, she used to dream of the past. And you are far more powerful than she. You must be special even amongst 'the elite,' as you put it earlier, special even to the Lux Casta."

"She is the Nexus," I heard Tyran say from the doorway. He was using his arrogant voice. The one he used when he was in control. It usually meant that there would be a considerable amount of gloating and snarkiness in the conversation. "The one prophesied to bring everything together. Can't you feel it? All the game pieces racing across the board in preparation for the final stage of the game."

"You have no proof I'm the Nexus," I contradicted smoothly for once.

"Your friend Winslow said you weren't, but we found where he had hidden the codex that the prophet Ahijah had written. I have read the entire prophesy. It is you, down to that sexy little birthmark on your lower back."

"How did—"

He put up his hand to stop me. "When I kidnapped you a few months back. I stripped off your clothing for the decoy. I lied. I did peek." He grinned crookedly.

I took an uneven breath and tried not to think about him seeing me naked. "I do hate you."

Morpheus gave me a warning look and squeezed my arm. I didn't care.

"Time to call," Tyran said. "How much did you get down her?" he asked Morpheus.

Morpheus held up two empties and exited the room.

Tyran sat in the spot Morpheus had vacated. He ran his finger down one side of my neck and up the other like he was studying a road map. Then it occurred to me that he was running his fingers over the blue veining. I hadn't seen myself in a mirror since the trade; I'd almost forgotten how altered I was. I must look completely inhuman at this point. He took a slow breath, and his mood seemed to shift, the bravado he'd entered with softened.

He held out the phone for me, but I shook my head as best as I could and swallowed hard. "I can't move my arms."

His jaw flexed. "All right. Give me the number." I recited it, and he dialed and hit the speaker, then held it between us.

"You are early," Gabriel answered, his voice a little more relaxed than the last time.

Tyran replied, "You asked for two hours, I gave you one and forty-five. How is my brother?"

"He is improving."

"Let me speak to him."

"Let me speak to Aleria," Gabriel retorted.

Tyran put the phone closer to my face. "I'm here," I said as loud as I could.

"How are you?" he asked, the tension in his voice increasing.

"No need to rush," was my only reply, my tone eerily calm. I could feel I had mere hours left.

"Aleria?" Gabriel asked.

I closed my eyes and didn't reply. I listened as Tyran spoke again.

"My brother," he ordered, ill-tempered.

"Tyran," Bowen answered, sounding stronger than before.

"I suppose they have you chained like a dog now that you are feeling better."

"No, as I have said before, I am not being treated like a prisoner. Of course, the Slayer-to-vampire ratio is greatly in their favor."

"How many Slayers to abate their fears?"

There was a pause—perhaps he was asking for permission? "Four," Bowen finally answered. I hoped that meant Kez was okay. Gabriel was one. I was guessing Samael and Uriel were the other two, although I did recall them saying another Slayer was coming to town.

"How long until they release you?" Tyran asked with a strange mixture of concern and impatience. I opened my eyes.

"They would like to keep me under observation until sundown."

Tyran cast his eyes at me, his lips downturned. "Cutting it close."

There was another long pause. "How is she, really?"

"We may need to get the surrogate back. Contact in four hours." He hung up the phone.

This time I did sense something—a wave of emotion overpowered me that was clearly from Bowen. Tyran moved to the other side of the bed and stretched out next to me. The room was silent, save the sound of our breath. Mine shallow, his deep and controlled.

A short time later, I sensed something else and gasped. Joshua was in pain, emotional and physical. I wondered what had happened, and then I realized only one thing could have happened: Gabriel had lied to me. Joshua was sick. It was the same sort of pain I'd sensed from Bowen.

I was distracted when I felt Tyran shift on the bed. "What is it? Can I do something for you?"

This was bad. He was being nice.

"I'm fine," I said, and then thought for a moment. I drew in a breath. "Actually…"

"Yes?" he asked curiously when I didn't finish my sentence after a while.

"Talking helps distract me. Would you tell me something? It's personal."

"The end must be near if you want to know anything about me," he said, with an odd mixture of emotion that I couldn't place. Maybe there wasn't; I didn't know if I was reading him well. But I was going to assume that the dream I had was real.

I debated on how to begin. "I'm not the first of the Lux you've had dealings with, am I?"

He was quiet for a long moment. "No," he finally replied, his voice low.

"You loved her."

He rolled onto his side, propping himself up on one elbow, and looked down at me. "You are fishing," he said, his voice dismissive, but his eyes weren't. I saw the vulnerability the seer in the dream had seen. A different Tyran than I knew.

"What was her name, the red-haired girl with freckles?"

"You read about her."

"I was told that no member of the Lux had ever been captured. Did the Watchers know?" I paused, then added one more descriptor. "She had a long scar all the way across her torso."

His face clouded. "You can't know that."

"What was her name?"

He sat up, looking haunted. He pulled up the left side of his shirt. "Áine," was tattooed in a Celtic looking script on the side of his ribcage.

"How do you say that?" I asked.

"Awn-yuh. It means 'radiance,' like the sun." He paused, "And your last name means 'fire.'" He pulled his shirt back down.

I squeezed my eyes shut for a brief moment, and then met his eyes, my voice wavering, "Did you kill her?"

"How could you know this?" he whispered, as if he couldn't quite catch his breath.

"I had a dream. I was there. I was in her, or was her. I felt what she felt."

"She was just using me," he said, an edge of bitterness in his voice.

Energy came from somewhere, and I hurriedly pushed the words out. "Is that what you convinced yourself? You know that isn't true. You were ready to betray everything. If she'd asked you to run that night, you would've, wouldn't you, knowing that your own mother would have ordered your death?"

He looked like he wanted to lash out and hit me. "Yes!" He yelled and shot up from the bed. He paced back and forth, centuries of stuffed emotion rolling off of him. I followed the movement with my eyes, making me dizzy.

"She loved you enough to allow herself to be sacrificed. The Lux are supposed to kill themselves if captured. She betrayed that for a chance to stay with you."

He stopped moving and looked at me. "She loved me," he said half-questioning, half-confirming.

"Tyran, I have no reason to ease your pain in any way. I would've preferred that she was using you. But for some reason, I am compelled to tell you the truth. My eternal flaw, I guess."

"She always told me the truth." He paused, "Your kind, no good can come of any of you. You will ruin my brother like she ruined me. I have tried to drive him away from you. You will be sacrificed, and there is no recovery for that."

"You killed her," I stated.

"I had to—" His voice broke. He looked at me pleadingly.

"Did your mother know how you felt?"

"It wouldn't have mattered. She is single-minded."

I felt anger well up in him as if a bomb was exploding inside. He strode over to the dresser in the corner, and with one swipe of his hand, he smashed it into pieces. "Is this what you do to my brother? I have never told anyone about her. You...you get into heads." He poked at his temple.

There was a voice on the other side of the door. "Sire?"

"Leave me. I'm fine," he barked as his chest heaved with breathlessness. Suddenly, he was on the bed with me, his face inches away.

"I knew what you were the second I tasted your blood, but it was too late; you already had your hooks in my brother. Instead of offering him a deal, I should have taken you straight to my mother and have been done with you. And now he will hate me forever for saving him from you."

"You are broken, aren't you?" I said before I could stop myself. *Idiot.*

"No," he replied hoarsely. "But some things we can't change."

"We have free will. Áine told you something at the end. She said, 'Remember how this felt. You make your future. You do not have to be trapped by it.' Make your own future, Tyran." He narrowed his eyes at me, and then he was gone. The door was wide open, and I could hear something being smashed in another room. *Good job. Way to go.*

Now that the conversation was over, I realized the pain had grown stronger. Any energy I had was burned up during the exchange. I struggled to close my eyes, and when I did, I waited for the end to come. I expected darkness to swallow me up, but it didn't. I laid there, an unmoving rock on the bed, listening to everything.

Praying for…something.

20

INVISIBLE

A passionate discussion was being waged outside my door. Morpheus was saying that they needed to bring me with them to pick up Bowen, that it was imperative that they give me the antidote as soon as possible.

Tyran agreed, but only after he accused Morpheus of being soft on me, that Morpheus was overly concerned. Morpheus' response was strong enough that Tyran backed off. I personally thought Morpheus remained neutral; he simply had some decency. Who knows? It could all be a ploy to protect his brothers.

Sleep eventually came, and when I woke, I could feel Tyran pressed up against me. His arm was wrapped tightly around my waist, and his face nestled in the hollow behind my ear. He made some soft sounds like he was dreaming. I'd thought maybe our last conversation had chased him off. *Not that lucky, I guess.*

Despite my deeper understanding of him, I still didn't want him touching me. Even if I decided to forgive him of the atrocious things he'd done to me personally, he'd still killed three of my friends, two of those in front of me.

I assessed myself. Horrible pain: check. Inability to move: check. Irritability: check. I couldn't even open my eyes; I think that was what bothered me the most. I was able to take shallow breaths, which meant I could still smell. Unfortunately, all I could smell was Tyran. I stopped breathing.

The alarm on his phone chimed. He moved, it was silenced, then he settled back in. A few minutes later, it went off a second time; he stirred and exhaled down my neck, pulling me a little closer. *Apparently, I'd wrecked my karma at some point.*

The alarm went off again, and he really woke this time, but he didn't move right away. He finally disengaged himself from me and rolled to the other side of the bed. He nudged me.

"It's time to call." There was a long pause. I felt him shift on the bed; I assumed he was looking at me.

He placed his hand on my chest. I wanted to cringe away, then I realized he was checking for breathing. I took a breath, but he'd already lifted his hand. He ran his hands over my face. I managed to part my lips, but I don't think he noticed that either, because he was lifting my head. His hands slid up my face, and he opened my eyelids. He let out a sigh of relief.

"Your pupils still dilate," he breathed. There was genuine worry on his face, and his eyes were soft and vulnerable like in the dream. At this moment, it would've been hard to tell him and Bowen apart. Of course, he wasn't worried about me, he was worried about his precious sacrifice dying before they could kill me.

I felt his weight leave the bed and watched him stalk out of the bedroom. A couple of seconds later, I heard something break in another room. I wondered what was going on, although trying to figure out Tyran seemed a useless waste of energy… time…whatever.

Suddenly, he was back and sitting next to me. He peered into my eyes; they felt dry from my inability to blink. "Can you move your eyes from the left and to the right?"

I looked to the right.

"Good. Right is 'yes,' and left is 'no.' Will the last number we called go through?"

I looked to my right a little. He let out a relieved gust. He held the phone in front of him and had it on speaker. He glanced over at me. My eyes were burning and must have appeared red. He gently put his fingers on my lids and closed them. *That was almost nice of him.*

Gabriel answered after the series of clicks. "Yes?"

Tyran's voice was tense. "We need the antidote. Now. No games. No time to waste."

"We would still like to keep him under observation for another hour."

"I-we-she—" He stopped. I don't think I'd ever heard him at a loss for words. "I need to show you. Do you have video on your phone? Or can I text you a video?"

They discussed logistics for a moment and hung up. A second later, Tyran slid in behind me, propping me up in front of him, my temple pressing against the side of his jaw. His phone rang about three minutes later.

I wondered if Gabriel had gone topside to use the video conference App on one of the cell phones. They talked briefly. I felt Tyran move slightly, and then I heard Gabriel gasp over the phone. *Now that couldn't be good.*

Gabriel said rather sharply, "How do I know she is still alive?"

Tyran opened my eyes and held his palm to my forehead, keeping my head upright. He asked me to move my eyes back and forth. Of course, I didn't want to since he was the one asking, but I wouldn't do that to Gabriel. I complied, and afterwards, noted Gabriel's worn appearance. My eyes watered, but I was unable to blink to clear them, so tears streamed unchecked down my cheeks.

Gabriel's voice was rough. "We will drop him near Trinity College in forty minutes. It is the best I can do. Aleria, don't you dare give up."

My eyes flitted downward, and then returned to his image on the phone. He paused for a long moment, looking at me as he pressed his lips into a hard line, and then disconnected the call. *I stand corrected—Gabriel is capable of using a contraction.* It made me worry even more.

There was a soft knock at the door, and Morpheus poked his head into the room. "They've returned." I wondered if Icelos and Phantasos had gone somewhere.

"I'll be right down."

Morpheus nodded and closed the door.

Tyran lowered me into the crook of his arm, his face riddled with conflicting emotions. He gently placed his fingers on my lids and closed them—for this I was grateful. Despite the tears a moment ago, my eyes were stinging.

I thought he was going to ease me the rest of the way onto the bed, but he raised me up again and pressed his cheek to mine. After a minute, he released me and placed my head on the pillow. The door snicked closed almost immediately thereafter.

Sleep, that's what I wished for—or oblivion. Maybe even the sound of splintering wood from an invading army of zombies. Scratch the last. I didn't think I wanted someone to eat my brain, although that might be preferable to Tyran snuggling up beside me again. Bring on the zombies! I sighed internally; forty minutes—that was how long I needed to last.

The door swung open. I caught Tyran's scent, then felt his weight on the bed again. He pulled me onto his lap. He felt warmer and smelt of fresh blood. Icelos and Phantasos must have brought him someone to feed on.

I wondered if it was a familiar or an unfortunate soul in the wrong place at the wrong time. *Would he have drained the donor in order to have extra strength to sustain me? Was another death on my hands?* I tried to shove the spiraling thoughts out of my mind. I was experiencing an odd sense of delirium, like my control was very thin.

After prying my mouth open, I soon felt a warm gush of blood flood into my mouth, but I couldn't swallow. I wanted the blood, despite the source, but I couldn't will myself to force it down. *This is it, the end.*

He pulled his wrist away from my mouth when some dribbled down the side of my face. Then I felt the tips of his fingers on my throat. He gently massaged. Soon, the warm blood trickled down my throat, and the panic that was starting to well up inside of me subsided.

He continued until all of the liquid pooling in my mouth had drained. The tingle of increased energy filtered through me and I was able to lift my lids. They felt thick and heavy, but I was able to do it under my own power. I felt pathetic for being so happy over something so small.

I glanced up at Tyran. His expression was once again unreadable as he wiped up the blood that had dribbled down my chin. I wondered which Tyran was beneath the mask. He nodded at me, then placed his wrist in my mouth again.

This time, my body reacted, and my fangs pierced his flesh. I released the hormone; he was being kind, so I returned the favor. I watched as he slumped back against the headboard, but his eyes never left me. I closed mine, not wanting the connection. Soon, I could wiggle my fingers and toes; I was sure I could've moved my arms too.

He was weakening. He ran the fingers of his free hand over my forehead and said, "Enough." As I released him, I resented the fact that I didn't have enough strength to kill him.

Tyran chuckled. "I can feel you wanting to kill me."

I swallowed hard and wondered if I could speak. I tried once, and a garbled sound escaped my lips. I coughed and tried again. This time I managed, "What do you want from me?"

His jaw flexed. "I don't know."

I nodded. I believed him. His confusion was rolling off of him, but the word that repeatedly came to the surface, almost haunting me, was *forgiveness.*

"You are in love with my brother."

"Not that kind of love," I replied, but there was a tinge too much defensiveness I couldn't hide.

"That's a lie," he said coolly.

"I am in love with Joshua."

"You are in love with both of them. In your eyes, if you admit it out loud, it will make you bad. You know yourself too well not to realize how you feel. Something is holding you back."

"You're wrong," I said, but even I didn't believe my voice.

"People fall in love with more than one person all the time."

"That doesn't make it right. I've made my choice." I paused, feeling breathless. "Please stop," I pleaded.

"Inflicting pain, it tears you up, doesn't it?"

I closed my eyes and turned my face away. I replied, without any real venom. "I hate you, Tyran."

To that, I heard another chuckle. "Tell me how you really feel," he said, his tone lighter than I expected.

"I'm too polite to use that kind of language." My tone still didn't have the acid of the past.

He reached around, placing his fingers under my chin, and turned my head back towards him. I opened my eyes to meet his gaze. He looked like he wanted to say something. His face had become serious, but he remained silent.

I decided to ask him a question. "If you could do it over again, would you have run with Áine?"

His face clouded over. "If I could go back, I would have run with her long before that night." He glowered. "Orson Welles said, 'If you want a happy ending, that depends, of course, on where you stop the story.'"

"Story isn't over," I stated.

"Time to go," he growled, then he picked me up.

The sun had barely set as we took two vehicles to the meet. Icelos and Phantasos were in a black Mercedes with the special coating on the windows. I figured wherever they were planning on taking Bowen was a long distance from here. I rode in the back of a normal, boxy European sedan I didn't recognize. Morpheus drove while Tyran kept his arm around me. He held my head to his chest, keeping me upright. I noticed the school clock tower in the distance, shortly after we pulled into an alley. We were only a few minutes' walk at human speed from the college.

Icelos and Phantasos exited their vehicle and made a sweep of the alley. Then I noticed Icelos nod at Tyran and disappear. Five minutes later, he returned with hotel keys that he held up between his index and middle fingers. Tyran opened the car door, and the night air flooded inside. I didn't want to go into a building again. Tyran took the room keys and handed one to Morpheus. "Hold the elevator for us."

Morpheus nodded in agreement and vanished. Tyran plucked me from the backseat, and I felt the rush of air as we moved preternaturally fast through a side door and into the elevator, joining Morpheus. The wall panels were made of mirror, and I caught the first look at myself in a few days. The bluish striations in my skin were so dark that it almost looked like bad theatrical makeup, but the translucent nature of the rest of my skin made it far too real. I turned my head towards Tyran's chest, not wanting to look at myself, not wanting anyone to see me.

The elevator opened, and we followed Morpheus down the

hall to the room. He opened it and made a security sweep before Tyran and I entered.

"I'll check the halls and stairwells again." He patted Tyran on the shoulder as he left the room. This was the first time I'd seen a physical gesture of friendship between them.

Tyran placed me on the bed, keeping me bent forward while he propped some pillows behind me. He eased me back with enough gentleness that I felt confused by it. "How long?" I asked him, keeping my voice low.

"We should hear any time now."

"You're going to keep him away from me, aren't you?"

He frowned. "That was the plan."

"Your plan?"

"It doesn't matter," he replied.

Just then the door opened, and Morpheus returned to the room. "All clear. I believe they will keep their word." He had two walkie-talkies with him.

Tyran's phone rang. He quickly held it to his ear. "Yes...Yes... I'll be down. He knows where to meet us."

Morpheus turned on both of the walkie-talkies and handed one to Tyran. "Click the blue button, and we will hear everything going on. If there is trouble, I will have her out of here before they get past the first floor."

Tyran gave me one long, last look and vanished from the room. Morpheus sat the walkie-talkie on the side table next to the bed and pulled a cushioned armchair over to less than a foot from the bed. He leaned back and rested his right foot on the mattress.

I peered over at him. "Are you really expecting trouble?"

He shrugged. "When dealing with the Council, no. But if anyone from the Conclave got wind of this, yes. Better to be prepared."

I didn't respond, but that sounded about right. Even the

vampires knew which humans to trust.

The walkie-talkie crackled to life on the other end. We heard a soft thump, like it was being set down on a hard surface.

"Give me the antidote," Tyran demanded, sounding hurried.

"I *am* the antidote," Bowen's voice calmly replied.

"Don't jest, brother; I need to get it to her now."

"*We* need to get *me* to her."

"*You* are needed elsewhere. You need to leave with Icelos and Phantasos."

"I wasn't joking. I am the antidote, and I need to see her now."

Tyran made a sound that fell somewhere between angry and impatient.

"Were you going to separate us?"

"We need a sample to replicate."

"The Watchers didn't trust you; we are to use my blood. Why are you delaying me? Where is she?"

There was a shuffling sound.

"I don't have anything," Bowen hissed. "Stop." *Was Tyran searching him?* Morpheus and I looked at one another, probably thinking the same thing.

Tyran made an exasperated sound. "I should have known there was no way to keep her from you. Room 306. Morpheus is with her."

There was a knock at the door seconds later, and when it opened, Bowen had a key in his hand. "Morpheus," Bowen greeted him cautiously. "How is she?" he asked, his voice barely audible.

My eyes flicked to Morpheus, who only moved his eyes towards the door; he had his elbows on the armrests and his hands steepled in front of his face. "I wouldn't waste time," he replied. "I'll watch the hall."

He exited, leaving me alone with Bowen for all of three seconds before Tyran and Icelos entered. Bowen had taken a few steps in my direction, and his face fell when they entered, but he continued to my bedside. He sat and pulled me into his arms.

My limbs felt hollow as I tentatively reached up and placed my hand on his face. He pressed my palm to his cheek and closed his eyes. It felt like it had been an eternity since he left. I shouldn't be this happy to see him. He glanced at Tyran, and then Icelos, and then back to me.

"The antidote worked—my blood will work—but I need to warn you, it wasn't pleasant."

I frowned. "Joshua was sick. You tested it on him," I stated, my voice even. I didn't need to ask; it was the only reason I could explain Gabriel's hesitation, and the fact that Joshua was in pain hours after I felt Bowen's pain.

"Yes," he replied in a grave tone. I didn't know if that was because things didn't go well in the lab, or if he was nervous about what I was about to go through.

He offered me his wrist. I felt so emotionally upended that I couldn't will my fangs to unsheathe. A moment later, Tyran was standing there with a small blade in the palm of his hand. He made a tiny cut on Bowen's wrist. Once I'd tasted his blood, my body finally decided to work, and I fed.

I could see Tyran looking intently at us from the corner of my eye. All I could think about was him saying, "*You are in love with my brother.*" I tried not to think about it. I tried not to think about how good Tyran's blood tasted either, though not as good as Bowen's.

Bowen's blood was better than anything I'd ever tasted. Last time, my human life was hanging by a thread, and I didn't notice, but then again, I didn't have a comparison at that point either. It raised desires in me, and I cursed myself for even thinking about any of this—for thinking of Bowen as anything other than a friend. I stopped and sealed the punctures, despite the fact that I wasn't done. I couldn't handle the intimacy.

The strength in his blood hit me, but I'd expected to feel something—more. I felt a familiar sensation of my heart beating a few times, the same as I had every time I'd fed directly from Gabriel.

Bowen waited a moment, and then he bent down. His lips felt warm next to my ear. "This was your husband's idea. Crush it between your teeth. It's the catalyst." He pulled his head back for a moment and made eye contact.

There was a flash of hurt in his eyes as I blinked up at him, but I was too distracted by the fact that he knew I was married to comprehend what he was about to do.

He lingered, his face about a foot from mine, then I saw the edge of his mouth twitch upwards, like he found something humorous, before he pressed his lips to mine. I felt dense until the words sank in, and I realized that he had something in his mouth. He was giving me the other part of the antidote—the catalyst.

I was startled for a split-second, then sank into the kiss. The experience I'd had months ago of waves crashing inside me returned and overwhelmed me. I let out a small murmur against his mouth as my breath became uneven. He gathered the back of my shirt in his hands and pulled me closer, and with what little strength I had, I responded, latching onto him.

Then my mind caught up to what I was doing, and guilt bubbled up. He kept his lips pressed to mine, but I felt him moving something in his mouth. He used his tongue to slide a capsule the rest of the way into my mouth and then drew away. I felt dizzy and had to close my eyes for a moment to concentrate on steadying my breath.

I stared up at him wide-eyed as I moved the capsule farther

back in my mouth, positioning it to where I could crush it with my molars. When I broke the capsule, I cringed as a sticky substance oozed from it and seemed to bond with my teeth. I wanted to gag as the pungent taste sparked both my taste buds and nerves.

Heat started coursing through me, and I took some gasping breaths as pain seized every cell in my body. Bowen grabbed onto me, turning me so my back was to his chest and held me when I tried to thrash. I started to scream, and he placed his hand over my mouth to muffle the screeching that tore through me. I bucked and kicked and writhed, but he held onto me, protecting me like a fortress in a storm.

My skin became slick with sweat. The moisture had a horrible cloying smell, kind of like the capsule had tasted.

He pressed his mouth to my ear. "It won't last long. Breathe... just breathe..."

After several minutes, the pain started receding as quickly as it had spread. It had the same intensity I'd felt when I'd been exposed to Aurora, but the pain now was so short-lived that there was no comparison. I lay limp in his arms while the disorientation threatened to turn my stomach. Nausea hadn't been a problem since I'd been turned.

After a short while, I started feeling a little more like myself. He slid the hand that covered my mouth to cradle my face. I squeezed his hand that was still on my torso.

"Thank you," I half-moaned.

I felt him shrug, and then he crawled out smoothly from behind me and sat in the chair Morpheus had moved next to the bed. I laid on my side and returned his gaze. The room was thick with emotion.

Bowen spoke over his shoulder. "I need to speak with Aleria alone for a few minutes."

"No," Tyran clipped.

"We won't be planning an escape. This is personal. I need a few minutes."

Tyran made a sound that was the cross between a grumble and a growl. He looked at Icelos, who'd been standing so quietly next to the window, I'd forgotten he was there.

Then Tyran spoke. "We will wait in the hall. Five minutes."

They exited reluctantly, and the door closed.

Bowen glanced at the closed door. "Why didn't you tell me?" he whispered. Hurt-anger-betrayal—all were present.

I struggled to a sitting position on the edge of the bed, feeling a little more energy. I didn't want to have this discussion laying down if I had the strength to sit up. We sat with our knees almost touching.

"He told you?" I finally whispered in return.

"No. I asked. I thought about your word choice the other night. You said, 'I love you. I just *can't* the way you want me to.' You didn't say *'don't,'* you said *'can't,'* like something was preventing you. Not that those feelings aren't in you. It wasn't a hard conclusion to draw. Suddenly, everything made sense. The way you'd mourned Joshua, and the way you kept your distance from me. When I saw him and spoke with him in the lab, all the pieces came together."

"I—" I broke eye contact and fastened my eyes on my feet.

"You should have told me. I would never have done anything to you. I—"

"No...not you." My head snapped up, and I cringed. "My secrets should not be your burden. I wasn't trying to deceive *you*. I was scared, scared to even utter the words out loud."

"You didn't trust me," he said, all the hurt in the world evident in his voice.

"Not trust you? How could you think that? Of course I trust you. If I didn't, I would never have suggested sending you to Gabriel. He and the people you were with are my family—even now. I wouldn't risk their lives for my own—ever. I wanted to tell you, but then I thought he was dead, and that it didn't matter. The longer I waited, the worse it got. Then, I just couldn't."

"If you'd wanted to, you would have," he responded flatly.

In the loudest whisper I could manage, I angrily snapped, "You weren't there!" Alarm gripped his face, and he leaned back. "Night after night, your brother came to me. Fed on me. If I close my eyes, I can still feel his weight on top of me. If he knew I wasn't a virgin, that his sacrifice had been tainted, you're telling me he wouldn't have done more than just feed? Maybe he wouldn't have, but I didn't know. I was protecting myself. I learned a long time ago that if you want to keep a secret, you don't tell anyone." My bottom lip started trembling, and my voice softened. "I am sorry."

Bowen leaned forward and took both of my hands. I looked at him nervously, not liking the pause he was taking to formulate his thoughts; but he was looking down at our hands, so I couldn't read his expression.

"I need to know something." He paused for an uncomfortable amount of time. He met my eyes, and seriousness held his features. "I need to know if you love me."

When I started to pull away, he slid his hands to my wrists and held me firmly in place. He wasn't going to let me avoid the question.

I looked up at him beseechingly. "Why are you asking me this?"

"I need to know."

"I can't." I felt breathless.

"How do you feel about me? I need to hear it."

"I can't cheat," I choked.

"I'm not asking you to," he replied, a small tremor in his voice.

"Bowen, I…"

"*Please.*"

"You know I love you."

He sighed, exasperated, "You know what I mean."

I grimaced and panic slipped into my tone. "You know how much I care about you. Why are you doing this?"

"Are you in love with me? I need to know," he said pleadingly, looking into my eyes. He looked fragile, like glass that could be broken with my response. Despite that, I wanted to lie, but I couldn't.

"Yes! Are you happy? I said it. Please let go of me." But he didn't. Instead, he pulled me onto his lap and held me to his chest, wrapping his arms around me and tucking my head beneath his chin like Joshua had done so many times. I clutched a fistful of his shirt; he smelled like the shampoo they keep in the shower at the lab.

"Thank you," he murmured, so softly I wasn't sure he'd really said it.

"Everything got so complicated. I hate this, but it doesn't change anything. It doesn't matter how I feel about you. He is my husband. I love him, I won't cheat, and I won't leave him."

Bowen was quiet for at least a minute. His breathing was labored, and then suddenly, it calmed. "Your loyalty is one of the reasons I love you." He kissed the top of my head.

I exhaled slowly. "Does knowing make you feel any better?"

"As I said before, I am very good at being patient."

"You're trying to torture me, aren't you?"

He chuckled and kissed me on top of the head again. "I hate to tell you this, but you smell dreadful."

I laughed, but it came out as a partial sob.

He nudged me. "Go get cleaned up. Your friend Peter sent some of your things. Phantasos was searching the bag when I came up. I'll find it. It will be good to get you in some clothes that you haven't lived in for days."

He helped me to my feet, and I was able to walk on shaky legs to the bathroom. I left the door unlocked so someone could drop off my clothes.

It took vigorous scrubbing to rid myself of the smell. It was like all of the toxin had been pushed through my pores, but since I'd been turned, I hadn't been able to see any of the pores in my skin. I wondered if that was why my skin felt so tender.

A soft knock at the door pulled me from my thoughts. "May I come in?" Bowen asked.

"Yes."

"I'll leave everything on the side of the sink."

"Thanks."

I stepped out as soon as I heard the door shut again. My clothes were neatly folded on the basin with a toothbrush on top. After brushing my teeth, I almost felt like a whole new person. I took a deep breath to center myself before having to face Tyran again.

Steam billowed into the room as I entered. Tyran and Bowen were facing one another, each of them leaning aggressively towards the other with only a few feet between them. They stopped speaking when I entered, but their expressions were strained. The tension was suffocating.

Bowen turned slightly so his back was to me and focused on the carpet. The muscles in his back were so strained that I could see them through his dark blue t-shirt. Tyran's hands were tightly fisted, and his jaw was clenched so tight, I thought his teeth might shatter. I took another step towards them, and they didn't move. Drips of water ran down my back from my wet hair.

"Take her," Tyran said.

Bowen's head snapped up.

Tyran turned to me. "Stay with him. Don't go to your Watchers. I think there is another informer besides Crina

Rousseau. I don't know who it is. I don't think it is someone you have contact with, but they have power. You both need to be invisible."

I moved next to Bowen and grabbed onto his arm, not believing what I was hearing. "You should come with us," Bowen answered firmly.

Tyran shook his head, "I can better help you here." He pulled a blade from his boot and handed it to Bowen. "Your turn, brother."

Bowen took the blade in his hand. It was a Durateus throwing knife.

"Get it—" Tyran didn't finish his sentence.

The door opened with a crack, and the lights flickered as Dagan swept into the room. I'd forgotten the sense of awe there was being in his presence. Paralyzing fear crept up my spine as all thought and movement halted.

Tyran stepped towards him. "Dagan, I—"

Dagan raised his hand towards Tyran and placed his palm flat on Tyran's chest in what seemed like a minimal gesture. Tyran flew backwards into the wall, as if he'd been catapulted. Dagan looked at me, and I heard him speak, but his lips didn't move.

"You should have stayed away."

I looked at Bowen and realized that I was the only one who'd heard him.

When I opened my mouth, nothing came out.

Bowen raised his hands in surrender. He spoke reverently. "All I ask is that you allow me to come with you. I won't challenge you."

Dagan knit his brow as he put his hand on my shoulder, only saying a single word to me: "Sleep."

Instantly, I felt my body go limp and Bowen's hands catch me. Then, there was nothing.

21

WHAT IS TO COME

When I opened my eyes—there was only blackness and more blackness. My mouth was thick with an odd metallic taste. I blinked and sucked in a breath, feeling my lungs expand, burning from disuse. I wondered how long I'd been out. Obviously, I hadn't been breathing. Blinking again, the thought crossed my mind that I'd gone blind.

Rolling onto my hands and knees, I felt the ground: cold stone, smooth or worn, no mortar. I struggled to suppress the terror that was spreading through my bones like poison as I felt my way through the darkness.

I scrambled to summon up my memory—those last minutes seemed fragmented. Tyran, unconscious on the floor with plaster fragments from the wall littering his body. Bowen, raising his arms in surrender—*Bowen*. I let out a shaky breath and started feeling around. Several feet from where I'd started, I hit a wall, but it was jagged rock—a cave maybe?

In the distance, drips of water reverberated off of the walls. The area was sizeable. Then the musty odor of dirt and water, heavy with minerals infiltrated my senses. I could also smell...

Bowen. He was here. I continued to test the air for his scent, and after about a minute, found him unmoving on the ground.

"Bowen?"

Nothing. I shook him, but there was no response. I placed my ear over his mouth to see if I could pick up on the faint sounds of breath, but nothing. I wished there was some light so I could see his eyes. I hunched down farther and placed my head on his chest, willing him to wake.

After some long moments, he let out a low moan and rolled towards me. My heart went into a sprint. *Wait. My heart?* It was beating. I placed my hand over my chest, pressing hard. My entire body was shaking with each beat. There was no mistaking it. My heart was truly beating.

How could this be? Was I still...? I thought about blood for a moment: my fangs unsheathed, and I was filled with a devastating amount of desire, for blood, for Bowen. So much so, that I sat up and started to push myself away from him. I felt his hand on my ankle. When I tried to pull away, he tightened his grip.

"Where are you going?" he asked, disoriented.

"I need to get away from you. Something's wrong." My voice choked off as my heart hammered painfully, and all I could think about was biting him or kissing him or both or worse. I squeezed my eyes shut.

He moved closer, not heeding my warning. "What's wrong?"

The pitch black of the room felt suffocating as I tried to ferret out the words to describe what I was feeling. "I don't know. Something changed. I feel like there is too much power in my body for me to contain." A panicked sound escaped me. "Too much emotion—too much *want*." I started panting, eyes still cinched shut.

I felt his hands on both sides of my face. "Slow down. Breathe."

"Where are we?" I wheezed, trying to distract myself.

"We have to be at one of the Hellmouths. And from the smell of this place, it's Northern Ireland. It's the wrong scent for Italy, and they wouldn't have taken us to South America."

I tried to acknowledge what he conjectured, but I ended up moaning instead.

He paused. "Am I hearing...?" I pulled his right hand from my face and placed it over my heart. He gasped.

"So I'm not crazy," I breathed, half-relieved and half-terrified.

As if he didn't believe it, he pressed his ear to my chest, placing his hands flat on my back, and listened. He breathed in my scent. "You don't smell human."

"I'm not. I don't know what I am." My delicate control started slipping away, and I once again began to tremble. "Back away from me," I begged.

Bowen released me, but I could still feel him directly in front of me. "Why?" he asked.

I opened my eyes, and in the tiny bit of light that emanated from them, I could see him no more than two feet away.

My mouth watered with him so close, and moisture began to bead up on the surface of my skin. Sweat. Now that the antidote had worked itself through my system, I shouldn't be sweating. I was so caught up in all the sensations I was feeling that I didn't realize I hadn't answered him.

He moved even closer. "Why don't you want to be near me?"

I scuttled a few feet backwards on my palms and heels, letting out a whimper. "I'm afraid I'm going to hurt you. Something's wrong. I feel like an overcharged battery. I don't know what to do with all I'm feeling. It's like when I was a newborn vampire, but twenty times worse."

"You won't hurt me," he stated confidently.

"I'm not in control. I feel stronger—I'm *different*." I scooted backwards until I hit the wall and could no longer see him.

Though I could hear him taking halting breaths a few yards away. Pain burned through my body as I tried to resist. I yelled out—half-cry and half-wail—searching for release. I screeched and rolled onto my belly, pressing my face to the chilly ground, then howled and started hyperventilating as I pulled my knees under my body, curling into a tight ball.

Bowen's scent grew stronger. He must've been moving closer. "Back up."

"Let me help you," he beseeched.

I forced the words out. "Don't you understand? I want to feed on you—right now—and not in a good way. I won't be able to stop."

"I won't let you."

I sucked in a breath and said the next words in a rush of breath. "You know that if I pump enough of the hormone into you that you will gladly let me drain you." I raised my voice. "Back UP."

He didn't.

The last wisp of control I had melted away, and I launched myself towards the last location of his voice. I hit him with such force, I heard his head thud on the ground and the scent of his magnificent blood wafted into the air.

While he was stunned, I tore the shirt away from his neck and bit down. My brain was screaming for me to stop. He threw me off before I could release the hormone, but it didn't feel like he was able to do it from sheer strength—it felt like leverage.

"Stop me, please," I begged, a second before I tackled him again.

We rolled, and I ended up on top of him. I grabbed his left arm, twisted it upwards, and held it behind his head. I sank my teeth into the base of his neck once again, but he countered. He grabbed my other arm at the elbow and bit down on me, while my teeth were still in his neck. I felt the hormone surge through my body, and with my newly beating heart, it traveled fast. Calm tried to take hold, but I was too frenzied. I was desperately trying to fight my impulses, my body seemed to move independently of my will.

He gasped, and then slid his hand down and caught my wrist, twisting my arm behind my back hard. The tendons were straining in my arm and shoulder, but I still couldn't will myself to stop. Tears sprang from my eyes because of the pain, but I started to drink and kept drinking. Frantically, I tried to think of a logical reason why I was as strong as he was now.

Bowen twisted away enough that I had to unclamp my jaw. I went for his throat again, but he thrashed his head back and forth and tried to buck me off. I bent around, aiming for the other side of his throat. He turned his head quickly, and his lips brushed mine, sending a wave of electricity down my spine. I pulled his arm tighter behind his head, and he twisted my arm tighter behind me.

"Aleria." His voice was surprisingly calm.

We were deadlocked in struggle, and I had all the advantage. I shifted my weight and tried yet again for his neck, then he turned his head again, but this time, he pressed his cheek hard to mine, effectively keeping me from reaching his throat.

"Aleria, fight it." His voice was silky and reminded me of all the months he'd spent training me to resist my impulse to kill when I was first turned.

My cheek slipped against his, slicked from my tears that hadn't stopped streaming. I whimpered again, but was unable to stop straining against him.

He was tiring. He still hadn't fully recovered and was losing blood. I hadn't sealed either neck wound and didn't know how quickly he was healing. Whatever had happened to me had made me stronger. I was getting closer and closer to his throat.

"Aleria...please." Strain slipped into his tone.

"I'm trying."

As I still had him pinned to the cold earth, he continued to crane his head to the side until there was no space for me to get to his neck. I pulled back slightly, and feeling his heated breath on my face, I kissed him. My fangs sliced the edge of his lip, and when I tasted his blood again, I lost myself. I released his arm as my hand drifted to his hair and grabbed a fistful.

The kiss was ravenous, and he returned it as he shifted under me. He released my arm, and I twined the fingers from that hand into his hair too, my shoulder aching. I heard the sound of fabric ripping and realized my fingers were in the hole I had torn earlier, tearing his shirt away.

Abruptly, he managed to flip me off of him and roll me onto my belly. Immediately, he moved on top of me and deftly encircled each of my wrists, stretching my arms above my head. His knees dug painfully into the backs of my calves, as his full weight pressed down upon me.

I turned my head to the side, and he pressed his cheek to mine once again. He had leveraged himself so that I couldn't get any traction, but I continued to pant and struggle against him. My mind was still screaming to stop.

"Aleria, slow down your breathing, just like before. You can control this," he purred.

Once again, I tried to yank my wrist out of his grip, and he stretched my arms out farther.

"Aleria, please. Save your energy to fight your way out of here. Don't fight me."

After a few more ragged breaths, I tried to struggle from his grip one more time. I could sense his exasperation, but he remained steady. My fight was leaving me—the last bit of energy I had drained away.

Despite stopping my struggle, he remained on top of me, pinning me to the cool ground. *A wise choice*, I thought. I couldn't guarantee that I wouldn't go for his throat the moment I caught a second wind. My lids started to feel heavy as a confusing amount of static seemed to split my head open. I squeezed my eyes shut, and I felt myself slip into an abyss of darkness.

It was a dream. I stood at the top of a great temple. The blood-red sky roiled, casting shadows like phantoms running across the land beneath. A battle raged below—blood flowing from the opposing sides.

Evil was pushing at the seams beneath our feet—wanting out —wanting to play. I searched the faces of the warriors, and with each death, I could see alterations in the future, for better and for worse. Then the faces shifted and became familiar, the past morphing into the future, chainmail into leather and Kevlar. Fates. I could see their possible fates.

I watched Phineas fighting alongside Samael. I could see that if Phineas lived, the Conclave would grow in power. If he died, it would weaken. I turned my eyes on Samael. If he died, then Neka would never be whole again.

Turning, the queen strode into view with a sword, moving lithely towards a Watcher I didn't know. If she died, her attempt to unify the covens would be scattered for years. I felt as if I was watching a puzzle cube being twisted and turned.

Tyran was watching the action, but not engaging. His possible fates flashed before me, and I gasped, turning away from him in shock. He was linked to so many fates.

Then there was the horrible sound of static reverberating in my head once again, followed by a shift, as if time had backed up. I could sense the battle coming, like feeling the earth anticipate a hurricane before it hits landfall—the fighting hadn't started yet.

The scarlet tint of the sky seemed to stain everything red, even darker than before. I'd been here before. I looked at my hands, and this time, the body I wore was my own. My North Star charm was bouncing against my chest as I struggled to free my arms from two vampire guards dressed in leather battle gear. They danced back and forth, trying to hold me in place. Their eyes glowed as they scowled and flashed their fangs at me. I was in that same white gown made of thin fabric, making me feel vulnerable and naked.

Directly ahead, the queen mounted the steps in front of me. She grabbed my face and examined me with a raised brow, while her fingers dug into my cheeks. I refused to grimace and stared defiantly back at her as the guards held me in place. The guard on my left feared the queen.

Bowen's voice came from behind me. *"Maman...s'il te plaît.* (Mother...*please*)"

She looked over my shoulder at him. "It is far too late for that, my son."

"If you do this, I will never forgive you," he warned, his voice cracking.

"I know." Her tone was arctic, but I was close enough that I could see the muscles in her neck strain as she swallowed. If I hadn't known any better, I would've thought she was afraid. Whether it was from losing her son or something else, I couldn't guess.

Bending my knees, I twisted my body as hard as I could, knocking the guards off balance, needing to see behind me. Bowen was chained to an enormous pillar, carved into the side of the mountain. His back was to it, with his arms stretched tightly off to the sides behind him. Hefty shackles, as well as chains wound around him multiple times binding him to the spot. Four towering guards held vigil next to him.

I thrashed back and forth, surveying the area, seeing if there was somewhere to run if I broke away. There wasn't, but there was something I needed to do. Feeling a surge of energy, I twisted my arm free from the guard on my right, grabbing his wrist in the process. I jammed it backwards until I felt the bone splinter, then flung him screaming into the other guard. I caught a glimpse of the queen as I ran towards Bowen.

She didn't appear angry or upset, her face was wiped clean of emotion. I flew to Bowen and encircled his neck, pressing my lips to his ear. "I'm sorry." I wondered what I'd done to necessitate apologizing in that fashion.

Determined hands grappled my waist, pulling me from him before I could finish speaking. I kicked at the guards, knocking them backwards. A moment later, I felt a crushing blow to the head, leaving me senseless. Hands falling to my sides, I staggered a step back and fell to my knees hard. I looked up at Bowen one last time as he writhed against the chains, screaming my name. Then, everything swirled as the blood-red sky enveloped me.

The static seized my mind again and felt like nails down a chalkboard. When lucid thought returned, I could feel I was no longer in the future, without opening my eyes. I was on my hands and knees, the agony of the blow to my head lingering for a few more moments. Grass poked between my fingers and cool stone pressed against my shoulder.

"Ali?"

I looked up questioningly, wondering where I was. Someone said my name again, and the voice finally sunk in. Popping up, I rushed over to Gabriel, clinging to him in a tight hug. He returned the embrace, crushing me to him. "I'm here in your dream."

"Yes."

"Gabriel, I thought that was it. I never thought I was going to see you again; I thought I was going to die."

He didn't say anything in return. He simply hugged me harder.

"You are coming for me, aren't you?"

He released me and held me by the shoulders, looking at me penetratingly. "We have already mobilized; we believe you will end up in one of two possible locations."

"Northern Ireland. Bowen says we are in Northern Ireland. At the Hellmouth."

"You are there? Now?" He asked with an edge of alarm.

"Apparently, they found an Empath. They'll be here tomorrow. From what I've pieced together and what was in my vision, I—no, all of us—are to be sacrificed just after sunset."

"We will get you out of there."

I opened my mouth to respond, but I tasted blood as it dripped into my mouth. I wiped at my nose with the back of my hand.

"I need to tell you something. I had a prophetic dream. This is going to sound crazy, but if all this culminates in a battle, Tyran can't be targeted. If he dies, and you know I want him dead," I took a breath before continuing and wiped at the now gushing blood, feeling light-headed, "the world will be worse without him. There is change in him."

Gabriel cringed. I wasn't sure if it was because of what I'd told him or if it was because of the blood. "You need to wake," he ordered.

I nodded. "Will you sleep again, before then?"

He released my shoulders and ran his right hand through his hair. "I will try to sleep in the van on the way. I doubt I can do any more than that."

"If I find out anything else, I will try to break into your dream or Joshua's."

He gave me a tight-lipped smile and hugged me again. "Now wake," he said, a little more gently this time.

I did. I woke to Bowen's voice.

I groaned and tried to move, but Bowen still had my arms stretched out tight so I couldn't get any leverage.

"Aleria?"

I tried to say yes, it sounded more like, "Mpfhuhyee."

"Can I let you go?"

I assessed myself. I got my mouth to work and whimpered, "I don't know."

He sighed. "I'm going to risk it."

"I don't know if you should."

He paused for a moment in thought, then shifted his legs to either side of me. His knees had continued to dig into my calves, holding me down. He kept his hands ringed around my wrists, but pulled my arms closer to my body. We were still cheek to cheek. "You are bleeding."

"My nose. A dream."

"I'm going to get up. Are you doing okay so far?"

"Yes."

"If you feel it coming, just let me know." He rolled off of me, and I could hear him slide quickly across the ground a couple of feet away.

I felt stiff as I rolled onto my side and stretched before wiping my nose on my sleeve. "How long was I out?"

"A while. I think I may've fallen asleep at some point."

"It's almost sunset," I said, my voice blank.

"Yes."

"Your mother has everything to complete the ritual?"

He didn't answer for a little bit. "Yes. My mother wouldn't have sent Dagan otherwise."

"This sacrifice, it's happened before. Why didn't it work?"

There was another long pause. "You need live blood for the sacrifice. One of the Seven managed to take poison before he'd been strapped down. He was to be the last one sacrificed. By the time my mother got to him in the ceremony, his blood had gone cold. She finished the ritual, but it was too late. It didn't work. The cover stone had unlocked and slid away, but there was some sort of barrier. It looked like a liquid wall. It moved and responded to pressure, but was impossible to breach. We could see my father pushing at the barrier, but without the last of the live blood, it failed. The Hellmouth never opened."

"Did you know about Áine?"

"Who?"

"The Lux Seer who was sacrificed."

His voice was wary. "What about her?"

"Tyran was in love with her."

"In love with her?" he repeated as if he had to hear the words out loud in order to believe them. "He couldn't have been, he—" Bowen stopped short. He was quiet. "A marriage had been arranged for him around that time. We were to unite with another large coven in what is now the Ukraine, but there was an uprising in the area, and several members of the royal family were killed; she was among those slain. He didn't know her well, but he wasn't opposed to the match. She was beautiful, spirited, and they shared a common ideology."

He was quiet for another minute. "I remember one of the guard, Gareth, mocking him for taking up with a human soon after. Tyran had never done that before. If it was her, he spent months in her bed—many, many months." He paused again. "After the botched sacrifice, he changed. He'd always been harsh, but then he became cruel. He and my mother fought fiercely. I'd always thought it had to do with that. He never told anyone about the human, not even me."

"He loved her. Later convinced himself she'd used him to try to protect herself."

"How do you know this?"

"I saw it in a vision. I was her. I know what she felt. And I confronted him. He denied nothing, not even—"

"Killing her," he finished. Heaviness hung in the air, making it hard to breath.

I took in a shaky breath, wishing I could see Bowen. I changed the subject from the past to the present. "If Dagan will let you leave, I want you to find Tyran and go far from here. Leave me."

"You know I will not do that, and you want Tyran safe?" he asked, clearly shocked.

"Your own mother will kill you if you try to stop her and save me. And I don't want you to watch me die."

"So you are accepting this?" he snapped.

"I'm not saying I won't fight. I think there will be a fight. It's just that you will be caught in the crossfire. You will be targeted by the Watchers, as well as your own people, if you help me."

"I won't abandon you," he vowed. "You didn't answer me about Tyran. You want him unharmed?'

"I saw something. If it's true, the world is better with him in it."

"I find that hard to believe."

"I know."

"Sunset," he said.

Just then, a heavy door swung open and torches flared up throughout the room. Dagan's immense figure filled the doorway. He paused for a moment and stepped inside, closing the door behind him. He strode toward me, and I stood up in anticipation. He stopped to the side of me. When I looked over at him, I could see both Dagan and Bowen.

I caught his scent, and an epiphany struck me. The taste in my mouth when I woke. It was suddenly clear. Anger exploded inside me, and I swung at him, unable to reign myself in.

He caught my hand and held it in his vice-like grip.

I put my other hand on my heart. "You did this to me."

Bowen's mouth gaped in reaction to the way I was speaking to Dagan.

Dagan's eyes darkened.

"Why did you do this? I can't control myself."

"What did he do?" Bowen asked.

I grimaced. "He fed me his blood."

Dagan's scowl deepened. "I have made you stronger. Use it for what is to come."

"And what am I?"

"What you have always been—fire."

22

ENDS JUSTIFY

D agan's presence still lingered, despite the fact that it
must've been an hour since he'd left. He explained that
while both he and Moloch were Angels of Destruction, their
blood had the opposite quality, that of resurrection. He'd chosen
to give me his blood, activating bone marrow, restarting body
systems and my heart, because it had given me one advantage
—time.

I would now be able to do what no other vampire could:
produce blood, making it hard for me to ever completely bleed
out. My healing abilities would continue to keep me immortal,
but I would forever be altered. I would never be like other
vampires, I would be more. I was still trying to wrap my mind
around the implications of this, when Bowen's voice broke into
my reverie.

He stood on the far side of the cave, waiting for my reply. I
blinked at him, and then looked away, staring at one of the
torches that was sputtering; a blue flame sent sparks sprinkling
to the ground. Water dripped at a constant interval at the far side
of the cave, droning like a ticking clock.

I sat crouched on my haunches, not breathing. If I'd taken a breath, I would've smelled Bowen, even on the other side of the cave, and I was barely keeping my bloodlust simmering under the surface.

"Do you seriously need to stay that far away from me?" Bowen asked again, clearly frustrated.

I looked down and pinched the bridge of my nose. "Yes," I answered curtly, not able to add anything more to my argument. The single word was painful. I clenched my teeth as I gazed over at him.

He sighed and reclined against a large rock on the far side of the space, stretching out his legs and crossing them in front of him. Slowly, a grin stretched across his features. He laced his fingers behind his head. "I taste that good, huh?" His blue eyes sparkled.

I narrowed my eyes at him.

"I know, I know. You want me," he teased, his smile widening.

"Bowen...I—"

"Want me."

I rolled my eyes and rocked back, sitting down all the way. I shrugged my shoulders. "Meh, passable. I just don't have a lot of options in here. Don't flatter yourself too much," I replied, cracking a smile on the last part.

"Want me," he repeated one last time, still highly amused with himself.

I picked up a clod of dirt and chucked it at him. It hit the bottom of his shoe and exploded in a puff of dust.

He continued to grin.

I blinked slowly, while memories swept over me like a warm breeze. I must've gone down a rabbit hole, because I heard Bowen saying my name. I looked over at him. He'd dropped his arms and appeared concerned.

"You okay?"

I felt a ghostly smile on my face. "Yes. Just thinking about how things were when we met. All those weeks at the coffee shop teasing one another. Everything seemed so simple back then. I know they weren't on your end."

"You miss your home."

"Yes. I miss my family."

"When you survive this, maybe you can go back. Visit before they notice you aren't aging," he suggested.

It was a nice thought. I shook my head and tried not to sound too disappointed, but there was a small tremor in my voice. "I can never go back. They think I'm dead—funeral and everything."

"Without a body?"

"Your brother killed my friend, Gentry. She'd been my body double. She didn't have a family, so the Watchers used hers."

"I suppose that would be a problem."

I exhaled. "I should be buying a prom dress now. Picking out a boutonniere."

"I have a hard time picturing you in a puffy dress," he quipped, the crooked grin returning to his face.

I smirked and jutted out my jaw in mock arrogance. "I would rock the puffy dress."

Bowen's smile lingered, as if amused by the image of me in some horrendous prom gown.

I swallowed hard, past the cotton mouth. "Do you think it will happen tonight? It's after sunset."

His voice lost all emotion when he replied, "No. They would have started the cleansing rituals hours before sunset."

"What cleansing rituals?" I asked, dread and fear overwhelming me.

The look in his eyes became distant. "Just what it sounds like. My mother's handmaidens will bathe—" his breath hitched in his throat, and he wouldn't make eye contact, "the sacrifice." He stopped. I noticed he didn't say "bathe you," he said, "the sacrifice."

Bowen clenched his teeth and then resumed, "They will use rose water and fragranced oils. Once she is cleansed, priests will inspect the body. The sacrifice will then be clothed in white, representing the purity of the offering." He paused again, still avoiding eye contact.

"The cover stone has symbols that correspond with each required sacrifice and the lock they open. The priests burn the corresponding symbols from the cover stone into the body—"

He hesitated before continuing. "But the Seer is special; she represents the unlocking of the future. If found a virgin, another set is burned to allow the power, or life force, to transfer to Moloch, which would happen moments after his release. She is still alive when he—" He drew in a breath and shifted. "After the branding of the skin, she is cleansed with another set of oils. The sacrifice is then brought to the altar in preparation for the actual sacrifice."

Bowen shook his head and pulled his legs towards him, resting his elbows on his knees. After a few moments, he leaned his head onto his hands. It seemed an unnatural position for him to be in.

"Are you okay?" I finally asked.

He flinched infinitesimally. "Am *I* okay?" he asked, then looked up at me with an expression of such melancholy, I knew it would haunt me. "I feel powerless for the first time in my life. I don't know how to save you. I won't willingly go along with this, and I know that if I walk out that door, there will be enough guards to take down twenty of me."

"As I said before, I want you to go." I paused, working hard to keep my voice steady. "No good can come of you staying."

"As I said before, I won't abandon you."

"You won't be. Can't you understand that I don't want you to watch? Don't you see what it did to your brother?"

His eyes cooled. "I would never do what he did."

"I know." It was true. I took a steadying breath. "Why don't you see if they will allow you to go outside?"

"I will, but to survey, not to leave you. I want to see what I'm up against."

I gave him a withering look. Bowen walked to the massive door that looked heavy enough to keep a team of marauders out and tugged at the handle. To my shock, it was unlocked. He heaved it open and immediately raised his hands in surrender.

Warm light from fires filtered through the opening, as well as the shadows from several guards. I could make out at least five of them without having to move for a clearer view, but for Bowen to raise his hands that quickly, there must've been many more. The aroma of burning wood and freshly dug earth flooded inside as he stood there.

"Prince," a husky voice uttered in surprise. "I apologize. Men, stand down. We are only to keep the girl inside. We were told not to underestimate her."

I grinned at this, but then felt a sickening feeling spread through my limbs. It meant that their numbers must be great.

"Where is Dagan?" Bowen demanded.

"He is in the Chambers, Sire. Overseeing the preparations," the voice dutifully replied.

"When is the ceremony?"

"Tomorrow, my Prince. We are awaiting the arrival of the Empath."

"We have all of the other elements needed?"

"Yes, Sire. They are chained in the Keep," the guard revealed.

Bowen turned and looked at me for a long moment, his eyes anxious, and disappeared through the entry. When the door closed, the comforting smell of the fires died quickly.

Time moved slowly. The constant drip-drip-drip of the water infiltrated my consciousness again, like a clock counting down the final minutes of my life. I didn't like being in here alone. And as much as I wanted Bowen to leave—he wouldn't depart this place without me, and part of me was glad. I prayed for strength, but there was a smothering avalanche of fear that threatening to suffocate me.

I leaned back against the wall, and my eyelids drooped with an exhaustion so complete, I felt myself wanting to give up. In those last moments before sleep, I thought of Joshua. Suddenly, I was transported and found myself on my hands and knees. I could feel a wood decking beneath my fingers and hear crickets singing out in the night. The smell of orange blossoms and jasmine pricked my senses.

"Ali?" It was Josh's voice.

I whipped my head up. We were in the gazebo behind my parent's house. This was Joshua's location the last time I'd entered his dream. I leapt to my feet and ran to him. I wrapped my arms around his waist as he cupped my face, planting a desperate kiss on my lips.

The only thought I had in my head was that I was home, not home at my parent's house, but with him. He was my home—the stabilizing force that kept me going. No matter how twisted and complicated things got, he simplified everything.

"You're here? This is you in my dream?" he said between kisses, his voice hitched and uneven.

"Yes."

"It's not hurting you to be here?" he questioned.

"I—I don't think so. I didn't try to come here. I just fell asleep and ended up here." I thought for a moment, his hands still on my face, his eyes watchful. "I usually feel it when it starts to impact me physically. My nose usually bleeds in the dream too."

He ran his thumb under my left cheek and the other thumb over my neck. "Are these real?"

Pinning my eyebrows together confused, I lifted my fingers to my cheek. I felt the raised line under my cheekbone and nodded in affirmation. "Yes. Is it bad? I've only seen glimpses of myself in a mirror since it happened," I grimaced.

"No, it's not bad." He sounded truthful. "You're beautiful."

I looked down. Joshua placed his fingers under my chin and gently raised my face so my eyes could meet his.

"I would tell you that all the time if you didn't hate it so much. But you know I would love you no matter what." *He would.*

I nodded again and paused before I changed the subject. "You got sick." A statement, not a question.

"Yes."

"How bad?"

He pursed his lips. "It progressed quickly."

I thought about how quickly it had altered Bowen. I squeezed him a little harder. "But, you're okay now?"

"Yes. It was close. I don't think I would've survived much longer." He seemed to be debating something.

"What?" I pressed.

"Nothing." He smiled weakly. He swallowed, and his voice became strained. "You were right. Bowen isn't like the others."

I grinned. "So does that mean you would like him, if he wasn't in love with your wife?"

The corner of his mouth flicked upwards. "Something like that." He dropped his hands from my face and encircled me with his arms. "Are you okay? Have you recovered?" he quizzed, but I wondered if he was originally going to say something about Bowen.

"Yes, I'm better," but there was a hesitation in my voice that he immediately caught.

"The antidote worked, didn't it?"

"Yes, but…" I took a half-step back, and he released me. I took both his hands in mine; I could feel my heart picking up its pace. He looked at me anxiously as I raised his right hand and placed it over my heart.

His eyes tightened. "The prophecy said 'The unbeating will beat,' but how? From the antidote?"

I shook my head. "No. Dagan."

"Is he with you now?"

I frowned. "No. Something happened. I can't control myself. Bowen was with me, and I attacked him. He was barely able to fend me off."

"Barely? He should've—"

"I know. I bit him more than once. I'm stronger now. He was finally able to pin me, and I either fell asleep or passed out." My words started spilling out in a rush. "I had a prophetic dream, and then I was launched into Gabriel's dream. I was able to speak with him. Josh, I'm terrified I'll hurt Bowen."

"You won't. You'll get control."

"That's what he claimed, right before I tried to kill him," I replied, feeling completely defeated. His expression changed, and a second later, I felt liquid run down my face. My nose was bleeding again.

"You need to wake." He grabbed onto my shoulders.

"I don't want to go." My voice cracked.

"I don't want you to either, but you have to."

"I love you," I said, my voice finally steady.

"And I you." His lips met mine, and then he faded away.

I awoke to Bowen's voice for the second time this evening. I looked up. "You're back."

"Yes, and you have been dream hopping," he stated, and then he seemed to sense he was too close and took a few steps back, giving me some room.

"Not on purpose," I defended, as I struggled to clear my head.

I wiped now tacky blood from my face with the sleeve that was already crusted with old, dried blood. "What's it like out there?"

"You ever see any of the *Lord of the Rings* movies?"

"Um, yeeeaaah." My eyes widened. "No way."

The corner of his mouth quirked up. "No. There isn't an army of 10,000 Orcs, but there are over a hundred guards, as of today. Many of them are only a year or two old, but there will be more when the Empath arrives."

"What do you mean by more?"

"Dagan said another thirty will arrive in the next couple of hours. My mother's entourage will have close to fifty, and another twenty will be bringing in the Empath. We will be two hundred strong by tomorrow at sunset."

I gulped. When Gabriel said they were mobilizing forces, I hoped he meant a lot of forces. "Well, that's—"

"Apocalyptic."

"Hey, at least if it doesn't go our way, I'll be dead and won't have to deal with it." I meant it to sound light, but it didn't.

Bowen appeared aghast.

"Sorry."

My stomach twisted, lurching me forward onto my hands and knees. I pressed my forehead to the ground, giving the impression of bowing prostrate before a powerful being. I sensed him move towards me. "Stay back. For real this time."

"What can I do?"

"Not taste so good," I responded, laughing morbidly.

He let out a nervous chuckle.

I clawed at the ground as I pulled my arms inward to wrap them around my torso. I kept my forehead smashed to the cool rock. It somehow steadied me. "What? No pithy comeback about your awesomeness?"

"People wanting me goes without saying." But it lacked his earlier humor.

I moaned, and once again felt him move towards me. "Please, don't." I choked back a sob and felt angry with myself. "Bowen, I am so scared. All I want to do is be held right now, but if you touch me, I will hurt you." Somehow, admitting aloud that I was scared made it worse.

He was quiet for a while, so I finally rolled my head to the side and looked over at him. He sat with his eyes closed as he pressed his index fingers into his temples.

"Do you think a stake through the heart will kill me now? Or just paralyze me?" I was both trying to distract myself and discuss something that'd been nagging me since Dagan had left.

If Bowen had looked pale before, he was more so now. He pulled his mouth to the side in contemplation. "I hadn't thought of that." He paused for a moment. "You are healing more quickly than you did in the past. Your nosebleed stopped within moments of you waking from your dream. My guess, it will probably just paralyze you. Your heart would probably heal like any of your other body systems." He grinned, "But let's not find out."

"Easy for you to say; I've been staked three times just this month. It doesn't bode well for me."

"Three times?" He shook his head, incredulous.

"They aren't going to stake me as part of the ritual, are they?"

"No, wrists and ankles. They want all the blood to flow to the cover stone."

I pointed towards the door, sensing a new arrival. "Your brother is here, and he's none too happy."

He gave me a blank stare and was quiet for a moment, then asked, "You drank from him?"

I hadn't thought about what I'd said. The blood bond had only been one way before Bowen had left for the lab. I'd never drunk from Tyran. I felt like a stone dropped into my stomach. I exhaled, not knowing where to start, the part where I tried to kill his brother? Or the part where I repeatedly had to drink from him or perish? I opened my mouth to speak. "I—"

At that moment, the door swung open, and Tyran stepped inside, walking to the middle of the space, splitting the distance between me and Bowen. He looked back and forth between us, then moved a few steps closer to his brother.

Bowen remained seated and crossed his arms across his chest. "Speak of the devil, and the devil comes in."

I couldn't see Tyran's face, but his shoulders tensed. "You are going to fight them, aren't you?"

Bowen stared him down and didn't answer.

"This is your fault," Tyran hissed, as he turned and glared at me.

"I know," I answered. A look of surprise washed over Tyran's face. "Bowen, can I speak with your brother alone?" I nervously gathered the fabric on my shirt over my heart, clenching it in my fist.

Bowen rolled his lips inward, nodded, then exited without a word. When the door clunked shut, Tyran pivoted on his heels and took a few steps towards me.

I raised my hands. "Please, don't come any closer. I'm not under control."

"What do you mean?"

I shook my head. "It doesn't matter." I got on my knees in a show of humility. "Tyran, I have one thing to ask of you. Please, get your brother away from this place and keep him away. I am begging you."

"And what makes you think I could convince him to leave?"

"You are my only hope. He won't listen to me. I don't care how you do it—knock him unconscious, hypnotize him, woo him with your sparkling wit—just get him out of here." I paused. "And you need to stay away too."

"Saying things like that will almost make me think you care," he smirked.

"Think what you like. Will you do it?"

It was his turn to cross his arms over his chest. He considered, the conflict clear on his face. "I will do what I can for him. If he stays, only harm can come to him."

"Thank you." I sat back on my feet in relief.

"Don't thank me yet. This will not be easy." Then Tyran turned and left as abruptly as he'd come.

There was one last thing to do. I stretched out on the ground and rested the backs of my hands on my eyes stepping through the relaxation exercise Morpheus had taught me. My full concentration was on Gabriel, praying that he was sleeping in the van at this moment. My breathing slowed, and I felt like I was being pulled through a liquid tunnel. The sensation receded, and I felt my hands being pricked by grass once again.

When I lifted my hands away from my face, Gabriel was before me. He sat on a stone bench, his skin glowing in sunset light. "Ali, are you all right?"

This time I didn't pick myself up off of the ground. I remained on my back, smiling faintly. "Relatively speaking, yes." I paused, feeling a pang of loss. I wondered if this was the last time I would see him.

"I have information. The ritual will take place tomorrow, just after sunset. They will be approximately two hundred vampires strong, between the guards and other personnel. I also found out why the ritual didn't work hundreds of years ago:

"One of the seven managed to take poison before it was his turn to be sacrificed. They must have live blood for it to work." I took a halting breath. "I am the first to be cut, and the last to die. If it looks like their forces are too great, I want you to target me. If I die before the ritual can be completed, Moloch won't escape."

"Aleria, I cannot do that. You know I cannot."

"This is one of the few times that the ends justify the means. Gabriel, I give you my permission." I forced myself to stand and walked over to him. He immediately embraced me. Pressing my mouth to his ear, I said, "Thank you for being my family, Gabriel. I love you."

"I love you, kid." His voice thick.

"I'll see you tomorrow, then."

"Tomorrow," he repeated and squeezed me harder.

I woke to Dagan crouching over me. He took my right hand in his; he felt feverishly hot. "They have gone." I looked at him, confused for a moment. He added, "Tyran and Bowen."

"So, I'm alone," I breathed, not meaning to say it aloud.

He exhaled. I sensed conflict in him as he gave me a probing look. His eyes appeared almost black in the torchlight. He rose to his feet, took several steps towards the door, and stopped. His shoulders sagged slightly as he stood there silently. After a few long moments, he spoke, "*Alea jacta est.*"

I recognized it as Latin, and for some reason, it was familiar. *I should know this.* "Dagan, I'm sorry. I don't understand," I admitted, shaking my head, feeling stupid and a little hopeless.

"The die has been cast."

Then it dawned on me. I did know the quote; in reference to *Julius Caesar;* two years ago, my teacher had spent a half-hour analyzing that scene and the history around it. "You can't unthrow the dice."

"Yes."

"I remember now. Once Julius Caesar crossed the river, it meant war. There was no going back—win or die."

"The queen's play has been set in motion, and there is no deviating from it."

"Why? What is your loyalty to her? You obviously don't agree with the path she has chosen. Why are you submitting your free will to hers?"

His jaw flexed. "Some oaths are unbreakable."

I shook my head in frustration. "You referred to *Julius Caesar*. My teacher made us memorize part of one of his speeches:

"'I could be well moved if I were as you. If I could pray to move, prayers would move me. But I am constant as the Northern Star, Of whose true fixed and resting quality. There is no fellow in the firmament. The skies are painted with unnumbered sparks; They are all fire, and every one doth shine; But there's but one in all doth hold his place.'

"Here he was bragging about his constancy, and that no one could equal him, that in effect, his actions would make him immortal." I drew in another breath and rushed the words out before I lost my nerve.

"The irony was...they assassinated him in the next scene. It didn't matter. Remaining constant just to remain constant isn't always right. If you're a leader, you need to make sure you're on the right path, so you don't lead others astray." I was going to say something else, but without warning, he was standing inches from me. I lost my train of thought.

Dagan raised his hand and placed the tip of his index finger on the North Star charm hanging from my neck.

His voice was thoughtful. "You once asked me how I could give up heaven for this." He paused, "I shouldn't have." And with that, he was gone, the massive door closing soundlessly behind him.

And in that silence,
I found that I was truly alone...
and it was painful.

23

WHAT HAVE I DONE?

The sun had risen, the heat of it was shoving against the thick door of my confinement. *Restless*. It didn't begin to explain how I felt as the hours of the day ticked by. I hugged my knees to my chest and rocked. I attempted to break into Gabriel and Joshua's dreams again, but was unable. They were probably awake.

I also tried to see into the future—I hadn't purposely tried to do this before, so I was hoping that my inability to see anything didn't mean I was about to die. I continued to cling to some thread of hope that all would be well. It occurred to me that I'd never seen myself past tonight, save the dream where I was pregnant and with Bowen, although I wasn't sure if that was prophetic or not. I'd been too ill to tell.

Crossing my arms over the top of my knees, I rested my head. I may have dozed off for a little while. When the hair on the back of my neck stood on end, I raised my head and searched the cavern. Nothing appeared to have changed, but my unease remained.

It sounded as if a couple of doors unlocked, but it was

muffled, so I couldn't be entirely sure. Then, on the wall in the far corner, sheets of what appeared to be packed earth started crumbling away, revealing a tunnel and an open wooden door. It was made of the same heavy, ancient wood as the exterior one. It gave the impression that the clay-like dirt had been molded over it from my side to conceal its location. I wondered if I could've escaped through it if I'd known about its existence.

Two dark-haired guards clad in battle gear stepped inside, kicking the rest of the rubble out of the way, and at that moment, I laid eyes on the reason for my feelings of alarm: Zahra.

She was the female vamp that loved to hunt in the maze at the castle in France. Since she was female, she'd been forced to deliver my food when the male guards couldn't be trusted to be alone around me. She'd also been part of the ambush on our way back from the lab. Zahra had always carried contempt for me, though I'd never done anything to her.

Zahra strolled in; her whole presence sang of being pleased. She leaned triumphantly against the pillar closest to her location, her dark auburn hair swept over her shoulder. When she saw me watching her, her painted lips curved into a wicked smile.

"You are to come with me. It is time for the preparations."

"And if I don't?"

Her eyes narrowed in a dare. "Please, don't."

Part of me really wanted to tear into her, simply to wipe that smirk right off her face. And to make her pay for the people I was forced to watch her hunt. But it was still light out, and even if I broke free, I had nowhere to go. I would probably make it a hundred yards out the front door before I was nothing but ash and sputtering flame.

I clenched my fists until my nails cut into my palms. Bowen had told me to save my strength to fight my way out, and I would do just that. I would bide my time until I had a chance for a true escape and not tip them off as to my newfound physical power.

Standing, I walked towards her, keeping my eyes locked with hers, staring her down. Out of the corner of my eye, one of the guards reached for me. I snatched my arm away before he could touch me. "I can walk myself," I growled.

The other guard grasped my wrist, and before I could stop myself, I had spun around and seized his hand, twisting and bending it backwards until I felt a firm snap. He grimaced in both pain and surprise as he held his limp and broken wrist. Zahra walked over and harshly grabbed his arm and jerked it, setting the bone properly. He gritted his teeth and remained silent, but it was evident he wanted to cry out.

"Suck it up. It will be healed in a few minutes. Lead the way," she barked as she motioned for him to walk in front. Then she turned to me. "Aren't you full of surprises?" she commented, obviously itching for a fight.

"Like I said, I can walk myself." As I was speaking, I realized my fangs had elongated. My eyes must have been glowing, but Zahra didn't acknowledge it. Her eyes sparkled with scorn as she jerked her head to the side, indicating I was to follow the wounded guard. The other guard fell into place next to me, but avoided touching me. Zahra took up the rear.

We walked through the door and down several passageways that seemed to be natural extensions of the cave, save a heavy gate here or there. Then we reached a stone wall that was mortared together. The guard on point used his good hand to unlock the door and tug it open.

The room we entered appeared to be a large chamber in a deteriorating castle. Heaps of dirt were piled around the edges of it, and a path was worn clean through the middle. Heavy sheets of plywood were screwed into the walls with thick caulking messily filling the seams of the wood. I could only surmise that it was a crude way to block out the light so that we could move about during the day. We snaked through room after room, winding our way to our destination, finally reaching a door, where we halted.

Icelos was leaning next to that door, his short dark hair was damp. He grinned at Zahra as we approached. I'd watched Zahra and Morpheus hunt in the maze together, and wondered if there was something between them, but that split-second spark in Icelos's grey-blue eyes told me otherwise. The closeness to Morpheus had only been due to her connection to his brother.

"Is the passageway ready?" Zahra asked.

"They finished a few minutes ago," Icelos confirmed.

She stood silently in front of the door for a moment, a hint of hesitation in her dark eyes.

He twisted his mouth to the side, amused. "They tested it."

She gave him a haughty look and pushed through the door. A guard nudged me in the back to follow. I turned and glared at him, and he quickly allowed a little space between us. Icelos make a disgusted sound, and the next thing I knew, his hand was latched around my upper arm—he was dragging me forward.

"Take command of your prisoner," he scolded.

The humiliated guard uttered, "Yes, Sire."

Icelos's fingers were like barbs in my arm; his hand was jammed up in my armpit, controlling me from the shoulder. He was incredibly strong.

We walked down a passageway made entirely of plywood: ground, walls, and ceiling. All of the seams were caulked to block out the light. I counted fifty large steps through the passageway. We entered a vast circular room that must've been a turret. Seven cages were situated on the far side of the room—six of them were full—with well over a dozen guards loitering around the room.

At the same time as our arrival, an entourage filed in through the only other door to the room; they were enshrouded in daylight gear. We held our position just inside the room as they entered. I counted eight in the front, followed by two more who were holding a male prisoner. He had a black hood securely tied around his head and another eight guards filed in behind them. They proceeded to the vacant cage.

Once there, they shackled his hands in front of him, instead of behind, and removed the hood. I could only see his back as they shoved him inside the cell and locked the door. He turned, and my heart sank. The Empath. I knew him. It was Nigel Abacha himself; his normally close-cropped hair was a little longer, and his face was unshaven. His dark skin was slicked with sweat.

I wondered how they had gotten to him. I thought the members of the Council and Conclave had gone underground. I'd only met Mr. Abacha twice; he had the kindest eyes I'd ever seen. He was a good man. When we'd met in California, he'd been the only senior member of the Concilium that had shown concern for my well-being, besides Sebastian.

We made eye contact, and his eyes filled with recognition and sorrow as his nostrils flared. In that moment, I realized that he and Amara had the exact same cinnamon brown eyes.

Icelos moved me towards a tall, broad-shouldered guard that looked like he was in charge. "Gareth, where would you like her?"

The guard turned and fastened his unsettling yellow eyes on me. He did a double-take; his eyes widened slightly as if he'd seen a ghost. As quickly as the expression flickered across his face, it dissolved. I could see him assessing where to put me as he looked around the room.

"They will be here to collect her soon. The Chambers are almost ready for the cleansing. Shackle her to post next to the new arrival's cage."

"It won't hold her," Icelos warned.

Another guard stepped up behind the one in charge. He too had yellow eyes—they were obviously related, I assumed brothers. The one in charge, Gareth, looked slightly older, but it was hard to tell. Both of them looked vaguely familiar, their physicality, the way they moved.

And then I realized why: In the warehouse in California, they'd been part of the contingent the queen had left. They were the two yellow-eyed vamps that'd thrown Uriel through a skylight and had almost killed her. It had to be them. I hadn't met any other yellow-eyed siblings. They had been so involved in the fight, I doubt they'd ever really seen me.

Then I noticed both sets of their eyes were on me as they spoke to one another. The older one, Gareth, had his hand firmly around his brother's bicep. I looked away, trying to avoid the odd, probing looks.

I'd been so carried away chasing down my sense of déjà vu that I'd missed the rest of their conversation and stumbled when Icelos yanked me towards the post to shackle me. He pressed down on the top of my shoulder, forcing me to sit down hard on the ground, then pulled my arms behind me and put irons around my wrists, with another set on my upper arms, cinching me as flush as possible to the post. My shoulder blades rubbed painfully against it, and I couldn't lean forward so much as an inch.

Icelos bent down and spoke in my ear. "Try anything, and I promise I will make you pay. None of your protectors are here to spare you." He drew back and looked at me coldly.

I shivered and choked back my emotional response. I glared back at him, willing myself not to cry. When he walked off through one of the tunnels, I wiggled around as best I could so that I was facing the cages instead of the staring yellow-eyed guards, then clamped my eyes shut. I took a few deep breaths, trying to regain my composure.

The room was abuzz with conversations. I flinched when I felt a warm hand on my ankle and opened my eyes. Nigel Abacha had moved to the corner of his cage closest to me. He was seated not two feet away. My feet were only inches from his cage, so he could reach me with ease through the bars. His mild North African accent was melodic, as he spoke in hushed tones. "I am sorry to see you here, Miss Hayes."

"Mr. Abacha," I whispered. "Why are you here? I thought only the females in your family were Empaths."

He nodded. "A misconception we never corrected."

"How'd they find out?"

He shrugged and squeezed my ankle. "It is of no matter now. It is done."

"I guess so." I paused for a few beats. "And I'm sorry about your niece, Amara. I liked her very much."

He shifted his bottom jaw forward slightly. "It is a great loss," he said, closing his eyes for a moment.

There was a shift in the room, and the talk petered out. I strained to look over my shoulder. Females dressed in golden gowns were funneling through the doorway through which Mr. Abacha had just arrived. There were four humans and four vampires among them. Glancing quickly around the room, I noticed that all eyes were on me. I swallowed hard, and my breath hitched in my throat.

"What is it?" Mr. Abacha asked.

"They're here for me. Apparently, I get the special treatment," my nerves clearly showing in my voice.

"Stay strong, sweet girl," he encouraged, lifting his chin.

Tears threatened to tumble down my cheeks. I blinked them back. "You, too."

The younger yellow-eyed vamp came over and unchained

me. I rubbed at my wrists and upper arms now that I was conscious of how deeply the fetters had dug into me. I stood slowly and took one step forward, then grabbed onto two of the bars on Mr. Abacha's cage. I freaked, not wanting to let them take me, and squeezed the iron so hard that I could feel it groan in my fisted hands. The guard put his hand on top of my shoulder and began to pull me away, but I shook him off.

A different guard stepped in from my peripheral vision and hit me with something incredibly hard, and my knees buckled, pitching me forward into the cage. I let out a small squeal of pain, but I still held fast to the bars. I felt the yellow-eyed one move closer and the presence of more guards surrounding me. Mr. Abacha rose to his knees and placed his hand on top of mine. I looked into his benevolent eyes.

"Save your fight," he mouthed.

I nodded and reluctantly relinquished my grip. He knew, as well as I did, that there was a fight coming. It was like an electrical current underpinning everything.

The younger yellow-eyed guard hauled me alongside him, holding my upper arm the same way Icelos had, making it hard for me to resist. He kept glancing down at me as we walked through the room, making me wonder what he was thinking. We marched, side-by-side, through one of the plywood tunnels, where Gareth joined us. A few other guards fell into position to join the escort, but Gareth waved them off. I noticed a look pass between the brothers as we exited.

Once through the tunnel, we walked through several rooms and finally arrived in a space that reminded me of a Roman bath. A large, steaming tub the size of my bedroom was the focal point of the entire chamber. Steps disappeared into the milky-colored water swirling with rose petals. It smelled like earthy oils such as sandalwood. We came to a halt at some stone benches a few feet from the water.

"Cadeyn, they will be here momentarily," Gareth said.

At the same moment, the younger brother, Cadeyn, spun me around to face him and held onto my upper arms. "Rosemond, was she something to you?"

I sucked in a startled breath. "My g-great-grandmother," I stammered. I wasn't sure why I'd answered his question.

A litany of emotions seemed to pass over his features: hurt, followed by anger, and then what seemed like desire. After a long moment, he ran his hand down my arm to my wrist and raised it to his nose and breathed me in. He closed his eyes, and while he did that, I spied Gareth over his shoulder, looking anxious by the entrance. Cadeyn opened his eyes and grinned down at me.

"She was a clever girl." His features smoothed, and he released my wrist just as an entourage of women entered the room, some human, some vampire.

They had to be the queen's handmaidens. The one who appeared to be their leader, a vampire, approached me and ran her fingers down the side of my face, cocking her head to the side, examining me. I jerked back from her touch, but Cadeyn held me in place.

She chided me. "Are you going to be a problem? Or should I request the guards to stay?"

I inspected the area: the women, the bath, the white gown awaiting me, and then Cadeyn, who obviously had some sort of history with my great-grandmother. He had a look in his eyes that almost dared me to resist. I swallowed hard. "No problem."

She gave me one confident nod, then turned to the guard and said, "Cadeyn, you can wait outside." He flashed me a grin that seemed to have a little disappointment in it and abruptly turned on his heel and strode from the room; his brother followed.

The vampire who'd dismissed the guards turned towards me

again. "I am Persephone. I have been charged with your preparation."

One of the humans walked towards me, and hunger erupted inside me. My fangs shot out grazing my lip. Shaken, I turned and sat down on one of the benches, gripping the edge. I squeezed so hard that a chunk of stone came off in my left hand.

Persephone walked behind me. She ran her fingers through my hair and twirled it into a ponytail. "The humans are at your disposal. They are here for you." One of the women came and knelt on the ground next to me and offered her wrist. I let out a gasp and closed my eyes. I felt Persephone's lips on my ear. "This is what you are. Don't fight it."

"I won't be able to stop." I hesitated. "Something happened to me." I saw a brief flash of worry on the girl's face that was kneeling next to me.

Persephone assessed me for a moment. "You don't like taking human life."

"I've never taken one," I replied through clenched teeth, fighting the temptation.

She raised her brows in surprise, and then pursed her lips. "We," she motioned to the other three vampires in the entourage, "can help you stop, if that is your wish."

"Yes, please," I answered.

"So be it. The queen wishes you to be strong," Persephone informed me, and the human placed her arm on my lap.

I took a deep stuttering breath and reluctantly fed. As promised, they helped me stop—not once, but *three* times. I was shocked at the amount it took to abate my thirst. *What did Dagan do to me?*

After the feeding, I felt better—almost too good, like all the new blood was humming in my veins. I was deep in my own mind, going through a checklist of the things I was experiencing, when Persephone broke into my thoughts.

"Please remove your clothing," she repeated.

My hand went to the neck of my black shirt, and I glanced at the door. She followed my gaze and smiled. The sun was still up; I had nowhere to go, and she knew it.

She motioned for her assistants to help disrobe me. I held up my chin and allowed it, though I was pretty sure that I could've slain them all—maybe. Persephone would've been formidable, she was not a young vampire, like I could sense the others were.

Down the steps I went, sloshing into the fragrant water. Rose petals rippled away on the surface as my body displaced the water. Three of the handmaidens followed me into the vast tub while Persephone oversaw the proceedings. Every inch of me was cleaned. I pretended I was in an exotic spa getting a body scrub and tried to concentrate on the wonderful aroma of the soaps. Eventually, I was prompted to leave the tub. I stood still, completely naked, while I was rubbed with oils, just like Bowen had warned me. Warm damp towels were used to remove the excess.

They dressed me in the sheer, white gown I'd seen draped over one of the benches. The lack of undergarments made me feel even more vulnerable than the thin fabric. This gown was different than the ones in my dreams. It was a sleeveless robe style with fasteners on different sections of the dress. They clipped one together over my bosom, and I exhaled in relief, not feeling as exposed. Then they fastened the skirt portion that was so low, anyone could completely see my hipbones and belly. The middle section was wrap around; they tied it shut, effectually concealing my entire torso. I stood on the damp stone floor in bare feet, wondering what was next.

Persephone paced over to the wall and rang an embellished gong. Almost immediately, the door opened, and Icelos stepped into the room. He had the same I-can't-wait-to-see-you-sacrificed grin on his face that I'd seen before. I didn't let him get to me this time.

"It is time for her to be escorted to the priests in the Chambers," Persephone informed him.

He made a tiny bow towards her, then departed down the hall in a flash. Not a minute later, he returned with six guards and escorted me to another room. We arrived at the Chambers and I stopped only two steps into the room with such quickness that the guard behind me crashed into my back. The two vamps at my arms latched onto me harder, but I resisted as I beheld the room.

There were three men in black robes with hoods that obscured their faces standing behind a large stone table. A vast fire pit smoldered behind them, glowing embers had slim rods sticking out of it. My heart hammered against my ribs as I was pressed forward towards the table.

Icelos laughed behind me, making me want to turn and lash out at him, but was marched forward. I started to struggle against them, and suddenly there were five sets of hands on me as I was tilted horizontally and lifted onto the table.

I threw back two guards and rolled off the table and onto the floor, landing on my knees, but before I could stand, Icelos had wrenched me up. He was behind me and had one hand locked around my ribs and the other around my neck.

He pressed his mouth against my ear. "It is daylight; you have nowhere to go but to your destiny. This will happen. The sickness you cause in my kin will be burned from you."

I was confused. "Sickness? Your kin?"

He scoffed and spoke with venom. "The chieftain that my mother wed was a direct descendant of Queen Agrona herself. In effect, she is my aunt, and my cousins are the ones you infect and weaken with your humanity. My own brother seems to—" He stopped.

"I'm not human anymore," I whispered, clearly shaken.

He shuddered and the hand that was around my throat went to my hair. He twisted a knot of it in his hand and used it to turn me around to look at him. His eyes were set just like Morpheus', but they were almost navy blue. He had the same chiseled nose, but Icelos was wiry and thin, as compared to his older brother's bulky musculature.

He peered into my eyes with so much hatred, it seemed to surpass anything I'd ever seen in Tyran. For a moment, I wondered why he'd turned me around, and then his other hand drifted to my chest. As my thudding heart seemed to register, he replied, his voice hoarse, "I don't know what you are."

He shoved me away harshly into the slab table, knocking my upper body over the top. My right cheekbone struck the stone before I could stop myself. I whipped around again, but he grabbed me by the throat, forcing me down onto the table again; this time his men helped. I'd been so focused on him, I'd forgotten anyone else was here.

Heavy irons were clamped around my ankles, wrists, and neck and were cinched tight. I pulled against them, but it was useless.

The guards stepped backwards, and the priests shrouded in black stepped forward, one on each side and one at my head. They had white hands, gnarled with age and the translucency of aged vampires. I would've cringed away from them if I could.

They each carried a stone bowl with what looked like a paintbrush. I heard the faint sound of rustling fabric and looked to my left. Persephone had reappeared. She loosed the wraparound portion over my torso and abdomen, and I felt a rush of chilled air. Then she folded my skirt up to the uppermost part of my thigh. "She is ready, my lords," she said as she bowed to them, then backed away until I couldn't see her.

I trembled and felt totally exposed. My dress was opened to

the point that I only had a small swath of cloth over my breasts and bikini area—nothing else. I strained against the chains again. Simultaneously, the priests withdrew the brushes from the bowls and started painting swirling symbols all over my body in a hue close to the brown of henna.

From toe to fingertip, every bit of exposed flesh was traced with the light touch of their brushes, everything except my face. When they were finished, they replaced their brushes in the bowls again with a synchronicity that made it appear as if they shared the same mind.

The bowls were put aside, and they started inspecting my body with their icy fingertips, starting at my head. They were speaking in unison. It made my heart crystalize with fear. There was coldness in their words—or incantations—or whatever it was. It was something *evil*.

I clenched my teeth as they worked lower and lower. I realized they were about to do the examination that Bowen had warned me about. I closed my eyes and concentrated; I wanted to be away from here. I felt a vision blur my mind, and I welcomed it. I welcomed the pressure and pain that came with it. It was taking me away from here and from the horrible hands on my body.

I was walking forward into a men's restroom. The door squeaked on the hinges as stubby, hairy hands pushed it open. I was a man. I recognized the bathroom; it looked identical to the one in the underground lab out in the country, except as a mirror image. I glimpsed his identity in the bathroom mirror as he walked to a stall; he was one of the lab-techs I'd met briefly.

I...he pushed open the large stall to find Joshua draped over the toilet, looking more ill than I'd ever seen him. His skin was beyond pale, and a roadmap of veins marked every inch of his skin. He had bruise-like hollows under his eyes, and his face was drawn, hollow, and horrible. He was almost unrecognizable.

Joshua stared up at the man blankly for a moment, and then I felt embarrassment flush the man's face. "Oh, umm, I'm sorry. I didn't realize." He started backing away, humiliated. The blood rushed through his system.

Then I saw Joshua's eyes change. They glowed an opalescent green—a color I had never seen them. Josh was so sick, and then to my terror, he was on the man. Fangs latched onto his neck, and Joshua was feeding. There was no control in it. I felt the lab-tech's pulse begin to slow. His heart strained after a short time. He wasn't going to live.

Joshua wasn't slowing down. The man's heart was barely beating: thump—pause—thump—pause—thump. Darkness enshrouded his vision, Joshua still at his neck, and then there was nothing. I fought to stay in the vision. But my vessel was dead. *Dead. Josh had taken a human life. Not on purpose; he was sick. But what did this mean?*

I fought again to stay there. I needed to know what had happened. Then suddenly, I was outside the bathroom again and rushing inside at inhuman speed, chasing the smell of blood. As the door was pushed open, I saw Bowen's reflection as he passed the mirror, traveling a few steps into the bathroom. He reached the large stall, then stopped short as he took in Joshua, sitting with the man on his lap, tears running down his cheeks.

Joshua choked, "What have I done?" over and over again. He looked up imploringly at Bowen. I could feel the complex set of emotions that Bowen had about Joshua, but the one that rose to the top was compassion, the one that meant he would help.

I...Bowen spun around and rushed to the door, locking it. He was remarkably calm. He moved towards Joshua, whose inner agony was spilling all over the room. Bowen pulled down the shower curtain, placed it on the floor, and took the body from

Joshua's lap. He placed the dead man in the middle of the curtain and wrapped the corpse in it. He then snatched a rag from under the sink, mopping up the small amount of blood that had spilled onto the floor, and tucked the rag in with the body.

After cleaning up, I could feel Bowen's inner distress as he paced back and forth, deciding what to do. His thoughts were on both Joshua and me. He was worried that if the Watchers did something to Joshua because of this man's death, that it would crush me. Memories of my grieving Joshua rose to the surface before Bowen could lock them down.

Bowen glanced back over at Joshua, who was slumped against the wall and looking at the blood on his fingertips. Bowen thought through who was outside and decided to bring in Gabriel. He slipped outside and hedged in front of the restroom for a minute.

I felt Bowen's awkwardness as he quickly scanned the lab for Gabriel; he waited to catch his eye, not wanting to stray too far from the restroom. Gabriel was standing next to Beth, discussing a variation of the antidote. She was saying something about a modification for Joshua. Both Kez and Uriel were on the other side of the lab table listening, their backs to Bowen.

Gabriel looked up and met Bowen's eyes. Bowen jerked his chin towards the bathroom. Gabriel cocked his head to the side questioningly. I felt Bowen mouth, "Joshua." Gabriel nodded and moved towards him. Bowen returned to the men's room with Gabriel close behind. He held the door open for Gabriel in an effort to show that he wasn't trying to corner him.

Gabriel entered, and his eyes shot to Joshua sitting inconsolably on the floor with blood on his face and hands, and then to the body wrapped in the plastic shower curtain. Gabriel winced and looked away, cursing under his breath. He motioned for Bowen to shut the door. Bowen closed it swiftly and locked it again.

Bowen spoke at a volume only those in the bathroom would hear. "I can help you. It is your decision. This is your world."

"Help how?" Gabriel growled, then relaxed his shoulders a little. "I apologize; this is not your doing." He turned his gaze on Joshua and looked pointedly at him.

Bowen continued, "If you can get rid of the body, I can make everyone forget the man was even here, make them believe he was on vacation, or anything of your choosing."

"Alter their memories," Gabriel uttered.

"If this news gets to your Conclave, what will be the result?"

"Joshua will be executed," he responded flatly, the pain evident on his face.

"Will this help your cause? Will it help Aleria? You?"

Gabriel looked at Bowen. "It would help you."

Bowen didn't flinch, but I could feel his guilt in even entertaining the idea for a moment. "I fight fair, and I would never knowingly allow..." Bowen stopped for a moment, then rephrased. "I was with her when she mourned him last time." He shook his head, and I felt the waves of emotion surge through him. I saw his memory of me and what I looked like during that time. "He's sick; this wasn't his natural choice," Bowen stated.

"No. You are correct. It will serve no purpose. It would be senseless," Gabriel agreed.

"And your Slayers? Will they agree with you? Or do I need to..."

"Slayers are resistant to glamours."

Bowen frowned. "Not to me," he said simply.

Gabriel's head snapped up as the words sunk in. "But..."

"Don't worry, only a few of what you call 'the Ancients' have the ability. I doubt it would work on someone with your bloodline, but the others, yes."

"Then Uriel will have to agree. She is of the Angels of the Four Corners, too."

Bowen nodded.

Gabriel moved over to Josh, grabbed onto his upper arms and hoisted him up, forcing him to walk towards the sink. Josh followed him woodenly, obeying like a child. Gabriel leaned him against the wall and used a damp rag to help Joshua clean up; Gabriel's face was fixed into a scowl the entire time.

After all the blood was wiped away, Joshua looked at Gabriel, wholly lost.

"I've lost my soul. There's no—"

Bowen made a guttural sound in the back of his throat, effectively stopping Joshua from speaking. "I was born like this. Do I not have a soul? All of the terrible things I have done over the millennia...do you think I will go unjudged for them when my life is finally extinguished? Do you think your God would allow me to go to nothingness and not pay for my crimes? If you think so, then you have less faith than I do."

"You believe that?" Gabriel asked.

"I cannot imagine a God that would not punish me." I felt Bowen shrug. "I could never wash my hands clean of the blood I have shed. You have damned your soul—not lost it."

"Then..." I heard Joshua say, but something started wrenching me from the vision.

Pain...horrible...horrible...pain. I felt pressure on my torso and screeched as the flesh over my rib cage was being seared. I opened my eyes to find all three priests bending over me. They each had a red-hot rod in their hands and were moving in unison again. They completed a symbol, stepped back, and watched.

I could feel myself healing, and I could see them shaking their heads. They were speaking rapidly in French. One of them motioned to the door, the sleeve of his robe flapping from his sweeping motions.

Less than a minute later, I heard Persephone's voice. "How may I help you?"

A craggy, haunting voice hissed out from beneath the hood of one of the robes. "The vessssel is healing too quickly. Thisss wasss to be a *human* sacrificcce. The sssymbols will not remain."

"The queen feared this and has a contingency plan, my lords. I will be back momentarily." She backed out of my sight, then returned shortly thereafter. "If you will allow me to approach?"

"Yessss," slithered a voice from another priest.

As she came into view, she held a test tube containing bluish liquid that seemed to be almost glowing. A silvery-blue shimmer swirled around inside, like it was alive. She held it over my lips. I turned my head away and clamped my lips shut. "Miss Hayes, this will happen one way or another."

I had a feeling I was about to regret my refusal, but I couldn't help myself, and pressed my lips together even harder.

Persephone's voice was liquid. "May I please see one of those?" There was a pause. "Thank you." Suddenly, she jabbed one of the red-hot rods into my side. It sliced through my skin as the scent of burning flesh filled the cold air. I screamed through my clenched teeth, still keeping my jaw locked. Tears burst from my eyes.

She removed the poker and started with another. Almost simultaneously, strong hands gripped the sides of my face like a vice and forced my head back to center. My eyes snapped open, and then I narrowed them to slits when I took in Icelos' visage leaning over me.

Persephone started with a third rod, and I couldn't take it anymore. A blood-curdling scream bellowed from the depths of my soul, and my mouth was instantly filled with that vile liquid. Icelos forced my jaw closed, holding his hand over my mouth until I swallowed. A grin twitched in the corner of his mouth, and then he disappeared.

My chest was rising and falling in short bursts as I panted, trying to see through the pain.

Persephone addressed the priests, "My lords, this will slow the healing. We were anticipating this. We were afraid that she would heal before we could drain her in the sacrifice. Please continue at will."

The priests murmured to one another in French once again. Then they began with their incantations in unison. Knowing what was coming next, I wished so badly for another vision to take me away from this place—*any place.*

I tried to brace myself for the upcoming onslaught of pain, but there was only so much the mind and body could take. When they returned to branding my skin, I no longer felt the relief of my healing abilities. The marks continued to burn. I screamed until my voice gave out; after that, all that emanated from me was a low, hoarse whine.

In what seemed like an eternity, they finished. But to my surprise, they hadn't traced all of the original markings. They'd only burned in the ones on my torso, abdomen, and lower chest. My arms, legs, and neck were untouched by their instruments. I sucked in a breath through my teeth, trying to swallow the pain.

Another gong rang out, followed by the rustle of fabric. My attention went to the priests. One of them had removed his hood to address whomever had entered. I didn't bother looking at the new arrival; I was too transfixed on the priest.

He was bald, with bulging blue veins all over his head. His head and neck were as gnarled as his hands. He glanced down at me, and his eyes were a pale shade of bluish-silver. So light, in fact, that it took a moment for the color to register. I quivered.

"Our tasssk is complete," he informed the new visitor.

"The markings are incomplete," he replied. It was Morpheus.

"She was found impure. Only the markings for the sacrificcce itself were completed. Would you like us to inform the queen?"

There was a pause. "No, she will find out soon enough."

"As you wishhh."

Then all three of them backed away in the same synchronized fashion. I swiveled my head back to look at Morpheus. He was inches from the table, his expression stoic. I watched as his eyes followed the tearstains down the sides of my face.

His eyes softened "Are you ready?" he said, his voice seemed a little unsteady.

I let out a huff of air.

His grey eyes looked stormier than ever. "I am going to unchain you. I wanted you to have a moment to collect yourself. The guards are outside. Icelos disagreed, but—"

"You're the older brother," I finished, touched by the kindness in this world so immersed in evil.

He unlocked everything and helped me sit up. I tentatively took a few stuttering breaths and scooted to the edge of the table. When my feet hit the ground, my legs felt like straw, and I started to tumble forward. Morpheus caught me.

"You're in shock since you aren't healing. It will pass." He threaded his arm around my waist and started moving me towards the door. "For what it's worth, I'm sorry." He sounded sincere.

"Thank you."

He stopped. "One more thing," his voice uneven. "Tyran and Bowen were stopped by the queen's escort when they tried to leave. They are here."

The dream of Bowen chained to a pillar came rushing back to me. "No good can come of this," I said in a shaky breath. "No good can come of this."

TEST OF OUR LOYALTY

Morpheus and I stepped over the threshold, and the cold air raised gooseflesh all over my body. A wave of terror hit me as the hard reality came crashing down around me: I was walking to my death. *This can't be it...this can't be.*

I clenched my jaw and raised my chin defiantly, trying to retain some sort of dignity, but I had to pause as I felt my knees wanting to buckle from the weight of my world being torn to pieces. Morpheus squeezed me a little tighter to his side, for which I was exceptionally thankful, though it caused a flair of pain from my burns.

Sucking in a breath, I looked towards the heavens. The sky was clear overhead, and my eyes found the North Star. My chest constricted. I wanted Joshua. I needed him—his strength. I tried to sense if he was near or on his way, but my fear was dampening everything. I couldn't sense anything besides my death approaching.

In the distant sky, clouds were brewing and rolling in at an alarming rate. It reminded me of that *Close Encounters* movie I'd watched with my dad, but the coloring was different. The clouds looked black and heavy with rain as they closed in the early night sky, but their underbelly was a deep red, reflected from the recent sunset.

After another another calming lungful of air, my eyes dropped from the sky to my immediate surroundings. I instantly noticed the cover stone of the Hellmouth, the seven people-shaped slots in a semicircle around two-thirds of the stone, and, finally, the sacrificial altar. Its design was very close to that of my dreams, with manacles imbedded into the stone.

Beyond the sloped courtyard, a formidable line of guards stood with their backs to us. I counted twenty in total, and then noticed that was just the top row. Just like in my dream, wide steps spilled down the steep hillside. Row upon row of guards stood vigil below that. The old stone stopped, at a circular area at the base of the steps. I realized then, that the courtyard with the Hellmouth was at the top of an ancient amphitheatre.

Beyond the amphitheatre was a worn cement staircase with a metal railing that appeared to be left over from a tourist stop. The narrow steps went all the way down to the base of the hillside where they joined a paved path and disappeared into a forested area. The rest of the hillside was all rocky soil, with clumps of grass growing out of any available space.

My head cleared a little, and I was suddenly able to feel something beyond my own fear—Bowen's fear. I raked my eyes to the left, and there he was, chained to a pillar fifteen feet or so from the altar to which I was being escorted. Our eyes met, and the tears I was trying so hard to abate came stinging to the surface.

Red-rimmed gashes pierced his shirt, and blood matted the side of his hair and face, but thankfully, no other sign of physical trauma. He'd already healed. I pressed towards him, but Morpheus straightened my path and moved me towards the table.

Morpheus bent to me. "Don't make it worse for him."

Looking up, Morpheus' eyes bored into mine, but they were pleading.

"What happened?" I mouthed.

He pursed his lips and glanced around uncomfortably. He proceeded to turn me into him and pressed his lips to my ear, his voice so low that not even another vampire could hear. "When he and Tyran were detained, he staked his own mother in the heart in an attempt to stop the sacrifice. They almost took his head right then, but she wanted to make him watch as part of his punishment." Morpheus sighed. "She will decide afterwards if he will live."

I squeezed his arm and swayed a little, my terror growing. Peeking over at Bowen, I felt angry with him. *How could he do something so stupid?* I wanted to ask about Tyran, but Morpheus straightened up and nudged me forward towards the stone altar.

He pushed me along until two guards came to take over. As opposed to Morpheus, I didn't care if I got the guards into trouble, so I resisted once more. I moved my right arm in a windmill motion, broke the guard's grip on me, and spun around behind him. I shoved his body so hard into the other guard that they both toppled over, gasping in surprise.

In the blink of an eye, I was with Bowen. I grabbed onto the thick chain around his chest to anchor myself; I knew they would try to pull me away. Pressing my cheek against his, my voice broke, "Why? Why did you do it? Attacking your mother?" I hissed angrily.

"You sent me away," he fired back.

Two sets of hands grappled my shoulders and tried to peel me away. I held firm while the chain in my hands groaned.

My words were rushed. "I'm sorry. I didn't want this to happen. I saw it. I didn't want you to be harmed."

"This is bigger than the two of us."

Nodding, the weight of that truth was crushing. I knew that the Watcher's effort was not to save me but to stop Moloch, at any cost. I just prayed that I'd be killed or saved before the sacrifice was completed. My desire was to live, but would accept my death if it was for the greater good.

At that moment, I felt a blow to the back of the head. I jerked forward and felt the crack of the stone pillar against my forehead, followed by the feeling of blood trickling lazily down the back of my head through my hair.

Bowen was shouting at them to stop, but my mind was fuzzy and the ringing in my ears overshadowed everything. I sagged and was only able to keep myself upright by hanging onto the chain. Fingers dug into my shoulders and tried to pull me away again, but a deep voice cut through everything, even my confusion.

"Release her. Let them speak." It was Dagan.

I turned and squinted at him through the pounding pain in my head.

"Consider these your last words. You have thirty seconds," he said with finality.

The guards bowed reverently and backed up, obeying him. Bowen looked at me in anguish. Even now, with his face filled with terror and regret, he looked beautiful. I composed myself and cupped his face with one hand, pressing my cheek to his. "If you can get away, do it. Don't give your mother another reason to—" I couldn't say it.

"I wouldn't be able to live with myself if I did nothing."

"You have to. Promise me." I begged.

Bowen slowly exhaled and nuzzled me. "No."

"I am so, so sorry I could never give you what you wanted." The knot in my throat made it hard to speak. "I do love you."

"I know," he responded, his voice thick.

A heavy hand gripped my shoulder again. Quickly, I placed

my other hand behind his head and kissed his cheek. He shuddered. I kept my lips there until they ripped me away.

To decrease my ability to fight them, both guards lifted me up off the ground until only my toes scratched at the earth as they moved me towards the altar. The guards then plopped me on the table, and the taller one shoved my shoulder downwards, forcing me to lie down. I searched the hillside, desperately wanting to see some indication of hope—someone coming—but there was nothing.

My burns made me want to scream in agony, so I clenched my teeth. Claustrophobia set in as the irons were clamped around my ankles, wrists, and upper arms. I was grateful that my neck wasn't chained this time so I was still able to look around.

Almost instantly, Persephone was at my side. She reopened the middle section of my dress. Her delicate face frowned, and she wiggled her fingers at someone out of my view. One of the attendants in a gold dress stepped forward into my sightline. She had another vial of the blue and silver liquid and handed it to Persephone, then backed out of my vision. Persephone grinned at me and said, "Cheers," a little too cheerfully.

I closed my mouth firmly and looked away, my face fixed in a sneer.

"This again?" She sighed, and then bent to my ear. "Last chance, or…" I heard a muffled scream of pain from Bowen. She took a step to the side so I could see him. Her attendant had driven a small dagger into his side. She had no remorse on her face and was poised with another blade ready to go.

Glaring at Persephone, I opened my mouth.

"I thought so. I was told about your predictability."

I forced the liquid down, coughing and gagging from the aftertaste. But something was wrong; a burning sensation tunneled through my veins. My thoughts remained clear, but everything seemed to slow down, like time itself decided to crawl.

I glared over accusingly at Persephone. "What did you do to me, you b—"

She placed her index finger over my lips and smiled innocently. "Slowed your healing again and slowed your body. The queen wanted you to understand everything that was happening, but not be able to move quick enough to do anything about it…pity."

Blinking at her, I pictured my fingers wrapping around her perfect little neck. She reached under the edge of the table, and it appeared as if she were turning a crank. The end of the altar began to sink as the table tilted towards the Hellmouth. There were two pivot points on the sides of the table with stationary pedestals about the size of stools. After she turned the crank a dozen times, there was a clunk as the table was set in place at a forty-five-degree angle. She pulled out plugs in the table where my blood was to drain into the metal-lined crevices leading to the intricate designs carved into the cover stone.

Again, I scanned the forested area at the bottom of the hillside, and for a moment, I thought shadows had melded into one another, but it may have been a trick of the light.

Shuffling feet echoed off of the stone walls of the courtyard behind me. They were too heavy and clumsy to be a vampire's. Within moments, people dressed in simple brown robes, each escorted by a vampire guard, drifted by me on both sides. They were quickly manacled into their spots. Nigel Abacha was in the last position, and if it was the same as in my dream, he would be the last sacrificed before they came back full circle to me.

A soft rhythm from a drum began, marking the beat in two-second increments. Glacial fingers swept down my arm, and I swiveled my head to look at who was touching me, but he or she was shrouded in a black robe similar to those of the priest, although it was a young hand instead of gnarled and ancient.

The chill of a new presence filled me with dread, and the hair on the back of my neck stood at attention. The queen had arrived—I could sense her behind me.

She sounded unearthly, as if two people were speaking at once. "Are we ready to begin?"

The robed entity next to me bowed. "Yes, my queen. Everything is in alignment."

The queen made a pleased sound in her throat, and then appeared a couple of yards off in my peripheral vision. Her heavy golden gown was exquisite and embellished with precious stones lining runes identical to those on the cover stone.

Her smile melted as she looked down at me hungrily. She ran her fingers over my arms, then pulled the dress up to expose my legs. Next, she rested her hand flat on my belly, over the branding. The chill of her hand felt good on the markings that still carried heat.

"What is this?" she asked, incredulous. "The markings are incomplete."

The robed figure bowed again. "My lady, I am sorry you were not informed. The sacrifice was found to be impure." His smooth voice was betrayed by a tiny tremble.

"*Impure,*" she snarled, and then a scream erupted from her that I feared may have stopped my heart.

Suddenly, the queen was on the other side of the table, bending the priest backwards over the pedestal, pressing the back of his head hard into my stomach. Her ice-blue eyes began to glow and become white. She tore the front of his robe open, the fabric hanging in a large flap as she leaned over him. He was trembling so violently that it felt as if I was trembling too—maybe I was.

She held him firmly by the neck, with her left hand, as if he were some small animal. Then raised her right into in the air for a moment. She rolled her eyes back into her head and chanted something. As she spoke, she slowly lowered her raised hand to the priest's chest.

When her fingers made contact to the bare skin over his heart, his entire body convulsed. Slowly, the little color he had drained away from his body, and I watched as deep, blue veins appeared from beneath her fingers, spiraling outwards. His body seemed to shrink ever-so-slightly as the map of veins eventually covered every bit of skin I could see. A hissing sound seemed to rush from his lungs and he convulsed one last time.

She released him, and he slid to the ground like silk fabric, landing lightly, an empty vessel. Eyes closed, she slowly regained control as I watched, horrified.

Within seconds, she returned to the in-control, despotic queen I despised. She stepped back, and her eyes traveled to her son. "Did you do this? Did you *taint* her? Knowing it was against my wishes?"

Slowly, I rolled my head to see Bowen. He simply stared his mother down and didn't answer. I looked at him pleadingly. It was obvious he shouldn't anger her any more than he already had.

I returned my gaze back to the queen when she took a breath to speak. Despite the cool exterior, her boiling rage was still bubbling right beneath the surface. "Sacrifice her—here, now—and I will spare you. You will be released at this instant."

His face smoothed over for a moment, and then he grinned and laughed. He shook his head in disbelief. After a long pause, he said a single word: "No."

For the first time, I noticed Tyran. He was lingering in the shadows, not far behind his brother. His expression and emotions so locked down that it was impossible to read them. His eyes met mine, and he held my gaze. A single tear streaked down my cheek. His nostrils flared, and he broke eye contact to look at Bowen.

Then Tyran moved silently into the background until I lost sight of him behind another pillar. He'd been clenching and unclenching his fists, but I couldn't tell what he was thinking, not even through the blood bond.

My attention returned to the forest below searching for any sign of hope, and unexpectedly, I witnessed shadows moving. It hadn't been my imagination earlier. But this time, I wasn't the only one who noticed. An entire garrison of guards had been dispatched towards the tree line.

The smell of vampire blood drew my interest, and a second later, a guard appeared a few feet away. His eyes were wild, but he first bowed to the queen in supplication, or maybe fear, or both.

"Speak," she demanded.

"Slayers, my queen. They have come up, through the caverns, beneath the castle, and have taken the lower level and the entire east wing."

"How many?"

"I don't know, my queen, maybe all of them. I recognized a few of them from the line of the Angels of the Four Corners. The neophyte vampires can't withstand them."

"They must. Hold them back. We need more time. If this fails, none of you will be spared."

His voice shook when he answered, "Yes, my queen. We will fight down to the last. We are yours." He bowed again and disappeared; I assumed back into the castle. I smiled—the Angels of the Four Corners—I knew Gabriel was in there, along with Uriel and Raphael.

She turned and scanned around her. "Morpheus." She motioned for him to approach.

He stopped a couple of feet from her and bobbed his head. "Yes, my queen."

Her voice lowered. "Help with the defense inside the castle. I need more time." Morpheus seemed to hesitate for a moment, and the queen did something that shocked me—she uttered one more word: "Please."

He nodded. "Yes, my queen. It will be done." And with that, he vanished into the castle.

The queen drew my attention once more when she started chanting something under her breath very quickly; it sounded ancient in origin. She stopped at my side, and fastened her eyes on Bowen. "Your chance for freedom," she offered, lightly holding an ornate knife with a curved handle.

Bowen cast his eyes to the side and cursed.

Something cold pressed against my lower forearm, and when I looked down to see the reason, saw that Queen Agrona had sliced my wrist horizontally and vertically, making a cross. Blood gushed from the wound. I expected the incision to hurt, but the blade was so sharp, it merely felt like pressure.

The blood streamed across the surface of my skin, making me itch. She turned my wrist in the shackle so that the incision was on top of the hole to catch my blood. I observed my blood as it raced down the crevice towards the Hellmouth. It was only a small amount, but it was flowing like it had a purpose. It reached the outer ring and started running clockwise towards the next sacrifice.

She stepped away from me after she'd repeated the process on my other ankle, one half of my body now done. Then she advanced to the first position on the Hellmouth, continuing her invocation. Two more priests joined her, and I caught the worried look they exchanged between them as they joined her side. They pulled their hoods up onto their heads, adding their voices to the queen's eerie refrain.

Agrona stood in front of her intended victim and made the same slices in his wrists, then the feet, as she had with me. I watched his blood flow and join with mine, accelerating the progress of the blood en route to the final channel that led directly to the inner ring on the cover stone. When his blood entered it, Agrona took the dagger and stabbed the man in the heart.

He cried out briefly, and then fell silent. She recited something else and moved onto the next person. Again and again, I watched her drain the blood and proceed to take the life of each of the other sacrifices. Every time, I prayed they wouldn't be able to complete the ritual.

Then she came to Nigel Abacha. New tears plummeted from my eyes as she took his wrist and made the incisions. I wanted to hear a battle cry or something to interrupt what came next. His blood reached the outer ring, and then ran to the inner one.

Once it mingled with the blood from all of the other sacrifices, Agrona held up the knife and recited her chant more triumphantly than she had for the others, as she finished Nigel. She glanced at me, and a fresh layer of cruelty spread across her features.

She moved to my other side and stood by the table. She took my wrist in her hand and looked once more at Bowen. "Belenus, this is your final chance. Finish her, and all will be forgiven." I didn't hear a response, but I did feel her begin cutting my other wrist. I didn't watch.

After a few long moments, I peered over at Bowen. The fear and pain that gripped his face melted away, and his eyes softened when he realized I was watching him.

He parted his lips like he wanted to speak, but he didn't. We continued gazing at one another in this wordless communication as the queen finished slicing my right wrist, and then the vein on my ankle. Bowen tugged at his fetters, but they didn't move.

In defeat, he mouthed, "I'm sorry."

New noises filtered up from the bottom of the hill, so I searched the lower base of the incline, my head woozy from blood loss. The garrison that had entered the forest had never come back.

A battle cry of what must have been a hundred people split the air as they began rushing towards us and met the second wave of guards. A clash of steel and sparks lit the night. A crack of thunder drowned out all the other sounds, and I looked up at the sky once again. The blackened clouds had closed in the entire sky and, to my shock, the scarlet hue from the sunset hadn't waned. It looked as if the sky itself was running with blood.

The queen moved to the side of the altar closer to Bowen and leaned against the table, her body pressing against my thigh. "Bring him to me," she commanded.

The guards paused for a split-second, as if in disbelief that she wanted Bowen unchained, probably because he'd tried to kill the queen just hours ago. The chains clanked heavily to the ground. Bowen was dragged forward towards his mother. He was only a few feet away from me when they stopped.

Agrona stood up the rest of the way, and her entire presence altered. The regal air she had, melted and became lethal. She held her hand in the air like a cobra ready to strike. "I will ask you again. Did you defile her? Did you take your father's only chance to absorb her power?"

Bowen's face was a mask of defiance and something else. I stared at him as the guards held him locked in place, and I finally placed his other emotion—hurt. Despite everything, she was still his mother, and her disapproval and accusation stung. She didn't know her own son at all.

She sighed after a moment when he did not answer, her hand still hanging in the air. "Open his shirt," she commanded. The sound of buttons hitting the ground immediately followed. Bowen didn't look surprised, but he did struggle against the two guards holding his arms—a vein in his forehead began to bulge with the effort. Instantly, the two yellow-eyed brothers appeared behind Bowen and clamped onto his shoulders. The two of them, along with the original two guards, were able to hold him steady.

Without any other warning, the queen struck Bowen over the heart. She pressed her fingertips against his chest, and I watched as blood began to seep from beneath her digits and lethargically run down his chest. A tremor shook his body, and the color was leeched from his skin until he looked like bluish-white parchment.

The same veining I'd seen on the priest snaked across his skin, radiating from her hand. His knees buckled and his expression dulled, but he continued to stare her down. A small exhale escaped from his lips as I watched the light begin to fade from his eyes. It was then that I realized I was screaming.

Agrona leaned closer to Bowen. "Your brother couldn't keep himself out of the last Seer's bed, either."

At that moment, I felt a surge of emotion from Tyran, so strong that I gasped loud enough to draw Agrona's attention.

I said the words that came to me from Tyran, as clear as if I had seen them written on paper. "You knew about Áine?"

To my surprise, she answered. "Of course, I knew."

Not two seconds later, her body moved awkwardly, and the hand that was draining the last of Bowen's life went limp at her side.

Slowly, a blade emerged through her chest. I recognized, at once, that it was one of the Watcher's Durateus daggers. The queen was being stabbed from behind. She was dragged backwards two steps, and then I watched as Tyran straightened up behind her. He held the blade in her back and wrapped his other arm around her shoulders so he could speak into her ear.

"You knew I loved her, yet you had me kill her? Watch, as her life drained away in front of me?" His voice cracked.

She couldn't answer due to the paralysis, but he continued his questioning.

"And you were going to do the same to my brother? Some sadistic test of our loyalty?" He paused and made a pained sound. Holding her up by the blade in her back, he reached to his side and drew out another dagger. This one was adorned with markings of the French coven on it. He pressed it to her throat. "If I do this, I will take your throne and tear down everything that reminds me of you."

Though paralyzed terror was evident on her face, only air escaped her lungs—she couldn't form a single word.

Tyran started to make a deep cut in her throat.

At that moment, a familiar voice cut through *everything*, including the clash of weaponry all around us.

My heart began to beat unevenly in alarm. I yanked against my confines painfully hard, needing to escape. *No, no, no!*

"The throne is not yours to take, my son."

25

WORTHY

Time seemed to stand still for a moment. Tyran swallowed hard, but didn't remove the dagger from his mother's back or release her. Tyran kept his mother between himself and faced the man behind the voice.

The Hellmouth had opened, to no one's notice. The battle being waged around us and Tyran's assault on his mother had drawn all focus.

Moloch was standing at the base of the altar, the edges of his black wings visible, a terrible angel poised for destruction. He wore the golden breastplate adorned with the owls, horned beast, and other symbols that I'd seen so many months ago.

He was blond, blue-eyed, and breathtakingly beautiful, like his sons, but the cruelty that seemed to charge the air around him filled me with unspeakable terror. In juxtaposition to everything around him, he appeared serene, unaffected by the chaos threatening to swallow us up. His leisurely pace screamed with the arrogance of supremacy forged through countless battles fought and won against mortals and immortals alike.

Moloch turned his eyes on me; he blinked lazily as his mouth quirked up on the sides. "Aleria, I have been looking forward to our meeting," he said in a pleasant tone, and then took a predatory step forward.

He placed his hand on my bare foot, running his fingers over it in a few small circles, avoiding the cuts on my ankles. He proceeded to slowly walk alongside the rest of my body, while running his hand up my leg. The heat of his palm was feverish. He stopped and rested his hand on my naked hipbone. I sucked in my stomach, trying to shrink away from his touch.

He tilted his head to the side, watching my reaction as he ran his fingers over the branding on my belly. "You are more beautiful in person than in the dreams I invaded. It's almost a waste." I felt light-headed, both from the blood loss and the frantic beating of my heart.

Involuntarily, I let out a small cry under my breath, and he smiled. But Moloch's amusement was short-lived when his gaze turned upon my limbs. He probed my arms, and then stepped back to my legs, pulling my dress up to my knees.

He growled at the queen, his wife. "She was to remain untainted." His composure began to slip as rage festered beneath the surface. I didn't want to be there if he did lose control.

"Father, please don't do this," Bowen said, more breath than voice.

The guards had released him. He was on his hands and knees, unable to stand. It looked as if it took effort to hold up his head.

Moloch scoffed. "You sound as if I have a choice—even though I have been denied her power, her sacrifice is necessary."

"You are out—it's not necessary. Spare her," he pleaded.

"I will never be sent back. Her heart is the key to destroying the curse forever."

I felt confused for a moment, wondering what he meant by needing my heart, and then the edges of my eyesight dimmed as I felt myself rocketed into a vision.

. . .

I was in the chambers again, but the weather was hot and humid. The room was very similar to the one I'd been in, but I was certain this was the past. I could hear drumbeats and chanting outside. Whoever I was inhabiting looked down at her body. Her clothing looked like something straight out of a Cleopatra film, and she was chained to a table.

She had the same Henna-type markings all over. Moloch prowled towards her. His presence was all-encompassing, and when he touched her, calm surged throughout her body, but not her mind. She was terrified to the point that I could feel her mind cracking, and he was savoring her every moment of fear.

When Sebastian and Gabriel had told me about the fourth chamber months ago, I'd wondered what had happened to all the sacrifices. Now that I was experiencing it, all I wanted to do was to be freed from my vision and never experience it again, especially first-hand, in real-time.

He loosed her and pulled her body aloft, holding her against him. He looked her straight in the eye; he was hypnotic, and she couldn't look away. When he grinned, I could see the tips of fangs, and a horrible realization hit me: he was the first vampire.

He wasn't just an Angel of Destruction; he lived on blood and sacrifice. He held her hair, twisted her neck to the side, and breathed her in, running his nose down the side of her face and neck. Then he fed, drinking long and deep.

When her heart started straining, he stopped and leaned her against the table. Moloch made her watch as he drew a knife and carved another symbol over her heart. She shrieked out in pain, and he reveled in it. He looped his left arm around her body and held her head again, forcing her to watch, and he pressed the fingers of his right hand into the skin directly over her heart. She continued to cry out and plead as he chanted something under his breath.

With the speed of a viper, he pulled back his right hand and struck her chest. I watched as his fist emerged, bathed in crimson. She gaped at his hand for a moment, then down at her chest where her heart had been, then everything went black.

Screaming awake, I found his eyes on me, but I couldn't contain my reaction. *Moloch was going to take my heart—take it.* I hadn't seen what he did with it, but images of ancient cultures eating the hearts of enemy warriors blotted out all other thought. More than one of those cultures believed that they would absorb the power of the fallen warrior. *What if this was where that idea had come from?*

When I tugged at the manacles, I could tell there was still a horrible lag between what my mind was ordering and what my body was doing. As I panicked, I prayed the adrenaline would help burn off whatever they'd drugged me with and that it would be soon enough for me to do something.

Looking around, I tried to see what I'd missed while having the vision. No one was looking at me any longer. Tyran had backed alongside Bowen, who was still unable to stand; in fact, he looked worse. The queen was still Tyran's captive, unable to move. Tyran was arguing with Moloch, but I couldn't focus on any of the words.

Down the hillside, swords clashed and sparked as they met together in battle, and I saw flashes of movement that appeared to be from hundreds of bodies caught up in the melee between good and evil.

I observed as a Watcher spun around and made a small slice on the arm of a vamp. From my location, it didn't look like it was anything more than a scratch, but the vamp cried out in pain and crumbled to the rocky earth. As I saw the tortured expression on the vamp's face, I knew what I was seeing—they were using

Aurora as a weapon. His screams only intensified as the minutes ticked by, but I couldn't force myself to look away. I could still feel the memory of the incomprehensible burn surge throughout my entire body. Within a short while, he was nothing but ash on the ground.

My heart began hammering when I realized there were more and more vamps in the same condition. It took minutes, and they were gone, just a spot of scorched earth where they'd finally succumbed to flame. They must've increased the potency of the toxin or changed something. There was no way I could've survived what they were brandishing now. I was both thankful and terrified by what I was seeing.

A familiar shape caught my attention amongst the mayhem below. Maybe a hundred yards away, Kez was carving a path up the hillside. He had a sword and a dagger and was spinning and weaving his way through, dispatching the young vampires with wicked efficiency. He kept looking just past me to my left; I finally tore my gaze away from the battle to see what he was so focused on.

After viewing the scene around me, I knew there was only one thing or person that he'd want with that much intensity: Tyran. Even though the queen gave the order, Kez held Tyran responsible for Amara's death. I wondered if the message to spare Tyran had gotten out. My guess was that even if it had, Kez didn't care.

As five vampires went for Kez at once, I became distracted when I felt a warm hand on my upper arm. The shackle fell away, and a second later, the one on my wrist was gone too. Then in the blink of an eye, found that Moloch was half-seated on the pedestal next to me. He had my wrist in his right hand, while he ran his left hand up and down my arm, caressing it. He glanced over and saw that I was watching him. "Your wounds have closed already. Impressive," he murmured.

Only irritated, pink lines and trace amounts of blood remained where she'd cut me. The drug that had slowed down my healing enough for the bloodletting seemed to be finally wearing off. Weakness still held me back, but I'd begun recovering more quickly. I tugged at the shackle on my other arm, and there was definitely less of a delay between body and mind.

Moloch brought my captured wrist to his nose and breathed in. I resisted the desire to pull away. For an instant, I thought I saw a flicker of anger in his eyes and wondered if he sensed Dagan's blood running through my veins.

I checked on Bowen again. He was on his side and barely moving at all. He didn't appear to be healing. I rotated my hand and squeezed Moloch's fingers to get his attention. I had nothing left to lose, so I forced myself to be bold and asked, "Do you have the ability to heal him? To stop what your wife did?"

Moloch cocked his head to the side like he was curious, but he didn't answer. Instead, he reached across my body, removed the bonds on my other arm, and pulled me to a seated position against him. The power that seemed to crackle around him was so palpable, it was almost dizzying being so close to him. He circled my shoulders with his arm to keep our conversation private.

"Please, I know how this ends. I won't fight you—spare him."

"What if I told you that your blood would heal him? But it would take it all."

It felt like my stomach dropped to my feet, but my voice remained steady. "Then take it," I rasped. I had no doubt that I was going to die at this point. Gabriel wasn't going to make it to me on time. If I could save Bowen, then at least I could do something.

"You would do that for him, knowing he is my son?" Moloch asked, taken aback.

"Yes," I answered, staring him square in the face.

The malicious grin returned to his face. "But if this is a negotiation, you have nothing to offer me that I cannot take for myself."

"No, just a willing sacrifice. And he is your son."

He looked at me expressionlessly, not commenting.

After an awkward pause, I asked, "So, is it true? Will my blood really heal him?" I didn't know if he was toying with me.

He didn't answer, but peered down at Bowen with an unreadable expression. Then Moloch queried his wife, "What incantation did you use, my love?"

The Queen was still incapable of speaking, but her eyes tightened.

A low chuckle escaped Moloch from deep in his chest. "You have always been a jealous creature, haven't you?" He stared at her a moment longer, and I realized that they were communicating.

Just a few days ago, Dagan had spoken straight into my head; Moloch must have that same ability. He tilted his head towards me, glancing at me from the corner of his eye.

"Yes, I believe your blood will do."

"Then release me and let me save him."

Bowen's eyes were glazed over, and though it seemed he could hear us, there was no visible reaction. I regarded the queen with so much hatred, that I felt it burning in my chest.

Moloch grabbed the hair on the back of my head and forced me to look him in the eyes. "I want both my sons at my side when I rise to power. What she did was against my wishes. However, saving Belenus will not spare you—you are mine."

"Let me save him then. Afterwards, you can rip my heart from my body, just like you planned to do from the beginning." I sounded stronger than I felt.

He laughed. I didn't think anything could be creepier than his smile, until now. "Never underestimate a Seer," he said and unclasped the bonds from my feet. He stood, removing himself from my side, which allowed me to swing my legs over the side of the table.

My balance off, and I tumbled forward onto the ground. I only had shaky control of my limbs. Once I could sit up straight, I fumbled with the ties in the middle of my dress and haphazardly knotted them together. There was still a delay between my movements and cognitive functions, but it was lessening, even from just a few minutes ago.

I took a stuttering breath, knowing I was unable to walk, then planted my hands next to me to crawl to Bowen. The stones beneath my hands and knees were cool and smooth. I covered the three yards to Bowen, practically collapsing on top of him. Tyran took a step to the side, still holding his mother, to give me more room.

After resting for a moment, I sat with my legs curled beneath me, hunching over Bowen's upper body. As I pushed back the damp hair from his forehead, he gazed at me, but there was an unnerving vacancy in his expression as if he was barely there.

"Please, don't give up." I begged him to stay with me, pressing my wrist to his lips, but there was no reaction.

I willed my fangs to elongate so I could reopen the wound on my wrist, but I couldn't think clearly enough. Until that moment, I hadn't realized how scared I really was.

I bit my bottom lip hard to make myself concentrate on the task at hand, and then everything came back into focus. Tyran had a small knife in his boot. I grabbed it and sensed someone step towards me, but they stopped when I put the blade to my own wrist and made a quick cut.

The knife clattered to the ground next to me while I forced my bleeding wrist into Bowen's mouth. I leaned down, pressed my temple to his, and continued to murmur my pleadings to him. After a good thirty seconds, I finally felt some weak pulls on my wrist and breathed a sigh of relief.

Moments later, the edges of my eyesight began to dim. If it really would take all of my blood to heal him, I prayed he would finish me so Moloch couldn't use me. I closed my eyes, feeling consciousness slip away.

I woke, limp in Moloch's arms. My head was tilted back over his forearm, making my world seem upside-down. Both Bowen and Tyran were yelling in anger, drawing my attention. I gazed over at Bowen from the corner of my eye; he was still on the ground and looked horrible, but he was alert.

Moloch began walking towards a billowing heat—a dry heat rising up from the ground. Then I caught sight of the source; he was standing right next to the Hellmouth. It seemed as if the rest of the world had been temporarily veiled.

I couldn't hear anything beyond the sound of my breath and his. He dropped my legs and held me upright, with his arm looped around my waist. My upper body was arched away from him, as if he was dipping me in a dance. His free hand rested gently on my cheek, and I raised my eyes to his face, taking in all of his terrible beauty.

The warm glow from below bathed him in a glorious light, and his blond hair fluttered slightly as the hot air moved upwards past us. He ran his hand slowly down my neck, over my sternum, and stopping over my heart. It was at this point that I could no longer hold open my eyes. He began speaking in the ancient language that Agrona had been using earlier.

At first, I felt nothing. Then, there was a soft hum, and I could no longer hear my breath or even the beat of my own heart. There was only Moloch's deep voice, as if he were speaking directly into my brain, and the pressure of his fingers over my heart that I could only assume was still beating.

Suddenly, I was jarred to the side, and Moloch's hand was no longer pressing against my chest. I felt another arm behind my back, but I couldn't seem to shake the heavy feeling of my body, and my lids refused to open.

It was Dagan's voice that cut through the wall of nothingness. "I cannot allow you send her to hell as your replacement. It was the punishment you earned."

"You can—and will."

"I fulfilled my oath; our agreement is at an end."

"You are mine to command," Moloch roared.

"You should never have convinced me to follow you, Semjâzâ." Dagan paused. "I should have never followed. I have been bound by what I despise for far too long."

"He will never accept you back. You have fallen. There is no return. No redemption," Moloch spat back.

"So be it. It does not change what happens at this moment. I accept my fate and the punishment I deserve. Forgiven or not—I no longer stand by you. Release her."

I sucked in a breath, feeling as if some control Moloch had over me dissolved with his distraction. I was able to open my eyes, and I was shocked at the situation I found myself in. Dagan had a firm grasp on Moloch's wrist, holding his arm in the air and preventing him from finishing the ritual. I didn't know what to do. Each one of them had an arm around me. They were both so powerful that I could've been torn in half without any effort on their part.

I grabbed onto Dagan's sleeve and felt his fingers respond against my ribcage, but he didn't take his gaze off of Moloch.

They continued arguing, but the language was unlike anything I'd ever heard. I remembered Gabriel's reaction to Dagan's note, saying it was written in the language of the angels. I wondered if this was its spoken form.

Moloch dug his fingers in a bit harder, pulling me his way,

and I cried out in pain when a couple of my ribs crushed from the pressure. Moloch's head snapped down to look at me.

That seemed to be the only distraction that Dagan needed. He let go of my back and Moloch's arm at the exact same moment. There was a flash of movement as he unsheathed the sword on his back and drove it through the armhole in Moloch's armor, while he simultaneously thrust his arm between my body and Moloch's, spinning me behind him.

Dagan held me protectively behind him for a few beats, his hand on my wrist. I felt the rush of something transfer between us, or maybe more specifically, to me. Then he pushed me backwards, away from him several feet, just as Moloch removed the sword. I knew I should've looked around for a means of escape, but I couldn't take my eyes off of them as they struggled.

They danced back and forth on the edge of the Hellmouth, almost plummeting into the opening several times. The light from the opening seemed to increase as they fought; it cut through the night sky like a beacon, piercing the billowing clouds of scarlet encircling us.

The intensity of the light forced me to avert my eyes for a moment. I heard two sets of snaps that sounded like fabric being sharply flapped in the wind. When I turned back, I was awestruck.

Both Moloch and Dagan had spread their magnificent, black wings. They were already larger than life, and now it seemed as if the earth could not hold them. The ground itself seemed to tremor in fear of them and the power behind their fight.

There were cracks of thunder directly above us, and I caught a glimpse of lightning as it struck the forest below. It felt as if the world was being pulled down around my ears.

My attention was diverted when I heard Icelos's voice say, "Command vehicle," in the distance. My heart reacted spastically at the words. I'd been so focused on Moloch and Dagan that I hadn't been concerned with anything beyond it.

I listened intently as he gave orders. "Find them. We have already lost too many. Break their coordination. I am sending Zahra and your brother. Cadeyn, do not fail me. No survivors: everyone in their command vehicle dies."

I looked back at Dagan and Moloch, just as a wave of energy threw me backwards to the ground. I struggled to see through the light, but of one thing I was sure: Dagan had planted a blade in Moloch's chest, straight through his armor.

Then, I wasn't sure if I could trust my eyes. It seemed as if the ebony color of Dagan's wings was washed away. I saw a flash of what looked like a shadow fall into the opening of the Hellmouth, a glimpse of white wings, and then all the light vanished as the Hellmouth itself closed.

Breathless, I sat on the ground, temporarily blinded in the newly darkened landscape. Then reality caught up with me. I got to my hands and knees just as an arm came from behind, looped around my waist, and pulled me to my feet. For a moment, I prepared to fight, until I caught the faint spice of his scent mingled with sweat and blood; a sob immediately rose in my throat.

"Gabriel," I cried as I turned, pressing myself to his chest. At that moment, fear seized me, and my instinct was to push away, afraid that I would lose control again and hurt him.

"Can you stand?" he asked.

When I tested my legs, I realized that not only was I able to stand, but my ribs had already healed. I had complete control. Even with his warmth and smell, I didn't have the desire to drain him as I had with nearly every entity, vampire or human, since I'd ingested Dagan's blood. Gabriel shook me a little, prodding an answer.

"Yes." I paused. "Wait—" I knew there was something

important; two words rose to the surface. My thoughts came out fragmented. "Command vehicle...Icelos. He sent Zahra and Cadeyn and others."

Gabriel immediately hit the button on his comm unit. "Josh, get to Sebastian now." He listened. "No, I have her. Go now. Take Samael."

I had this horrible sinking feeling. "Sebastian isn't alone, is he?"

Gabriel's eyes tightened. "No."

Peter was with him. They wouldn't have let him fight, but he would have insisted on helping. I was about ask him to take me there when Gabriel lurched forward and fell to his knees just as I was grabbed from behind. I clutched the arm around my neck, readying to battle.

Then I heard Icelos's voice boom in over my thoughts: "Do as I say, Seer."

I looked over, and blood was gushing from the side of Gabriel's head where he'd just been struck. Icelos had a blade poised behind Gabriel's back, just itching to pierce his heart. When I didn't react straight away, he pushed the blade in a little. Gabriel didn't make a peep, but I could smell the additional blood and read the pain on Gabriel's face.

I closed my eyes for a second, then nodded, realizing that Phantasos was the one holding me. I opened my eyes and looked around to see why Icelos appeared so desperate.

My gaze fell on Tyran. He was still holding his mother tightly in his arms with the dagger tight against her throat. Bowen was standing behind his brother, with his hand on Tyran's shoulder. It seemed like he still needed some assistance to stand.

Icelos addressed Tyran. "It is not too late, Cousin; all can be forgiven. Release your mother."

"You have no power here, Cousin," Tyran replied. "There is no forgiveness for what she has done, only payment."

"You are her blood and her sworn servant."

"She is not worthy of my love or service. Stand down."

Phantasos moved closer to his brother, dragging me with him while twisting my left arm above my head. Icelos kept one blade in Gabriel's back and put another to the side of my ribcage. "You have let her infect you, just as your brother did. Do you care for her too? If you slay the queen, I will stop the Seer's heart and take her head. Your vengeance or your brother's loyalty—your choice."

The knuckles on Tyran's hand turned white, and his eyes narrowed. He was going to seek his vengeance. I shifted on my feet, and Icelos pushed his knife farther into Gabriel. My mind raced with all the possibilities, but there was only one of which I could be sure—she had to die.

I found Tyran's eyes on mine and mouthed, "Kill her," then I added, "for Áine," as that last little push.

I looked wide-eyed at Bowen and felt in my gut what he was about to do. His hand dropped from Tyran's shoulder, and faster than I thought possible, Bowen launched himself at Icelos. I sucked in air between my teeth as I felt the knife in my side pass between two of my ribs towards my heart, and then abruptly stop. I unclenched my teeth when I heard the knife clatter to the ground.

Out of the corner of my eye, I saw the queen's head fall to the ground separately from her body and Tyran blurring towards me.

When I was ripped from Phantasos' grip, I crashed to the ground on my side. I opened my eyes and Bowen was lying on his side, deathly still, just a few feet from me. His eyes were closed as I crawled towards him, the skirt on my dress making it hard to move forward.

To my left, Gabriel and Icelos were fighting, and behind me, Tyran was trying to wrestle Phantasos back. Tyran was pleading with him to hear him out, but Phantasos was repeatedly screaming, "You murdered her."

When I reached Bowen, I pressed my palm to the side of his face, leaving black smudges from the ash all around us. A relieved gust of air left me when he sleepily opened his eyes. "You're not healing," I said, fear slipping into my tone.

"I am," he whispered, "just slowly." He sighed. "No one has ever survived my mother's ability before." He let out a humorless chuckle. "I'll be fine. I used everything I had to get to Icelos." He put his hand over the top of mine and glanced at Gabriel. "Go."

"Come with us," I more implored than asked.

"You know I can't." He blinked slowly as if he could drift to sleep.

"Please," I pleaded weakly.

"Help Gabriel and go—but spare my cousin."

I swallowed and nodded, forcing myself to choke back the emotion that threatened to sink me, knowing full well this could be the last time I would ever see him. It was obvious that we both felt the weight of it; for a few more seconds, we stared at one another without saying a word. Then I pushed myself up from my knees to my feet.

Icelos and Gabriel were deadlocked in a fight. Icelos had a dagger above their heads and was trying to force it downwards towards Gabriel, but Gabriel was too strong and held him at bay. I picked up Gabriel's Durateus blade that he'd dropped when Icelos had first reached him and lunged at Icelos.

I hit Icelos from the side, preventing him from slashing at Gabriel at the last second. I'd taken him by such surprise and force that he hadn't had time to react.

He held tight to his blade, but it was useless to him; I'd already reached around and plunged the blade into his heart before we both smashed onto the ground. I rolled off of him, shoved him onto his back, and pressed the dagger in until I felt it hit stone.

When I was positive I'd immobilized him, I jumped up and spun around in a circle to make sure no one else was advancing on us. Our path seemed to be clear for the moment. Almost instantly, Gabriel took me by the elbow and started leading me away. I followed without question, but glanced quickly over my shoulder at Bowen. He'd pushed himself onto an elbow and was shouting something in French at Tyran and Phantasos, who were still arguing and grappling with one another.

Bowen seemed to sense my gaze and met my stare. I could see, as well as feel, the sadness in his eyes. When I tore myself away, I felt as if part of me would never recover.

The last look he gave me would forever be emblazoned on my mind.

26

COST

S cenes flashed by like pictures in flip-books as I followed Gabriel towards the van's location. It almost seemed surreal. I tore by vampires dropping to their knees in agony as Aurora burned them from within. Watchers were lying on the ground, cringing as their blood seeped into the soil beneath them.

More than anything, I wanted to shut down, but there wasn't time for me to wallow in emotion. I pressed on with renewed determination, forcing out the unwanted images in an effort to get to the van.

I only paused once, to rip away the bottom of my dress to allow for better movement. Time after time, both human and vampire guards tried to stop us, but we sliced through the obstacles, hardly slowing at all. I fought alongside Gabriel with a singular purpose; we often moved as one, backing one another's moves.

We made it to the base of the hillside and into the forested area at the bottom. I could sense that something was horribly, horribly wrong—I just knew it in my bones. Joshua had to already be there, and his alarm was clawing at my insides. Gabriel broke into a sprint once we entered the tree line and were past the French coven's forces. I wondered if he could sense it too.

I navigated my way through the trees as we blurred past them. We reached a small hill. The van was nestled into the trees at the top of it. I would've missed it if the scent of blood hadn't been so strong. Somehow, Gabriel seemed to move even faster than before.

We reached the van, where bodies littered the ground like crumpled and discarded cups after an out-of-control party. We started picking our way through the carnage, assessing threats and looking for wounded friends. Gabriel identified each as he passed ahead of me: "Theirs, theirs, theirs, ours..."

I paused at the "ours" when I recognized the lifeless body of one of the other recruits that'd been at Signum Academy with me. I gritted my teeth and pressed on.

Gabriel pointed to a body on his right, his voice sounding husky. "Check him."

Then Gabriel peeled off and went in the opposite direction to board the van. My eyes shot to where he pointed, and I covered the space in half a heartbeat when I realized it was Ian. It felt like it had been a lifetime ago since I'd seen him.

The trip to Germany and his saving my life flashed through my mind as I pressed my ear to his chest, trying to hear his heartbeat. It was faint, but he had one. I probed his wounds; no major organs appeared to be damaged.

He'd been utterly and totally beaten—to the point that I wondered if they'd tried to extract information from him. His right arm was still bleeding heavily. I tore another strip of fabric off the bottom of my dress and began to wind it around the wound, but the blood bubbled up through it unimpeded. I debated what to do for a moment.

Finally, I took a deep breath and prayed he hadn't been exposed to any vampire blood as I unwrapped the wound and lifted his arm to my lips. I squeezed the edges together and ran my tongue down the wound to seal it up quickly. I was worried he would bleed out without assistance. I watched as the wound healed before my eyes. Once closed, I gently placed his arm at his side. Then, worked on the next wound.

"Ian, can you hear me?" I asked, feeling vulnerable out in the open. I wondered if there were any enemy assailants lurking amongst the trees. A soft moan escaped Ian's lips, capturing my attention, but he went back under. There was nothing else I could do, so I decided to check in with Gabriel and headed towards the van.

When I reached the sliding door, Gabriel appeared in the entrance with a wild look in his eyes and fresh blood smeared all over the front of him. I opened my mouth to speak, but he cut me off.

"They have Samael and Peter. Samael is wounded. Joshua took off after them. It's five to one. We—"

He didn't get to finish; I grabbed a Durateus sword from the ground to match the dagger in my other hand and was off.

"Stop Sebastian's bleeding," I yelled behind me. I didn't sense Gabriel behind me, which told me two things. One, that Sebastian was in bad shape. And two, that there was a possibility he would survive.

I traversed my way down the other side of the hill, instinctively knowing I was headed in the right direction. I picked up on a blood trail, Samael's blood, and accelerated. I could feel rocks tearing into my bare feet, but I ignored the pain. I was close. The sound of my heartbeat was loud in my ears, as well as the sound of wind as I flew over the landscape.

When I came to the edge of a clearing, I skidded to a stop. Eight people with aggressive postures were at a standoff. A flash of lightning struck the ground at the far side of the heath and temporarily made everyone a silhouette. Almost instantaneously, a roll of thunder rumbled, blotting out all other noise. Birds took flight from the trees next to me, screeching into the air. I hunched down to assess what was happening before charging in.

There were two groupings, divided into three and five. In the smaller group, Samael had his arm wrapped tightly around his torso, and I could see the blood leaking out from under it. He was pushing Peter protectively behind him, using himself as a shield to keep Zahra from him.

The other grouping had Gareth, Cadeyn and two others were circled around Joshua. I stood paralyzed, not knowing who to help first. I decided four-to-one odds were the least favorable. I darted towards Joshua. I saw a flash of Gareth's yellow eyes as he turned to see my approach, but he noticed too late. I struck and took his head.

I spun around and planted my dagger in one of the other vamp's hearts, then whirled around to face Cadeyn. He stood protectively in front of Gareth's corpse. His agony apparent, Cadeyn hesitated for a split-second before he raised his sword to engage me, but Joshua intervened, having already dispatched the fourth guard. Joshua and Cadeyn were equally matched, so I turned on my heel and headed straight towards Samael and Peter, but there was no sign of them. They'd vanished.

I picked up on Samael's blood trail and tracked it back into the woods. I found Samael unconscious, but still alive, a dozen yards into the tree line. I left him there, smelling a new blood trail that could only be Peter's. I came around a giant boulder and found Zahra crouched over, feeding on him.

"Get away from him," I screeched.

She dropped his body to the ground, narrowing her eyes as she licked the blood from her lips. I glanced at Peter, his blood was saturating the ground, both from the area around his abdomen and from the punctures on his neck. Zahra stood while wiping a bit of blood that had run beneath her chin, her face framed by her wild auburn hair. Her fangs were elongated, but her dark eyes didn't glow; they looked completely black, no whites at all.

"He's your friend, isn't he? Is that why he tasted so good?" She grinned.

"Get away from him," I said again with deadly calm.

She took a half-step to the side and drew the sword she had on her back.

"Moloch is dead, and so is your queen. I'll be happy to dispatch you to them."

"You're lying," she challenged.

I grinned and shrugged. "You can believe what you want. I really don't care. If you stay here, I will kill you."

She hedged for a moment, and then her eyes appeared to focus on something behind me. She seemed to vanish like vapor. I wanted her dead, but Peter was more important. I raked my eyes over the trees in front of me, but didn't sense any immediate danger.

I dove to Peter's side and cupped his neck with my hand, trying to stop the onslaught of blood; she had torn at him savagely. He tensed his muscles, obviously racked with pain.

He met my heavy gaze, but his eyes were glossy and faraway. I moved my eyes to his torso and examined the wound on his abdomen with my other hand—dark blood gushed out over the tops of my fingers. I recognized the color difference even in the darkness. He had internal injuries, and his liver had been punctured. I pulled him onto my lap and cradled him, knowing there was nothing I could do for him.

"Peter?" I croaked, barely able to get a word past the lump in my throat.

His eyes fluttered, and he seemed to refocus, but his face

tensed with a new wave of pain. "About time you got here," he said, with a faint smile.

"You were expecting me." I tried to sound light-hearted, but it came out as a half-sob.

"You wouldn't leave a friend behind." Then his whole body seemed to stiffen and curl inwards.

"I can take the pain away," I offered and pushed the hair out of his eyes. The curls were getting tangled in his eyelashes.

When he didn't reply, I drew in a breath and pulled him closer. I sank my fangs into the wound on his neck and pumped in as much of the hormone as I could. His heart was laboring and beating unevenly. After a moment, his body relaxed, and his pain eased. The blood bond snapped into place and the rush of the emotional connection overwhelmed me.

He half-smiled. "So that's what it's like," he said, the euphoria of the bite clear on his face.

"Peter, she punctured your liver and took too much of your blood. There is nothing I can do to save you..." I paused, "Unless?"

I heard him suck in a breath, and then shake his head. "No, don't. It's okay. No regrets."

"This is my fault." Tears tumbled down my cheeks, and landed on his face. I wiped them away.

"Not your fault." He looked at me with clear eyes, totally at peace, and pressed the tip of his index finger to the charm on my necklace. "Your star was meant to burn brighter and longer than mine."

"No...no...no. This can't," I choked on my tears.

"Just let me go." He took a stuttering breath. "I love you."

"Love y—" I whispered, but the light went out of his eyes before I finished saying it. *Why could he always see everything more clearly than I could?*

I kept rocking him back and forth, saying his name, telling him how much he meant to me, willing him back to life.

But there was nothing occupying the body in my arms anymore. His soul was gone, and I could feel its absence. I didn't realize I was making a low wailing sound until I felt the hand on my shoulder. I hadn't felt anyone around me, and even though I was utterly surprised, I didn't flinch or move.

The voice I heard was gentle. "Love, he's gone."

I melted a little as Joshua knelt behind me and tried to pry my fingers off of Peter's shoulders. It was then that I realized that he'd been there the whole time. That's why Zahra had fled without a fight.

He moved around in front of me when I didn't relinquish my grip. He kissed my temple as he slid his hand under Peter's body, then waited a moment. "Let's bring him back." He patiently waited while I took my time to surrender the body.

I finally nodded, but was unable to speak. Josh lifted Peter from my arms and began the short journey back to the van. Halfway there, we found Samael sitting up with the aid of a tree. I held out my hand, offering to help him up.

He looked as beaten down as the rest of us. And when he noticed Peter, his face crumpled. He'd done everything in his power to protect him. His shoulders sagged as he exhaled a long, slow breath and took my hand. When he stood, I pulled his arm around my shoulders, and he hobbled alongside me the remaining distance.

As we stepped into the clearing, Gabriel sat heavy in the doorway of the van. I stopped, and Samael stood under his own power, dropping his arm to his side. I felt the blood retreat from my extremities, and my stomach sink. My bottom lip trembled as I broke into a trot, closing the rest of the distance between myself and the van.

When I reached the vehicle, I attempted to climb in, but

Gabriel caught me around the waist and pulled me to him. He didn't say anything. He simply pressed my head to his shoulder and wrapped his arms around me. I fought him for a second, still trying to get past him, feeling desperate. I denied what I already knew to be true. When he refused to loosen his grip, I gave up as I felt sobs well up from deep within me.

"I need to see him," I pleaded.

"No, you will not. You do not want that to be your last memory of Sebastian."

"But," I protested one last time and felt my brow cloud over. I twisted Gabriel's shirt in my hands and felt Gabriel's sorrow mingled with my own.

The radio in the van cracked to life, with Uriel's voice: "They are retreating. We have taken the castle."

A crunch of gravel under booted feet came from not far away. Gabriel shifted, and then relaxed. I didn't bother looking at the people approaching; I just held on.

Joshua was speaking about Ian needing attention and Peter being gone. Then I realized it was a medical team accompanied by a Slayer. I felt safer with the extra protection around and closed my eyes, sinking farther into Gabriel's arms. He held me for a long while, and when he finally stood, he passed me off to Joshua.

I buried my head in Josh's chest. *I wasn't strong enough for this. We'd won, but at what cost? I'd lost half of my family.* When my knees gave out, Joshua picked me up and walked in a large circle, comforting me. I knew I wasn't being fair; he'd lost them too, but I had nothing left.

My last thought was of a Greek proverb my great-grandmother had always quoted to me when I struggled,

"It is not good for all our wishes to be filled;
through sickness, we recognize the value

of health; through evil, the value of good;
through hunger, the value of food;
through exertion, the value of rest."

When the darkness came, I welcomed it. Somewhere in all of this, I would find value, but for now, I needed rest. I closed my eyes and knew that wherever I ended up, I would be alive and with the family that I had left. And for the first time, I allowed myself to shut down.

I was with Joshua.

I was home.

27

EPILOGUE —AETERNUM

I was not myself. I examined my hands, feeling the familiar confusion of being in someone else's body. I knew the hands well—Bowen's hands. He was leaning back in what I thought was a bed. But then, his arm brushed a metal railing, and I realized it was not a bed but a gurney. When the sterile smell of the room infiltrated my consciousness, I knew exactly when and where he was. This was the past; he was at the lab.

I heard Joshua's voice; it was weak and hoarse. "I need you to promise me something."

Bowen opened his eyes and looked at the ceiling. His chest constricted as a rush of emotions flooded his mind, almost choking him.

He was tempted to make a snide comment, but refrained. He didn't hate Joshua, but he sure wanted to. He slowly rolled his head to the side and met Joshua's eyes. Josh's appearance was startling; worse than I'd seen in the previous vision. And worse than anything, he appeared to have no hope. Bowen didn't say anything.

Joshua continued. "I will take your silence as a yes," he said softly. "Promise you will take care of her. All this," he moved his eyes in an arc, indicating the room, "It's temporary. She's going to outlive them, outlive Gabriel and the others. I need to know you will—" He didn't finish. He sucked in a breath, cringing in pain, and closed his eyes. I didn't think it possible for him to look sicklier, but suddenly he was. This wasn't an emotional response; he was dying. I knew he'd made it, but it was almost unbearable to see him like this.

"She can take care of herself," Bowen replied. It took me a moment to assess the emotion behind his comment. After a beat, I realized it was rejection. No. That of one tired of being used. After everything we'd been through, Bowen felt like I didn't really care about him. I couldn't understand how this was possible.

"I'm not saying she isn't strong. She bears things that would break most." Joshua paused again, and this time, it was emotion that was strangling his words. "When I'm gone, she will need you —" His voice broke.

"She has family amongst the Watchers," Bowen responded, refusing to believe what Josh was trying to say. He had a hard time understanding why Joshua would bother; he broke eye contact and focused on the ceiling again.

Josh sighed, clearly getting frustrated. "That is not what I mean. She's always had lots of friends. People are drawn to her. You've seen it. It's been that way her entire life. She's a leader who doesn't want to be. I think it half irritates her. But she needs someone looking out for her; she has this innocence—even now. Her hope, that wanting to see the best in people, it can be a weakness. And, not just that. Despite the large group of friends, she only lets a handful of people truly in.

"Besides the family that thinks she is dead, there are five people in her life now that I know she would die for, without hesitation." Josh took a labored breath, and the gurney creaked beneath him. "Peter, Gabriel, Sebastian, me, and..." Josh waited so long to say the last name that Bowen looked back over at him. There was sadness in Joshua's eyes when he finished with the word "you."

"No. I helped her, she feels indebted." Bowen believed it, was convinced of it, and it killed me. He always said he was very patient, but something must've happened. Between leaving me and this time in the lab, Bowen had stopped believing in my sincerity.

A heavy silence descended. It was suffocating. Joshua put his hand over his heart and pressed into his chest with the heel of his hand. "There is one question I never asked Ali when she returned from captivity."

After more silence, Bowen asked hesitantly, "What was that?"

"If she loved you—and not the love of friendship." He paused. "I knew the answer, and I couldn't bear to hear it." Joshua closed his eyes.

I wanted to hear, to feel Bowen's response, but instead, I felt a horrible pressure inside my head, so much so that it pulled me from the dream.

There was a voice. "You need to wake, Aleria." I rubbed my eyes and refocused. I was no longer in the lab. Confused, I focused on the figure of the large man in front of me.

"Morpheus? What are you doing here?" The painful pressure stopped.

"I broke into your dream. You cannot stay here. You need to wake."

I shook my head, trying to clear the cobwebs. I looked down at myself. I was in a hospital bed, but I couldn't really be here— there was sunlight streaming through the window. I would be a charcoal briquette by now. I gritted my teeth and lay back against the pillow. "You didn't answer me. What are you doing here?"

He pursed his lips. "I stumbled on you three days ago in a shared dream. You didn't realize I was there. It happened again yesterday. I tried speaking with you, but you were unresponsive. It was as if you were in a trance or under the influence of some sort of potion. I became—" he fell silent for a brief moment, "concerned."

The corner of my mouth quirked up. "So you decided to check up on me again?"

He reluctantly nodded in affirmation.

"Morpheus, that sounds dangerously like a gesture of friendship."

His shoulders slumped slightly and shook in a slow, silent ironic sort of chuckle. He raised his stormy grey eyes to meet mine. "We will call it...limited friendship. I make no apologies for what I am, and I know you do not agree with the way I live."

"No, but it sounds better than just not being my enemy," I smiled weakly. After a short pause, I asked, "How is he?"

"He..." Morpheus stopped and carefully chose his words. "He has been coronated king."

I stopped. "But, he wouldn't want that."

He sighed, "No, he didn't, but the elders refused to allow Tyran to ascend since he was the one who extinguished his mother."

"And there wasn't someone else?"

Morpheus angled his head to the side and regarded me like I was a puzzle that was missing some pieces. "Bowen was reluctant, but he believed it was for the best."

"Wouldn't you be next in line?"

A strange look passed over his features, then he grinned at me. "I am not an option."

I opened my mouth to ask him why, but he gave me a warning glance. I changed the subject. "Is he okay?" I asked cautiously.

"There is a power vacuum after the queen's demise. Tyran is supporting his brother's rule, but it is an unstable situation." He pursed, "My brother, Icelos, married Zahra. The only reason I can see for this is to strengthen his position to make a play for the throne. They have been mates for two-hundred years, and he is not a romantic. It was a calculated move."

"I thought Icelos and you were close? Would he actually do something to his own cousin?" I asked confused.

"Power can be intoxicating. I pray I am wrong, but fear I am not."

"Morpheus, if Bowen is in trouble, will you tell me?"

"If there is something that you can do to help, then yes, I will."

I was happy with what I could get. "Thank you." Morpheus turned to leave. "Morpheus?"

"Yes?" he said, turning back to face me.

"I help my friends. If you are ever in trouble, I want to know."

A brittle smile passed briefly over his features. "Wake, Aleria. I'm sure they are worried about you." It felt as if he gave me a push and, as he did, passed more information to me.

Almost instantly there was a deafening, whirring sound. I sucked air into my lungs like I was a swimmer that had been under for too long. The air burned, and I couldn't get much into my lungs. I clenched my teeth, biting onto something, and kept my eyes pinched shut while rolling into the fetal position, pulling tubes with me. It seemed like my head was going to explode.

I didn't think a vampire could get headaches, but maybe that was a result of my free-fall into dreamland. A warm hand cupped mine, and my eyes shot open. I went to speak, but I choked. I felt panicked. There were large tubes down my throat.

"Ali, wait. Just relax; we will take it out." Gabriel turned and yelled outside the door. "Jess—I need you!"

Jess's statuesque figure almost instantly appeared in the

doorway. I recognized her as Gabriel's friend who'd given me an ultrasound after my poisoning and had removed the tracking device from me. She patted my shoulder and said soothingly, "Just lie back. I'll remove the feeding and breathing tubes."

Relaxing, I did as ordered, noticing the almost empty pint of blood hanging above me where an IV drip would normally be. I then glanced around the room. It appeared we were in the basement of a large house. I'd been placed on a twin bed, and three chairs were positioned around my bedside. It smelled like old carpet and rubbing alcohol.

As Jess removed the last of the tubes, she told me, "I would normally have you drink some water to ease the pain in your throat." Her kind, blue eyes were concerned.

I swallowed a few times, trying to moisten my throat. "Thanks, I'll be fine. I acquired super healing since the last time I saw you," I croaked. When I started to sit up, and Jess grabbed some spare pillows and shoved them behind me. I fingered the large, pastel-blue men's dress shirt someone had put me in.

She smiled and tucked a strand of her dark blonde hair behind her ear that had loosed itself from her chignon. "Yes, I wish all my patients healed as quickly." She turned towards Gabriel. "I'll check on Ian one more time before I head out for the night. I'll be back tomorrow around noon." She squeezed my arm. "I'm glad you're awake. You had us all worried."

"Thanks, Jess."

"I didn't think I would need a breathing tube," I commented before she could leave. The feeding tube made sense.

"We weren't sure what to do—your heart is beating now. It was like you were in a coma, and the deeper you went, the less you were breathing. When you stopped breathing all together, your heart started straining. We thought it was the best thing to do."

I nodded in response. She gave me one last squeeze, then patted Gabriel on the shoulder as she headed out the door.

"How long have I been out?"

Gabriel paused as ran his hand through his hair. His face was covered in almost healed cuts and bruises. "Another few hours, and it would have been four days. You had us a little more than worried, kid. You were completely unresponsive; your pupils did not even dilate. If your heart had not been beating, we may have lost hope."

I felt horrible for worrying them. "I'm sorry. I think I was lost. I don't know when I would've found my way back," I said, obviously preoccupied. I wondered what would've happened if Morpheus hadn't pulled me out.

"Don't know when?" he repeated, confused.

"Morpheus—he found me and helped me back." I blinked at Gabriel a few times, my mind finally catching up. "Where's—"

"Cleaning up. He has been at your side every minute. He was still covered in filth from the battle. I told him if he did not bathe immediately that I was going to have Jess tranquilize him, and he would not appreciate what would follow."

A smile flickered on my face picturing the exchange. I eyed the seat on the opposite side of the bed from Gabriel. There was definitely evidence of a grimy person taking residence in it.

Gabriel put his other hand on top of the one he was holding. "How are you feeling?"

I shook off the question. "When I didn't wake, did you run tests on my blood?"

"Yes."

"What am I?"

He blew the air out of his lungs out in one big gust. "Straight to the chase, eh?"

"You know me," I shrugged.

"Beth is still working on it, but honestly, we do not know. She seems to think that when your body was breaking down from Aurora, the necrosis literally caused gaps in your cells. Her only explanation is that something got through the gaps and was able to add its own code to your DNA."

"Does the Concilium know?"

He pressed his lips into a thin line. "No." He paused. "It will stay that way...for now."

"It was Dagan—his blood—he said he made me stronger. I'm more powerful, but when it happened, I lost all control. Things. Umm," I paused. "I will need to talk to Joshua first." I felt shame burning in my chest. At that moment, the smell of soap and conditioner wafted from the door, and it overwhelmed my senses. I didn't know how long he'd been standing there, but it was at least long enough to hear my last comment.

Gabriel nodded. "I will leave you two alone." He quickly ducked out of the room.

Before I could even open my mouth, Josh was sitting at my side, and I was in his arms. He was holding me like he was afraid I was going to slip back into oblivion, and really, I couldn't blame him.

After a few minutes, he eased back, cupped the side of my face, and looked into my eyes, his face fixed with anxiety. "What's done is done. You don't need to tell me anything. You're alive, and I have you back now," he paused, his voice becoming throaty, "If back is where you want to be."

My mouth dropped open, and I emphatically stated, "All I wanted was to get back to you." I closed my eyes. "I deserve that, though. Something did happen."

He dropped his hand from my face.

I broke eye contact. "If I was in my right mind, it never would've happened, but it did. After Dagan did whatever he did to me, I lost control. I kissed Bowen. I'm so, so sorry. Well, technically I tried to kill him, and then I kissed him. And when I say 'kill him,' I would have drained him dry without hesitation. I just couldn't stop." I started feeling more nervous and began speed talking when Josh didn't react.

"When I did it, Bowen was eventually able to throw me off and pin me down on my belly. I actually had the upper hand when I initially attacked him. It may have saved his life. I don't know. I am so, *so* sorry. If you can't forgive me. I understand. I'll go. I—"

He kissed me. Afterwards, he pressed his forehead to mine and spoke. "I am not saying it doesn't hurt, but this is what I know. One: you would never willingly harm Bowen; therefore, you were out of control. Two: I know you have feelings for him, but I cannot blame you. You thought I was dead. I know you would never have let him in otherwise. And three: I know you chose me. I just had to make sure."

I raised my eyes to meet his. The corners of his mouth were pulled downwards. "Always. I always choose you."

We sat for a long while, with arms encircling one another, until Gabriel returned.

"I'm sorry to interrupt. Ali, did Morpheus do anything besides help you back? Did he give you any information?"

"Yes." I cleared my throat. "Yes, he did."

"Would you like to clean up? Then we will debrief."

"Yes."

"Morpheus?" Joshua asked.

"Can I tell you in the debrief?" I asked, not wanting to have to go through everything repeatedly.

"Okay, I'll show you to the shower." He took my hand and led me from the room, down the hall, and up a staircase. We arrived at the bathroom, and I stopped short two steps inside, placing my hand over Joshua's before he could flip on the light. I started to tremble. I could feel his confusion.

"Okay."

He turned on the light. I could feel his eyes on me, but I was looking in the mirror. Maybe it was vain of me, but I hadn't seen myself since Tyran had cut me, or for that matter, since I'd been branded.

I walked forward and turned my head to the side, examining the scar on my face. It wasn't bad—it traced the angle of my cheekbone into the deepest part of the hollow. I let out a shaky breath, relieved. I'd pictured something puckered and bumpy and horrible. It wasn't much more than a slightly indented pink line. I was sure even that would fade with time. The cut on my neck was the same.

I put my hands on the top button of the dress shirt and stood there—a silent monument. Joshua interrupted my thoughts.

"Do you want me to stay? Or would you like to be alone?" I tore my eyes away from the mirror and looked at him. There was no confusion on his features any longer; he looked at me with unfettered love. So much so that it made my lip tremble.

"I…" I didn't know what I wanted.

"Jess and I removed all of the inked markings. It doesn't look nearly as bad without them."

I studied my arms, remembering the henna-type dye they'd used to mark my skin. Joshua closed the gap between us and placed his hands on either side of my face.

"I think you are beautiful, inside and out. It doesn't matter what was done to you. It doesn't change anything." He kissed me, a slow, tremulous kiss filled with emotion.

I clung to him for a couple of minutes, gathering his shirt in my hands and pressing my forehead into the middle of his chest. He leisurely rubbed my back. Very softly, he asked, "Would you like me to stay? Or would you like some space?"

"I don't know what I want."

"How about this: I will go and get you some clothes and give you a few minutes alone. Then I'll be back. You can let me know if you need me to stay."

I nodded mutely and released his now crumpled shirt. He bent down and kissed my cheek before leaving.

Frozen, I stood in front of the mirror with my hand poised on the top button again. I opened my shirt and stood staring at myself. My entire torso looked—embossed. If the patterns hadn't been burned into my body, I may have thought them beautiful. I ran my fingers over the skin. The raised portions felt glossy, like normal scarring. I took a halting breath and broke myself free of the sight of myself. I finished undressing, then climbed into the shower and let the warm water wash away the sterile smell of whatever Josh and Jess had used to remove the ink. I imagined that the water was carrying away all of the pain and grief. I knew it wouldn't last, but for now, I felt better.

The air pressure in the bathroom changed when Josh opened the door and came inside, even though his entrance was silent. "How are you doing?" he asked.

I assessed myself for a moment. "Better than I thought I'd be."

"I'm glad. Do you want me to stay?"

"If you don't mind, I don't really want to be away from you —*ever.*"

I could hear the smile in his voice as well as relief. "Me either."

A short while later, Joshua led me to a room downstairs for the debriefing. When we entered, Sebastian's absence stung. Part of me expected to see him sitting in an armchair, stroking his greying beard, his eyes twinkling at me over his wire-rimmed glasses.

I felt as if a great weight pushed me into the chair. Then I was startled by the presence of someone I hadn't seen since I was in California. I suppose I should've expected someone from the Council in Sebastian's absence.

Sydney Sato stood and strode over to greet me. Her silky, black hair was swept up into a knot on top of her head, like it had been the last time I'd seen her. Wisps of hair gently framed her face as she looked at me with her pale blue eyes.

"I am pleased to meet you again, Aleria—though I wish it was under happier circumstances. I've been dispatched as your contact with the Council and to assist with the debriefing. They thought you might be more comfortable with me since we'd met before."

"Yes," I replied, almost swallowing the word. I had liked her before, had felt I could trust her. But recent events with Crina Rousseau had made me a little more discerning, not that I'd ever trusted Rousseau.

My eyes darted to Gabriel. He nodded at me, but his eyes tightened, almost imperceptibly. If I didn't know him so well, I would've dismissed it. Unfortunately, I didn't know what it meant.

Sydney returned to her seat with an expectant expression. "Shall we begin?"

"Where would you like me to start?" I asked.

She picked up a thick file from the table next to her. Small flags were teaming out of the side in an array of colors. Apparently, there'd been a sale, because it had enough to ring the planet a couple of times. I sighed. She was going to have a lot of questions.

"I think we have a good picture of everything that happened up until Bowen was cured and sent back to you."

I swallowed and shifted in my seat, remembering events from what seemed like a year ago. She asked me to start after all of Tyran's erratic behavior towards me, and I was relieved.

There were things I would explain later to Gabriel and Joshua—things that didn't need to be in this report. I explained how Bowen returned and that the antidote worked quickly, but that is was also excruciating. I revealed that Tyran was planning on saving some of the antidote to replicate it, but their alternate delivery method worked in avoiding that. I took a moment to glare at Josh. He shrugged and gave me a tight smile layered in mixed emotions.

I paused, remembering the tense conversation between Bowen and I that had followed that exchange. His asking me if I loved him, and my desire to lie so he could be free of me. He would've seen through the lie. I gulped down a breath and skipped the conversation. I went over Tyran's attempt to let us go and Dagan thwarting it with his arrival.

Then I described everything that followed: the cave, attacking Bowen, Zahra, Icelos, Persephone, the priests, the cleansing rituals, the visions, Moloch, the betrayal—all of it. I held it together until I remembered Peter's weight in my lap as I watched the last of his life trickle away, unable to stop it. I didn't sob; tears just leapt from the rims of my eyes quietly as my voice stayed strong. I talked until there was nothing else to say about that night. I closed my eyes and waited for the barrage of questions.

It was Gabriel who prompted me. "You said that you did not wake on your own. That Morpheus found and helped you."

I nodded. "Yes, he said he found me there multiple times and became concerned."

"He cares for you?" Sydney asked.

I paused and rolled the thought around in my head. "I would say care is too strong a word. He feels connected to me. His mother was a Seer, one of the Lux, to be specific. We are not friends, but somewhere between, not quite enemies, yet not quite friends."

"Do you trust him?" Sydney asked.

"I, uh, sort of? He likes being a vampire and all that comes with it. But he prefers to live in the shadows. He doesn't want to rule the human race. And he doesn't wish me any harm. That is all I can really say."

"So he would help you again?" she asked.

"Maybe, probably. I think so? He certainly wouldn't sacrifice himself for me, but he would warn me of danger if he could without fear of compromising himself."

"You said he gave you information," Gabriel prompted.

I then gave them the information of Bowen's kingship, the power vacuum, and Icelos as a potential threat. I paused suddenly, feeling sick.

Josh squeezed my hand. "What else did he tell you?"

I furrowed my brow. "He said that when one Hellmouth opens, they all open."

All noise in the room instantaneously ceased.

Gabriel swallowed. "Did I just hear you correctly?" I could see his pulse in his temples.

"Yes," I replied, feeling as if the air was being sucked from my lungs. "And," I paused, taking a steadying breath, "right before Dagan killed Moloch and tossed his body back into the Hellmouth, he called him 'Azâzêl.' I thought I was told his angelic name was Samyaza, the leader of the 200 fallen angels." I was met with more silence. "What does that mean?"

Sydney looked at me, her silvery blue eyes were unreadable. "It doesn't mean anything." A thin smile twitched on her lips, but it didn't reach her eyes. It was then that I knew she was very good at masking her emotions. I noticed I was tilting my head to the side and staring at her. She seemed to sense my disbelief; she nodded no more than a half inch. "It is a battle for another time —another place."

I could accept that. I nodded, but remained silent.

Sydney clicked her pen shut and rested her hands in her lap. "I don't have any other questions for you." She turned to Gabriel. "Do you?"

"No, I believe she has earned some down time." He looked at me warmly, with exhausted eyes. I wondered how much sleep he'd gotten since the battle. How much more burden had been placed on his shoulders with Sebastian's absence.

I had one more question. I cleared my throat, trying to clear away the uncomfortable feeling gripping my esophagus. "Where is the surrogate?"

Gabriel broke eye contact and looked at his lap, his jaw fraught with tension. He didn't answer, and Joshua squeezed my hand. I looked to Sydney.

Sydney took a short breath. "She is safe. Members of the Conclave felt it necessary to hide her away in a safe house. They have expressed their desire to keep her out of harm's way until the balance of power settles. If your daughter carries your ability, she will be valuable to our efforts and desired by our enemies."

"A daughter," I confirmed.

"Yes, you didn't know?" She caught herself. "I apologize, of course you wouldn't. You've been away."

My eyes went to Gabriel again. He still wasn't looking at me, or saying anything for that matter. His face smoothed, and addressed Sydney. "Do you still need to return tonight?"

"Yes."

"I'll have Uriel escort you back to Council." He turned and used the phone.

Sydney stood and ironed out the sides of her skirt with her hands. "Thank you." She stepped over to me. "Aleria, it was nice meeting you again. I will see you soon."

I shook her hand and watched her as she gracefully swept from the room with the files and notepad clutched on her arm.

Joshua stood and offered me his hand. I took it, allowing him to pull me up. He placed his hand on my lower back, ready to lead me from the room, but I paused when Gabriel didn't move.

"Josh, do you mind if I speak with Gabriel alone for a moment?"

He looked at me steadily for a second; I could sense his mixed emotions. "Of course," he said into my hair as he kissed the top of my head. He left the room without a sound, only the click of the door closing to mark his absence.

Gabriel still wasn't looking at me. "Are you okay with this? With the Conclave having the surrogate?"

He exhaled and finally made eye contact. "For now."

"Is—" I had a hard time saying the words, "our daughter a pawn in a power play by the Conclave?"

"She is probably safer now, where she is. That is all that matters." He finally stood, but there was an awkwardness between us. It had to be from speaking of the child. I still couldn't reconcile it in my head. I exhaled harshly and closed the space between us, wrapping my arms around his torso. He was my family now; and I refused to let the twisted actions of others change that. He relaxed and returned my embrace.

I chuckled softly and echoed Sydney Sato's words, "Another battle for another time."

"Yes, another time." He squeezed me a little harder.

"Gabriel?"

He pulled away and looked down at me inquisitively, his hands on my shoulders.

"Thank you for protecting Josh," I said almost inaudibly, not wanting Joshua to hear me in the hall.

He looked at me, confused for a flash, but then the realization of what I was speaking about settled onto his face. He frowned and nodded. "He told you?" he whispered.

I shook my head. "No." I bit my bottom lip. "I saw it. I know what you and Bowen did." I let out the breath I'd been holding. "Thank you. You did the right thing."

Gabriel stood silently, frozen in place, still holding my

shoulders. He finally seemed to resolve the conflict in his head. A faint smile crept onto his face as he pulled me close for a moment and hugged me again.

"Now go spend time with your husband. You are safe, the queen and Moloch are dead, and all is well." I stiffened, and he quickly added, "All is well, for now."

Backing up, I held both his hands and smiled genuinely at him. Though it was tinged with loss. There was still much to say, but was too choked up to say anything. He seemed to be thinking the same thing. He squeezed my hands and nodded at me, his deep, brown eyes finally looking peaceful as I left.

Joshua was leaning against the wall of the other side of the hall. He reached for me, and I took his hand, a coy smile curling my lips.

His cautious expression eased and was replaced by a shy grin. "You okay?"

I blinked. "The queen and Moloch are really dead." I felt tension leak from my body. I knew they were. I watched them die, but Gabriel just saying it again seemed to make it real. I hadn't been watching a movie. This *was* reality.

The light in his eyes seemed to increase. They weren't the dark emerald green they'd seemed to be of late. They looked lighter, like the glow of the Mediterranean. "They're really dead," he repeated, and he started drawing me down the hall.

We made a right at the end of the corridor and stopped in front of a painted white door. "This our room?"

He nodded as he pulled out a key and unlocked the door. I entered ahead of him and moved to the middle of the space. It wasn't much. A few boxes were stacked in the corner, along with a couple of duffle bags, and most importantly, a bed large enough for two.

He re-locked the door from the inside, then leaned against it.

The corner of his mouth was still curled in a faint grin, but his eyes were anxious. He didn't approach me.

I realized he was giving me space. After everything I'd been through, maybe I didn't really want to be touched. It would be an understandable response, but that wasn't how I was feeling. I wanted him to touch me; in fact, I wanted his hands all over me. Despite being unconscious for days, I was strong. I felt powerful and alive, my worst scars emotional, but even those would heal. Josh would help me heal. I was stronger than all of this.

Mischief danced in my eyes a moment before I ran to him. I jumped into his arms so hard, he lost half the air in his lungs. I wrapped my legs around his waist, while pressing my lips to his with feverish urgency. I had one hand tugging up his shirt and the other gripping his hair. He gasped and returned every bit of passion that was pouring out from me. His hands went up the back of my shirt as we stumbled towards the bed.

I clung to him as he eased me onto the bed and let his weight down on top of me. I tore at his shirt, unsuccessfully trying to get it off. He didn't hide his laughter at my eagerness and helped me remove it. When he returned my gaze after pulling it over his head, tears welled up in my eyes, and he stopped instantly.

"Are you okay?"

"Yes," I breathed, tears spilling down my cheeks. "I'm so happy, that's all. I'm sorry, I'm being a stupid girl." If I could've blushed, my embarrassment would've made me scarlet. He rolled off of me and pulled me on my side to face him.

"You don't have to be strong all the time."

I ran my right hand across the hard planes of his chest, over all of the perfectly formed muscle. He was so beautiful. I lightly kissed his lips.

"You make me so—so—so happy," I said between kisses, unable to articulate anything grander than that.

His hand went to the buttons on my shirt. I froze for a

moment when he opened it, shamed by the markings, and started to tug my shirt closed. But he shook his head. He kissed my forehead, my eyelids, my nose, and then buried his face in my neck. He was literally kissing my fears away.

"You will always be perfect to me." I released a shaky breath. He pressed his ear to my chest. "I didn't realize how much I'd missed this sound." He ran his hand down the outside of my figure, and my heart responded, thundering in my chest. He let out a low, husky laugh. "I definitely missed this."

I pulled him back to my lips and pushed away all the negative thoughts wanting to invade my consciousness. I melted into him, feeling a blending of both of our emotions. This was what mattered now.

I woke hours later, feeling the impending sunrise, and propped myself up onto my elbow, sleep hanging heavily on my bones. Rest had given me clarity. I could spend my existence worrying or I could live. There would always be evil to fight, but now I could face it with my family.

Joshua rolled over groggily. "Everything okay?"

The corner of my mouth twitched upwards. "Perfect."

He pulled me close, enveloping me with his arms.

I pressed my lips to his ear and murmured, "*In aeternum te amabo.*"

"My Latin isn't that good," he breathed.

I smiled. "I will love you for all eternity."

He cupped my face and returned my gaze. "And I you."

THE FALLEN PART I: CHAPTER ONE
A SNEAK PEEK AT BOOK FOUR

L ights, like a sea of flashbulbs, exploded in my vision, but when my eyes fluttered open, I realized it was all in my mind. My entire head was wrapped with some sort of cloth. I thrashed to loose it, but it was too tight. My senses were cloudy; I became aware that I'd been drugged. It took an effort to remember the last moments before my abduction, but only fragments resurfaced.

Rolling onto my back, I tugged at my bound wrists, but was met with agony. My restraints were coated with something that felt like a white-hot torch flaying my skin whenever I struggled. I clamped my teeth together to stifle my whimper.

A car door slammed, and only then did I grasp that I was in a trunk. Muffled laughter could be heard—the congratulatory kind. I sucked in a breath of anticipation. The trunk opened, and I was hoisted up. The hood on my head caught on something, and a puff of fresh air wafted under the cloth. It was cold...*and familiar*. My mind raced, trying to identify the scent.

It felt like I was being carried up a long staircase, then down an extensive hall. A set of doors opened, and from the hollow sound, it seemed as if I were now in a large space.

My head cracked on the ground after my body was roughly dumped on the floor. Disoriented and feeling vulnerable, I struggled onto my knees, balancing myself the best that I could with my wrists and ankles bound.

The moment I realized my location, the hood was ripped away.

My shoulders were grabbed from behind, and my forehead was pressed to the marble tile. One of my abductors growled, "Bow before your king."

I swallowed hard and looked up only using my eyes, resisting the urge to lift my chin. Bowen entered from a doorway behind the throne and stood with a shocked expression—his blond hair longer than the last time I had seen him. Instantly, he was in front of me, raising me to my feet. He let out a shaky breath, and before I could utter a word, he cupped my face and kissed me.

I jerked back, and his eyes locked on mine—his expression a warning.

"Remove her fetters," he rasped.

"My liege, she killed—"

"You question me?" he retorted with icy calm.

Instantly, and with trembling hands, one of my captors unlocked the shackles and backed away, not receiving the congratulations he seemed to expect.

There was a long pause. I rubbed at my wrists as they healed.

My captors were addressed. "Thank you for your service. See Morpheus for payment. You are dismissed." The king placed his hand on my shoulder as the mercenaries filed out of the room. Then he spoke to someone still lingering behind. "Cadeyn, did you do this?"

No response.

"Did you place a bounty on her head when I expressly *forbade* it?"

"Yes, Sire. Permission to speak freely?" Cadeyn asked in a reverent tone.

"Granted."

"I posted the bounty before you had told me not to do so. It was revoked after our discussion. As you are aware, many Seekers go dark once hired. Consequently, I was unable to verify the change in orders. I apologize. You should have been informed, and I accept any punishment you see fit."

"Deliver her to my quarters unharmed. We will discuss it later. I realize blood has been spilled, but her life is not yours to take. If you harm her, your life and any you have sired are forfeit. Am I *clear*?"

"Perfectly." Cadeyn's square jaw flexed as he looked at me. His unnerving yellow eyes narrowed to slits. He approached me and placed his hand around my bicep, squeezing harder than necessary. Then, he practically dragged me from the throne room.

I was on alert as we walked down a passageway to the grand staircase in the lobby. He glanced down at me as we ascended the stairs. There was no need to wonder what he was thinking. He wanted me dead, and he wanted to be the one to do it.

We approached a room at the end of the hall. I had never been inside, but I had seen the ornate doors with the gold filigree swirling around lions and fleur-de-lis before.

Two guards stood at attention.

"She is to wait in the king's apartment."

The one on the right nodded and swung his door open. We strode inside, and the door shut behind us. Cadeyn released me, and I quickly backed a few steps away. I knew I was as strong as he because of the power Dagan had given me, but I wasn't stupid. Revenge was a powerful motivator, and he was far older than I.

I forced myself to be still and returned his piercing, yellow-eyed gaze. Cadeyn didn't seem to be in a hurry to leave.

After an uncomfortable minute of staring, I decided to speak. "Did you love her?"

He blinked at me, and a little bit of the rage on his face seemed to be replaced with something else.

"My great-grandmother," I clarified. "The day I was to be sacrificed, you asked me if I was related to her."

"I know of whom you are speaking." His voice was much softer than before.

"Sorry," I whispered.

Cadeyn looked away, and I could see the memories drifting across his expression. She *had been* something to him, but his face darkened after a moment.

"You killed my brother, and for that, there is no forgiveness.

You cannot manufacture some sort of sentimentality with me because you look so much like her. You are *not* Rosemond."

I frowned. "I know. I was simply curious. She kept her younger years a secret. If you hadn't said something, I would never have known she had even seen a vampire…much less…" My words trailed when I realized I was speaking too much.

He stepped towards me and ran his index finger down my cheek, cocking his head to the side. I could sense his murderous rage still simmering beneath, but his words were soft. "The same lavender eyes. Same skin. Same dark tresses…" He took my hand and pressed my wrist to his nose. "You even smell like her, despite the fact that you are one of us."

I stood motionless and didn't respond.

"Your beloved Belenus will be along shortly. Do not attempt to leave." He then bent to my ear and whispered, "And know this: my respect for him and the throne are the only things keeping me from taking your head. And when that day comes, it will *not* be quick." He smiled thinly at me, and then vanished from the room as only an aged vampire could.

The moment the door closed, I searched my pockets for my phone and my hidden tracking device—nothing. I sat down hard on the upholstered trunk at the end of the bed, feeling sick that I couldn't contact Joshua or Gabriel.

It didn't take long for me to start pacing while I waited, still unable to put all the events prior to my capture in order.

When the door opened, I took in a breath to speak. His blue eyes flashed as he held up his finger to silence me. He walked to the wall and flipped open a panel, pressing a series of buttons. A low hum seemed to wash out all sounds beyond the room.

He looked over at me. "We can speak freely now."

I sucked in a breath, then asked, "Tyran, where is Bowen? You may be fooling everyone else, but not *me*."

Wide-eyed, he answered, "I don't know."

ACKNOWLEDGMENTS

Of course, I need to begin with my more than amazing husband who is my stabilizing force.

Beth, my biggest fan (don't tell you-know-who). I can't thank you enough for the endless hours of hashing through my less than perfect first draft. You are fabulous!

Rachel, thank you for your continued dedication to helping me track all the threads to make sure they don't unravel. I love your giant brain.

James Stewart, Amy, and Katie for helping me with different drafts. Each of you is so talented and I'm thankful for your insight.

Alexis, I appreciate you making the time in your hopelessly busy schedule to help with the final polish.

Much gratitude for my student editors and fan club: Rachel, Becca, and Jessie. You seriously helped keep me going. Also, thanks to Lisa, Rebecca, Rachel, Judy, Jessica, Tamar, Jessica, Kim, Kris, Mic, Roy, and Chris for giving me both feedback and encouragement. And to many of my students and former students, for enthusiastically being my focus group.

Vera Walker, for once again wowing me with a beautiful cover. As I have said before, you have mad skills.

And to Mom and Dad for your continued support.

BOOKS IN THE WATCHER SERIES

Fiction Books

Allure: A Watcher Series Prequel

The Unintended: Book One

The Nexus: Book Two

The Sacrifice: Book Three

The Fallen: Part One: Book Four

The Fallen: Part Two: Book Five

Light & Shadow: The Watcher Series Shorts & Extras

ALSO BY ROBIN WOODS

Creative & Fiction Writing Books

Prompt Me Novel: Fiction Writing Workbook & Journal

Prompt Me: Creative Writing Workbook & Journal

Prompt Me More: Workbook & Journal

Prompt Me Again: Workbook & Journal

Prompt Me Sci-Fi & Fantasy: Workbook & Journal

Prompt Me Romance: Workbook & Journal

Prompt Me Horror & Thriller: Workbook & Journal

Prompt Me Reading Log & Analysis: Workbook & Journal

Coming Soon: Prompt Me Mystery & Suspense

* * *

Thank you for reading. If you enjoyed this novel, please take a moment to write a review. It is the best way to help the authors you love. Blessings!

ABOUT THE AUTHOR

Robin Woods is a former high school and university instructor with two and a half decades of experience teaching English, literature, and writing. She earned a BA in English and an MA in Education.

In addition to teaching, she has published six novels, eight creative writing books (and counting), and has multiple projects in the works, including writing for a Hollywood producer.

When Ms. Woods isn't chasing her two elementary school kids around, she's spending time with her ever-patient husband, or sitting in a coffee shop wondering how vampires like their lattes.

For more information, an extended bio, free writing resources, and free extra scenes, visit her website at www.robinwoodsfiction.com